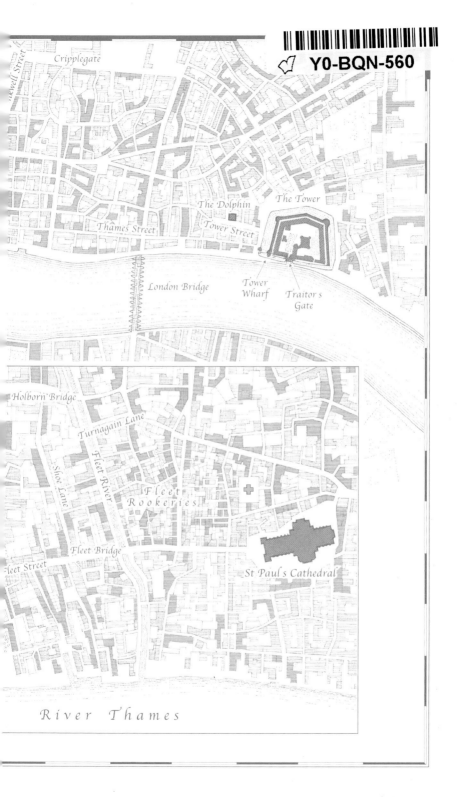

Cripplegate

The Dolphin        The Tower

Thames Street        Tower Street

London Bridge        Tower Wharf        Traitor's Gate

Holborn Bridge

Turnagain Lane

Shoe Lane        Fleet River

Fleet Rookeries

Fleet Bridge

Fleet Street        St Paul's Cathedral

River  Thames

# A Conspiracy of Violence

Also by Susanna Gregory

*The Matthew Bartholomew Series*:

# A CONSPIRACY
## OF VIOLENCE

## Susanna
## Gregory

TIME WARNER
BOOKS

TIME WARNER BOOKS

First published in Great Britain in January 2006 by Time Warner Books

Copyright © Susanna Gregory 2006

The moral right of the author has been asserted.

A CIP catalogue record for this book
is available from the British Library.

ISBN   0 316 73110 2

Typeset in Monotype Baskerville
by Palimpsest Book Production Limited,
Polmont, Stirlingshire
Printed and bound in Great Britain by
Mackays Ltd, Chatham, Kent

Time Warner Books
An imprint of
Time Warner Book Group UK
Brettenham House
Lancaster Place
London WC2E 7EN

www.twbg.co.uk

For Hilary Hale –
Editor, mentor and friend,
with great appreciation and affection

# Chapter 1

*London, December 1662*

Sleet pattered wetly on the dung-coated cobbles outside
Lincoln's Inn, and the biting wind had long-since blown
out the lamp that swung above the gate. The night was
so dark that it was difficult even to make out the craggy
outlines of the chimneys and turrets that topped the
ancient walls, and the sturdy gate was no more than a
looming mass of black.

Thomas Chaloner eased farther inside the doorway of
the Rolls Chapel, invisible in his black cloak and the blacker
shadows. It was bitterly cold, and his hands and feet were
numb from standing still so long, but he was used to that
kind of discomfort. Observing the movements of others
while remaining unseen was how he made his living,
because Chaloner was a government spy. Or rather, he
*had* been a government spy. He had been dismissed in
March, and his situation was fast becoming desperate –
he owed rent to his landlord, there was no food in the
larder and even his best clothes were beginning to look
hopelessly tatty. And that was why he was lurking outside

1

Lincoln's Inn on an icy December morning, waiting for dawn and the interview that might be his salvation.

The man he wanted to see was named John Thurloe. Thurloe had been Oliver Cromwell's Secretary of State and Spymaster General during the Commonwealth, and when that regime had collapsed following Cromwell's death, Thurloe had fallen with it, and had lost his position of power – although fortunately for Chaloner, he had retained a modicum of influence over his successors. The restored King Charles II immediately appointed good Royalists to form his new government, but they had scant idea how to run a country, and Thurloe's advice and guidance had proved invaluable, although few of the newcomers were prepared to admit it.

A group of leatherworkers slouched past, heading for the factory on Fleet Street, although none noticed the silent, motionless figure in the doorway. The factory was owned by a political fanatic called Praisegod Barbon, whose name had been adopted for one of Cromwell's more rabid parliaments, and so its goods were unpopular in Royalist London – no one wanted to be accused of supporting adherents of the old regime. Consequently, Barbon's men were shabbily dressed and resentful about their change of fortune. Chaloner sympathised with their plight, and wondered how many others were consigned to poverty because of circumstances beyond their control. He watched them pass, then turned his attention back to Lincoln's Inn, wishing dawn would come, so he could abandon his chilly vigil and go to meet Thurloe in his warm chambers.

Chaloner was not usually given to hovering outside the homes of former employers, but he was uneasy about the interview, aware that its outcome would effect the rest of his life. While he waited, he recalled how, when the republic had first started to shake itself to pieces, he had been in Holland, assigned to a diplomat named Sir George Downing. Downing had hedged his bets – offering his services to the flustered ministers of the old regime, as well as to the exiled King – until he was sure which side would emerge victorious. He had kept Chaloner on his staff for two years after the Restoration, because Chaloner's reports on the Dutch navy were useful to *any* British government and Downing was more than happy to take credit for them. But in March, Downing had left The Hague and returned to England, where he and Chaloner had quarrelled violently. In a fury, he had dismissed the spy in a way that had made it difficult for him to find other work. Now, after months of futile applications, Chaloner saw his only hope was to ask Thurloe to intervene, and see whether he knew any government officials who might require an experienced pair of ears and eyes.

The significance of the meeting meant he had been unable to sleep, and he knew the time would pass more quickly if he was doing something – even if it were only standing uselessly outside Lincoln's Inn. Also, he did not want his restlessness to communicate itself to his woman, who was sure to question him about it if it did – and he did not want Metje to know what he was doing until he was sure he had some good news. She was becoming irritated with his unsuccessful attempts to find work in the city, and he did not want to admit yet another failure if his interview with Thurloe failed to bear fruit.

Time ticked past slowly. The bells in St Clement Danes

3

chimed five o'clock then six, and the city began to stir. Smoke scented the damp air as fires were kindled, and lights started to gleam along Chancery Lane. Chaloner waited until a smudge of lighter blue appeared in the eastern sky, then crossed the road to Lincoln's Inn's stocky gatehouse. Lincoln's Inn was one of four foundations with the right to license lawyers, and had been built in an age when strong doors and high walls were a prerequisite for survival.

A porter answered his knock eventually, rubbing his eyes in a way that indicated he had been asleep. He was not used to visitors calling so early, and was more interested in his breakfast than in conducting guests to the chambers of residents. He waved Chaloner inside, then set about laying the fire in his lodge. It was too bitter a morning to be long without some warmth.

'Where are you going?' he called when Chaloner set off in the direction of Chamber XIII. 'I thought you were here to see Mr Thurloe.'

'Does he no longer live in Dial Court?'

The porter smiled fondly. 'He lives there – he loves those rooms, although they are too dark and gloomy for my taste. But Mr Thurloe walks in the gardens at dawn every day. Everyone knows that, and you have been here before – I never forget a face.'

Chaloner was impressed. 'It has been months since my last visit.'

The guard grinned, pleased with himself. 'I have a good memory, which is just as well, since we have to be careful who we let in – assassination is always a risk for men like Mr Thurloe. Even though it has been nearly three years since the King came home, and everyone knows Mr Thurloe means him no harm, there are still

4

those who want Mr Thurloe dead. But if you want to see him now, it will have to be in the orchard. Go past the chapel, then turn right at the library.'

Chaloner followed his directions, passing the rectangular chapel with its peculiar open undercroft, and the ornate library with its diamond-patterned brickwork. The garden, a pleasant tangle of old fruit trees, overgrown bushes and long grass, lay to their north. The sleet had abated, although the trees still released showers of droplets each time they swayed in the breeze. The air smelled of wet vegetation, sodden soil and the richer aroma of the compost heaps lined up under the library's windows. Chaloner tried not to shiver when the wind cut through his cloak, afraid Thurloe would interpret it as a sign of nervousness.

The man who was often credited with running Cromwell's government single-handedly could be seen walking along a path still strewn with old leaves from the previous autumn. He was slightly built, with medium-brown hair that fell to his shoulders. His blue eyes were often soulful, which led people to imagine him gentle or timid. He was neither, and there was a core of steel in Thurloe that had shocked more than one would-be traitor. But although he was ruthless and determined, Chaloner had never known him to be cruel or vindictive – not during his seven years as Secretary of State and Spymaster, or in the unsettled period since the collapse of the Commonwealth. As Chaloner approached, he coughed softly, to let the ex-Spymaster know he was coming.

'Thomas,' said Thurloe, relaxing the hand that had been reaching for his sword. 'You are early.'

'You said dawn, sir,' replied Chaloner, glancing up at

5

the sky. The east was definitely lighter than the pitch black of the west.

Thurloe raised his eyebrows. 'I suppose distant glimmerings might be considered dawn by some, although not by most. You have been away from England too long, and have adopted foreign notions.'

'I assumed you would be busy once it was light enough to read.'

Thurloe smiled. 'Well, let us stroll in the darkness together, then. I do not like these gloomy winter mornings, and your company will not be unwelcome. What can I do for you?'

'Do you have a gun, sir?' asked Chaloner, as they began to walk. He gestured to the walls. 'It would not be difficult to scale those, and a sword is no protection against a pistol.'

'Is that why you came?' asked Thurloe. He sounded amused. 'To ask after my personal safety?'

'No,' replied Chaloner sheepishly. 'I came to ask whether you might write me a testimonial, so I can apply for employment with the new government. As you know, Downing dismissed me in March, and . . .' He hesitated, not sure how to describe the awkwardness of his situation without saying anything rude about Downing. For all he knew, Downing and Thurloe were still friends.

'And he has never liked you, and declines to recommend you to his successor,' finished Thurloe baldly. 'Worse, he has put it about White Hall that you should never be hired again.'

'Yes, sir,' said Chaloner uncomfortably.

'And his malign influence stretches even further than that,' Thurloe went on. 'By declining to write you a reference, he is effectively ensuring you will never work for any respectable organisation again. Potential employers will want to know what you have been doing all your adult life, and your choice is either to admit an association with Downing, who will then say unpleasant things about you, or confess to being a spy, which is likely to see you killed.'

Chaloner nodded unhappily. 'But although I worked under him, you were my real master – not just for the past five years in Holland, but in France, Portugal and Denmark before that – and so you are just as qualified to give an account of my skills as he is. In fact, you are more so, because I shared *some* of my intelligence with him, but not all – anything particularly important was sent to you without his knowledge.'

'I would never tell him that, if I were you. He would think you considered him untrustworthy.'

'I did – and I was right,' said Chaloner, seeing there was no way to explain his situation without denigrating Downing – and if he and Thurloe were still friends, then that was unfortunate but unavoidable. 'He was sending information to the exiled King while professing loyalty to you, some of which served to weaken the Commonwealth and hasten its demise.'

'Hush, Thomas! It is not wise to make such comments, not even to me – especially since I happen to know you were no dedicated Parliamentarian yourself. Your loyalty lies with your country, not with its shifting governments, which is as it should be. But we should not waste time discussing Downing. What did you—?' He dropped his hand to his sword a second time when he became aware of someone moving through the trees.

'A messenger, sir,' said Chaloner. The dagger he kept hidden in the sleeve of his tunic had dropped into his hand several moments earlier, when he had heard a twig snap underfoot. 'From the General Letter Office. I recognise his livery.'

'It is young Charles-Stewart,' said Thurloe in relief, beckoning the boy forward. 'Named after the King we executed thirteen years ago – not that I had any hand in *that* business, I hasten to add. However, you and I worked for the men who did, which makes us both suspect.'

The boy approached Thurloe with a friendly grin that suggested he had delivered letters to Lincoln's Inn before, and handed him a satchel. While Thurloe asked after the lad's ailing mother, Chaloner tactfully withdrew. He was replacing the dagger in its hiding place when there was a blur of movement and Charles-Stewart dropped to his knees. Thurloe stumbled backwards with a cry, and Chaloner saw two figures running towards the wall. One carried the satchel. Chaloner was racing towards them almost before his mind had registered what was happening.

'Help the boy!' Thurloe yelled, reaching towards him as he flew past. Chaloner staggered, and almost lost his footing in the sleet-plastered grass when he tried to avoid colliding with the frantic ex-Spymaster. 'Do something! Hurry!'

Cursing under his breath, Chaloner skidded to a halt and knelt by the lad's side, watching the two men scale the wall with half his attention, while the rest told him there was nothing he could do for Charles-Stewart. The knife had entered the lad's chest and death would have been virtually instant.

'I am sorry,' he said to the distraught Thurloe. 'He is dead.'

8

Thurloe's face turned from appalled to dangerous as he hauled Chaloner to his feet and shoved him towards the wall. 'Then catch those villains,' he snarled. 'Catch them – at all costs!'

Chaloner ran as hard as he could, but was nowhere near fast enough to gain the ground he had lost while stopping to tend the messenger. The two robbers had turned right along the wide avenue called Holborn, and were almost to the bridge, where he knew they would disappear into the chaotic maze of alleys that crowded the banks of the Fleet River. He forced himself on. Then the shorter of the pair collided with a cart, and his accomplice screamed abuse at him until he could regain his feet. Chaloner began to catch up, but was still too far away to capitalise on the mishap. When he saw they would reach the labyrinth of slums unchecked, the taller of the two turned to give Chaloner a triumphant, jeering salute before ducking down a lane. Chaloner tore towards the entrance, but when he reached it, feet skating across the treacherous, dung-slick cobbles, he found it empty.

The alley was not for the faint-hearted. It lay close to the Fleet, which meant it reeked not only of sewage, but of the odorous fumes released by nearby tanneries, soap-boilers and slaughterhouses. Over the years, tenements had clawed their way upwards to accommodate the increasing demand for housing, and, with each new floor, they inched closer to the buildings opposite, so the sky was now no more than a slender grey ribbon high above. At street level the passage was a thin, dark tunnel, too narrow for carts, and the ground underfoot was soft with old rubbish, squelching and sticky from the night of rain. More lanes radiated off it – dismal, stinking fissures that never saw sunlight. The cluster of hovels known as the Fleet Rookery was the domain of beggars, thieves, ruffians and harlots, living half a dozen or more to one chamber, and only the foolish or unwary ventured into it.

Cautiously, Chaloner eased down the lane, feeling the onset of the familiar stiffness in his left leg that always followed vigorous exercise. Usually, the old war injury was no more than a nuisance – an occasional cramp when the weather turned damp – but a furious run, like the one he had just made from Lincoln's Inn, had set off the nagging ache he knew would plague him for the rest of the day. He tried to ignore it, concentrating on his surroundings as he allowed the dagger from his sleeve to slide into the palm of his hand for the second time that morning.

Out in the open, on the wide, bustling thoroughfares of roads like Holborn or the Strand, Chaloner was more than a match for any common cut-throat – time served with Cromwell's New Model Army before Thurloe had engaged him as a spy meant he knew how to use the weapons he carried – but the cramped, sordid confines of the capital's slums represented a different challenge. He knew it was rash to follow criminals into a place where its inhabitants would think nothing of killing a stranger and dumping his body in the river, but the simple truth was that he could not return to Thurloe and admit defeat – not if he wanted any sort of career in espionage.

He edged along the alley. Nothing moved, except rats foraging among discarded offal from an unlicensed butcher's shop and a few rags swinging on a washing line high above his head. The lane emptied into a larger street, and he hung back to assess it. To his right was a tiny square dominated by a rust- and slime-dappled water pump; to his left was a dung cart loaded with barrels for collecting the urine and faeces used by tanneries and gunpowder manufacturers. The cart was so wide that it filled the street completely, leaving gaps of no more than the width of a hand between it and the walls to either side.

Chaloner suspected the dung collector had been paid or forced to leave his wagon in a position that would prevent pursuit. The vehicle's stench seared the back of his throat, and he did not relish the prospect of scrambling across its top – he knew that as soon as he did, the driver would flick his whip and the whole thing would jolt forward. If he did not topple into the brimming barrels of his own accord, someone would give him a helping hand, or stab or shoot at him when he was struggling for balance.

He tensed when a window creaked above him, then stepped smartly under the overhanging façade of a towering, five-storied tenement. Swill from a chamber-pot splattered to the ground, joining the refuse and ashes that formed the foetid carpet under his feet. He edged forward, narrowing the gap between him and the cart until he was close enough to crouch down and peer underneath it.

He saw several pairs of human legs, and there was a low murmur of conversation, although he could not hear what was being said. He stood abruptly when an old woman with a donkey approached from the direction of the square. She released the low, mournful cry that every Londoner knew meant there was fresh milk to be purchased for children and invalids. Customers would answer the call with jugs, and the animal would be milked on the spot. The woman was not alone in advertising her wares. From somewhere deeper inside the labyrinth came the rising yell of a fish-seller, while the bass bellow of a tallow merchant offered the stinking fat that could be turned into cheap candles.

Chaloner considered his options. The robbers were confident now they were on home ground, lingering at the front of the wagon to chat with the dung collector. And they had good reason to feel safe: even if Chaloner did manage to scale the cart and lay hold of them, then what would he do? Their friends would never allow him to march them to the nearest parish constable, and besides, constables were notoriously corrupt if the right coins appeared, and just as likely to slip a dagger between Chaloner's ribs and release the thieves. The sensible decision would be to return to Lincoln's Inn and tell Thurloe that he had done his best, but the culprits had been too far away by the time he had been ordered to give chase.

But he could scarcely apologise to Thurloe for failing to catch Charles-Stewart's killers with one breath, and ask for a testimonial with the next. If he wanted to convince the ex-Spymaster of his worth, then he had no choice but to do as he had been ordered.

'Milk, mister?' came a voice at Chaloner's side. The old woman was moving towards him, hemming him in with her donkey. His fingers tightened around his dagger as he scanned the street for signs of danger, aware that she might have been sent to distract him while an attack was set up.

'Not today.' There was no one else in the street, so he turned his attention to the cart and the men to the front of it.

She eased closer. Her eyes were black and shiny, and gleamed in a face that was a mask of wrinkles. 'You will not catch them from here. Go down the alley by the pump, and turn left when you see the barber's sign. Left again by the ditch will bring you to a place where you can surprise them.'

Chaloner nodded his thanks, but did not imagine for a moment that she was being helpful. She was probably trying to send him into a trap. 'I will wait here.'

He crouched again, using the donkey as a shield from anyone who might be aiming a pistol at him. The milling legs behind the cart had been reduced to just three pairs as onlookers lost interest. One wore boots that had been polished a deep, glossy black. These, Chaloner knew, belonged to the shorter of the two villains – the one who had snatched the satchel. It was the taller of the pair, who now paced restlessly, that had stabbed Charles-Stewart. The third man wore shoes that were thickly crusted in excrement, and were unquestionably the dung collector's.

Chaloner assessed the cart objectively, noting the sturdy planking around its edges. If he kept to one side and moved quickly enough, he might be able to jump over it and surprise them. His best option would be to fight into a position where he could hold his dagger to the throat of the taller one and 'persuade' him to return to Lincoln's Inn, preferably carrying the satchel. One killer and the return of stolen property might be enough to secure Thurloe's good graces.

The old woman poked him with a bony finger. 'They

13

will have a knife in you before your feet touch the ground on the other side.'

Chaloner glanced up at her, surprised she should find his intentions so transparent. 'Is that so?'

Her face was bleak as she petted her donkey. 'They killed my son – my Oliver – so I will shake the hand of any man who slits their throats, but you will not do it by climbing across the cart. They will be expecting you.'

Chaloner did not think he looked like the sort of fellow who slit throats, but supposed his very presence in the Fleet Rookery was enough to make folk assume the worst. His leather jerkin, breeches and riding boots were worn and unfashionable, but they were of good quality and marked him as someone who had not always been poor. He was of average height and build, with brown hair and grey eyes. He had a pleasant face, but not one that was in any way remarkable, and he had worked hard over the years to make his appearance as unmemorable as possible. Outstanding features were a serious disadvantage for a man who made his living as a spy.

'Who will be expecting me?' he asked, watching his quarry intently.

The old woman tutted her annoyance. 'Snow and Storey. The men you are chasing.'

'Are those their names? They did not bother with a formal introduction.'

She made a wheezing sound he assumed was a chuckle. 'Snow wears good boots – he dyes them blacker every night. Storey has yellow hair and is taller. Murdering bastards!'

Chaloner wished she would go away.

'They work for Sir John Kelyng and his chamberlain,' she went on. 'They think that makes them better than

14

the rest of us, although most around here would say it makes them vermin.'

Chaloner had no idea who she was talking about. After a decade overseas, he was a virtual stranger in his own country, and he knew he would have to conceal his ignorance of local politics when he spoke to Thurloe. He did not, however, need to hide it from nosy old ladies in the Fleet Rookery.

'Sir John Kelyng?' he asked, his attention fixed on the feet behind the cart. 'Who is he?'

The old woman regarded him in disbelief. 'You do not know Kelyng?'

Chaloner turned to look at her. 'Should I?'

She continued to gape at him. 'He is one of the King's new sergeants-at-law, and was in prison for most of the last ten years, because he was so hearty a Royalist. Now he is out of the Tower, and is devoting himself to ferreting out traitors.'

'What kind of traitors?'

'Traitors to the King – men who prefer Cromwell's lot. His chamberlain scours the gutters for scum like Snow and Storey, and pays them to listen in taverns for anyone saying the wrong things.'

Chaloner was not surprised. Although the King had been restored to his throne with blaring trumpets and cheering crowds, his ministers knew perfectly well that he would sit uneasily for a while yet. Spies would be hired to watch for any hint of rebellion, and Kelyng was doubtless just one of many who had been ordered to hunt down potential troublemakers.

The old woman rambled on, giving examples of Kelyng's disreputable doings. 'Parson Vane was fined thirty shillings for saying the old king deserved what he

15

got, and they cut off the butcher's ear for agreeing with him. Snow and Storey have no friends around here.'

Chaloner pointed to the strategically positioned cart. 'But people are still prepared to help them.'

'Potts was too scared to refuse. But while they can force a man to block a road, they cannot make us do *everything* they want. You got here unharmed, although you were watched from the moment you stepped off Holborn. So, take the lane by the pump, and stick your dagger through their rotten gizzards. And when you do, whisper "Oliver Greene". Then they will know who sent you to kill them.'

Chaloner suspected it would be a bad idea to do as she suggested, and he was not for hire as an avenging angel anyway. But his other options were limited, so he nodded his thanks and walked to the alley she had indicated, aware of her approval.

The lane was home to some of the most ramshackle buildings he had ever seen. There was not a vertical line in sight, and he wondered whether she had directed him down it because it was in imminent danger of collapse. He began to run, dagger openly drawn. A man started to come of out of a door, but backed inside hurriedly when he saw Chaloner and his glinting blade. Then came the sound of a key being turned; in the Fleet Rookery it was always wiser to see and hear nothing.

A left turn took Chaloner into an alley so narrow that he had to turn sideways. It was a perfect place for an ambush, since he could not protect himself in such a confined space. But he met no one, and emerged into a lane that was considerably wider – large enough for a horse-drawn carriage to pass, although its wheels scraped against the houses on either side, producing showers of rotten splinters and earning yells of outrage from the owners. After another left turn, he saw the old woman was right: he could now see his quarry clearly.

Snow and Storey had moved with the dung collector, Potts, to stand outside an alehouse. These had been declared illegal during the Commonwealth, since they fermented sedition and disorder, but the one in the Fleet Rookery looked as though it had ignored the prohibition. The benches outside were worn shiny from generations of rumps, while the taps and barrels in the adjacent yard were in good working order. The three men were drinking, celebrating the escape. The two robbers looked hard, rough and villainous, and exactly the kind of lout hired by ruthless officials to root out treachery among the poorer classes. Snow still carried the satchel he had grabbed from Thurloe, although he had made no attempt to inspect its contents. Either he knew better than to try, or he could not read.

Chaloner slid into the shadows of a doorway, and reviewed the situation. Storey wore a sword and Snow had a pistol. It was the firearm that would be the problem: Chaloner was not afraid of being shot at – it was an old gun from the wars, of a type that was notoriously unreliable – but the noise of its discharge would draw unwanted attention. The alehouse was busy, despite the fact that it was not long past dawn, and at the first sounds of a skirmish, men would rush out to join in.

Potts climbed on to his wagon and scanned the lane Chaloner had recently vacated. 'You lost him,' he said, jumping down again. 'He was a constable, you say? Which parish?'

'Er . . . Whitechapel,' replied Snow, swigging his beer.

'You were thieving over there?' asked Potts, eyeing the

pouch. It was battered and old, but still not something Snow would have owned.

Snow was indignant. 'No, we were not!'

'Why was he after you, then?' asked the dung collector with cool logic.

Storey looked smug. 'Because we are loyal to the Crown. Traitors – like Oliver Cromwell's lickspittle son Richard – want to kill us, so they can start a revolt and behead another King Charles. We stand in their way, and they will do anything to be rid of us.'

'The King recruited us special,' bragged Snow. 'He hates rebels – you only have to go to Westminster Hall to see that.'

'I did go,' said Potts. 'I saw Oliver Cromwell's head on a pole, and a few others, too. King-killers, they said. Henry Thurloe was there – the old Spymaster.' He rubbed his chin. 'Or did Thurloe get a post in the new government? It is difficult to keep up with it all – not that it makes much difference to me. I still scrape dung, no matter who is in charge.'

'*John* Thurloe,' corrected Snow superiorly. 'And there *is* a difference between the King and the Commonwealth. There were no alehouses under Cromwell, for a start.'

Potts looked dubious, indicating Chaloner's assessment had been accurate: the Fleet tavern had ignored the edicts, and no one had bothered – or dared – to stop it.

'But Thurloe's head is not outside Westminster,' said Storey, eager to show off his superior knowledge of powerful men. 'Kelyng said the man had collected so much dirty information about Royalists when he was Cromwell's Spymaster, that no one dares move against him now, lest he reveals something embarrassing.'

18

'Kelyng told you that?' asked Potts. He looked more uneasy than impressed. 'Personally?'

'Well, he told his chamberlain, but we were meant to hear,' confided Snow. 'He also said that Thurloe was offered a post in the new government, but he rejected it, and sits at Lincoln's Inn reading books about the law, hoping to find a legal way to get rid of the King.'

'Well, Thurloe *was* a lawyer once,' Storey pointed out. '*He* says he refused the King's offer because of poor health, but Kelyng says he is lying. Kelyng means to bring him low anyway.'

Chaloner frowned, wondering whether their gossip bore any relation to the truth. He had assumed the theft of the satchel was simply that – two robbers opportunistically grabbing something that might be valuable – but now it seemed one of the King's officers had actually commissioned Snow and Storey to intercept Thurloe's private post. Thurloe had acquired many enemies during his years as Cromwell's most trusted advisor, so it was no surprise to learn that some remained determined to see him destroyed.

Potts's face assumed a wily expression. 'If that constable was Thurloe's man, then you owe me another jug of ale. I might have been killed helping you, and . . .'

In one sure, swift movement, Snow whipped a dagger from its sheath and had the man pressed against the wall with the blade under his chin. Terrified, Potts struggled to stand on tiptoe, to relieve the sharp pressure against the soft skin of his neck.

'You might be killed yet – for a traitor,' said Snow coldly. 'Shall I tell Kelyng that your loyalty to the King costs? Do you want to be hanged and quartered, like the regicides?'

19

'The what?' squeaked Potts in alarm. 'I do not know them! I am not one of their number!'

Snow sighed his disdain at the fellow's ignorance. 'The regicides were the men who signed the old king's death warrant – fifty-nine of them. Three had a traitor's death back in April, and unless you want to die like them, you will be satisfied with what you have already been given.'

He released Potts, who backed away, hand to the oozing cut on his throat. Without another word, the dung-collector clambered into his wagon and flicked his whip at the horse. The animal strained forward, then moved ahead, making the contents of its barrels slosh over the rims and forcing Storey and Snow to scramble into the alehouse to avoid the yellow-brown cascade. Inside the tavern, men huddled over their beer and pretended not to notice.

Storey and Snow ordered more ale, while Chaloner waited patiently. It was now obvious that his first priority was to learn as much as he could about Kelyng and that arresting the robbers came second – he could always hunt them out later and see them brought to justice. Eventually, the two men drained their flagons and left the alehouse, making obscene gestures when the land-lord suggested payment.

It was a dull day, with pewter-coloured clouds blocking out the sun and rendering the alleys even more dark and oppressive than usual. The dimness helped Chaloner, though, allowing him to follow his quarry more easily. Stalking was a skill he had honed to perfection, and neither man had any inkling that he was being pursued. He found a filthy blanket, crushed into the muck of the street and full of vermin. He pulled it over his head, stooping and exaggerating his limp as he did so. The hasty disguise was far from perfect, but it was sufficient to fool the likes of Snow and Storey.

It was not long before they were out of the Fleet's dark kingdom and back on Holborn, retracing the route along which they had been chased. Chaloner ditched the blanket, and retrieved the hat he had tucked inside his jerkin. Once he had donned it, and turned his black cloak inside out to display its tan-coloured lining, he was confident they would not recognise him should they happen to glance around. The pair swaggered down Fetter Lane, past the house where Chaloner rented rooms and, for a moment, he thought they might stop for yet more ale at the Golden Lion, a tavern popular with men who liked the fact that its landlord never asked questions about their business.

He ducked into the tavern's stable when he saw his neighbour, William North, striding towards him. He did not want to be waylaid with polite conversation, and he certainly did not want to explain why he was shadowing criminals. North was a Puritan, and his dark, plain clothes contrasted starkly with the flamboyant merchants around him who were dressed in the very latest fashions – cassocks with wide cuffs, petticoat breeches with cascading ribbons and frills, ruffled shirt sleeves, and the curly wigs popular at Court. He carried a Bible in one hand, but since he was also a moderately successful jeweller, there was a sheaf of accounts in the other. Preoccupied with his own affairs, the Puritan did not so much as glance towards the stable as he hurried past with his chattering colleagues.

Snow and Storey turned on to Fleet Street, then headed for the Strand, passing the Norman church of St Clement

21

Danes with its stocky tower of pale stone. The Strand was one of London's major thoroughfares, with handsome mansions on its southern side, and an unruly clutter of hovels and taverns lying to the north. Here, private carriages were more numerous than handcarts, ferrying the wealthy to and from their businesses and homes. Sleek merchants peered out, their elegant wives rocking next to them. Pickpockets slunk here and there, maimed soldiers from the wars begged for alms, and a band of drunken seamen staggered noisily towards their ship, shadowed by hopeful prostitutes.

At the end of the Strand was a spacious avenue leading to the Palace of White Hall, the King's London residence. This was a sprawling mass of buildings that included not only accommodation for the monarch and his retinue, but tennis courts, a bowling alley, gardens, a chapel, offices for his Ministers of State, and the Banqueting House – outside of which Charles I had been beheaded some thirteen years before.

The Banqueting House held a further significance for Chaloner. Like many men who had backed the losing side and been forced to abandon their property after the collapse of the Commonwealth, one of his uncles had converted land to coins and cached them. The elder Chaloner had secreted his treasure under a flagstone in the Banqueting House's main chamber. His reasoning had been that the new regime would be too busy with its survival to think about prising up a good marble floor, and his hoard would therefore be safe. On his deathbed, he had confided its location to his nephew, with the request that Chaloner retrieve the money and present it to his sons when the current wave of persecution was spent. Uncomfortable and wary in the city where he was so much a stranger, Chaloner had kept his curiosity in check, and had not even gone to see whether he could identify the right tile.

One peculiar characteristic of the Palace of White Hall was that the main road from the city to Westminster ran clean through its centre. The avenue – the southern part of which was named King Street in deference to the fact that it cut the sovereign's lodgings in half – was always thick with carts, carriages, horses, livestock, soldiers, merchants, courtiers and clerks, and the heaving throng made it even easier for Chaloner to follow the two robbers. The thunder of wheels, feet and hoofs on cobbles, the babble of conversation, and the various bells, gongs and rattles used by traders were deafening. The cacophony almost drowned out the ranting of the street preacher who stood on the stump of the old Charing Cross and the agitated yaps of a dog tethered outside the Angel tavern.

White Hall was even busier than usual that day, because the Banqueting House was set to be used for a ceremony in which Charles 'touched' his subjects in the hope of curing them of the glandular disease known as the King's Evil, or scrofula. He took such duties seriously, and the occasions always attracted crowds.

Chaloner was not surprised that Snow and Storey were taking the stolen satchel to White Hall, since, as a man apparently devoted to exposing the King's enemies, Kelyng might well work or live near the buildings from which the affairs of state were run. The two thieves did not enter the palace grounds, however. They stopped at a well outside, where they pretended to mingle with servants from the nearby mansions.

The area around the conduit was crowded. Some folk

carried containers that were suspiciously small, indicating they were there only because it afforded an opportunity to exchange gossip with the members of other rich households, while others pushed carts loaded with empty barrels. Chaloner had spent a good deal of time at such places in the past, collecting information that was then converted into cipher and sent to Thurloe. He eased into the throng, smiling at a young woman and engaging her in idle conversation. His naturally affable manner meant people seldom objected to his friendly approaches, enabling him to blend into his surroundings without raising suspicion. He made a show of listening to her lurid revelations about the wanton Lady Castlemaine – the King's favourite mistress – but most of his attention was on Storey and Snow. He could tell from their forced casualness that they were waiting for something to happen.

Within moments, a man wearing a livery of mustard yellow approached. He was in his late forties, with a lined, dour face. He carried himself erect, in the way of an old soldier, and there were two other details that rendered him distinctive: first, upon his little finger, he wore an emerald ring that looked altogether too expensive to be owned by a servant, and second, he was missing an eye.

He pushed his way towards the robbers, making no attempt to disguise the fact that they were his objective. Snow handed him the satchel and received a purse in exchange, while Storey attempted to create a diversion by jostling a groom. The groom's tunic was emblazoned with the arms adopted by Sir Richard Ingoldsby, a man known even to an outsider like Chaloner. Ingoldsby, a regicide, had convinced King Charles that he had not *meant* to add his signature to his father's death warrant – Cromwell had grabbed his hand and shaped the letters against his will. Contrary to all reason, the King had believed him, and even the most hardened of cynics were astonished to learn that not only had Ingoldsby been forgiven his crime, but he was to be awarded a knight-hood, too.

The groom whipped out a pistol, making bystanders scatter in alarm. Storey promptly fled, forcing Snow to race after him. Chaloner watched them go, but made no attempt to follow. He knew their names and a tavern where they drank; they would still pay for murdering the post-boy. But first, he needed to concentrate on the more immediate problem represented by Kelyng and why he should want to intercept Thurloe's private messages, so he turned back to the servant who had purchased the satchel. The fellow crossed the street and made for the Royal Mews – once stables but now converted to homes for senior court officials – and disappeared through a door that led to an ill-kept garden. Chaloner darted after him, and the man's jaw dropped in astonishment when the satchel was ripped from his hands.

'You have no right to come in here,' he began angrily, trying to grab it back. 'You—'

Chaloner drew his dagger, making him jump away in alarm. 'Who do you work for?'

The servant glanced behind him, although whether because he was looking for rescue or because he was afraid of being heard answering, Chaloner could not be sure. 'This is Sir John Kelyng's house.'

'Who is he?'

The man's eyebrows shot up, but he answered anyway. 'One of His Majesty's lawyers, famous for his prosecution

25

of regicides and traitors.' His hand started to edge towards his knife, but Chaloner saw the stealthy movement, and knocked the weapon from his fingers.

'Why does he pay ruffians to steal satchels?'

'His affairs are none of your business,' the servant replied irritably. 'Now give me that bag.'

Chaloner took a step forward, dagger at the ready.

'He told me to collect a pouch from the fountain,' replied the servant with an impatient sigh, seeing in Chaloner's determined expression that he had no choice but to reply. 'He did not tell me why, and I am not so reckless as to ask.'

'I do not believe you.'

'That is not my problem. Now, I have more important—'

Chaloner swung around when he heard the rustle of leaves behind him. A sharp hiss cut through the air, and instinct and training were responsible for his abrupt dive off the moss-encrusted path. A moment later, the servant joined him on the ground, a blade embedded in his chest and his single eye already beginning to glaze with encroaching death. Blood gushed from his mouth in a way that indicated a lung had been pierced. He turned his head slightly, and looked at Chaloner.

'Praise God's one son,' he whispered.

All Chaloner's attention was on the trees where the knifeman still hid. He did not reply.

'Praise God's one son,' said the man, a little louder. He coughed and tugged Chaloner's cloak. The ring flashed green on his finger. 'It is dangerous for . . . seven. Remember . . .'

Chaloner glanced at him and saw desperation in his face. 'Lie still. I will find help.'

26

The man revealed bloodstained teeth in a grimace that indicated he knew he was beyond earthly assistance. 'Remember to . . . trust no one. Praise God's one . . .'

'Amen,' muttered Chaloner mechanically, concentrating on the leaves that were beginning to tremble in a way that suggested another attack was about to be launched. He looped the satchel around his shoulder, gripped his dagger and prepared to make his move.

'You do not . . . understand.' Chaloner glanced at the servant a second time, and sensed he no longer knew what he was saying. 'I am . . . John Hewson . . . of seven . . . Trust no one, and praise . . .'

There was a sharp crack, as someone trod on a twig in the bushes ahead. Chaloner tensed, trying to see through the tangled undergrowth. He heard Hewson's breathing stop, and a detached part of his mind pondered the question of whether the knife had missed its real target, or whether Hewson had been killed because he was dispensing information. There was no way to know, although he was able to conclude, from the direction of the snap and the shivering foliage, that there were *two* men lurking in the thicket ahead. Knowing they would expect him to head for the gate, since it was the obvious route to freedom, he scrambled upright and ran in the opposite direction – towards the house that stood at the end of the garden. There was a loud pop as a pistol went off, and he hit the ground hard. His senses reeled from the impact, and he became aware of urgent shouting from the road. The King was coming. Then another shot rang out.

The discharge of firearms close to a monarch was a relatively unusual event in London, and, after a short, stunned

27

silence, chaos erupted. Footsteps clattered as people ran towards the Banqueting House, and voices clamoured to know what was happening. An agitated horse whinnied in a way that suggested its rider was losing control of it, and a dog barked furiously. The word 'treason' was suddenly in the air, and it was not long before folk were yelling that the King had been assassinated.

Inside the garden, Chaloner's attackers held a hissing conversation that suggested one of them had not associated the discharge of his own firearm with the commotion, and was keen to go to the King's assistance. The other rebuked him with a testy impatience that indicated it was not the first time his companion had drawn stupid conclusions. While they argued, Chaloner climbed to his feet, ignoring the protesting stab in his weak leg, and took refuge in a patch of nettles. The weeds were thick, but he was oblivious to their stings as he waited to see what his assailants would do, fingers wrapped loosely around his dagger.

He ducked when they moved along the path towards him. The one in front wore a white skullcap, a cloak of burgundy wool, blue petticoat breeches and a satin shirt with ruffled sleeves. His face reminded Chaloner of a wolf's, with pointed chin, wide mouth, sharp yellow teeth and close-set eyes. He carried a pistol in one hand and a sword in the other, and his face wore a fierce expression that turned to anger when he saw the servant.

'Jones is dead,' he whispered furiously, turning to his companion.

'So I see,' replied the other. Chaloner studied him carefully, sensing him to be the more dangerous of the pair. He was heavily built, and had massive fists, like hams. He was almost as finely dressed as the first man,

28

although his coat was last year's fashion and his wig looked as though it had been made using someone else's measurements. Rings adorned his fingers, and there was a pair of calfskin gloves tucked into his belt. However, his finery and the superior airs he gave himself did not disguise the fact that he had probably not been born to them, and that elegance and wealth was something he had acquired along the way.

'That is *your* dagger,' hissed the wolf.

The second man seemed unperturbed by what was essentially an accusation. 'Then the intruder used it to kill Jones. It is obvious.'

The wolf sighed angrily, but appeared to accept the claim. 'He will be heading for the back gate, aiming to escape into the crowds around the Banqueting House. Guard it, while I search the garden.'

'I would rather—' began the second.

'No, Bennet!' interrupted the wolf. 'I do not want your opinion. Just do as I say.'

Bennet's face was a mask of disapproval, but he slouched off in the direction indicated by his companion's pointing finger. The wolf, using his sword as a scythe to probe the vegetation, began to move towards Chaloner, who picked up a handful of dirt and tossed it into a bed of mint.

'Stay where you are,' ordered the wolf, when Bennet immediately turned towards the noise with a predatory grin. 'It is a trick.'

Chaloner grabbed a second fistful of soil and lobbed it at the gate, which had Bennet kicking at the brambles in a frenzied attempt to determine whether someone was hiding there. When the wolf turned to berate him, Chaloner leapt to his feet and ran full pelt towards the house. Another crack echoed as a pistol was discharged, and splinters flew from a nearby tree. Chaloner hurdled a bed of winter cabbages, jigged behind a tangle of raspberry canes, and raced into the steamy warmth of a kitchen. Startled scullions gaped as he pounded through their domain, his feet skidding on the grease-coated floor. He saw an exit at the far end and powered towards it, knocking over a boy carrying a tureen of soup; the bowl crashed to the floor, adding its contents to the already slick surface.

Chaloner found himself in a long hallway, at the end of which was a door. He heard Bennet shout behind him, ordering him to stop. A scullion grabbed his arm, but Chaloner felled him with a punch. He reached the door, and spent several agonising seconds pulling away a bar, praying it would not be locked, too – if it was, then he was a dead man, because there was nowhere to hide and even the most inept of gunmen could not fail to miss him at such close range.

The yelling grew closer. Bennet cursed foully as he lost his footing in the oily spillage and went flying in a whirlwind of arms and legs. Chaloner tugged at the door. It did not budge. The wolf was scrambling over Bennet and bringing a pistol to bear, triumph lighting his pointed features. Made strong by desperation, Chaloner hauled on the door again. Something snapped and it flew open. Then he was outside, disappearing into the crowd that was surging towards the Banqueting House.

Chaloner mingled with the throng, pulling off hat, wig and cloak and tucking them under his arm in an attempt to change his appearance and confuse his pursuers. He knew they would expect him to head in the opposite direction, to put as much distance between him and the scene of Hewson's – or was it Jones's? – death as possible, so he did the reverse: he allowed the crowd to take him back towards Kelyng's rear gate, and then on to White Hall. He listened to people's speculations as he moved among them, keeping his head down and working at being inconspicuous.

Everyone seemed to know that shots had been fired as the King had ridden from St James's Park to the Touching Ceremony, and some folk claimed to have heard them. A baker said there had been three loud bangs, but a woman swore on the lives of her children that there had been eight. Most believed an attempt had been made on the King's life, although an apprentice wearing a blood-splattered apron maintained that the King had shot one of his spaniels, to show his new government what would happen to them if they used him as they had his father. A fat vicar was of the opinion that the incident originated with Lady Castlemaine, whose husband had executed one of her many lovers. Chaloner recalled a comment his uncle had once made about how a mob could be controlled with rumours, but how dangerous it could be if the tales took on a life of their own.

He glanced behind him. The wolf was on the doorstep, scanning the street with one hand behind his back to conceal his reloaded weapon. He scowled when Bennet arrived and elbowed him to share the vantage point. Unlike his companion, Bennet made no attempt to disguise the fact that he was armed, and Chaloner was under the impression that he would shoot if he recognised his prey, regardless of the fact that he would probably hit the wrong person.

More people joined the crowd, and Chaloner was jostled by a thin, ungainly creature with red-rimmed eyes and the stooped shoulders of a scholar. In a gesture of apology, the man draped a comradely arm around his shoulders, and Chaloner, knowing he was less likely to be spotted with someone than alone, made no effort to shrug him off. When he glanced around again, the wolf was swimming against the crowd in the direction he imagined Chaloner would have taken, although Bennet continued to monitor the faces that streamed past.

'Do not be alarmed, friends,' called a chambermaid from a window above their heads. 'It is only Kelyng's men blasting at each other with pistols. They do it all the time.'

'It was the King!' shouted a grubby boy. 'His Majesty shot Kelyng.'

Another rumour was born, and people seemed pleased to learn the identity of this particular victim. Smiles broke out, and the butcher's apprentice pulled a flask from his jerkin and offered a toast.

'It does not surprise me that Kelyng's rabble are responsible,' said the thin man to Chaloner, raising his voice above the babble. 'It is common knowledge that he has been hiring felons and vagabonds these last few months. Such men will not be easy to control, and spats among them will be inevitable.'

'Why has Kelyng been recruiting such folk?' asked Chaloner.

The man grimaced. 'He *says* it is to protect the King against the remnants of the last government – rebels who remain loyal to Richard Cromwell – but I am more inclined to believe the story that he intends to take up where John Thurloe left off, and employ a legion of spies

32

that will make him the most powerful man in the country.'

Chaloner was thoughtful. Was that why Kelyng had sent men to intercept Thurloe's post? Did he realise that in order to create such an army, the vestiges of the last one needed to be totally eradicated? Yet Snow and Storey were overconfident and stupid, while the wolf and Bennet had hardly been a model of competence, either. Thurloe was more than a match for any of them. Chaloner's new friend was speaking again.

'I wish a pox on the lot of them, personally. We were promised a new order, but this government is no better for the common man than was the last one.'

'You do not look like a common man to me,' said Chaloner. He ducked away from the fellow's embrace; he was no longer in danger, and did not need to maintain the disguise.

The man inclined his head in formal greeting. 'William Leybourn: bookseller, printer, surveyor and mathematician. I live on Monkwell Street in Cripplegate, should you want to browse the finest collection of tomes in the city – including some written by me. And you? What is your trade, other than running for your life?'

Chaloner regarded him askance. 'Why do you say that?'

'I saw you race from Kelyng's house as though it were on fire, and I know what it means when a man removes hat, wig and cloak on a cold winter's day – he does not want to be recognised. I also saw the furious expression on Kelyng's face when he realised he had lost you.'

Chaloner was startled by the revelation. 'That was Kelyng?'

It was Leybourn's turn to be astonished. 'You do not recognise Kelyng?'

Chaloner cursed himself for speaking without thinking. 'I have not been in London long,' he explained, slipping easily into the role of country bumpkin; a good deal could be learned by pretending to be a clueless provincial. The ruse did not work, however, and Leybourn narrowed his eyes and regarded him suspiciously.

'Where were you before? The moon?'

Chaloner changed tactics, opting for honesty instead. 'The United Provinces of the Netherlands.' Bitter experience had taught him it was wise to be truthful when possible, since it left fewer opportunities for being caught out in lies.

'I see,' said Leybourn. 'Well, you will not learn much that makes sense from the Dutch. All they do is eat cheese and bathe in butter. Do not look shocked. You must have read the broadsheets telling us how wicked Hollanders are waiting to invade us – to kill our children while we sleep.'

'Yes, but I am not so stupid as to believe them.'

'And neither am I,' said Leybourn. 'But you did not know that when you spoke, and to admit that you reside in Holland, when there are rumours of a royal assassination, is wildly reckless. If I were to yell that you were a Dutchman, and that you had just shot at the King, you would be torn apart before you could say Rembrandt. People are afraid of the Dutch.'

Chaloner saw he had a point, although it was unsettling to hear emotions ran quite so high. The woman who had shared his bed for the past three years, and whom he loved dearly, was Dutch, and she had mentioned a growing antipathy towards her, even from friends. He had dismissed her concerns as the natural sensitivity of a foreigner abroad – he had experienced similar misgivings

34

himself in the past – but now saw he should probably take them seriously.

'So, you do not know Kelyng,' mused Leybourn. 'In that case, why were you in his house?'

'You ask a lot of questions.'

Leybourn grinned, unrepentant. 'I cannot help myself. It is not every day I see someone get the better of Kelyng, God rot his putrid soul.'

'What has he done to you?'

'He owes me money. He ordered several expensive legal texts last year – as a newly appointed sergeant-at-law, he needs them for his work – but now he refuses to pay.'

'Why?'

'On the grounds that he is using them to serve the King. It is flagrant extortion, but he says that if I complain, my comments will be considered treason.'

'Just for asking to be reimbursed?'

'Quite,' agreed Leybourn bitterly. 'Despicable, is it not? So, now you see why I detest the fellow and his niggardly ways. Any man who annoys him is a friend of mine.'

Their section of the crowd had arrived at the Banqueting House, joining the masses already there. Chaloner had never seen so many sick people, all hoping the King would cure them. Here more rumours circulated. Folk had seen the King arrive moments before, so there were no tales that he had been killed, although Chaloner was disconcerted to hear the claim that Dutch marksmen had been at large. Leybourn had been right to advise him to caution, and he saw how dangerous it was to be unaware of London's current bigotries.

He was listening with growing horror to an Anglican

35

priest, who was taking advantage of the gathering to bellow an impromptu sermon about the evils of any religion not consistent with his own, when another thin, stoop-shouldered man approached. Leybourn introduced him as his brother and business partner Robert, although Chaloner had guessed they were related: both had gaunt, pale faces and bony frames. Robert, more caustic than his sibling, matter-of-factly informed them that the shots heard near the Royal Mews had been due to the unpopular Sir George Downing falling off his horse – the fellow was so afraid someone might kill him, that he always carried three loaded pistols, and each had ignited when he had taken his tumble. The general consensus, Robert maintained, was that it was a pity one of the balls had not travelled through the man's black heart.

Chaloner's thoughts turned to the servant who lay dead in Kelyng's garden, who had said his name was Hewson, contrary to what his employer seemed to believe. He tried again to decide whether Bennet had killed Hewson deliberately, or whether he had simply missed his intended target. He did not have enough information to say one way or the other, but Hewson, along with poor Charles-Stewart, made two dead that morning, and it was barely nine o'clock.

'I should go,' he said, breaking into Robert's scathing tirade against Downing. He knew he should return to Thurloe as soon as possible, and not waste time listening to the gossip of a pair of booksellers, gratifying though it might be: having spent five years working with Downing, Chaloner doubted any Londoner could loathe the man as much as he did.

Leybourn caught his arm. 'You are leaving? Without

36

telling us how you came to be chased from Kelyng's house by the man himself? And you have not told us your name.'

'Thomas Heyden,' replied Chaloner, giving his usual alias. Thurloe had chosen the name because it was neither resoundingly English nor resoundingly foreign. 'I am a clerk.'

The last statement rankled, because it happened to be true. In the absence of other work, he managed the accounts for Fetter Lane's Nonconformist chapel, although it took only a few hours each week and the pay barely covered the rent. Puritans, so numerous and powerful during the Commonwealth, were becoming an ever-dwindling minority as people shifted back to traditional Anglicanism, and few sensible folk had anything to do with them. If Chaloner had not been so desperate, he would not have done, either, and leaving the Puritans' employ was yet another reason why he hoped Thurloe would help him.

'What kind of clerk?' asked Leybourn.

Chaloner was not about to admit to a link with an unpopular sect. 'A household clerk.'

'Whose household?' pressed Leybourn. He tapped his chin with a long forefinger. 'Not Downing's? You said you have been in Holland, and he is recently returned from there.'

'Then he predicted the collapse of the Commonwealth and became a Royalist,' elaborated Robert. 'However, no one likes a turncoat, not even one who turns to the King.'

He spat, leaving Chaloner wondering whether he had been cornered by a pair of rebels. Or were they Cavaliers, hired to ferret out potential traitors by encouraging seditious talk? He listened to their dialogue uneasily, heartily wishing he had a better understanding of affairs in his native country.

'And in order to prove himself, he did that unspeakably nasty thing which shocked Dutchmen and Englishmen alike,' added Leybourn. Chaloner kept his expression neutral: Downing's controversial action the previous March was certainly not something he was prepared to discuss with strangers. 'It meant he and his household were obliged to leave The Hague rather abruptly. Are we right, Heyden? Is Downing your master?'

After a moment's reflection, Chaloner opted for honesty again: he did not want to be reported as a suspicious character by declining to answer, and Leybourn was too astute for brazen lies.

'I worked for Downing,' he admitted, watching the bookseller's triumphant grin that he had been right. 'But he did not need a Dutch-speaking clerk in London, so I was released.'

'Consider yourself fortunate. No decent man should align himself with such a villain.'

'No,' agreed Chaloner fervently. 'He should not.'

'You do not like him?' asked Robert keenly.

Since very few people liked Downing, especially once they had met him, Chaloner had no qualms about voicing his real opinion of the man. 'I do not. He dismissed me without testimonials, because he said I was untrustworthy.'

'Why did he think that?' asked Leybourn curiously.

Chaloner shrugged. 'Well, I did carry on with his daughter's governess for a couple of years.'

'Did you wed her?' asked Robert, brazenly prying now. 'Or were you just trying to annoy a man who prides

38

himself on being able to seduce any wench who takes his fancy?'

'She still comes to me most nights,' replied Chaloner evasively.

'She will not take you, because you are poor,' surmised Leybourn with his annoying intuitiveness. He nodded at Chaloner's head. 'At a time when men are proud to display flowing locks, yours are short. You have good, thick hair, the kind a wigmaker might purchase from a man in urgent need of funds.'

'I usually wear a periwig,' said Chaloner, wondering how the man was able to draw so many accurate conclusions. It was disconcerting, and he did not like it. He pulled the headpiece, which the wigmaker had provided as part of the bargain, from his pocket. He hated it: it smelled of the horse whose tail had provided the raw materials, and had a tendency to slip to one side. 'But I was hot.'

'Where do you live?' asked Leybourn. 'If it is near Cripplegate, we can share a carriage.'

'*I* would rather walk,' said Robert, beginning to move away. 'The last time I treated myself to a carriage, the driver went to the Fleet Rookery and abandoned me there. I lost my purse and most of my clothes to villains who crept out of the shadows with staves and knives.'

'I will go by water,' said Chaloner, watching him disappear into the crowd.

'Then I will come with you,' said Leybourn, in the kind of voice that suggested objections would be futile. 'I fancy a jaunt on the river. How far will you be going?'

Chaloner regarded him coolly. Was he employed by the new government to watch men who had once been in Thurloe's pay? Or was he hired by Kelyng or Downing,

39

and his tirades against them were a ruse to gain the confidence of dissenters? Or was he just a nosy bookseller, and Chaloner had been an agent for so long that he was apt to be wary of everyone? He studied the thin, eager features as they walked, and all his experience failed him: he could not tell whether Leybourn was friend or foe.

The quickest way to the nearest pier – the Westminster Stairs – was through the Holbein Gate, a sturdy but shabby edifice that straddled King Street and was a major obstacle for carts. Drivers regularly clamoured for it to be demolished, but the King stubbornly resisted any attempts to reduce the size of his palace. The gate boasted several stately chambers, and their current occupant, Chaloner learned from Leybourn, was Lady Castlemaine. Chaloner suspected that most of the stories about the King's favourite mistress were wildly exaggerated. When he had visited his boyhood home in Buckinghamshire that summer, his brothers had told him she regularly amassed gambling debts of a hundred thousand pounds, and his sisters thought she was a secret drinker. Now Leybourn was claiming she was pregnant with another of the King's brats, although her meek husband declared it was his own.

'It is not, of course,' declared Leybourn, negotiating his way along King Street. For a major thoroughfare, it was wretchedly narrow. Vehicles were nearly always at a standstill, and the congestion sometimes had to be sorted out by armed soldiers. The squeal of metal wheels on cobbles was amplified by the towering buildings on either side and, combined with the yells of traders and the racket of cattle being driven to the slaughterhouses, Chaloner could barely hear Leybourn bawling in his ear. 'I doubt Lord Castlemaine has been within a mile of his wedding bed for years. That honour is reserved for those with the funds to buy her expensive gifts.'

They reached the mighty façade of Westminster Hall, where a small crowd lingered around the place where the heads and limbs of traitors were displayed. Chaloner looked away, not wanting to see the decaying remnants of men he had met in life. Leybourn led the way to a damp wooden pier that boasted a jostling flotilla of waiting boats. Immediately, another clamour assailed their ears, as rivermen vied for their custom, offering improbably low prices that would be inflated with hidden extras at the end of the journey. Leybourn seemed to enjoy the barter, and eventually selected a villainous-looking fellow with no teeth. Chaloner followed them down the slick green steps and into a bobbing craft.

He scanned the pier as he scrambled into the bow, alert for any indication that he might have been followed. He did not think Kelyng could have caught up with him, since he had rushed off in the opposite direction, but Bennet might have managed. However, there was nothing amiss, and he began to relax, grateful to rest his aching leg. Leybourn and the boatman continued to haggle as they moved away from the jetty and eased into the powerful current that carried them north and then east, towards Temple Stairs where Chaloner intended to disembark. He had no idea what Leybourn would do, since Cripplegate was a good way from the river.

Then he heard running footsteps. It was Bennet. The chamberlain seized a riverman by the shoulder, pointed at Chaloner's craft, and silver flashed. The message was clear: more would be given if the fellow caught up. The boatman grabbed his oars, clearly intending to have what-ever had been offered. Chaloner watched, aware that a vessel containing three people could not possibly outrun one carrying two, the driver of which was already hauling as though his life depended on it. It was gaining, while Chaloner's man was enjoying a niggardly debate with Leybourn about the cost of oysters. With nowhere to run, and no means to escape, Chaloner was trapped like a fish in a barrel.

# Chapter 2

Bennet knelt in his boat, bracing himself against the rocking motion, and took a pistol from under his cloak. If his riverman thought this irregular, he made no comment, and only continued to haul on his oars for all he was worth. Chaloner's own man faltered when he saw the weapon.

'Pull,' Chaloner ordered, scrambling forward and grabbing an oar. The boatman obeyed with mute terror, and they began to ease ahead. Then Chaloner saw Bennet extend his arm and squint along the barrel. Even the most dire of marksmen could not miss at such close range, and he braced himself for the impact.

But Leybourn hauled something from his doublet. 'Fireball!' he yelled, hurling it at the other craft. It landed with a thud that was audible even at a distance. Bennet's oarsman gave a shriek of horror and dived overboard. Bennet tried to maintain his balance in the savagely bucking craft, but soon disappeared with an almighty splash. Chaloner's man cheered wildly, and stood to make obscene gestures at the bobbing heads that surfaced a moment later. Leybourn sat with a satisfied smile stamped across his thin features.

'What was it really?' asked Chaloner.

'Tobacco,' replied the bookseller. 'A customer gave it to me in exchange for one of my pamphlets. I am sorry to see the Thames have it, but it cannot be helped.'

'It is a waste,' agreed the boatman. He elbowed Chaloner away, wanting the craft back under his own control. 'This will affect the fare, gentlemen. Me being threatened with firearms costs extra.'

'And you being you rescued from gun-toting lunatics does not come cheap, either,' retorted Leybourn tartly. 'I charge for that sort of service, so I advise you to stick to our original agreement or you may find yourself in debt at the end of the journey.'

'He was trying to kill your friend,' objected the boatman. '*You* endangered *me*, by making me carry you when Gervaise Bennet was after your blood. If you got on *his* wrong side, then you had no business asking me to take you upriver. I might have been killed.'

'You are mistaken,' said Leybourn smoothly. He pointed forward, to where another boat was in disarray, oars in the water as it rotated hopelessly out of control. A large, heavily paunched man in a red wig, and a pretty, fattish girl carrying a long-handled parasol were shrieking their alarm while their boatman paddled ineffectually with his hands. 'Bennet was aiming at them. It was my quick thinking that saved the day, but *they* were the ones he was trying to shoot.'

'I doubt it,' said the boatman, inspecting the stricken craft as they passed. 'The passengers are Sir John Robinson and his daughter Fanny. Bennet would never risk harming Fanny.'

'But he does not feel as benevolent towards her father,'

argued Leybourn. 'He might well want to put a ball in Robinson's heart.'

The names meant nothing to Chaloner. 'Who are they?'

'Robinson is Lord Mayor of London,' replied the boatman, regarding him askance. 'Every decent soul knows that. He is a powerful and wealthy merchant, with fingers in every pie worth eating.'

'Robinson is also Lieutenant of the Tower,' added Leybourn helpfully. 'Bennet wanted to marry his daughter, but his offer was declined in no uncertain terms.'

'Bennet is a chamberlain,' said Chaloner, surprised. 'Yet he set his sights on the Lord Mayor's daughter? I would have thought he was aiming somewhat above his station.'

The boatman nodded, relishing an opportunity to give his opinion. 'So it was no surprise when he was turned down.'

'No surprise to most folk,' corrected Leybourn. 'It came as a great shock to Bennet himself, however. Rumour has it that he dressed himself in his finest clothes and arrived bearing a bribe of forty silver spoons. Apparently, he was stunned when Robinson told him to leave.'

'I heard it was Fanny who told him where to go,' said the boatman, laughing. 'Robinson took a fancy to the spoons, and was seriously considering the offer.'

Leybourn waved a hand to indicate detail was unimportant. 'It is common knowledge that Bennet had decided to wed Fanny, so it was deeply mortifying for him to be publicly rejected.'

'Why did he think he had a chance?' pressed Chaloner.

He had guessed, from Bennet's clothes and demeanour, that he considered himself something special, and his attitude to Kelyng had verged on the insolent. But even with delusions of grandeur, it was still a massive leap from hired servant to the son-in-law of an influential merchant.

'Ambition and an inflated notion of his own worth,' replied Leybourn. 'And he was rejected for two reasons. First, because he is just what he appears: a bully in fancy clothes. And second, he is in the pay of Kelyng, and no one wants anything to do with *him*.'

'Why not?' asked Chaloner.

'Because he is a fanatic, and thus a man without reason. Although he is said to be fond of cats.'

'It was men with violent opinions who got the last king beheaded,' stated the boatman, giving voice to an inflexible view of his own, '*and* who got that traitor Cromwell on the throne—'

'Cromwell was never king,' said Chaloner pedantically. 'The crown was offered, but he refused.'

'Only because he knew he could never keep it,' said Leybourn acidly. 'I suspect he was sorely tempted by the thought of King Oliver.'

'Did you see him dug up?' asked the boatman conversationally, as he rowed. 'When I learned he was going to be prised from his tomb, I went to watch. I saw his corpse plucked out and taken to Tyburn for hanging.'

'I was busy,' said Leybourn distastefully. 'But Kelyng was there, laughing his delight. Inflicting justice on Roundheads – dead or alive – is the sort of thing he enjoys very much.'

Chaloner winced. He was not particularly squeamish, but very little would have induced him to witness such

46

a spectacle. To him, the Royalists' treatment of Cromwell's body had smacked of a spoiled child stamping its foot because it had been deprived of its revenge, and he recalled the revulsion of the Dutch when the story had reached Holland. He did not know how Englishmen dared accuse Netherlanders of debauched and grotesque behaviour when they hacked up old corpses to provide the public with an afternoon of entertainment. He could not imagine what a black day it must have been for Thurloe, to see the remains of his friend so barbarously treated.

When the craft bumped against the seaweed-draped Temple Stairs, Leybourn dropped some coins in the boatman's hand – enough to earn him a pleased grin – and clambered inelegantly to dry land. He waved away Chaloner's offer to pay half.

'Who *are* you?' asked Chaloner, as he and the bookseller walked along the narrow lane that divided the Middle Temple from Inner Temple. London's four 'Inns of Court' – Lincoln's, Gray's, Middle Temple and Inner Temple – were all solid, semi-fortified foundations that stood aloof from the teeming metropolis that surrounded them, and within their towering walls stood peaceful courtyards, manicured gardens and gracious halls. But the public alley that ran between Inner and Middle temples, and provided access to the river from Fleet Street, was a foetid tunnel with a gate at either end, and a world apart from the rarified domains it transected. 'You are no mere peddler of books.'

Leybourn was indignant. 'No, I am not! Robert and I print and sell books to earn an honest crust, but I am actually a surveyor and a mathematician of some repute. Have you never heard of me? I have written a number

47

of erudite pamphlets and treatises. You can come to see them in my shop if you do not believe me.'

Chaloner remained unconvinced. 'Who do you work for? The King?'

'I work for no man!' protested Leybourn. His expression became spiteful. 'It is a good deal safer that way, if you are anything to go by. First Kelyng was after you, then Bennet. What have you done to make such dangerous enemies?'

'It must have been a case of mistaken identity.'

'Really,' said Leybourn flatly. 'Well, do not underestimate them. They may be bumbling fools, but they are dangerous ones. Kelyng is so ardently Royalist that he sees conspiracies everywhere, and if he thinks you are an enemy of the King, he will not rest until you are dead. And Bennet is vengeful, mean and ambitious. You would be wise to stay out their way.'

'So would you. It was your tobacco that brought about Bennet's ducking. But thank you for the ride.' They were nearing the end of the lane. 'If there is anything I can do in return . . .'

'A generous offer,' said Leybourn sullenly, 'from a man who declines to tell me where he lives. I will never find you again, even if I do have a favour to ask.'

'You can leave a message for me at the Golden Lion on Fetter Lane.'

'I might, then,' said Leybourn. He forced a smile. 'I have enjoyed meeting you, Heyden. It is not every day I am obliged to rescue someone from waving pistols.'

'And it is not every day I owe my life to a well-lobbed ball of tobacco,' said Chaloner with a pleasant smile, passing through the gate at the end of the lane and emerging into Fleet Street. 'Good morning, Mr Leybourn – and thank you.'

Once through the gate, Chaloner limped towards St Dunstan-in-the-West, unwilling to visit Thurloe until he was sure he was not being followed. Fleet Street was perfect for tailing someone, because it was chaotic and busy, and the huddle of illegal stalls along each side provided ample opportunity for disguise and conceal-ment. Leybourn was adequate – he kept his distance and exchanged his wide-brimmed hat for a skullcap – but nowhere near good enough to fool Chaloner. Smiling, because he had suspected from the start that the encounter had been engineered, Chaloner ambled past the church, then ducked behind a carriage, using it as a shield to mask his entry into the game shop at the end of Fetter Lane.

Bright pheasants, pearl-feathered pigeons and dull-eyed rabbits swung from the rafters, while the limp bodies of deer were draped in the window, like curtains. The room smelled of the sawdust scattered on the floor and the cloying scent of old death: some of the corpses had been hung rather too long. Chaloner pretended to be inspecting a hare as he waited to see what would happen outside.

Within moments, Leybourn appeared, looking this way and that in mounting annoyance when he realised he had lost his quarry. Chaloner was puzzled. Who was he? The man had certainly saved him: Bennet could not have missed at such close range, and it had only ever been a faint hope that he could have been out-rowed. But why had Leybourn risked himself? Had Thurloe set a spy to watch a spy? But how could Thurloe have known

Chaloner would end up near White Hall when he was dispatched to follow the two robbers?

After a while, Leybourn gave up the chase and walked back the way he had come. Chaloner waited a moment, then made for the door. Escape, however, was not to be so easy. Blocking the exit was the largest bird he had ever seen and, unlike the other feathered occupants of the shop, this one was alive and looked dangerous. It fluffed up its green-brown feathers, and the bare skin on its neck flushed with bad temper.

'Do not move,' came a hoarse whisper from the back of the shop. 'If you do, it will have you.'

'Thomas!' cried another voice, this one familiar. At first, Chaloner could see no one, but then he spotted his neighbour's daughter, Temperance, crouching atop a cupboard and clutching her drab Puritan skirts decorously around her knees. He liked the nineteen-year-old, who was as tall and almost as bulky as he, but who had a kind face and gentle hazel eyes. He often thought that if her father had allowed her more social contact, then they might have been friends.

'What are you doing there?' he asked. It was unlike the demure Temperance to climb furniture.

'I am trapped,' she replied, although he could hear laughter in her voice. She thought her predicament amusing, unlike the raw terror of the first person who had spoken. 'That bird snaps at me every time I try to reach the door. Be careful. It is very vicious.'

'Is it a turkey?' asked Chaloner. He had read about turkeys, and had even eaten some at a feast given by Downing in The Hague once, but he had never seen one alive.

'It was supposed to have been delivered dead,' came

50

the whisper. Chaloner looked around the shop, but still could not locate the speaker. 'I am a *game* dealer. *Game* means someone is supposed to have shot it. How am I supposed to cope with living goods?'

Chaloner jumped back as the bird lunged at him, beak open in an angry gape and wattles bobbling menacingly. 'It will be dead soon enough if it does that again.'

'Really?' asked the voice eagerly. 'You would be doing me a great service if you were to dispatch it. My regular patrons are too frightened to visit, and the damned thing is ruining me. It has been here almost a week now, and you and Miss North are the first customers I have seen since Tuesday. Look out! Here it comes again!'

Chaloner took a piece of bread from his pocket – left from the meagre breakfast he had eaten while waiting to see Thurloe – and tossed it towards the bird, hoping to stall its relentless advance. The ugly head dropped towards the offering, then began to peck, flinging the bread this way and that as it broke it into manageable pieces.

'It is just hungry,' said Chaloner, watching it with pity. 'Do you have any seed?'

'I am not usually required to feed my merchandise, but I suppose I can make an exception,' replied the voice. 'Look in the cupboard behind you. There should be some barley.'

Chaloner eased towards the chest while the bird was occupied, and found the sack of grain. He scrambled away in alarm when a thick neck suddenly thrust under his arm in an attempt to reach the food. The bird was a fast and silent mover. There followed a brief tussle, in which the turkey tried to grab the bag and Chaloner resisted. When the bird's neck was stretched to full length,

51

the snapping beak was uncomfortably close to his face, and the furious cackling at close quarters was unsettling.

'Do not antagonise it!' cried Temperance, frightened for him. 'Let it have what it wants.'

'Turkeys will slay a fellow without a moment's hesitation,' yelped the voice at the same time. 'In New England, they are feared by man and beast alike.'

With difficulty, Chaloner managed to extricate a fistful of grain, and the bird's head followed his hand to the floor, gobbling greedily. He edged around it while it was feeding, and began to lay a trail. 'Where do you want it?'

'I want it dead,' said the voice. 'Use your dagger to cut its throat while its mind is on the barley.'

Chaloner studied the featherless neck without enthusiasm. He had never enjoyed killing, and suspected any assault on the turkey's life would end with them both being hurt, since he had no idea how to slaughter something of its ilk. Besides, there was something about the bird's bristling defiance that appealed to him. 'I will entice it out of your shop, but you can dispatch it yourself.'

'I cannot!' cried the voice in horror. 'Not a great, dangerous brute like that!'

'It can stay in here, then,' said Chaloner, watching it eat. It was clearly starving, and the barley was probably the first food it had seen in days. It was no surprise the creature was in such a foul mood.

The disembodied voice released a resigned sigh. 'Then lead it into the yard. But for God's sake make sure the gate is closed first. I do not want it to get into Fleet Street – I will be fined.'

'You are limping,' said Temperance, watching Chaloner entice the bird towards the back door. 'Did it bite you?'

'No,' said Chaloner shortly. That was something he would have to remember to disguise when he met Thurloe: the ex-Spymaster could not be expected to recommend anyone in a poor physical condition. 'There is grain in my boot.'

'Then get it out,' advised the voice. 'Or that greedy bird will chew through your foot to get at it.'

It was not long before the turkey was installed in a tiny garden with the rest of the barley and a bowl of water. A thickset, lugubrious man with a black beard emerged from under a bench to watch it through the window, while Chaloner helped Temperance down from her perch.

'Thank you,' she said gratefully. 'I was beginning to think I might be there all day. I knew it was a mistake to order one of those things for Christmas, but mother insisted. They dine on turkey in New England, you see, and she wanted to show kinship for our distant Puritan brethren.'

'If she wants to eat like them, then she is going to have to behead it herself,' said the shopkeeper shakily. 'You can tell her it is in the yard, waiting.'

The turkey incident had taken some time, but Chaloner was not entirely convinced Leybourn had really gone. He walked across the road to Praisegod Barbon's leather factory, and pretended to inspect the jumble of displayed merchandise. Barbon, only recently released from the Tower for anti-Royalist ranting, nodded a startled welcome to a rare customer, but Chaloner declined to engage in conversation, and lingered near the door while he waited to see whether the bookseller would reappear. It was the first opportunity he had had to draw breath since chasing Snow and Storey out of Lincoln's Inn, and he used the time to think carefully about the theft of the satchel and the stabbing of the post-boy.

Most of Thurloe's spies were now unemployed, and Chaloner would not be the only one wanting to be hired by the new government. Was the entire incident a test, to see who was the most efficient, and whose name should go forward? Chaloner would not put such a trick past the wily Thurloe. The question was, would returning the satchel with news that its theft had been ordered by Kelyng be sufficient, or would Thurloe expect robbers in tow, too?

Bells chimed, telling him it was noon, and that he had been gone more than four hours – too long. He donned the hated wig, and to ensure he was not being followed, took a tortuous route through the Clare Market to Lincoln's Inn. The market, recently established by the Earl of Clare, was a chaotic jumble of stalls, alleys, sheds and runnels. Chaloner held his sleeve over his nose when he passed the shambles, wincing at the rank, choking stench that emanated from the butchers' and fishmongers' shops. He emerged near the new theatre built for the Duke's Company in Lincoln's Inn Fields, although all the ornate plasterwork in the world could not disguise the fact that it had enjoyed a previous life as a tennis court. Checking for the last time that he was alone, he cut across the Fields to Chancery Lane.

The gate to Lincoln's Inn was answered by the same porter who had admitted him that morning. The man raised his eyebrows questioningly, and Chaloner brandished the satchel, feigning a buoyancy he did not feel. The porter grinned and waved him inside, letting him make his own way to Thurloe's apartments. Chaloner crossed a neat square that was bound by accommodation wings to the north, west and east, and the chapel to the south. It was dominated by one of the ugliest sundials he had ever seen. He weaved through knots of black-gowned students, then climbed a set of creaking stairs in the building that abutted on to the western end of the chapel, before knocking on the door to Chamber XIII.

Thurloe's suite comprised rooms on two levels, all boasting oak panelling and a comforting, homely odour of wax and wood smoke. On the lower floor were a bedchamber and sitting room, both with dark furniture that rendered them gloomy and sombre. Shelves lined the walls, bowing under the weight of books. Most were legal texts, purchased when Thurloe had decided to eschew politics and turn to the law again. Chaloner glanced at the spines, and wondered whether any had been bought from William Leybourn of Monkwell Street, Cripplegate. The upper floor comprised a garret for his manservant – an elusive, unobtrusive fellow whom Chaloner suspected was dumb – and a pantry where his meals were prepared.

When Chaloner entered the sitting room, he saw a fire blazing in the hearth and Thurloe sitting so close to it that there was a smell of singed cloth. That morning he had visitors, which was unusual: he was almost always alone, and there were rumours that his fall from grace had left him with no friends. One of the three guests Chaloner knew well, although it was not someone he would have chosen to meet. Ten years older than Chaloner, Sir George Downing was a florid man, whose expensive green coat failed to disguise the fact that he was growing fat. He was confident, aggressive, and cared

55

for no one's opinion – unless he thought the acquaintance might be useful, in which case he was greasily obsequious. Given that he had betrayed Thurloe by changing sides before the Protectorate had fully disintegrated, Chaloner was surprised to see the fellow in the ex-Spymaster's home.

The second man Chaloner did not know. He was in his fifties, and wore an eccentric arrangement of waistcoats and doublets. All were well made, suggesting he was wealthy. When he raised his handkerchief to dab his lips, the scent of oranges wafted across the room. The hand holding the napkin was unsteady, and Chaloner was under the impression that the knock at the door had startled him. He was accompanied by a lady who wore a dress that fell in sumptuous pleats, and with short, straight sleeves that ended in a series of elaborate ruffs. It was a style made popular by those wanting to emulate the sensuous Lady Castlemaine, and Chaloner knew the neckline would be indecently low. In this case, however, the suggestive plunge was concealed by a gorget – a decorous cape-like collar – fastened with a jewelled clasp. She was considerably younger than her husband, and her lively blue eyes and aristocratic posture suggested the gorget would be whipped off as soon as she was away from the company of prim men.

'Thomas,' said Thurloe, as Chaloner entered. 'You were gone so long I thought you had decided not to come back. What happened? Are you limping?'

'No, sir,' replied Chaloner, aware that Downing was regarding him with open disdain. He glanced down and realised his clothes were dishevelled and stained, and was annoyed the man should see him looking quite so disrepu-

56

table. He did not want him to have the satisfaction of knowing his refusal to provide a reference had reduced a former 'employee' to near destitution.

'You cannot hide it for ever,' said Downing spitefully. 'Being lame cannot make it easy to find profitable work. No one hires cripples, when there are whole men to be had.'

Before Chaloner could think of a suitable reply – the ones that sprung immediately to mind were far too vulgar to be uttered in Thurloe's genteel presence – the ex-Spymaster went to a jug on the table, gesturing towards the hearth as he did so. 'Sit, while I pour you a tonic, Tom. My physician recommended this potion of strengthening herbs, and it does help of a morning. Take that stool.'

Chaloner declined, knowing perfectly well that he would struggle to rise once he was down, and when Thurloe gave one of his small, secret smiles he inwardly cursed his stiff knee – the seat had been offered to test his fitness, and Chaloner's refusal had told the clever lawyer exactly what he had wanted to know. Thurloe handed him something brown in a silver goblet, which he accepted cautiously: as a man often in poor health, Thurloe tended to swallow a good many draughts that promised vitality and well-being. Most tasted foul and all were probably worthless.

'Have we met before?' asked the stranger, studying him. 'There is something familiar about you.'

'Your paths have never crossed,' replied Thurloe with considerable conviction. He held out his hand for the satchel. 'Did you buy my cinnamon, Tom? It is difficult to come by these days, and there is nothing like spice in hot milk on a cold winter's evening.'

'You have gone from diplomatic envoy to housemaid, have you, Heyden?' asked Downing with a sneer. 'Could you not find a better use for your talents after we parted company? You must have fallen on very hard times if that wig is anything to go by.'

'That is hardly his fault,' said Thurloe sharply. 'Clerks flocked to London in their thousands after the Restoration, and there is little hope for a man without proper testimonials, as you know very well – just as you also know that one from *me* would do him scant good, either. No household professing to be Royalist would employ a man recommended by a former Parliamentarian minister.'

Chaloner sincerely hoped he was mistaken.

Downing waved a plump hand, to indicate he did not consider Chaloner's predicament important. 'I dismissed nearly all my retainers last spring, because I want everyone to know that *I* only hire Cavaliers. Obviously, that description does not apply to the men who were pressed on me by *you*, John. We are friends, but I am sure you appreciate my point.' He shot Thurloe a meaningful glance.

Thurloe grimaced, and it was clear to Chaloner that he did not consider Downing a friend, and nor was he happy about the indiscreet references to matters of intelligence.

'You dismissed anyone you suspected of remaining loyal to Cromwell, Sir George?' asked the woman, regarding the diplomat with some amusement. 'How can you be sure you eliminated the right ones?'

'By ridding myself of the lot, except for some maids, women who . . .' Downing flapped his hand expansively.

'Come to your bedchamber when your wife is away?' suggested Chaloner.

58

'Whom I know to be firm Royalists,' finished Downing with a scowl.

'Why did you decline to write their testimonials?' the woman asked. 'Because you do not want other wealthy households to harbour deadly Roundheads under their roofs?'

'I gave them all testimonials, except Heyden here,' replied Downing curtly, not liking the tone of her voice. He glowered at her, while Chaloner recalled how he had thought Thurloe overly cautious five years before, when he had insisted that Downing should not know his real name. Now he was greatly relieved by it. In fact, Thurloe was the only man in London who did know and, given the rabid Parliamentarian convictions of one of his uncles – the most widely known and outspoken member of his family – Chaloner hoped to keep it that way.

'And what did poor Heyden do to incur your displeasure?' asked the woman with arched eyebrows. 'Provide an alternative bed for these Royalist lasses?'

'Sarah!' exclaimed Thurloe, shocked. As a devout Puritan, although by no means a fanatic, lewd jests were anathema to him. 'Please!'

'I do not like his handwriting,' replied Downing stiffly, although a shifty expression in his eyes indicated she was near the truth. 'And he made two mistakes with my accounts – minor ones, it is true, but a clerk must strive for accuracy.' He glanced at Thurloe, passing the message that if errors were made in this, then could Chaloner's espionage reports be trusted?

'Two small errors in the five years he served you is hardly serious,' said Thurloe reproachfully. 'And his other skills must have been of value to you – his fluency in Spanish, French and Dutch, for example.'

59

'Dutch?' asked the stranger with a sudden eagerness. 'How well can you speak Dutch?'

'Like a native, so they said,' replied Downing before Chaloner could answer for himself. 'He jabbered incessantly in the filthy tongue when he was in Holland, and I dislike servants having discussions I cannot understand. You never know what they might be saying about you.'

'*I* do business with the Dutch,' said the man. He raised his handkerchief to his lips again. 'It is rare to find an Englishman who knows their language. Perhaps I might have a place for you, Heyden. Visit my house on the Strand next week. Thurloe will tell you how to find it.'

'Once or twice, there was uproarious laughter,' Downing went on darkly, shooting the fellow a glance full of comradely warning. 'I am certain he was cracking jokes at my expense – making sport of me in the knowledge that I had no choice but to sit there and grin like a half-wit. Think very carefully before you make any decisions, my friend.'

'You told me to do all I could to impress The Hague's burgesses,' said Chaloner, neither denying nor confirming the charge. 'So that is what I did. And that particular alliance brought you a lucrative treaty, so I do not think you should complain about how I came by it.'

'You insolent whelp!' exclaimed Downing, struggling to his feet. 'How dare you speak—'

'Sit down, Sir George,' interrupted Thurloe sharply. He gazed steadily at the spluttering diplomat until he complied, then turned to Chaloner. He was angry, objecting to sparring matches carried out in his presence. 'You are pale, Thomas; perhaps you have taken a chill. Go to my bedchamber and lie down. I will see you when my business is completed.'

'I shall bring you some more tonic,' offered Sarah, going to fetch the jug and indicating Chaloner was to precede her into the adjoining chamber. 'I am not very interested in hearing their tedious discussions, and would rather have you tell me where I can buy good cinnamon.'

'Leave the door open so we can see you, then,' instructed her husband. 'And keep your voice down. We do not want a noisy analysis of condiments distracting us. *Our* business is important.'

Chaloner was uneasy. He did not want a woman quizzing him about spices when he had not the faintest idea where they might be purchased, suspecting he would be caught out in an instant. However, Thurloe's visitors seemed keen to rid themselves of him, and nodded approvingly when Sarah ushered him into the next room, leaving the door decorously ajar. Downing immediately began a malicious diatribe about ungrateful staff, and only desisted when Thurloe regarded him with unfriendly eyes. Then their voices dropped to inaudible murmurs, suggesting business was underway. Chaloner perched on the edge of the bed, while Sarah kindled a lamp.

'Do not sit there,' she advised. 'You will spread muck on John's clean blankets, and he will not like that at all.'

Chaloner moved to the hearth, watching her take one of Thurloe's night-caps and drop it in a pot that was warming over the fire; the ex-Spymaster was fastidious and liked hot water available all day. She rolled the steaming garment into a ball and handed it to him. He regarded it blankly.

She sighed impatiently. 'For your leg, to ease the ache.'

'There is nothing wrong—'

She slapped it into his hand. 'Take it – unless you *want* to give Downing cause to jibe you.'

'Thurloe will no more want grime on his night-cap than he will on his bedclothes.'

'We will burn it when you have finished. He has a dozen, and will not miss one. My husband seemed to recognise you, and he is usually good with faces. Where could you have met?'

'Nowhere,' replied Chaloner. He knew for a fact he had never encountered the man before – he would have remembered the orange-scented linen and the fellow's lumpy nose. 'He is confusing me with someone else.'

'Perhaps so. He is not himself at the moment – too many financial worries, I suppose. What shall we talk about? Cinnamon? Or would you prefer to tell me your problems?'

Chaloner was startled. 'What problems?'

'Downing hates you, and you are unlikely to secure another post as long as he refuses a testimonial. My husband will offer you work, but it will only be a matter of time before Downing makes him change his mind – he is a slippery, conniving fellow, and my husband always yields to him eventually. Were you one of John's spies? Is that why Downing is afraid of you?'

'I am not a spy,' replied Chaloner firmly. 'And Downing is not afraid of me – I only wish he were, because then he might keep his nasty opinions to himself.'

She took the cap and soaked it in the water again. 'It is no secret that John once employed an army of agents – or that some of them now want places in the new government. Downing sent him information about the political situation in the Netherlands, and I assume you

62

did the same, since you worked with him and you speak Dutch. Well? Am I right?'

'You have a vivid imagination,' said Chaloner, smiling because he did not want to offend her. 'I was just a clerk.'

She regarded him critically, head tilted to one side, then continued as if he had not spoken. 'Downing professes himself to be a Royalist now, and is keen to eradicate all evidence of his former loyalties. John will say nothing about him, because he and Downing share too many secrets. But can Downing be sure *you* will not? I suspect the answer is no, and *that* is why he is wary of you.'

Chaloner wondered if she was right. He and Downing had never liked each other, although they had kept their antipathy decently concealed until events in March had brought their true feelings to the surface, but it had never occurred to him that Downing might see him as a threat. He hoped she was mistaken: Downing was the kind of man to make life very difficult for those he considered a nuisance.

'Then why is he here?' he asked. 'Meeting Cromwell's old Secretary of State is not the best way to go about eliminating ties with the former regime.'

'John has been asked to provide reports about Britain's relations with various foreign powers,' she explained, 'and Downing was an ambassador to the Dutch. Therefore, being seen conferring with John is a good thing at the moment, because it means Downing is providing a vital service in the government. But we were talking about why Downing detests *you*.'

'Probably because of Metje de Haas,' he said, to lead her away from politics.

'Who is she?'

'His daughter's governess, whom I helped to evade his charms. He never did catch her.'

Sarah gave a grin that was at odds with her haughty demeanour. 'Good. I do not like to think of women violated by those fat, pawing hands. Where is she now? Holland? Or is she one of the secret Parliamentarians he dismissed when he returned to London?'

Chaloner saw no reason not to talk about Metje. It was safer than discussing whether the powerful Downing was a good Royalist. He glanced to where Thurloe leaned towards the portly diplomat, listening to a whispered monologue, and wished he would hurry up, so Sarah would stop trying to interrogate him. 'She is in the service of William North the jeweller – a companion to his daughter.'

'You mean Temperance?' asked Sarah, her face alight with sudden pleasure. 'I know her! She and her family came from Ely, just after the Restoration. We used to meet in St Paul's Cathedral and explore the traders' booths together, but then her father declared such places out of bounds, on the grounds that they sell ribbons – the kind of wicked fripperies that insult his Puritan sensibilities. We seldom see each other these days, which is a pity. I suppose he hired this Metje because Temperance was lonely after the ban on shopping. Do you still see Metje?'

He changed the subject, thinking it none of her affair. 'Your husband is a merchant?'

'He is John Dalton.' She looked at him in a way that indicated the name should be familiar, and sighed when she saw it was not. 'After the wars, he made his fortune in wine. This means he has the favour of the King, whose Court consumes rather a lot of it. Because the King approves of him, Downing is attempting to befriend him, too, although both are finding the process a sore trial.'

'Is your husband a difficult man to like, then?'

She glanced sharply at him, and he sensed he had hit a nerve. 'He can be awkward, but so are most men. I wish he were a handsome young soldier, but we cannot choose what we want in this life, and so must make do with what we are given. Do you really speak Dutch like a native?'

'Metje thinks I sound German, but that is preferable to an Englishman, given that we are on the brink of war with Holland.'

'On the brink of war?' she echoed in disbelief. 'We are not!'

Chaloner shook his head slowly, wondering why so many affluent Londoners were unwilling to see the truth – unlike the poor, who seemed almost eager for the conflict. Personally, he considered the looming Dutch crisis a serious problem, and was more than happy to talk about it – and if she passed his concerns to her husband, then so much the better. 'We will be fighting within three years unless someone takes steps to stop it. We would be fools to challenge the Dutch – they have more ships, a navy in which men are actually paid, and better resources. We cannot afford to take them on.'

But she was not particularly interested, and her expression became mischievous as she thought of another question. 'Did you really say malicious things in Dutch when Downing was actually present?'

'Of course not. That would have been the height of bad manners.'

She seemed disappointed. 'Well, you should not take

his malice to heart. He hates everyone, and the feeling is wholly reciprocated. I think he was despised *before* March, but what he did to those regicides earlier this year was despicable – discovering their hiding places in Holland, and dragging them back to be hanged and quartered. What sort of man does that to another human being?'

The descriptions that sprung into Chaloner's mind were unrepeatable. He affected nonchalance, although she had chosen another subject about which he felt strongly. 'Downing supported Cromwell for ten years, and needed a spectacular way to prove himself loyal to the King. What better way than presenting His Majesty with three former friends to be sentenced to a hideous death?'

She regarded him silently for a moment. 'Were you with Downing when he caught them? He said you parted company last spring, and that was when those men were apprehended.'

'Is there any more tonic?'

'You refuse to answer. Why? Because you helped Downing? Or because you decline to be associated with his shameful behaviour?'

Chaloner glanced towards the door. 'Because I do not want to engage in such talk when the man is within spitting distance of us.'

'Spitting is the best thing to do to him. My husband went to watch those poor men die, but I could not bring myself to join him. Did you go?'

'No,' replied Chaloner shortly. 'Shall I stoke up the fire? It is cold in here.'

'It is not cold,' she said softly. 'So, I surmise from your reaction that you objected to what he did, and you argued

66

about it. That is why he hates you, and why you are so open in your disdain for him. It is nothing to be ashamed of – there are men who would shake your hand for defying him.'

'And there are others who would hang me for angering a friend of the King.'

'Downing is no man's friend. The King was angry about what happened to those particular regicides – I heard him myself, telling the Earl of Clarendon how wrong it was to demand the return of criminals from a foreign country. He said it made us look stupid, for allowing their escape in the first place.'

'The Dutch refused the extradition at first,' said Chaloner, relenting and recalling the tense negotiations that had taken place between government officials and Downing. 'But he bullied, cajoled and bribed, and eventually they capitulated. One clerk told me it was just to make him go away. And John Okey, Miles Corbet and John Barkstead paid the price.'

'Did you meet the regicides? I suppose you did: Englishmen abroad naturally gather together, no matter what their political affiliation.'

Chaloner frowned: first Leybourn had questioned him, and now Sarah Dalton was doing it. He was tempted to tell her to mind her own business, but if she was close enough to Thurloe to refer to him as 'John', then it would be unwise to alienate her.

'They were not interested in talking to clerks,' he replied vaguely.

She poked the embers with a stick. 'I have always wanted to see Holland, but my husband tells me it is too far. I doubt I will ever go – at least, not as long as I am married to him.'

'You could always go to East Anglia instead. There is not much to choose between them in terms of bogs and flat fields.'

She raised her eyebrows, amused. 'I see I am talking to a true romantic.'

Chaloner was relieved when Thurloe came to tell Sarah that her husband was ready to leave. He waited in the bedchamber until they had gone, unwilling to endure another spat with Downing. His encounter with Sarah had been perplexing, but now he needed to muster his wits and convince Thurloe that he would be a worthy addition to the new government's intelligence services.

'They have gone,' said Thurloe, beckoning him into the sitting room. 'Dalton is a decent soul, but Downing is a sore trial. I cannot imagine how you managed to put up with him all those years. I should have paid you double, to compensate you for such unpleasant working conditions.'

'He has his good points,' replied Chaloner, walking carefully so as not to draw attention to his stiff leg. The chamber still reeked of Dalton's orange water.

'Name one,' challenged Thurloe. Chaloner hesitated. 'You cannot, because he does not have any – except perhaps a fondness for good music. The man is a disgrace, and what he did to Barkstead, Okey and Corbet was truly wicked. I understand he tried to do the same to your uncle – who also signed the old king's death warrant.'

Chaloner nodded, but made no other reply.

Thurloe regarded him closely. 'Your uncle was my friend. I would like to know Downing had nothing to do with his end.'

'He died of natural causes months before Downing

indulged his penchant for persecuting regicides.' Chaloner glanced uneasily at Thurloe, wondering why Downing had been visiting him, and whether they had traded secrets. 'He still thinks my name is Heyden.'

'And I recommend you keep it that way. It would be extremely unwise to let *him* know you are the nephew of a king-killer. He will almost certainly use it against you, and my influence is on the wane, so I may not be able to stop him. What did he say when he learned death had cheated him of his prize?'

'That he was going to excavate my uncle's grave and cart the body to London. I thought he was jesting, but then I learned it had happened before – that Cromwell had been exhumed and his skeleton ceremonially hanged before a crowd of spectators.'

'You are not the only one to be shocked by that,' said Thurloe, reading the distaste in his face. 'I had supposed we lived in civilised times, and was appalled to see corpses defiled. However, there are men in the new government who consider that sort of thing perfectly justified, so we should keep our opinions to ourselves. Are any of your family likely to visit London?'

'No, sir. They know former Parliamentarians should stay low until the frenzy of purges is over. They will remain quietly in Buckinghamshire.'

Thurloe indicated Chaloner was to sit opposite him, then huddled close to the fire, as if the discussion had chilled him. 'Downing really is a selfish scoundrel. He suggested I order you back into his service just now. He detests you, and the feeling is clearly mutual, but he could not bear the thought of Dalton having a clerk who can speak Dutch, while he does not.'

Chaloner was hopeful, prepared to put up with

Downing if it meant gainful employment. 'Is he planning to return to The Hague soon?'

'No – and I strongly suggest you decline any post offered by him. He cannot be trusted and you will not be safe under his roof. *I* will never tell him your name and family connections, but that does not mean he will not learn them for himself.'

Chaloner was disappointed by the advice. 'We will be at war soon, and Britain needs intelligence agents – preferably experienced ones – in place as soon as possible. I could do a lot of good for our country, if the government would only send me back.'

'Unfortunately, that is easier said than done, as far as you are concerned. You need an official diplomatic post in order to operate efficiently, but our government has appointed its own people and dismissed the ones I hired. It is a ridiculous – not to mention dangerous – situation, since it takes years to cultivate reliable informants, as you know. But I cannot force Williamson to take you, even though it would be in England's best interests.'

'Williamson?'

'Joseph Williamson, a clever tutor from Oxford. He is in charge of intelligence now. He is astute, quick witted and will do well in time, but I have no influence over his decisions. All I can do is offer names to the Lord Chancellor – the Earl of Clarendon – and hope he passes them to the right quarters. I have had scant success so far: none of the spies I recommended have been hired by Williamson.'

'Because he does not trust people who once worked for you?'

'Almost certainly, and I do not blame him. I would be wary myself, were I in his position. You are in an

70

unenviable situation, Tom: you cannot return to Holland alone, because you need the cover of an ambassador's entourage for your work, but Downing declines to recommend you to his replacement in The Hague. As I see it, the only way forward is to prove yourself first by working here.'

Chaloner was unhappy. 'But in Holland I watched shipyards, monitored the manufacture of cannons, stole nautical charts, and started rumours to damage Dutch alliances with France and Spain. I did not spy on my fellow countrymen, and being an agent in a foreign country is not the same as being a spy here. I do not have the right skills for such work.'

Thurloe sighed. 'We live in changing times, and only those prepared to adapt will survive. I will suggest you are used where you will be most effective, but I doubt my advice will be acted upon – at least, not immediately. You may find the choice is reduced to doing what you are told by the new government, or abandoning espionage altogether.'

Chaloner stared at the fire. He had known the situation was unpromising, but had not imagined it to be quite so bleak. He thought about his encounters with Kelyng, Bennet, Snow and Storey, and then being questioned rather more keenly than was appropriate by Leybourn and Sarah Dalton. He did not understand London's tense, bitter politics, and disliked not knowing whom he could trust. It was a bad position for a spy to be in.

'Who is Sarah Dalton, sir?' he asked after a while. 'She asked a lot of questions.'

'I trained her well, then.'

'She is one of your agents?' Chaloner supposed he should have guessed.

Thurloe nodded. 'I would have told you – both of you – before I left you alone together, but it was impossible under the circumstances. If she quizzed you, then it was on my behalf. Even though I am no longer Spymaster, a faithful few still supply me with gossip. I am lucky they do, or men like Downing would have had my head on a block months ago. As it is, I am too knowledgeable to kill.'

'I am glad to hear it, sir.'

'If anything happens to me, and you need a friend, you can turn to Sarah. I am not in the habit of divulging my agents' identities, but England is turbulent, and everyone needs someone he can trust.'

'She supported Cromwell, was a Parliamentarian?'

'Not really. Like all of us, she witnessed the undesirability of civil war, and wants to ensure we do not travel that road again. What she supports is stability and peace. I imagine you feel much the same. Most of my people do.'

'Do you know a bookseller called William Leybourn, sir?' asked Chaloner, after another pause.

Thurloe nodded. 'I buy legal pamphlets from him on occasion, although he is best known for his erudite contributions to mathematics and surveying. Why do you ask?'

'He also asked a lot of questions.'

'It seems you have had a busy morning, fending off all these interrogations. Shall I summon a physician to tend your leg, or was Sarah able to help?'

'There is nothing—'

Thurloe's voice was cool. 'Do not lie, Thomas. I dislike being misled, especially since it has already cost me my favourite night-cap.'

Chaloner regarded him uneasily. Thurloe could not possibly have seen what he and Sarah had been doing

72

from his fireside chair. 'How did you—?'

'Because it was not on the pillow where I left it, there is a suspicious pile of ashes in the hearth, and your breeches are damp around the knee – where I know you were hit by splinters from an exploding cannon at the Battle of Naseby. You were sixteen, and should have been at your studies.'

'Yes, sir,' replied Chaloner, trying to mask his annoyance. The last statement had told him exactly who had revealed the secret he had been to such pains to conceal for the past seventeen years: his uncle, the regicide. The older Thomas Chaloner had dragged his nephew from Cambridge, very much against his will, and later claimed he had joined the New Model Army of his own volition. Chaloner had not been expected to live after Naseby, and by the time he had recovered and learned what had been said about him, it was too late to correct the story.

Thurloe settled more comfortably in his chair. 'You seem surprised I know about your private life. You should not be. First, your uncle and I were friends, and so of course we discussed our families. And second, I was particular about my agents, and investigated them very carefully before I hired them. I know more about you than you imagine. I know about a lot of people. Why do you think my head is not on a pole outside Westminster Hall?'

'I assumed because of your detailed knowledge of foreign affairs, sir.'

Thurloe smiled enigmatically. 'Well, there is that, too.'

A knock at the door preceded a visit from some of Thurloe's relations, who filled the room with boisterous shouts and laughter. Thurloe sat amid the chaos like a king, revered by the men, fussed over by the women and clamoured at by noisy children. He said little, but reached out to ruffle a boy's hair here or chuck a giggling girl under the chin there, and it did not seem possible that such a quiet, mild man held secrets that could destroy some of the most powerful men in the country. Chaloner withdrew to a corner, although it was not long before the whirlwind of happy voices had retreated – they were to travel to Thurloe's own wife and children at his manor near Oxford later that day – and he and the ex-Spymaster were alone again.

'Marriage is a splendid institution,' Thurloe observed smugly, knowing he was unusually fortunate. 'And children are a blessing from God. Do you have any plans in that direction?'

Chaloner felt like retorting that he probably knew the answer to that question already, given that he seemed to have probed so many other private aspects of his former spy's life. 'Possibly.'

Thurloe seemed about to reply with something equally tart, but then changed his mind. 'Tell me what happened this morning. You retrieved the satchel, so I conclude you had some sort of encounter with the villains who murdered poor Charles-Stewart.'

The pouch lay on the table, and Chaloner noted it had not been opened. 'I chased them to the Holborn Bridge, where they disappeared into a maze of alleys and—'

'The Fleet Rookery,' interrupted Thurloe grimly. 'It has an alehouse, where plots were hatched to kill the Lord Protector. I went myself once, and overheard one plan discussed in the most brazen manner. It has been a breeding ground for rebels for years, and I suspect it will continue so, regardless of who sits on the throne.'

'People tried to kill Cromwell?' As soon as he saw the flicker of surprise in Thurloe's eyes, Chaloner knew he should not have asked the question.

'I forget you are unfamiliar with your own country – although I had not imagined you to be quite so uninformed. There were many assassination attempts, although most were the bumbling efforts of amateurs. But let us return to today. You chased the thieves into that festering hotbed of treachery . . .'

'I overheard them say they were in the pay of a powerful lawyer, so I decided to find out who. They went to White Hall, where a servant wearing a yellow doublet paid them—'

'Kelyng dresses his retinue in yellow.'

'You know Kelyng?'

This time Thurloe made no attempt to disguise his astonishment. 'Surely you have heard of Sir John Kelyng? Really, Thomas! How can I recommend you to the government when you do not know its most infamous officials? How long have you been back?'

'Since March, sir, but not all of it in London. I spent several months in Buckinghamshire.'

'I know,' said Thurloe dryly. 'It was I who suggested you visit the siblings you have not seen in a decade, if you recall. Families are important, and you had been away too long from yours. However, your absence is not a valid excuse for such ignorance. Continue.'

The interview was not going well. Now Chaloner felt he was lacking in two areas: his weak leg and his poor knowledge of current affairs. 'Kelyng and his chamberlain were in the garden – presumably awaiting the arrival of the satchel – and there was a skirmish. The servant

75

was killed.' He saw the shocked expression on Thurloe's face. 'Not by me. Bennet threw a dagger.'

Thurloe stared at him. 'They killed their own man?'

'Kelyng referred to him as Jones, but *he* claimed with his dying breath that his name was Hewson.'

Emotion burned briefly in Thurloe's eyes, but was extinguished so fast Chaloner was not sure whether he had imagined it. 'Most men call for priests or physicians, but this fellow told you his name? Did he say anything else?'

'That we should praise the Lord, and that it was dangerous for seven.'

'Seven what?'

'He did not say. I think he was raving.'

'That was all? He mentioned no other names, no messages for loved ones?'

'No, sir,' said Chaloner, wondering why Thurloe should be so interested in a death that was essentially irrelevant. The ex-Spymaster was silent for a moment, then indicated that Chaloner should continue. 'Kelyng shot at me, but I escaped. The crowds at the Banqueting House assumed the gunfire was Downing's doing – falling off his horse in his haste to ride next to the King.'

'A whisper. That is all it takes to start a rumour. Your uncle taught me that.'

'Which one, sir?' asked Chaloner archly, not wanting Thurloe to think his entire family consisted of the arrogant, witty hedonist who had signed the previous king's death warrant. 'James? Peter? Robert?'

Thurloe pursed his lips. 'I forgot your grandfather sired an inordinate number of brats. Eighteen, was it, from two wives? But I only knew one of them. Your Uncle Thomas used to amuse himself by fabricating a tale, then timing how long it took before the gossip was repeated back to him in a garbled form. It sounds foolish, but it taught me how powerful rumours can be. Then what happened?'

'Bennet followed me until I was able to lose him.'

'I wondered at the time whether that pair of cut-throats might be in Kelyng's employ. It is a pity they killed Charles-Stewart: he was only a boy, and his mother will be devastated.'

'Their names are Snow and Storey, sir, and they will be easy to catch. I can go to—'

'No,' said Thurloe tiredly. 'If we send them to Newgate for hanging, Bennet will only replace them with others, and we will have lost the advantage of knowing who they are. Let them be for now. They will face justice soon enough – God's justice, if not man's.'

He stared into the flames and appeared to be lost in his thoughts. Chaloner glanced at the pouch again. 'Are you going to look inside the satchel, to see if everything is there, sir?'

Thurloe shook his head. 'There is no need, because I know exactly what it contains. Nothing.'

'Nothing?' Chaloner was confused.

'Nothing. It is empty.'

Chaloner did not know whether to be angry or amused that Thurloe had sent him on a fool's errand. He started to stand, thinking it was time he drew the interview to a close. Thurloe had already said he could not arrange his return to Holland, and there was no point in lingering.

Thurloe waved him back down with an impatient flick of his hand. 'I wonder you managed to send me all those detailed reports, if you are in the habit of tearing off in the middle of conversations.'

77

Chaloner tried not to be irritated. He did not know Thurloe well – they had only met on a handful of occasions, and most communication had been in the form of letters. Each had ended his missive with polite enquiries after the other's family, and occasionally they had confided various worries or concerns, but the general tenor had been brisk and impersonal. He began to think it was easier to serve Thurloe from a distance, and that he would probably dislike the man if he ever broke through his cool reserve and came to know him better.

'I have had a trying morning,' said Thurloe, pouring himself more tonic. 'First, Charles-Stewart. Then Downing foisting himself on me, trying to make me attend meetings in which I have no interest and asking questions about you. And now Hewson. I thought I had finished with murder and subterfuge when I was dismissed from power, but they seem to follow me around.'

'You will never be finished with them, if you arrange for empty satchels to be delivered to you, sir,' said Chaloner, rather acidly. 'Such activities smack of skulduggery.'

Thurloe grimaced. 'Downing said you were insolent, and he was right. But let us return to Kelyng, before we both say things we may later regret. Ever since the Restoration, he has vowed to destroy me – he accuses me of planning a revolt, with Richard Cromwell as its figurehead.'

'The King does not agree. If he did, you would be in the Tower.'

Thurloe nodded. 'And the truth is I no longer have any interest in politics. Kelyng is wrong about me, and most people know it, thank God. However, he keeps trying to catch me out.'

'By intercepting your post?'

'Yes, although I arranged alternative methods of receiving letters months ago, and lads with satchels are a ruse. However, I confess I was surprised to learn he is brazen enough to order one snatched from my very hands.'

'You were lucky his men did not kill you, too.'

'He would not dare. The new government still needs my advice, and as long as I am useful, I am safe. He would not harm me physically, and risk incurring the wrath of his king.'

'But the men he hires are stupid – one might disobey him or knife the wrong man. Or he may try to damage you in other ways, perhaps by putting forged documents in these pouches.'

'He has done that already, but I was able to exchange them for some laundry bills. Kelyng is more nuisance than danger, although I would be a fool to ignore his antics completely.'

'Is there anything I can do?' Chaloner had not worked for Thurloe without incurring some sense of obligation, and disliked the notion of Kelyng trying to bring him down by underhand means.

Thurloe smiled, pleased. 'Thank you, Tom. There are two things that would help enormously. First, I would like to be told of any rumours concerning Kelyng or his men. They might allow me to stay a few steps ahead of the wretched fellow.'

'Of course, sir.' Chaloner supposed he had better start frequenting taverns and listening to more street gossip. 'And the second?'

Thurloe raised a finger. 'Before we discuss that, we should assess your situation. You are eager to return to

79

your duties – preferably in Holland – but that is out of the question at the moment. Downing's replacement will not hire you, given what Downing wrote in his official report. However, that is not to say that we cannot take steps towards your eventual reinstatement. The first stage is to have you noticed by the right men.'

'Williamson?'

'Williamson, yes. But I do not know him, so I will send you to the Lord Chancellor instead. Once established at White Hall, you will have to work hard to prove your worth – and even then, you may never be trusted. But it is a chance, and I know you will make the best of it.' Thurloe studied the younger man thoughtfully. 'Your young lady is Dutch, is she not? What is her name?'

'Metje de Haas,' replied Chaloner, wondering whether the relationship would count against him; the Earl of Clarendon might think his loyalties were divided. 'Her mother was English,' he added, although it occurred to him that the ex-Spymaster might know more about Metje than he did. He and Metje seldom discussed families, because she did not like hers and he had been under-cover with a false name, so not in a position to say much about his own.

'I imagine it was useful to have a Dutch citizen in tow when you went about your duties for me?'

'I never involved her, sir. It was safer that way – for both of us.'

'Very wise. How does she feel about being a foreigner in England?'

'She likes being a companion to a jeweller's daughter, but complains about the growing antipathy towards the Dutch in London.'

Thurloe nodded. 'If we go to war with Holland, she

may find herself in considerable danger. But this is none of my affair.' He cleared his throat and became businesslike. 'So far, I have sent only six intelligence agents to the Earl – five spies experienced at rooting out rebellions, and an investigator by the name of Colonel John Clarke. None were passed to Williamson, unfortunately.'

'I met Clarke once, when he visited The Hague.' Chaloner had quarrelled with him. 'He tried to seduce Metje. When she repelled his advances, he turned his attentions to Downing's wife.'

Thurloe pursed his lips in disapproval. 'He promised he would mend his ways after that scandal involving Cromwell's niece. I am his kinsman, you see – his new wife Joan was married to my half-brother Isaac Ewer. Isaac died of fever in Ireland ten years ago.'

Chaloner regarded him in surprise. Isaac Ewer was one of the better-known regicides, which meant Chaloner was not the only one unlucky enough to own kin who had executed a monarch.

'Clarke was a fine investigator, despite his fondness for other men's wives,' Thurloe went on. 'But he was murdered last week.'

Chaloner hid his shock. 'By the Lord Chancellor?'

Thurloe was startled by the suggestion. 'Of course not by him! He is eager for good spies, and you do not demand the cream of the crop and then kill them. He is as angry about this as I am.'

'What about the other five?' asked Chaloner uneasily, wondering what he was letting himself in for by going to White Hall. 'Are they still alive?'

'Alive and impressing the Earl with their diligence – he sent me a note praising them only this morning. You will be the seventh man I recommend, although I am uneasy about doing so, knowing what happened to Clarke.'

'What did happen, exactly?'

'He was stabbed in the belly, although White Hall did not want itself tarnished by the reek of murder, so Clarendon spirited the body out of the palace and dumped it by the Thames. Everyone assumes Clarke was murdered by footpads, and very few know what really happened.'

'But the Earl told you?'

'Yes, he did. He feels guilty that I sent him a man – a friend – who was then killed.'

'A friend?'

Thurloe's expression was cool. 'I do have some, Thomas, despite rumours to the contrary. I was fond of Clarke, and when I write to Clarendon, I may ask him to let *you* find his killer. You offered to help me, and this is the second thing you can do.'

'Me?' Chaloner was uncomfortable; it was a long way from reporting the movements of Dutch ships.

'You have investigated murders before – Downing said you solved at least two when you were in The Hague. Be careful, though. White Hall is a pit of vipers, no matter which government occupies it, and I shall be vexed if you take unnecessary risks. And then, when you have discovered the identity of the killer, please come to me with the answer. Do not tackle Kelyng alone – that might endanger both of us, especially if any animals are involved. He has a passionate liking for them.'

'So you have already decided Kelyng is the guilty party.'

Thurloe gave a humourless smile. 'It stands to reason he is involved: he knows Clarke and I were related, and that I held him in brotherly esteem. Perhaps he stabbed him in the hope that I would become careless with grief, and let slip with something incriminating. However, you must not let my opinion cloud your judgement – Kelyng is not my only enemy. And Clarke's death may have nothing to do with me, anyway. He may have been killed over whatever he was doing for Clarendon.'

'I will do my best to find his murderer, sir.'

'I know you will, Tom. But you cannot go to Clarendon dressed like a pauper, so buy yourself a decent cassock-coat and a new wig.' Thurloe passed him a heavy purse. 'I would not ask you to do this if there was anyone else I could trust. Your uncle would not approve of me shoving you into the lion's mouth.'

Chaloner was not so sure. His uncle had done a good deal of shoving himself, and had made it perfectly clear that he considered the youngest son of a younger brother to be a readily disposable asset. He had not enrolled his own boys in the wars that had almost claimed his nephew's life, and nor had he encouraged them to become intelligence agents in countries that would shoot them if they were caught. 'He would have understood.'

Thurloe gave a grim smile. 'He was a practical man. I asked my other agents to send me reports on Kelyng, too, but Clarke was the only one who did. I thought Simon Lane might oblige, but he obviously thinks it is too risky – that communicating with me might be miscon-strued.'

Lane was a smiling, cheerful man whose tuneful bari-tone had often accompanied Chaloner's bass viol. 'If I see him, I will ask.'

'No, he has made his choice, and it is the sensible one under the circumstances. You may feel the same way in a week, although I hope you will not forget me entirely – that you will find time to visit.'

Chaloner wondered whether there might be truth in the whispers about Thurloe's lack of friends after all. 'If you like, sir.'

Thurloe regarded him appraisingly. 'Go shopping, then – and throw that wig in the river at the earliest opportunity. It smells of horse.'

# Chapter 3

The following day, Chaloner took Metje with him when he went to purchase clothes to impress the Lord Chancellor. However, it was not long before he wished he had left her behind. Her idea of what was suitable did not match his own notion of buying the first thing he saw, and the business dragged on far longer than he felt it should. By the time the garments were ordered, he was tired, irritable and painfully aware that nearly all the money Thurloe had given him was gone. Since he was late with the rent and there was not so much as a crust of bread in the larder, clothes seemed an outrageous extravagance.

'You cannot meet the Lord Chancellor dressed in rags,' argued Metje, speaking Dutch as she always did when they were alone. 'He will not employ clerks for the Victualling Office who look poor enough to help themselves to the navy's supplies.'

Chaloner had allowed himself to fall into an awkward situation with Metje. To her, he was Thomas Heyden, a diplomatic envoy. This had worked perfectly well in Holland, when their relationship had been superficial, but it was different in London, when he had come to realise that she was the woman he wanted to marry. He was not looking forward to the time when he would be obliged to confess that he had misled her for the past three years, suspecting she would be hurt and angry.

She knew he was struggling to find a new employer, and nagged him incessantly about his lack of success when *she* had experienced no such problems, so she was delighted when he mentioned the possibility of an interview at White Hall. Because she had been so pleased to hear he had finally done something right, he had broken one of his own rules of secrecy by confiding that the man he was to meet was the Earl of Clarendon. She saw the post would be a considerable improvement on part-time clerking for the Puritans of Fetter Lane, and was determined to do all she could to ensure he created a good impression, waving aside his concerns over paying the landlord.

'I could move to cheaper accommodation, but then you would not be next door,' he said, trying to think of ways to alleviate the problem. 'And you cannot walk across half of London to visit me at night.'

She agreed. 'Nor can you come to me. My room is directly above Mr North's bedchamber, and you have only to breathe on the floorboards to make them creak. He would find us out in an instant, and I do not want to lose my position because he thinks me a harlot. You must keep those rooms if you want to see me. And what about your viol? You play it most evenings now, because the Norths like hearing it through their walls, but if you moved, your new neighbours might complain.'

'I should cancel the order for the cassock,' he said, looking back to the tailor's shop.

She took his arm and pulled him on. 'Consider it an investment, which will reap its own returns in time – and you *must* find work, Tom. You cannot live like a pauper for ever. Or would you rather I returned my new fancy apron, so we can purchase cheese instead?'

He smiled. 'I cannot imagine when you will wear it, when North forbids lace in his house. He told me the Devil's underclothes are made of lace, although he declined to explain how he comes to be party to such an intimate detail.'

'He is a dear man,' she said affectionately. 'Did I tell you more of his chapel windows were smashed last night? He was so upset that he is talking about leaving London again. I hope he does not, because what would become of us? Will you visit him this afternoon? He was asking for you yesterday – something to do with whether the community can afford to replace the glass.'

'People remember the time when it was Puritans defacing churches, and they want revenge. North should sell the building, and hold his prayer meetings in someone's house instead.'

'It is wicked that people cannot attend chapel without fanatics lobbing bricks,' said Metje angrily. 'I am not a good Puritan – or I would not visit you night after night – but Mr North is. I shall always be grateful to him for employing me – a destitute Hollander in a hostile foreign country – when no one else would give me the time of day.'

They walked to Fetter Lane, where she returned to her duties. Although North would have dismissed Metje instantly had he learned she was carrying on with a man, he was not a strict taskmaster and afforded her a good deal of freedom. He seldom questioned her when she announced she was 'going out', and her life as a paid companion for Temperance was absurdly easy.

When Chaloner was sure Metje was safely home – it was a Saturday and apprentices were drunkenly demanding of passers-by whether they were true Englishmen – he went to find North. The Nonconformist chapel was an unassuming building halfway along Fetter Lane, a short distance from North's house and the rather less grand affair next door in which Chaloner rented an attic. Despite its modest appearance, it attracted much ill will, mostly from Anglican clerics who had been deposed by Puritans during the Commonwealth, and by apprentices who enjoyed lobbing rocks. Occasionally, larger missiles were launched, and there had been threats of arson.

The door was barred, so Chaloner knocked. North answered, and his dour expression cracked into a smile when he recognised his accounts clerk. North was not an attractive man, and his plain clothes did little to improve his austere appearance. He had dark, oily hair, a low forehead and his stern face was rendered even more forbidding by a burn that darkened his chin and the lower half of one cheek.

He waved Chaloner inside the chapel, which comprised a single room with white walls and uncomfortable benches. It was dominated by the large pulpit in which the Puritan incumbent, Preacher Hill, stood to rant of a Sunday morning. Hill ranted at the daily dawn meetings, too, when his flock came to pray before they went about their earthly business, and he ranted in the afternoons when the hardy few appeared for additional devotions. In fact, he ranted whenever he had an audience, no matter how small, and Chaloner had once caught him holding forth to a frightened baby.

'I tried to catch you yesterday,' said North, ushering Chaloner towards the small gathering that sat near the pulpit. These were the chapel's 'council' – those with the time and inclination to argue about funds, building repairs and which psalms to sing. 'Were you looking for work again?'

'Will you leave us if you are successful?' demanded a large woman who wore a massive shoulder-width brimmed hat and voluminous black skirts. Faith North was clearly annoyed that her community might lose the man who acted as their treasurer. 'We were in a dreadful mess before you came along, and I do not want to go through *that* again. I have better things to do than juggle money, and we cannot let Temperance do it, not after the chaos she created last time.'

Temperance blushed and stared at her shoes. 'I told you I was hopeless at book-keeping, but you insisted I do it anyway. It was not entirely my fault things went wrong.'

'I thought it would do you good,' sniffed Faith. 'Make you a better wife when the time comes.'

'No harm was done,' said North, laying a sympathetic hand on his daughter's broad shoulder. 'Heyden untangled the muddle, and we are making a profit now – enough to maintain our chapel, buy food for the poor and pay Preacher Hill.'

'The Lord,' boomed Hill, making several people jump. The preacher wore drab, slightly seedy clothes, and his pinched face was entirely devoid of humour. His small eyes glinted when he spoke of his love of God and his hate of blasphemers, two subjects that merited identical facial expressions, and a large mouth accommodated his shockingly powerful voice. 'The *Lord*

89

allowed us to make this profit. Heyden had nothing to do with it.'

Faith sighed wearily. 'So you tell us every week, Preacher. But it is cold in here, and I want to go home, so we should turn our attention back to the business in hand. You can tell us about the Lord's fiscal omnipotence later, when we are in front of a fire with a hot posset in our hands.'

North indicated Chaloner was to sit next to him. 'Two more windows were smashed last night, and we have been discussing whether or not to replace them.'

'You have sufficient funds in the—' began Chaloner.

'We should not,' stated Hill with great finality. 'The Lord broke them for a reason, and we must bow to His will. We shall spend the money on Bibles for the poor – to keep them warm this winter.'

'The Lord broke them?' asked Chaloner. 'I thought it was apprentices.' He did not point out that if Bibles were offered to the needy with the addendum that they were to provide warmth, then they were likely to end up on the fire.

'Be quiet,' ordered Hill indignantly. 'Only true believers are allowed to speak here.'

'Hush, Preacher,' said North reprovingly. 'Heyden has given us several good ideas – such as putting wire in the windows to repel fireballs – and we do not want him to resign because you insult his religious convictions. God works through unusual instruments, and he may well be one of them.'

'Very unusual,' agreed Hill, eyeing Chaloner coolly. 'But if he were to accept the Truth, and follow the Way of the Light, then I might—'

'Windows,' prompted Temperance. 'I do not see why

we should suffer when we have the money to rectify the problem, and, despite what Preacher Hill says, I do not think God wants us to be miserable. I have never known a more bitter winter – snow already, and frosts that threaten to freeze the great Thames itself.'

'The *Lord* will freeze the Thames,' proclaimed Hill dogmatically. 'Not frost.'

'These acts of violence worry me,' said North, twisting around to look at the holes in the glass. 'As you know, our only son was killed three years ago – the victim of bigoted ruffians – and I cannot bear the thought of losing anyone else in such a way. We have not been in London long, but already people have turned against us. Perhaps we should return to Ely . . .'

'Your son is with God,' said Hill, softening his voice to indicate sympathy. 'In Heaven.'

'We know that,' said Temperance, while her father struggled to control the grief that always bubbled up when he spoke of his boy. She took his hand and squeezed it comfortingly, then glared at Hill. 'But we still miss him.'

'Glass,' said Faith in a voice thick with emotion. 'We should be talking about glass.'

The discussion ranged back and forth while Chaloner wondered why decent people like the Norths had anything to do with Hill. The preacher was the kind of man who had caused so much strife with his inflexible opinions during the Commonwealth, and associating with him was dangerous at a time when even moderate Puritans were regarded with suspicion and dislike. It was cold in the chapel, and Chaloner tucked his hands inside his jerkin when Hill started to hold forth. He wished the man would shut up, so he could go home and sit by the fire, but then remembered he only had one log and, with no money to buy more, was obliged to save it until Metje arrived later.

When Hill's diatribe blossomed into a tirade against debauchery – which coincidentally included a selfish hankering for new glass – Chaloner stopped listening and considered his own circumstances. He was earning a pittance from an unpopular sect and was prevented by Downing's malice from doing the work he did best. It was frustrating to see relations with Holland disintegrating so rapidly, when he knew he was better qualified to arrest the slide towards war than the men who had been hired to replace him. He had seen Dutch merchants pelted with mud that morning, and Metje had been upset when one of the local rakers – street cleaners – had asked whether she bathed in butter, like all Netherlanders. He itched to be involved again – either in Holland or monitoring known Dutch spies in England – and hoped with all his heart that his interview at White Hall would be a success.

'. . . and I am not sure Heyden would agree with *that*,' he heard North say.

'Yes,' he said, jolting out of his reverie and seeing expectant faces waiting for an answer. 'I do agree.'

'Thomas!' cried Faith in disgust. 'I thought you were a sensible man! Now we shall all spend the most miserable winter imaginable – and it is *your fault*.'

Hill was smug. 'The Lord made him agree with me. He *does* work through unusual instruments.'

Temperance, Faith and North were cool with Chaloner when the meeting ended, and he saw they felt he had let them down. They walked home in silence, the Norths marching arm-in-arm in front, and Hill and Chaloner behind. But Temperance was not the type to bear grudges, and it was not long before she dropped back to join him.

'Have you slaughtered your turkey yet?' he asked, before Hill could spout more religion.

'It is still at the game shop,' she replied. 'Eating enough grain to feed London, apparently.'

'It *is* a big bird,' said North, overhearing. 'But not, perhaps, God's loveliest creation.'

'All God's creations are lovely – it says so in the Bible,' bellowed Hill. He reconsidered before anyone could take issue. 'However, turkeys *are* conspicuous by their absence in the Good Book.'

'What do you think, Thomas?' asked Temperance. Chaloner could see mischief glinting in her eyes, although her face was the picture of innocence. 'Does God love turkeys as much as doves?'

'Be careful how you answer that,' advised Faith, glancing significantly in Hill's direction. 'You could find yourself in deep water.'

'Not as deep as the poor turkey,' replied Chaloner. 'Will you really eat it at Christmas?'

Faith nodded grimly. 'The game dealer claims he has fulfilled his end of the bargain – to supply a bird – and says turning it into dinner is our business. So, I shall kill it when it is delivered today.'

'The Lord guide your hand and protect you from evil,' intoned Hill. He took a deep breath and his voice became alarmingly loud. 'The Lord leads the righteous, but the wicked He will cast—'

'I had never seen one before,' interrupted Chaloner quickly. 'A turkey, I mean. Not alive, at least. I did not know they grew to such a great size.'

'I think our game dealer procured us an exceptionally

grotesque one,' said Faith, thus beginning a debate with Hill as to whether any of God's creatures should be so described. Chaloner took North's arm and drew him away.

'It is dangerous for you when Hill rants in the street. Your religion is no longer popular, and it is unwise to draw attention to yourselves. So far, the smashed windows have been confined to the chapel, but it will not be long before they turn on your home. I do not want to see you hurt.'

North sighed. 'God will protect us.'

Chaloner was tempted to point out that God had not protected North's son from vengeful fanatics, but it was too raw a subject to use for scoring points. 'The new Bill of Uniformity has expelled men like Hill from the Anglican Church, and it will not be long before other laws are passed that will make your religion illegal altogether. You *must* keep a low profile.'

'I will speak to Hill again,' promised North, although he did not look enthused by the prospect.

When they reached North's door, Metje was emptying slops into the street, but Chaloner did not return the secret smile she shot in his direction. He was worried, afraid that Hill's intemperance might bring trouble on North, which would draw attention to the fact that not only was he a Puritan, but that one of his household was Dutch. And then broken windows might be the least of their troubles.

'Not in front of *our* house, dear,' said Faith, when she saw what her employee was doing. 'Walk across the street and dump it outside the Golden Lion instead. They will never notice.'

Metje screwed up her face in the endearing way she

94

had when she had made a mistake. 'I am sorry,' she said in her melodic English. 'I keep forgetting swill always goes outside the tavern.'

'It does not matter,' whispered Temperance. A delicious smell of smoked pork and new bread emanated from the house as she opened the door. 'The maids do it all the time – just make sure no one is looking.' She shot Metje, then Chaloner, a conspiratorial grin before going inside.

Metje reverted to Dutch. 'I *was* right,' she said when they were alone, referring to a topic they had debated at length the previous night. 'She *does* have a hankering for you.'

Chaloner thought she could not be more wrong. 'I am neither rich nor Puritan enough to catch her eye. Will you come later?' It was not just a selfish desire to lie with her that prompted the question: he did not want her to spend the night in North's house.

'Yes, but do not fall asleep before I arrive, like you did yesterday. And do not fall out of any carriages, either.'

She shot him an arch glance as she went inside, to let him know she had not been entirely convinced by the tale he had invented to explain his sore leg. She knew he had an old war injury, but she also knew it plagued him only when he had been doing something unusually taxing. It was becoming increasingly difficult to deceive her, and he sensed yet again that it would not be long before he was forced to admit he had been living a lie for the past three years. He saw her inside the house, then climbed the stairs to his attic next door – quietly, so as not to attract the attention of the landlord.

He was halfway up the second flight when Daniel Ellis appeared on the landing. Ellis was a short man with straight silver hair that fell in a gleaming sheet around his shoulders. His dark eyes were beady, and he had an annoying habit of entering his tenants' rooms when they were out. Naturally, Chaloner had assumed he was a spy, paid to send information to the government about his lodgers, but the traps and devices he set to catch Ellis out quickly proved he was just a man who liked to indulge in superfluous – and usually inconvenient – 'home improvements'.

'Mr Heyden,' Ellis said, clasping his hands in front of him. 'A small matter of the rent.'

Chaloner passed him two crowns, everything left from Thurloe's advance with the exception of a shilling and a few pennies. 'I will pay the rest next week,' he promised, reading the disapproval on the man's face.

Ellis was sceptical. 'You have said that before. Do you have *any* hope of employment, or should I offer your quarters to Mr Hibbert instead? *He* would never be late with payments, and nor would he waste hours scraping away on a tuneless viol.'

'The Victualling Office,' replied Chaloner, repeating the lie he had told Metje. The department that issued supplies to the navy was a large building near the Tower, and its officials were numerous and relatively transient, which meant it would be difficult for anyone to check up on him.

Ellis was pleased. 'Good. Did you hear a whore last night, by the way? I swear I heard one laughing, although there was no trace of her when I went to investigate. Occasionally, the front door has been left open by mistake, and they have found their way inside.'

'I heard no whores,' replied Chaloner, making his way up the stairs and supposing he would have to warn Metje to keep her voice down – again. It was not easy, when one of the best aspects of their relationship was the fact that they made each other laugh.

Playing the viola de gamba, or bass viol, usually relaxed Chaloner, because it forced him to push all else from his mind. That night, however, music did little to quell his growing unease for the safety of the North family, or his concern that Metje was finally beginning to want to know more about him than he was able to share. His leg hurt, too, a residual throb from the dash to the Fleet Rookery. Even so, he was still asleep long before Metje arrived. After they had talked for a while by the flickering light of the fire, she went to bed, but he found himself wide awake. He lay next to her, listening to the clocks chime the hour until, unable to lie still any longer, he went to sit in the window. The bells struck five, then six o'clock, and he drew the blanket more closely around his shoulders as pellets of snow clicked against the glass. It was bitterly cold.

'Come back, Tom,' called Metje drowsily. 'It is freezing in here without you.'

'You should leave soon, or North will be at his morning prayers before you.'

She stirred reluctantly, and he reflected that she had changed little since they had first met. She had been a respectable widow of thirty, with black curls that were the envy of women half her age, and dark eyes in an elfin face. As governess to Downing's hopelessly stupid daughter, she had been miserable and lonely, and Chaloner's first encounters with her had been in the kitchens during the depths of night – she warming wine in the hope that it would bring sleep, and he returning

97

from nocturnal forays on Thurloe's behalf. He had been wary at first – being caught keeping odd hours by a Dutch citizen was not a good idea – but she had accepted his explanation that he was smuggling spices for Downing, and it had never occurred to her that it might not be true. Unwittingly, Downing had supported the lie by summoning Chaloner to furtive meetings, in which they discussed the reports they would send to Thurloe.

Gradually, the late-night discussions became more intimate, and she had amazed him with her increasingly imaginative ideas for visiting his room night after night without being seen. Downing, still hopeful of seducing her himself, would have dismissed her had they been caught, and the fact that they had carried on undetected for so long was a miracle of subterfuge. Then Downing had returned to England, and Metje had been dismissed when she had declined to sleep her way into his good books. As a Netherlander in London, her prospects had been bleak, and she had been fortunate North and his family did not share the current antipathy towards all things foreign.

'It will be light soon,' said Chaloner, watching her fall asleep again. 'Do not grimace at me, when you are the one who seems to enjoy this ridiculous charade.'

'I do not enjoy it,' she countered drowsily. 'It is just convenient. And we have no choice, anyway. You cannot support me – you can barely feed yourself.'

Chaloner was unhappy with the situation, and had been since she had first suggested it. 'I did not mind deceiving Downing, but I dislike doing the same thing to North. He deserves better from both of us. And while we have managed to mislead the poor man so far, we cannot do it for ever.'

'Why not? He thinks I am a pious woman, who likes rising early to prepare the chapel for morning service. He even gave me a key to his front door, so I can go out without disturbing him, and he trusts me to the point where he has never checked whether I really do leave my room at dawn – or whether I abandon it a good deal sooner. My solution to keeping you *and* my job is working brilliantly, so do not look for problems where there are none.'

'He will catch us one day,' warned Chaloner.

'Why should he? We have fooled him since spring.'

'I was away all summer.'

'For the last couple of months, then. You have been here since October, trying to find work – which you had better do soon, or you will starve. The only thing in your cupboard is a cabbage long past its best.'

Chaloner saw there was no point in arguing, so let the matter lie. He gazed out of the window, to where people were emerging from the Golden Lion. Some kind of meeting – obviously an illicit one, judging by the furtive way the attendees were leaving – had just ended, and he wondered whether they had gathered for politics or religion. The tavern's landlord was known for turning a blind eye to his patrons' business and, for a small fee, he would also act as an unofficial post office for those who craved anonymity. It was a service Chaloner used for all his correspondence – although, he realised with a pang of alarm, he would not be able to do it for much longer, because he did not have the funds to pay for it.

Metje took a deep breath, then slid from under the covers, dashing across the floor to where her clothes lay in an untidy pile. Chaloner watched her for a moment, then turned his attention back to the street. Fetter Lane was reasonably affluent, and most householders obeyed the aldermen's edict that lights were to be kept burning in ground-floor windows during the hours of darkness. It meant parts of the street were very well illuminated, something a spy always liked around his home. Additional lights flickered in most houses, where servants were up setting fires for their masters and starting their daily round of chores. The cobbles, swept the previous day for the first time in a month, were carpeted in snow, although it was a thin dusting that would melt once trampled by feet, hoofs and wheels.

Chaloner opened the window and leaned out to inspect the North property, eliciting an angry howl from Metje about the icy blast of air.

'Speak English,' he suggested mildly. 'If North hears Dutch being screeched in my room, he will wonder what you are doing here.'

She winced at what could have been a serious blunder. 'Is he awake?'

Chaloner nodded. 'Reading his Bible. It is slippery outside. Do you want me to come with you?'

'And risk the leg you damaged falling out of that carriage?' She grabbed her skirts and wriggled into them, jumping up and down in an attempt to stay warm at the same time. 'Besides, he will wonder how I come to have an escort at such an hour. What would I say?'

Chaloner shrugged. 'Tell him I have asked you to be my wife.'

She sighed. 'And how will we live? They will not keep me once I am wed, because Faith believes a wife's place is in her own home.'

He smiled, a little sadly. They had this conversation at least once a week, and her answer was always the

same. 'I hope the Earl of Clarendon sends for me soon.
I do not want to wait weeks for a summons, and Ellis is
demanding the rent.'

'You should visit that other man you mentioned – the
merchant who smells of oranges . . .'

'John Dalton.'

'Dalton, yes. Government posts are too much at the
whim of personalities, and you should consider other
options.'

Chaloner did not think he would fare much better
with Dalton. Dutch merchants invariably spoke English
or French, and he did not imagine there would be a vast
amount of work for a translator. He said as much, but
Metje disagreed.

'If there is a choice between Clarendon and Dalton,
you should accept Dalton. You will find it is more secure
in the long term, and I would give a great deal to feel
secure.'

'You are uneasy?'

She regarded him in disbelief. 'Have you not been
listening to me these last few months? You *know* I am
uneasy. I am a Dutch citizen living in a country with
which we may soon be at war, and my lover is unemployed. If there is a conflict, I will need protection, and
*you* will not be able to afford it. Perhaps you should ask
Downing to take you back. He likes you.'

Chaloner was startled, both by the suggestion and the
assertion. 'He detests me.'

She pulled a face. 'He does *now*, thanks to what you
said to him in March when he arrested those regicides.
But you managed to conceal your dislike before then,
and he paid you well. Since he dismissed you, you never
buy wood for the fire, I cannot remember the last time

101

there was decent food in the larder, your clothes are wearing out. You could rent cheaper rooms . . .'

'We discussed this before. I would never see you if I move – unless you hide me in your attic.'

'But then Temperance would know – she watches you like a hawk. I *will* win our wager about her infatuation, Tom, just you wait and see.' She swayed towards him, a pert, elegant figure, even in prim chapel-going garb, and came to perch on his knee. 'But she cannot have you, not while I am here.'

He rubbed the soft skin of her neck, then glanced out of the window again. 'Lord, Meg! North is leaving his house early. He will arrive at the chapel before you.'

She shot to her feet. 'Damn! He will not believe I am taking bread to the homeless again – especially since he offered to go with me next time.' She pulled on cap and cloak. 'Go and distract him, but please do not pretend to be a beggar this time – your last performance distressed him horribly, and he was quiet all day, reflecting on the horrors of destitution.'

'I will tell him I have the plague,' said Chaloner. 'That will drive him back inside his house.'

'At your peril! He is terrified of sickness, and carries a club to repel infected people. What is wrong with talking about the weather? I do not understand this desire for the dramatic, Tom. You did it in Holland, too.'

Chaloner supposed he had, since discussions about the climate tended not to be a good way of keeping people's attention in his line of business.

She indicated he was to hurry, so he grabbed his cloak and set off, leaving her to follow. Outside, the street smelled of snow and smoke, and he was suddenly reminded of one Christmas at his family's manor in

Buckinghamshire. All his siblings had been there, and the house had been ablaze with candles. It was before the first of the civil wars, so his parents had been alive, smiling at each other and holding hands in the absurd, affectionate way they had had with each other. His oldest sister had jokingly arranged everyone in a line according to height, and they had processed out of the house into a white Christmas Eve for midnight mass. It had been a happy time, full of laughter and light, and Chaloner had never understood why Cromwell had wanted to eliminate the festival.

The memory of candlelight and singing faded abruptly when his foot slipped on the slops Metje had dumped the previous day – now frozen into a hard, slick plate – and he took a tumble.

'Heyden!' exclaimed North, hurrying towards him. 'I was going to warn you about the ice, but you were down before I could shout.'

'Christ!' muttered Chaloner, trying to climb to his feet. It was not easy with a leg that was unwilling to bear his weight.

'There is no need for blasphemy,' admonished North severely.

North was wearing his Sunday best, which entailed a black suit that was even plainer than the ones he favoured during the rest of the week. In the semi-darkness, the burn on his face was more noticeable than usual, a dark patch across his chin and cheek. Temperance had told Metje that he had been set upon by a mob at the Restoration: when the King had made his triumphal return, people were keen to demonstrate their new loyalties, and North had not been the only Nonconformist to suffer an unprovoked attack. Sadly, the assault had occurred just months after a similar incident had deprived North of his only son, and Temperance had confided that both parents had clung even more fiercely to strong religion afterwards, as a way of dealing with their misfortunes.

Chaloner accepted the outstretched hand. 'I am sorry if I offended you.'

'You offended God,' replied North. 'But I shall escort you to your rooms, where you can rest and pray for forgiveness.'

Chaloner could see Metje just inside the door. 'There is no need—'

'Nonsense,' said North, moving forward and hauling Chaloner with him. 'It is no trouble.'

Metje shot back up the stairs, making so much noise that North glanced up in alarm.

'Rats,' explained Chaloner, leaning heavily on the man's shoulder in an attempt to distract him. 'They come in to escape the frost.'

'They must be very big ones,' said North nervously.

'Huge,' agreed Chaloner, moving slowly up the steps. 'This is very kind of you, sir.'

'It is no more than my Christian duty.' North shivered when they reached the bedchamber. 'It is colder here than it is outside. Do you have no firewood?'

'I forgot to order it.'

'Then I shall lend you some,' declared North. 'I will fetch it now.'

Before Chaloner could decline, North had gone, and Metje emerged from under the bed, quaking with laughter as she dusted herself down. 'Next time, give me more than half a minute before creating your so-called diversion. I could hardly believe it when you brought him all the way in here.'

'It was an accident. I slipped on some ice.'

The humour faded from her face. 'Are you hurt?'

'My dignity suffered a fatal insult. I shall never be able to look him in the face again – a man half his age wallowing on the ground and unable to rise. But you should go before he comes back. Take care not to meet him on the stairs.'

The summons from the Lord Chancellor arrived early the following morning. Fortunately, Chaloner's new cassock and wig were ready, and with them he wore a wide-brimmed hat that he hoped would make him look more Cavalier than Roundhead. He disliked dressing up, but impressions were important at Court, and it would be foolish not to try to make a good one. With an hour to spare, he used most of the last shilling from Thurloe's advance to lay in a supply of firewood, taking care to return more to North than he had been lent – but regretted carrying it himself when he ended up with sawdust on his finery. Metje left the Norths' sitting room in exasperated disgust at his carelessness, while Faith and Temperance fussed with brushes and damp cloths.

'You look very elegant,' said Temperance warmly. 'Although I do not like this current trend for wigs. I suspect they were invented by a *man* who is *bald*.' Somewhat abruptly, she removed her bonnet to reveal shining chestnut tresses. Chaloner regarded them in surprise, having had no idea that her prim headwear concealed such a splendid mane. She saw his reaction and smiled. 'I could sell it and pay for new windows in the chapel.'

'Temperance!' exclaimed Faith, shocked. 'Replace your clothing at once!'

105

'Do not sell it,' said Chaloner at the same time. 'It looks better on you than it would on a bald man.'

Faith looked from one to the other with sudden suspicion, and it did not take a genius to understand the line her thoughts were taking.

'I should go,' said Chaloner uncomfortably. 'Or I will be late.'

'I told you so,' said Metje, coming to escort him out of the house. Behind the closed sitting room door came the muted murmur of motherly advice. 'Temperance adores you.'

'She has more taste,' said Chaloner, catching her hand and raising it to his lips. 'Not like you.'

Metje laughed. 'My father always said my choice of men would lead me to a bad end. He was right: my first husband died fighting a duel over a neighbour's barking dog, and you have no money.' She reached out to straighten his hat.

'I will if I prove to be good at victualling.'

'I doubt *that* will happen. Downing said you were terrible at household accounts, although I suppose Mr North is happy with your work, so you cannot be overly dire. But I still think you should see what Dalton has to offer, and ignore the Lord Chancellor. You are better suited to translating than book-keeping – it is easier work for a lazy man.'

These comments sometimes stung, although he told himself she probably would not have made them had she known the truth about him. 'I can do both,' he said, a little coolly.

She laughed, rather derisively. 'Can you? Well, it will keep you busy, but I would rather see you once a week in a warm room than five times in a cold one. I acquired something for you yesterday.'

106

Chaloner disliked the occasions when she changed the subject before he could defend himself from her cutting remarks, and nor did he like her use of the term 'acquired'. It sounded as though she had stolen it. 'What?' he asked suspiciously.

'A lamp – a really good one. It means you will be able to read your music at night, and I will be able to dress without groping around in the dark.'

Chaloner regarded her sceptically. 'Where did it come from?'

She shoved him in the chest, disappointed by his response. 'A friend – one of the chapel council – gave it to me. She bought another and offered me the old one. And I am giving it to you.'

He did not want to appear ungracious, but buying fuel for such an extravagance was currently out of the question. He forced a smile. 'That is kind.'

'Mr North is taking Faith and Temperance to a jewellers' meeting in Goldsmiths' Hall today, so I should be able to smuggle it to you with no one seeing. You will like it, I promise. It is *massive*.'

He smiled again, amused she should think size had anything to do with quality, and his irritation at her began to fade. 'Thank you.'

She hugged him. 'It is a reward for accepting a post with Dalton. Be careful if you visit Mr North tonight, though. The turkey is due to arrive this evening, and I have a feeling Faith will not have the courage to put her knife to its throat.'

The icy snap of the last two days had given way to the dank fogginess that often afflicted London in the winter months. Clouds hung low overhead, covering houses and

107

trees with a film of fine droplets. Smoke from thousands of fires and the noxious industries along the Fleet became trapped in the mist, creating a yellow-brown pall that caught at the back of throats. Beggars were out in force, displaying wounds and sores, and appealing piteously for extra alms because of the dismal weather. One revealed fingers that looked frost-bitten, and Chaloner wondered whether he had allowed them to freeze on purpose, so he would have an injury to show passers-by. He gave the man one of his last pennies, sorry he should be forced to such desperate measures.

He walked briskly, concentrating on not stepping into the piles of ordure that littered the streets and on staying out of the path of carts and horses. Traders yelled every inch of the way, selling pies, ribbons, nails, pots, candles, cure-alls and fruit. Men in sober clothing screamed that God demanded repentance, and gaudily clad courtiers were jiggled along in sedan chairs. A massive bull, brought for slaughter from the nearby village of Islington, had escaped and was running amok, tracked by several baying dogs and an amorous cow. Its owner shadowed the menagerie nervously, calling for its return, but the bull had other ideas, and continued along the Strand on a bucking, chaotic mission of its own.

As Chaloner neared White Hall, the streets became more crowded, and he learned from the conversations around him that there was to be an exhibition that day – some of the paintings acquired by the King for his private apartments were to be publicly displayed. The Banqueting House had been chosen as the venue, and visitors were invited to inspect the collection for the very reasonable price of sixpence. Since he had some time to spare, Chaloner stepped inside, deciding at last to locate the stone under which his uncle had hidden his money.

The Banqueting House was one of the most imposing buildings in the city, a mammoth, rectangular edifice designed to look like an ancient Roman meeting hall. It had two tiers of massive oblong windows, and Chaloner recalled vividly the old king stepping through one of them to meet the executioner's axe thirteen years before. Inside, he gazed up at the riot of colour in Rubens's famous ceiling, although some of its the panels were already stained with soot from the many lamps that were needed to illuminate the room at night.

That day, every spare patch of wall boasted a work of art, and boards had been set up along the middle of the chamber to hold more. Sombre Dutch masters rubbed shoulders with the lighter, softer colours of the Venetian schools, and there was an atmosphere of hushed awe from the spectators. Chaloner turned his attention to the floor, which comprised squares of red and white marble, all in sad need of a scrub. He made for the far end of the hall and began to count: seven tiles from the door, and three from the second window. His uncle's slab was slightly different than its neighbours, because the mortar holding it in place had been scraped away. Dirt had dropped into the resulting gaps, but it looked as though no one had raised it since the older Chaloner had deposited his five hundred silver crowns there the night he had fled the country. It would make a pleasant surprise for his sons one day – but not yet. There were still too many unfriendly eyes on the regicides' families, regardless of the fact that most had been powerless to prevent what their kinsmen had done.

Chaloner left when a steward demanded the entrance fee, and headed for the Court Gate, which stood just north of the Banqueting House. He had never been inside White Hall palace, although he had travelled along King Street often enough, and he was obliged to ask the way to the Lord Chancellor's offices. The soldier issued directions that were difficult to follow, sending him across the spacious yard known as the Great Court, and into a chaotic huddle of buildings that were mostly occupied by the Queen's servants. He turned left when the soldier should have said right, and found himself in a second yard, this one boasting an individual buttery, pantry, wood shed, coal shed, stable, kitchen and laundry for virtually every White Hall resident. He passed through a gate that then locked behind him, so was unable to retrace his steps when he realised he was heading in the wrong direction. It was not long before he was hopelessly lost.

He continued to wander, confused by the palace's jumble of buildings and alleys. Some houses were ancient and verging on ruinous, although they had probably been splendid in their day, while others were rambling Tudor monstrosities, all irregular angles, brick chimneys and thick timbers. Others still were modern, hurled up quickly and cheaply, without regard to function or style. The result was a messy village populated by scurrying clerks, aloof retainers, arrogant courtiers and a smattering of clerics. Eventually, he found someone willing to escort him, and was conducted to an elegant wing overlooking the manicured expanse of open ground called the Privy Gardens. The Lord Chancellor was in good company, Chaloner's guide informed him, because he had Prince Rupert as a neighbour on one side, and the King on the other. The clocks were striking ten as Chaloner knocked to be admitted.

Clarendon's quarters were impressive, as befitted a

110

principal advisor to the King. They boasted several cartoons by famous Flemish artists, and a Renaissance sculpture of Hercules. Chaloner was admiring the latter when the Earl entered, so soft footed in velvet slippers that he did not hear him arrive, and spun around in alarm at the sound of a voice so close behind him. His reaction startled Clarendon, who dropped the vase he was carrying. It shattered with a crash on the marble floor, and the guards in the hall immediately burst in, pistols at the ready.

'Intruder!' yelled their captain, spotting Chaloner. 'Shoot him!'

'No!' cried the Earl, waving short, plump arms as they aimed their weapons and Chaloner dived for cover behind him. 'It was an accident. A vessel slipped from my fingers.'

The captain regarded Chaloner with narrowed eyes. 'How did you get in?'

'I admitted him, sir,' said one of the soldiers uncomfortably. His voice took on a wheedling tone. 'He has a written invitation.'

'Give it to me,' ordered the captain. He snatched the proffered missive and read it several times, while Chaloner watched uneasily, hoping no one had made a mistake. Eventually, it was handed back with a curt nod, and the captain turned to Clarendon. 'It is lucky you stopped us, My Lord, or we would have killed him. He is not on the visitors list you submitted on Friday.'

'He is from Thurloe,' said the Earl in a whisper, although his voice was still loud enough for Chaloner to hear, and probably some of the soldiers, too. He gave a slow, meaningful wink. '*Thurloe.* We do not include *his* men on our official lists.'

'Another spy,' said the captain flatly. 'Well, I hope he

111

is better than the last one. Mind your feet, sir. You do not want to cut yourself through those thin slippers. What did you drop? A wine jug?'

'A crystal vase,' said Clarendon, inspecting the mess sorrowfully. 'I always said it was a bad idea to use exquisite art for everyday use, but the King likes to be surrounded by fine things.'

'I had noticed,' muttered the captain. He spoke a little more loudly. 'I shall fetch a brush, sir. Meanwhile, I advise you not to walk about.'

The Lord Chancellor nodded then waved a chubby, ruff-clad hand to indicate the soldiers were to leave. While they shuffled out, Chaloner studied him covertly. Sir Edward Hyde, recently dubbed Earl of Clarendon, was short, fat and fussy, and did not look at all like the kind of man who had navigated a disenfranchised king through years of bitter exile. He wore a fluffy wig that made his face look pouchy, and his clothes were tight and unflattering. Chaloner had heard that younger, wittier courtiers had no respect for Clarendon, although he was reputed to be a man of principle, and that they teased him about his obesity.

'Philip Evett is a good sort,' said Clarendon, once the door had closed. 'He has been with me for years – ever since I went into exile with the King – and it is good to have a trustworthy man in charge of my personal safety. Did you see how quickly he dashed in to protect me?'

Chaloner nodded, not pointing out that if the sound had been a discharging gun, then the captain would have been too late. 'Yes, My Lord.'

Clarendon lowered his voice. 'Did Thurloe tell you what happened to Colonel Clarke? He was murdered – his belly sliced open like a pig's. It happened not far from where you are standing now.'

112

'Did it?' asked Chaloner, wondering whether the Earl was trying to unnerve him by describing what had happened to his predecessor. Was it some sort of warning, or perhaps a threat?

'In a corridor that leads to the servants' quarters. The poor maid who found him screamed herself hoarse with fright. I had asked him to investigate a series of thefts from the kitchens, so I imagine he was stabbed because he had uncovered the villain. I found papers in a secret pocket in his tunic, but they were written in cipher, and I have not been able to break the code.' The Earl rummaged on his desk and presented Chaloner with several slivers of parchment. 'Can you do it?'

Chaloner could: it was the common substitution code he and other agents used for sending routine messages to Thurloe, and was familiar enough to allow him to read it without a crib. One message was short, and informed the recipient that Seven were in considerable danger. The other was longer: *It hath pleaysed God hitherto to give alle men an opportunitaye to Praise God's One Sonne above alle else, and I am with greate passion to see it donne.*

'These were concealed in Clarke's clothing?' he asked, thoughts tumbling in confusion. 'Praise God's one son' was the phrase Hewson had muttered as he had died; Hewson had also made mention of the number seven.

The Earl nodded as he took them back, stuffing them carelessly inside a drawer. 'Yes. I assume they relate to the investigation he was conducting for me, but I cannot be certain until I have their meaning.'

'Perhaps I could look into the matter for you, sir,' suggested Chaloner, trying to sound as though the idea had just occurred to him.

113

'No, thank you,' said Clarendon curtly. 'He was Thurloe's kinsman, sent to me as a favour because I asked for a good spy. I feel responsible for his death, and consider it far too important a matter to entrust to someone I do not know – no offence. I will order Evett to work on it with me.'

Chaloner tried again. 'I have some experience with—'

'I said no,' said Clarendon firmly. 'If you see him, you can tell Thurloe that he need not fear the culprit will go unpunished, because *I* am looking into the crime personally. Now, since we are alone, we should take the opportunity to talk privately, Heyden. Or do you prefer to be called Chaloner?'

Chaloner kept his expression blank. 'Either is acceptable, sir,' he said, assuming Thurloe had told him his real name, although he could not imagine why. His family connections would hardly encourage the Earl to hire him, which meant he would not be able to do what Thurloe had asked.

Clarendon pursed his lips. 'I expected to see *some* reaction when I mentioned the fact that I know your uncle signed the warrant that killed the King's father.'

'I did not condone my kinsman's actions, sir. I would have stopped him, had I been able.'

'Brave words, but unfortunately not ones that will see you safe from vengeful hands – and there are far too many of those around these days. Thurloe did not tell me, in case you wonder how I come to know – your uncle did. I met him in France once, where he mentioned a nephew of the same name who was Thurloe's Dutch agent. I drew my own conclusions when Thurloe described your career. Besides, you have your uncle's eyes – a fine dark grey. However, this information will remain with me alone, and in White Hall you will be known as Thomas Heyden.'

'Very well, sir,' said Chaloner, wishing his uncle had been less verbose. Between dragging him to war and telling Royalists he was Cromwell's spy, it was almost as if the man had wanted him killed. He might have assumed that were the case, had it not been for the fact that he was the only one entrusted with the secret of the hidden silver.

The Earl sighed irritably. 'You could at least pretend to be grateful for my magnanimity. Do you know why I am prepared to keep your identity quiet?'

'Because Thurloe said that knowing a secret about someone will ensure he will never betray you?'

Clarendon's eyebrows shot up. 'He most certainly did not! He said the key to loyalty is making sure people are paid on time, if you must know. But I am prepared to protect you because our country has an urgent need for reliable men, and we are not in a position to be choosy. I understand you know a great deal about Holland, and you speak the language well enough to pass for a Dutchman.'

'Yes, sir.'

'Good. Thurloe thinks you should return there as soon as possible, because he says there will be a war soon. The problem with that plan is that Cerberus – that is what I call George Downing, because he is such a two-faced dog – does not share Thurloe's good opinion of you, and Joseph Williamson, who has taken charge of the intelligence services, declines to hire men with dubious testimonials. Thurloe suggests we put you to the test – we use you here for a few months and allow you to prove yourself. Will you accept the challenge?'

115

'Yes, sir,' replied Chaloner, feeling as though he was selling his soul – and to a man who did not know that the mythical Cerberus had three heads. 'What would you like me to do?'

Clarendon smiled. 'Here-comes Evett with the brush, so we shall have no more talk of regicides and spies in Holland. I shall tell you what I want, as soon as we have cleaned up this mess.'

The captain had brought the kind of broom that was used to sweep leaves from the garden, and was wholly unsuitable for collecting small shards of glass from a marble floor. Neither he nor Clarendon seemed aware of the fact, and a good deal of effort went into something that should have been completed in moments. The Lord Chancellor tutted and fussed over the breakage.

'Can this be repaired, do you think, Heyden?'

'No, sir. It has shattered into too many pieces.'

'Well, collect them up anyway, and I shall work on them this evening. The King is hosting another masque. It is bound to end late, and I shall need something to keep me occupied, since the racket will keep me awake.' He dropped to his knees. 'Put the larger bits in my handkerchief. Come on, or we shall be here all day.'

Chaloner knelt and began to gather splinters. He was unhappy, worried by the fact that his uncle had been very loose tongued to members of an enemy court, and wary of the panting, sweating man on the floor beside him, suspecting there was more to the Earl than he allowed people to see. The desire for deception meant he was potentially dangerous, and Chaloner began to see what sort of life he might lead if he followed through with the challenge.

116

He stood to collect one or two fragments that had somehow landed on the desk. As he did so, he noticed that among the scattered papers were reports from the five agents Thurloe had sent. For example, Simon Lane's familiar scrawl read: *C talked all through church with Jo.* Leaving such communications lying around was careless at best, and criminally negligent at worst. Pretending to pat the table for more shards, Chaloner shoved Lane's missive under another document for safety, but was startled when his tampering revealed a paper on which PRAISE GOD'S ONE SON was printed in large, capital letters. The words were brown, and the parchment scorched: they had been written in lemon or onion juice, which needed to be heated before it became visible. Some of the letters were similar to ones in the notes the Earl had found in Clarke's clothing, suggesting they had been penned by the same person.

He crouched behind the table to hide his consternation. Who had sent the Lord Chancellor a missive containing that particular phrase, and what did it mean? Or had it been intended for someone else, and the Earl had intercepted it? And why had Clarke converted the same words to cipher and hidden them in his secret pocket? Were the Earl and Clarke associated with John Hewson, who had ordered Chaloner to praise God's one son as he lay dying, or was that coincidence? Chaloner did not think so. He was beginning to think there was an important message in those four syllables, something vital enough for Hewson to gasp with his last breath.

'I think that is all of it,' said Evett eventually, standing with his cupped hands full of glass.

'Put it on the table by the window, if you please,' said the Earl, following him, to make sure he did as he was told. 'Perhaps I shall work a miracle tonight, when the

King and his courtiers chase each other around dressed as wild animals.'

'Wild animals?' blurted Chaloner, unable to help himself. He was disconcerted and uneasy, already regretting his promise to do the Earl's bidding. It would be safer to walk away and have no more to do with any of it. And do what? The notion of being a burden to his family was a powerful reason to see the thing through. He tried to gather his scattered, disorganised thoughts, before he made a mistake or said something best kept to himself.

'The masque,' said the Lord Chancellor, as if that explained everything.

'They dress up,' added Evett in a disapproving undertone. 'Skins, feathers and furs have been arriving all week, and most of them stink. No one will be allowed in unless he or she is in the guise of some wild beast. The King will be a lion, naturally, and Lady Castlemaine will not tell anyone her chosen creature. She says we must wait and see.'

'A fox, most likely,' said the earl. 'Or a wolf. It will be nothing cuddly, you can be sure of that.'

'There is a rumour that the Duke of Buckingham will be a pig,' said Evett with a perfectly straight face.

Clarendon chuckled. 'A boar, Philip, not a pig. No, do not withdraw. Come and enjoy a cup of tea by the fire. It arrived fresh this morning.'

'Tea?' asked Evett with infinite suspicion. He was Chaloner's age, with a head of reddish curls that tumbled around his shoulders. He wore the loose breeches and short doublet of the palace guard, and there was a thin scar on his left cheek that looked as though it had been made by a duelling sword. It was not disfiguring, and

118

added a certain dash to his appearance; uncharitably it occurred to Chaloner that he might have put it there himself.

'It is a beverage,' explained the Earl. 'Popular in Portugal. Come – do not stand on ceremony with me. You to my left, Heyden on my right. There. Now we can all enjoy the warmth of the fire.'

He leaned forward and poured a thick, brown liquid into three glasses. Leaves rose to the surface of each, where they formed a floating mat. Clarendon handed them to his guests.

'We *drink* this?' asked Evett, regarding it warily. 'Are you sure?'

'Yes, yes,' said Clarendon cheerfully. 'The Portuguese ambassador tells me it is excellent for the spirit *and* the digestion. Come on, man! Do not be shy.'

Obediently, Evett took a tentative sip. Leaves dappled his moustache as he chewed and then swallowed. 'Interesting,' he said in a way that made it clear he thought he had been misled.

'Actually, sir,' said Chaloner, wondering whether he should just drink the stuff, or whether it was a test to ascertain whether he was a sycophant, 'the Portuguese usually strain out the leaves.'

'Do they?' asked the Earl, his face falling. 'Well, I suppose I can use my handkerchief as a sieve. It is relatively clean.' He tipped the tea back into the jug, and wiped each glass with his sleeve. Then he placed the handkerchief across the top of one beaker and poured. The volume of leaves was so dense that the material soon became clogged. 'Dash it all!' he cried.

'It might be better to start again,' suggested Chaloner. 'Using less tea.'

119

'Have you been to Portugal?' asked the Earl, following his instructions. 'I expect it was nice.'

Chaloner glanced at him, trying to assess whether there was some inner meaning to the question. He could read nothing in the guileless pale blue eyes. 'Yes, sir. Very nice.'

'Good,' said the Earl. 'Did you like the United Provinces, too? Or do you prefer France?'

Evett's eyes shone. '*I* like France – those mighty castles in the south, perched on their great cliffs. We would not have lost the wars to Cromwell, if we had had a few of those to fight from.'

'We have the Tower,' said Clarendon. 'That has never fallen to an enemy. And you can show it to Ch . . . to *Heyden* tomorrow. Or perhaps the day after. Depending.'

'The cellars,' said Evett. 'To look for buried treasure.'

Chaloner began to wonder whether they were both mad – that they had engaged in one culinary experiment too many and that whatever they had imbibed had addled their wits. When a half-naked man dressed in a baboon's head burst into the chamber, he suspected the rest of the place was affected too, and that the entire country was in the hands of lunatics.

'Be off with you!' shouted the Earl crossly. 'I am engaged in private state business.'

The baboon waggled its head and made an obscene gesture, but reversed hastily when Evett came to his feet with his sword in his hand.

'That was Buckingham,' said Evett angrily, when the door had closed with the baboon on the other side. 'Still, he is a monkey in life, so why not come to the masque as an ape, too?'

'Be careful, Philip,' warned the Earl. 'Walls have ears.

120

Now, let us drink this tea, and then we shall discuss business. This is a very pallid mixture, Heyden. Are you sure there are enough leaves? My original brew was much thicker and blacker.'

'This is how the Portuguese drink it.' Chaloner disliked tea, but was loath to say so. He could not read the Earl, and did not know whether he would be offended if his offer of hospitality was rejected.

The Earl downed his portion in a single gulp, then sat back as though waiting for something to happen. 'I do not feel noticeably refreshed,' he announced after several moments.

'It is nasty,' pronounced Evett, setting his half-empty cup on the hearth and pulling a face. 'Tea will never catch on in England. It has a vile, bitter flavour, and in no way compares to ale.'

'I agree,' said Clarendon. 'I will pass the rest to the Portuguese ambassador, since he likes it.'

'Give it to Buckingham,' said Evett venomously. 'The leaves might choke him.'

'Now,' said the Earl, turning to Chaloner. 'Thurloe informs me that you are a good spy, and said that once or twice your reports prevented an exchange of hostilities with the Dutch. He also said you solved a series of thefts from Cerberus's house *and* you caught the man who murdered the Dutch king's favourite page.'

'Those cases were not as difficult as they—'

'Modesty,' said the Earl, regarding Chaloner with a smile. 'That is something I do not often encounter. Thurloe praises your talent for finding the truth, and recommends I use you to look into Clarke's murder, but I have a different task in mind – one better suited to your abilities.'

121

'Yes, sir?' asked Chaloner, beginning to be anxious again.

'It revolves around missing gold,' said Clarendon. 'Seven thousand pounds' worth of it. It is said to have been buried in the Tower of London and I want you to find it for me.'

# Chapter 4

Chaloner had experienced misgivings about the Earl of Clarendon from the moment he had set eyes on the fellow. He was superficially pleasant, but there was a stubborn inflexibility in him that suggested he would make a dangerous master. Chaloner had trusted Thurloe implicitly, confident that his role as intelligence agent in the various countries to which he had been assigned would never be revealed, and that his reports would either be destroyed as soon as their contents had been absorbed, or filed in such a way that they could never be traced to their sender. The Earl, on the other hand, left *his* spies' missives lying on his desk, and Clarke's death might well have been a result of his carelessness.

'This missing gold,' Chaloner said cautiously. 'Does it belong to the Crown?'

'Yes and no,' replied the Earl cagily. 'You can tell him how we came to hear about it, Philip. You have been more deeply involved with it than I, and know more of the details.'

'It started on the thirtieth day of October,' began Evett obligingly. 'A man named Thomas Wade of Axe

Yard came to us with a tale. He said an elderly woman by the name of Mother Pinchon had approached him the previous night, and said she knew the whereabouts of a great hoard of treasure – and for a hundred pounds, she would tell him how to get it.'

'Why?' asked Chaloner, already suspicious. 'If seven thousand pounds were hidden, why would she settle for a hundred? Why not dig it up for herself, and keep it all?'

'Because the treasure is buried inside the Tower,' explained Clarendon. 'We do not allow women to start excavating *there* whenever they please! It is full of rebel prisoners for one thing, and for another, it is always wise to restrict access into such places. No one goes in or out without an escort, so this woman could never have reached the hoard without official help. Besides, a hundred pounds is a fortune to a servant, and I imagine she thinks she has secured herself an excellent bargain.'

'How did she know about the gold in the first place?' asked Chaloner sceptically.

'She was in the service of Sir John Barkstead,' replied Evett. 'Do you remember who Barkstead was?'

'He fled abroad after the collapse of the Common-wealth,' replied Chaloner, becoming even more uneasy. 'And he was one of the men Downing brought home to be executed last March.'

'Yes, he was a *regicide*,' said the Earl, looking at Chaloner as if to remind him of the secret they shared. 'And as such, he did well for himself during the Protectorate. One of the posts he held was Lieutenant of the Tower.'

Evett took up the tale. 'And that means he had access to all parts of the castle. Mother Pinchon says that the night before he was ousted, he and she packed this seven thousand pounds – all his moveable money – into butter firkins.'

Chaloner nodded, thinking about his uncle's hoard. It was not only Parliamentarians who had hidden what they could, and there were tales of Royalists returning to the country they had abandoned after the wars and setting out with spades. Some had found their caches undisturbed, but many had not, and accusations were rife.

'When they had finished, and all the containers were sealed, Barkstead told her where he planned to bury them,' said Evett.

'Why?' demanded Chaloner. 'If he hid his money, he obviously thought he would have an opportunity to collect it in the future. Why would he share such a secret with a servant?'

'Good,' said the Earl, nodding vigorously. 'Your questions show an enquiring mind. But the answer is simple: he was fond of this woman. He said that if he could not retrieve it himself, then she should have it instead. She waited eight months to the day from his execution, then approached Wade.'

'Who *is* Wade?'

'The Tower's victualling commissioner,' said the Earl. 'He was the perfect fellow for this woman to see – not so mighty as to refuse her an interview, but well enough connected to ensure her request was acted upon. So, she told Wade her tale, and Wade came to us. I mentioned it to the King—'

'Who happened to be entertaining the Earl of Sandwich,' interrupted Evett. He sounded disapproving. 'His Majesty and Sandwich were deep in their cups, and they reached an agreement I am sure the King regretted the following day.'

'That Wade should have two thousand pounds as a finder's fee; Sandwich should have two thousand because he is a good fellow; and the King should have the remaining three,' explained the Earl. 'It was a simple division. Philip went to the Tower with Wade the very next day.'

'Did you find it?' asked Chaloner, intrigued despite his reservations.

'Obviously, they were obliged to visit Sir John Robinson first,' said the Earl. 'Do you know Robinson? Thurloe tells me your knowledge of city's officials is sadly lacking.'

'The Lord Mayor of London,' replied Chaloner, rather defiantly.

'He is also Lieutenant of the Tower,' added Captain Evett. 'He took over Barkstead's old post.'

'We needed his agreement to dig up the cellars, you see,' explained the Earl. 'Once we had it, the captain, Wade and Sandwich's clerk . . . what is his name, Philip? A fat-cheeked, obsequious little fellow, who says one thing and thinks another. You can see the truth in his calculating eyes.'

'Samuel Pepys, sir.'

'Yes, Pepys,' said the Earl, nodding. 'Sandwich commissioned Pepys to represent his interests. Meanwhile, Philip stood for the King, and Wade was there for himself and Mother Pinchon.'

'Wade had clear directions from Pinchon, so he knew exactly where to look,' Evett went on. 'He located the arch she described with no trouble, and we dug all afternoon. But we found nothing.'

'Mother Pinchon was not with you?' asked Chaloner,

surprised. 'Surely, it would have been best for her to point out where the hoard lies, rather than rely on her spoken instructions?'

'They were very good instructions,' said Evett defensively. 'And we had every expectation of finding the treasure that day. But we did not.'

'So, next you asked Pinchon to come to the Tower, and say exactly where—' surmised Chaloner.

'She refused,' interrupted Evett. 'She had served a regicide for twenty years, and Wade could not persuade her to set foot in the Tower again. Since she comes to Wade, and he does not know where she lives, her expertise was unavailable to us.'

'It was very disappointing when they were unsuccessful the first day,' said the Earl. 'But, undaunted, they returned the following morning to try again.'

'Because it was such a huge sum, we felt we should not give up too soon, so we excavated half the cellar,' said Evett. 'By this time, I confess I was beginning to be sceptical. We arranged a third dig for the following week, but were unlucky again. Then Wade suggested we try near the old Coldharbour Gate, since it has an arch that vaguely matched Pinchon's description, but we still found nothing.'

'Not even an empty butter firkin?' asked Chaloner.

'Nothing. Pepys thinks Barkstead lied to Pinchon – told her about the treasure and her chances of getting it, so she would continue to serve him after he no longer had the free cash to pay her.'

'You knew Barkstead,' said the Earl to Chaloner. 'Would he have done such a thing?'

Chaloner considered his brief acquaintance with Barkstead. They had met once before his arrest, and there had been several long discussions when he was in Downing's custody. 'He was ruthless and devoted to the republic, but I do not think he would have misled a faithful retainer so callously.'

Clarendon shot Evett a triumphant glance. 'There! I concur, because *I* think Barkstead was telling the truth, too. So, since seven thousand pounds is a lot of money, I want you to find it, Heyden.'

'You want me to dig again?'

'I doubt that would do much good. If Philip says the gold is not in the Tower, then it is not there. It is some-where else, and you must discover where.'

Chaloner did not like the sound of this assignment. 'How?'

'That is for you to decide. Philip will answer questions, but you are free to undertake the task as you see fit. All I ask is that you keep me informed. And there is one other thing: I do not want you to tell Wade or Pepys what you are doing.'

'But I might have to ask them about—'

'No!' declared the Earl emphatically. 'If you find this money on your own, then Sandwich and Wade have no claim on it. The King can have his three thousand, and I shall use the rest to . . . to replace those religious statues smashed by Puritans during the Interregnum.'

'I see,' said Chaloner, wondering whether it was wise to involve himself in a plot that would defraud a powerful noble like the Earl of Sandwich – and what would happen if the King learned he had been granted less of the money than his Lord Chancellor?

'You must not tell Thurloe, either. Did he ask you to report the outcome of this interview?'

'No, sir.' Thurloe had asked for information about

128

Clarke and Kelyng, which was not the same thing at all.

The Earl regarded him closely. 'I do not believe you.'

'But it is true, sir. He no longer dabbles in politics.'

Clarendon sighed. 'Then he is a wise man who knows when it is time to leave the stage. But you will not tell him about Barkstead's treasure. The only people who know what I have asked you to do are in this room – and Philip and I will not break our silence.'

'Neither will I, sir.'

'Good,' said Clarendon, rubbing his hands. 'All is settled, then.'

Once away from the grandeur of White Hall, Chaloner hauled off his new wig and scrubbed at his hair, glad to be rid of something that was hot, itchy and uncomfortable. He wanted to consider the implications of his allotted task, and reflect on the man who had assigned it to him, so began to walk to his favourite coffee house, thinking about the Lord Chancellor as he went. On first acquaintance, Clarendon came across as genial and slightly absurd. However, he had taken the precaution of investigating the spy recommended by Thurloe, and had learned something very few men knew, which suggested some degree of competence. Had he discovered a secret about Clarke, too, who had then been killed because he was deemed unsuitable? Would Chaloner also be found stabbed in a White Hall corridor – because he had failed to locate the gold, because he *had* located it but the Earl wanted no witnesses, or because the Earl did not want the nephew of a regicide in his employ?

Tucked away near Covent Garden was Will's Coffee House. It was a large, noisy establishment, patronised by officials who worked at White Hall and merchants whose

129

premises were on the Strand. Like most coffee houses – and more were being built each year – Will's was the exclusive domain of men, and was consequently a hearty, smoky place. Chaloner liked the pungent scent of tobacco as it mingled with the acrid odour of burning wood in the hearth, and there was something pleasantly heady about the exotic aroma of coffee beans. Will's was also a good place to go, because its owner allowed his customers to buy pots of coffee on credit.

Chaloner was about to open the door when he sensed something amiss. It was nothing tangible, more of a tingling at the back of his neck, but he had not survived ten years by ignoring such warnings, and had learned to trust his instincts. He moved away from the door, and when a handsome coach decorated with the Duke of Buckingham's crest collided with a brewer's cart, he capitalised on the chaos to slip into a wigmaker's shop. From a shadowy corner near the window, he had a good view of the road, but was invisible to anyone looking in. Moments later, the door clanked to admit a woman, while outside, two men peered through the glass, making a pretence at examining the displayed merchandise.

'Mr Heyden,' said the wigmaker, a Frenchman named Jervas. His expression was one of agitated consternation, which intensified when he saw curls dangling from Chaloner's pocket. 'Are you dissatisfied with the piece I sold you Saturday? Or have you come to demand your own hair back? If so, then it is too late – I have promised it to another client, and he has been in for fittings.'

The door opened and the two loiterers strolled inside. They were Snow with his jet-black boots, and fair-headed Storey. Chaloner glanced through the window, and saw the stout, menacing presence of Gervaise

Bennet across the street, distorted to monstrous dimensions by imperfections in the glass. He shot an apologetic smile at the wigmaker and addressed him in his native tongue, confident the two louts would not be able to understand him.

'I am eluding creditors, Monsieur. Tend your other customers and ignore me.'

Jervas tapped the side of his nose in manly camaraderie, and moved away to speak to the woman, a tall, elegant lady who carried a fan and whose expensive dress had more ruffles and frills than Lady Castlemaine's boudoir. With a jolt of unease, Chaloner recognised Sarah Dalton. She glanced at him out of the corner of her eye in a way that made him sure her presence there was no coincidence. Surely *she* could not be working with Bennet and Kelyng?

Meanwhile, Snow and Storey sauntered to the rear of the shop, where they began to try on the more expensive hairpieces. The way to the door was clear, but Bennet was standing with his hand inside his coat, and Chaloner saw through their plan in an instant – he was not about to be herded out of the building and into the sights of Bennet's pistol. The dagger in his sleeve dropped into the palm of his hand, and he moved silently to where Storey was sniggering at the sight of Snow in an elaborate auburn affair that reached his waist.

'I recommend the black wigs today, Snow,' he said, speaking in a low voice, so the man almost jumped out of his skin. He had not expected Chaloner to approach him. 'The red ones have lice.'

'*I* do not need a wig,' said Storey, fingering his oily yellow locks with pride. He glanced at his friend's dour expression, and collected himself, belatedly pretending

131

to be surprised that Chaloner should address him. 'Who are you? We have not met before.'

'Why are you following me?' asked Chaloner, in the same low voice. He did not want to attract Sarah Dalton towards a situation that might end in violence, no matter whose side she was on.

'Bennet hired us to ask you a few questions, then kill you,' replied Snow, seeing there was no point in continuing the charade: they had been exposed and that was that. 'He paid us two shillings.'

Chaloner was taken aback by the bald confession. 'Why does he want me dead?'

'Kelyng probably told him to arrange it,' replied Storey. 'But we never asked why.'

'You commit murder for them, and they do not bother to tell you the reason?' Chaloner asked, making his voice drip contempt. 'They must think very little of you.'

'It is because you killed One-Eyed Jones,' snapped Storey, nettled. 'They want revenge.'

'But they want questions answered first, you say? What do they want to know?'

Storey smiled, revealing a set of unexpectedly white teeth. 'That is more like it. Cooperation. They want the names of John Thurloe's six brothers.'

Chaloner was taken aback at the bizarre nature of the enquiry. 'What for?'

Storey's grin vanished. 'How should I know? They just want names and the places where they might be found. If you tell us, I will kill you quickly – you will not feel a thing.'

Chaloner was surprised Kelyng should need anyone to furnish him with such information – Thurloe was fond of his family, and their identities were no secret. 'Well,

132

there is Thomas, who lives in Becket,' he said, scratching his head. 'Then there is another John, this one from Gaunt, and there is Guy from Fawkes. Would you like me to continue?' He waited for the inevitable eruption of anger.

Storey shot him an apologetic grin, while Snow counted off the names on his fingers. 'We cannot remember all that, and it would not do to get it wrong. Would you mind writing it down?'

Bemused, Chaloner went to where Jervas kept his pens and ink, and began to scribe. He was aware of Sarah watching him curiously. 'This is a very strange thing to be asking.'

Storey agreed with a sigh. 'There is no fathoming the likes of Kelyng and Bennet. Still, they do what they must to rid London of traitors, and it is not for us to question their tactics.'

'How did you find me?'

'Bennet saw you coming out of White Hall,' said Storey, prepared to be helpful in his turn. 'We have been watching the area, although we had little to go on – a lame man with short hair.'

Chaloner was furious at himself for making two elementary mistakes: removing his wig and forgetting to disguise his limp. They combined to make him easily identifiable, and the area around the Royal Mews was sufficiently busy that Bennet had obviously predicted it would not be long before his quarry appeared. Just because Chaloner had put the incident in Kelyng's garden to the back of his mind did not mean Kelyng had done so, too.

'How do you know *I* killed Jones?' he asked.

Snow indicated he should continue writing, so he added

William the Conqueror and Francis Bacon. 'You stabbed him with Bennet's dagger, and we were paid to get rid of the body.'

'Get rid of the body?' echoed Chaloner, finishing the list with Julius Caesar and handing it to Snow. 'Why would Kelyng feel the need to do that, if Jones was killed by an intruder? The only reason for hiding a corpse is so no one learns what really happened to it. What did you do? Drop it in the river?'

'We are a bit more clever than that,' said Storey smugly. We—'

'We followed orders,' interrupted Snow sharply, throwing his companion an ugly glance. 'But we do not have time for more talking. Say your prayers.'

He drew a pistol, but dropped it with a yelp when Chaloner struck his wrist with the hilt of his dagger. A short lead pipe appeared in Storey's hands, and he brought it down in a savage arc that would have meant instant death had it met its target. But it was a predictable move, and Chaloner had no trouble in stepping out of its way. The weapon smashed one of the wigmaker's model heads, sending shards and dust across the shop and the hair cartwheeling towards the window. Jervas came dashing towards them with a wail of horror, Sarah at his heels.

'That cost four pounds!' Jervas cried. 'And the hair came from the prettiest whore in Southwark! You must pay for the damage. You—'

His tirade ceased abruptly when Storey turned on him, pipe clutched in both hands. He raised it high in the air, and then began to bring it down as hard as he could. Chaloner shoved him, so he stumbled into Snow, and the blow went wide. Both robbers crashed to the floor amid a cascade of heads and hairpieces. Snow gave a muted yelp when a particularly heavy model struck his temple; he tried to stand, but fell back amid the chaos. Chaloner started to kick the pistol out of reach, but Storey grabbed his leg while he was off balance, and then there were three men on the ground. Suddenly, the gun was in Storey's hands, and he was pointing it at Chaloner's chest.

Chaloner sensed Sarah was nearby, but did not realise she had joined the affray until the lead pipe landed sharply on the top of Storey's skull. The thief collapsed as if poleaxed, and the gun skittered from his nerveless fingers as he hit the floor. Chaloner scrambled to his feet and snatched the bar away from her when she looked as though she might use it a second time. Her grip was powerful, and she was not easy to disarm. At first, he thought she was inflamed with the kind of bloodlust he had seen on the battlefield, when it was difficult to stop men from fighting, but then he saw the stricken expression on her face. Hastily, he seized her arm, afraid she might faint.

'He was going to kill you,' she whispered, her eyes huge with shock. 'Shoot you.'

'He would not have succeeded,' he said, escorting her to a bench. He showed her the weapon, and when she did not understand what it was telling her, added, 'It is not primed.'

She looked as though she might be sick, so he set the hollow cranium of one of the broken models in her lap, not wanting Jervas to have even more of a mess in his shop. The wigmaker sank down next to her, appalled by the violence in his domain.

135

'I did not know,' said Sarah unsteadily. 'I saw the evil expression on his face . . .'

'His determination did not match his skill,' said Chaloner, speaking calmly to reassure her. 'That pair is incompetent, and should not be allowed out without supervision.'

Jervas disagreed, and poked Storey's leg with his foot, as he might prod something unpleasant. '*He* was not incompetent. He would have killed me, had you not pushed him over. And I am an innocent bystander – you are the one with debts.'

Sarah swallowed hard. 'What shall we do? If you let them live, they may try to harm you again.'

'But if I dispatch them, their master may send others who are better. It is safer to let them live to fight another day – although I suspect it is too late for Storey. I think the blow crushed his skull.'

'You mean he is *dead*?' breathed Jervas, aghast. He crossed himself in an automatic but imprudent demonstration of his native Catholicism. 'God help us! Bodies in my shop, my wigs destroyed! I wish you had not chosen my premises in which to hide from these creditors, Mr Heyden.'

So did Chaloner, who was sorry for the trouble he had caused. 'Do you have a back door?'

Wordlessly, Jervas pointed, and watched as Chaloner hauled first Snow and then Storey into the alley outside, laying them side by side in the sticky mud. When he had finished, Chaloner rested his hand on the pulse in Snow's neck. It was strong and regular, and the fellow stirred in a way that suggested he would soon be awake. Storey did not, however, and although he was breathing, his face was waxen beneath his crushed pate. Chaloner suspected he would never regain his senses.

136

'Oliver Greene,' he said loudly, remembering the old woman with the donkey. 'And young Charles-Stewart, too.'

'What are you doing?' asked Sarah, watching him collect Snow's hat and Storey's cudgel. She had not moved from the bench, although she was no longer so pale. Jervas understood, though, and was busy with a brush, sweeping evidence of the fight under the counter. 'A third man is waiting across the street, and he looks horribly like Gervaise Bennet. You should not be lingering here. I thought you planned to *escape* through the back door, not trot back and forth with bodies.'

'We cannot leave these men with Jervas. It is not his fault I hid with him, and he should not have to bear the consequences when Snow wakes up.'

'Will you pay for his damaged wigs as well?' she asked unsteadily.

'I wish I could, but I do not think threepence will cover them.'

She placed several gold coins in the startled wigmaker's hand, and, quelling his effusive gratitude, walked outside to stand with Chaloner in the alley. She was no longer trembling, although he noticed she declined to look at the two crumpled forms, one of which was beginning to groan as he came to.

'Were you following me?' Chaloner asked her.

'Not exactly. I – along with half of London – went to see the King's paintings today. I imagine that is why you are wearing your best clothes, too. When I spotted you leaving White Hall, I decided to see where you went.'

Chaloner was nonplussed. 'Why would you do that?'

'Because of something John said – that if ever I am in trouble, I should turn to you. I love my brother, and trust his opinion on most things, but I like to make up my own mind about who will be a friend in times of crisis.'

'Your brother? Thurloe is your *brother?*'

She regarded him askance. 'I know some of his spies consider him an exulted being – an aloof, iron man with no kith or kin – but he told me *you* regularly asked after his family in your letters.'

'He never mentioned a sister to me, or a brother-in-law called Dalton.'

She seemed surprised. 'Did he not? How odd. I married a decade ago – John advised against the match, but it was hard to refuse a wealthy vintner with six houses and a personal carriage. I have since repented my greed, and wish I had waited for a handsome soldier, but one learns by one's mistakes.'

'Why did you not tell me this on Friday?'

'It was none of your business. I only left John's sitting room to talk to you because I thought I might learn something that would help him in his struggle against Kelyng.'

Chaloner was beginning to dislike Sarah Dalton. 'And did you?'

'Not really. You were too careful. What are you going to do next? Kill Bennet? He is probably the leader of this unpleasant threesome.'

'I thought I would stroll over and thrust my dagger into his chest. No one will notice.' He saw her nod agreement, and experienced a flash of irritation. 'Of course not! I have just explained why it is better to leave them alone.'

'Do not yell at me when I have just saved your life.'

'The gun was not loaded, if you recall.'

'But I did not know that when I raced to your rescue. It still counts.'

He suspected there was no point in arguing. 'All right,' he said tiredly. 'Thank you.'

She seemed satisfied with his capitulation. 'Will you escort me home, or do you plan to leave me standing in this filthy lane until that man wakes up and strips me of my virtue?'

'I doubt they would dare,' muttered Chaloner unchivalrously.

The Dalton house on the Strand was a grand affair of yellow brick. It was set back from the street, separated from it by a strip of garden that had been planted with blocks of herbs. Lavender, mint, lemon balm and rosemary stood to attention within their designated enclosures, although their sweet aroma did little to mask the pungent stench from the urine barrel that was waiting to be emptied. Judging by its overflowing state, the collectors were late.

Inside, the scent of freshly baked pies filled the hall, which was a pleasant place lit by coloured-glass windows on either side of the door. Servants hurried to take Sarah's hat and cloak, and she indicated with an imperious gesture that Chaloner was to follow her along a corridor. Chaloner was about to say he had other business when a door opened, and Dalton came out on a waft of oranges. There was also something less pleasant, a hint of burning, which made Chaloner wonder whether he had been destroying documents.

'Where have you been?' he demanded of his wife. 'I have been looking for you.'

Since Chaloner had last seen him, Dalton had undergone a transformation. He looked pale and troubled, and there were rings around his eyes that suggested he slept badly.

'To see the King's paintings,' replied Sarah coolly, clearly annoyed by the tone of his voice. 'I told you at breakfast. Had you forgotten?'

Dalton rubbed his face and relented. 'I wondered whether you had gone to visit your brother.'

'I am worried about him. Did he tell you Kelyng tried to steal his post again? That man will not leave him alone.'

'Sweet God!' breathed Dalton, appalled. 'Why does Kelyng not concentrate on men who mean the King harm *now*, rather than ones who took Cromwell's side during the Protectorate? It makes no sense to me.' He shook his head, and changed the subject. 'Did you like His Majesty's paintings?'

'Not much,' replied Sarah. 'There were too many naked fat women in them – like on the Banqueting House's dismal ceiling.'

'Rubens,' said Chaloner, surprised. 'Most people admire his use of colour and light.'

She waved a dismissive hand, and turned back to her husband. 'Do you remember Heyden, dear? He visited John sporting a horsehair periwig on Friday, and now he wears none.'

'Wigs are a sore trial; I would just as soon go bareheaded.' To prove it, Dalton whipped off his own, revealing a few grey wisps on a balding pate. He looked twenty years older, and Chaloner was treated to a stronger waft of burning. The merchant had definitely been wearing his hairpiece when he had been near a fire.

'Put it back on, dear,' said Sarah, taking it from him

140

and jamming it firmly on his head. It was not quite straight, although he did not seem to care. 'Or you will take a chill.'

'Have you come about employment, Heyden?' Dalton asked. 'I recall inviting you, although my mind is full of other problems at the moment. Business,' he added hastily, as if he were afraid Chaloner might think his concerns ranged along other lines. 'All about business – and a clerk with a knowledge of Dutch would be a great asset, although Downing tells me you are dishonest.'

'He is a fine one to talk!' exclaimed Sarah. 'A more disreputable snake does not exist.'

'Quite,' agreed Dalton. 'Which is why I usually ignore his opinions. Thurloe speaks highly of you, though, and that is a fine compliment. He approves of very few men.'

'There are not many who deserve his approbation,' said Sarah dourly. 'Kelyng, Downing, Bennet, the Duke of Buckingham. None are men *I* would choose for decent company.'

'I do not need you yet, Heyden,' said Dalton, ignoring her. 'But come next Monday, and I shall have some documents ready for translation. And now I should leave you, or I will be late.'

'Late for what?' asked Sarah.

'Downing summoned me to an urgent meeting,' said Dalton unhappily. 'I do not want to go, but I cannot plead illness, because he has seen me up and about this morning.'

'You need not do everything he says,' said Sarah. 'John resists his charms, and so could you.'

'But your brother has nothing to lose,' said Dalton. 'He was Secretary of State and now he is a lawyer – you cannot sink much lower than that. But I have a great

141

deal of money tied up in this city, and cannot afford to aggravate important men without good reason. Still, I am loath to go, after what happened this morning. I shall see you for dinner, Sarah. Good day, Heyden.'

'What happened this morning?' asked Chaloner, when he had gone.

'Over the past few weeks, he has been spotting old friends who are dead,' replied Sarah unsympathetically. 'These "turns", as he calls them, are probably induced by worry over his new Dutch contract. If it is successful, it will bring him great wealth – not that he needs more. Will you accept his offer and translate for him?'

'Probably.' It sounded dull, but would be a good deal safer than working for the Lord Chancellor. Also, there was the fact that Metje had encouraged him to accept anything offered by Dalton, and he did not want to disappoint her.

Sarah regarded him thoughtfully. 'My brother never – *never* – discusses his spies with me, but he often talks about you and says I can trust you. I think he is more concerned about Kelyng's machinations than he is willing to admit, and is making the kind of preparations that suggest he considers himself to be in mortal danger. He wants his friends to know each other.'

'I am not his friend,' said Chaloner, startled. 'Just someone he hired.'

'You underestimate the affection he holds for you – you do not write to a man every week for ten years and not come to feel something for him. If John is in danger from Kelyng, will you help him?'

Chaloner was surprised by the appeal, and imagined Thurloe would be horrified if he knew what his sister was doing, dignified and private man that he was. He nodded, although he suspected he would not be of much use, given that London and its people were such a mystery to him. 'If I can.'

'Thank you,' she said softly.

As soon as he had escaped from Dalton's house, Chaloner retraced his steps along the Strand, and was amazed to see Bennet still standing opposite the wigmaker's shop. He estimated his skirmish with Snow and Storey had occurred nigh on an hour ago, and was astonished the chamberlain had not guessed something was amiss and gone to investigate. Chaloner certainly would have done, since the only reason for Snow and Storey not to have appeared with bloodstained hands was because they had become victims themselves. As he had nothing particularly pressing to do, he took up station near the New Exchange, with its double galleries of booths and stalls, and waited to see what would happen.

Bennet was becoming impatient. He stamped his feet and blew on his fingers, indicating he had been standing still too long, and his hand strayed frequently to the bulge under his cassock where his pistol lay. Once or twice, he seemed about to brave the traffic and go to see what had happened, but he was indecisive, and ended up doing nothing. Eventually, Chaloner glimpsed a pair of very black boots making their way towards him. It was Snow, swaying unsteadily and with his hand to his head.

Chaloner was some distance away, but did not need to hear what was being said to understand the gist of the conversation. Snow approached obsequiously, adopting a submissive posture, like a weak dog in a pack of hounds; Bennet swelled at the sight of such brazen subservience. Snow said something, and Bennet's every

143

gesture expressed his anger. Snow cringed, as if he was afraid of being struck. Then he handed over the piece of paper containing the names of Thurloe's 'brothers', and Chaloner braced himself for fireworks. But Bennet only pocketed the note, indicating with a nod that Snow was dismissed. The felon lurched away, while Bennet continued to wait.

Eventually, Bennet was joined by another man. It was Kelyng, who seemed surprised to see his henchman leaning against a wall in a bustling part of the Strand. Chaloner watched Bennet pass him the paper, then laughed when Kelyng went rigid with rage. Spitting his fury, Kelyng ripped the note into tiny shreds and began to scream abuse that was audible even at a distance, most of it centred around the fact that Bennet was so stupid that it was not surprising the Lord Mayor's daughter had refused him. Wanting to hear what transpired when Kelyng's temper was spent and his voice dropped to a more moderate level, Chaloner edged closer.

He was fortunate: Kelyng hauled his chamberlain towards the ramshackle premises of a grocer – an ancient, rickety affair jutting into the street in a way that had recently been deemed illegal because it interfered with the free flow of traffic. Chaloner eased towards them, making his way past rough shelves that displayed maggoty cabbages and tough turnips, eventually taking up station behind a teetering pyramid of apples. Kelyng shoved Bennet into a corner and continued to rail, while the grocer slunk to the opposite end of his domain and pretended not to notice. He studiously ignored Chaloner, too, clearly thinking that those who eavesdropped on Kelyng and Bennet did so at their own peril.

Bennet did not take kindly to being manhandled, even

144

by the man who paid his wages. He freed his arm with a glower, but Kelyng was too interested in giving vent to his own spleen to notice the dangerous expression on his chamberlain's face.

'. . . a disaster,' he was snapping. 'Thurloe probably knows by now.'

'He already knows you intend to bring him low,' replied Bennet tightly. 'This latest incident with the limping agent will not surprise him.'

'But I do not want him on his guard,' snarled Kelyng. 'It will make my task all the more difficult.'

'The damage was already done,' argued Bennet. 'The agent will already have told him what happened in your garden. What occurred today makes no difference one way or the other.'

'But *why* did you try to kill the spy?' demanded Kelyng furiously. 'His death will serve no useful purpose, and might even prompt Thurloe to take some sort of revenge against us. I do not want hired assassins after me when I am trying to cleanse London of traitors.'

'I was trying to disarm a loose cannon – to rid us of a man who might cause problems later.'

Kelyng switched to another topic, pacing restlessly in the narrow space and sounding as though he was talking more to himself than to his henchman. 'I *wanted* the letter in that satchel. I *needed* it to build my case, and we came so very close to getting our hands on it. Damn that spy!'

'What was in it?' asked Bennet, sounding as though he did not much care. 'A missive from one of Thurloe's foreign agents?'

Kelyng made a face, to indicate he thought Bennet a fool for asking. 'All those are forwarded straight to Williamson these days. I cannot find any fault with

145

Thurloe's conduct there – unfortunately. But I have reason to believe this latest satchel contained something pertaining to his brothers.'

Bennet was nonplussed. 'You mean his half-brother, Isaac Ewer, whose widow married Clarke?'

'No, stupid,' snapped Kelyng. Chaloner saw the chamberlain bristle, and suspected Kelyng would soon have a problem: Bennet disliked the way he was being treated, and was fast reaching the point where he would rebel. 'Ewer has been dead for years. I mean his *other* brothers – and we are not talking about St Thomas à Becket, Julius Caesar or Guy Fawkes, either. Fool!'

'His other Ewer kin are nothing,' said Bennet, rigid with barely controlled anger. 'I looked into them myself: they are poor farmers with no interest in politics.'

'That is why I wanted that satchel!' Kelyng snarled. 'I *know* the Ewers are irrelevant, but Thurloe has six other brothers, and I believe the contents of that pouch would have told me their names. The limping agent might know, too, but *you* let him escape. I told you to arrest him, but instead you take matters into your own hands – interviewing him yourself, then trying to kill him. You are an idiot.'

Bennet gritted his teeth. 'I *will* kill him for you.'

Kelyng sighed in exasperation. 'I do not *want* him dead: I want him in custody. However, I doubt he knows much. He is a hireling, like you, and obviously not trusted with important secrets.'

There was a tic at the corner of Bennet's mouth. 'With respect, *sir*, he made a fool of you—'

'He made a fool of *you*,' shouted Kelyng. 'And watch where you are putting your great clumsy feet, man! You almost trod on that dog.'

146

'A dog! I *do* apologise,' breathed Bennet almost inaudibly. He glowered at the mutt, and for a moment, Chaloner thought he might strike the back of Kelyng's head when he bent to pet it.

Kelyng seemed oblivious to the fury that was boiling in his accomplice as he swept the animal into his arms. 'Thurloe is so close with his secrets that even Dalton cannot worm them out of him.'

'Dalton?' asked Bennet. His temper was under control, but Chaloner thought he looked more dangerous for it.

'His sister's husband. He is doing his best, but Thurloe trusts no one, and the documents Dalton manages to steal for me have been next to useless – defunct property deeds and letters to physicians.'

A funeral procession rolled past outside. The cart carrying the coffin clattered on the cobblestones, and the two women at the front leaned on each other and wailed in a way that suggested they would never overcome their grief. They wore veils and black flowing cloaks, and Chaloner had seen them before: professional mourners, employed to put on a good show when the next-of-kin felt they were not up to the task. Others followed more sedately, talking among themselves in the way of people who have not seen each other for a long time. Their good-humoured chatter and the women's howls drowned out the discussion between Kelyng and Bennet, and Chaloner was obliged to wait until the cortège had passed, hoping he did not miss anything important.

He thought about what he had learned so far. Thurloe trusted his sister, but he had said nothing about her husband. Did that mean he knew Dalton was betraying him? Thurloe was astute, and might well have recognised his kinsman's treachery. Or was he blissfully

147

unaware, and would be shocked when he found out? The procession finished eventually, and Chaloner was able to hear again.

'. . . that Thurloe should walk free when he served Cromwell.' Kelyng spat the last name, which frightened the dog into scampering away. 'It is because of Thurloe that the Commonwealth lasted as long as it did. Without him, one of our rebellions would have succeeded, and we would have had the King back on his throne years ago.'

'I know.' Bennet's bored tone suggested he was used to this kind of rant.

'I will not rest until he is in his grave – him and *all* the evil minions who helped him, no matter who they are or what they did.'

'So you have said before. Many times.'

'So, there are six to go,' concluded Kelyng. 'I think—'

'Is that Tom Heyden?' came a voice from the other side of the apples. Chaloner winced when he recognised William Leybourn, the inquisitive bookseller. 'That is a handsome cassock. Can I assume you dressed up to see the paintings?'

His voice was loud, and Chaloner glanced towards Kelyng and Bennet, to see whether they had heard his name brayed so cheerfully. Fortunately, they were more interested in their own discussion, Bennet listening intently to what his master had to say. Chaloner wished he could hear, too, but that was not possible with the bookseller clamouring about which picture was the most valuable.

'I am busy, Leybourn,' he interrupted tersely. 'Perhaps we could discuss this later.'

'You are inspecting apples,' said Leybourn, startled. 'How is that so pressing?'

148

Chaloner itched to shove him away, but did not want to create a scene. 'Another time.'

Leybourn was offended. 'Very well. I apologise for breaking into your reverie on fruit, and I shall certainly think twice about approaching you in the future.'

'Good,' breathed Chaloner under his breath. But by the time Leybourn had gone, Bennet and Kelyng had left the grocer's and were climbing into a carriage that bore them away. His eavesdropping was over.

Deep in thought, Chaloner retraced his steps to Will's Coffee House, only to find the building mostly empty. It was well past the time when men gravitated towards such places for their midday meals, and only the stragglers were left.

The establishment was managed by a man named William Urwin, who played the violin to his patrons and recited mediocre verses of his own composition. He was also the proud owner of a collection of 'curiosities', which included the mummified body of an ape, a German clock with chimes, and a psalter said to have belonged to the Venerable Bede.

The coffee house's lower floor also served as a barber shop, where patrons could be shaved and, if necessary, be bled and have teeth drawn. The upper level was more conventional, and comprised a large room full of tables where men could dine with companions, and small booths around the edges if they craved solitude. The upstairs was devoid of customers that day, most preferring the diminishing company of the lower chamber, but Chaloner opted for a booth anyway. He drew the curtain to repel anyone who might want to talk, and sat stirring the thick, murky brew in front of him. He continued to stir and to think, until the coffee grew cold and the venison pastry on the plate at his side congealed in its viscous gravy.

Until that March, his life had been straightforward – the wars, his studies at Cambridge, a brief spell as a clerk in Lincoln's Inn, and then duties overseas. He had only ever served one master – Downing did not count, because Chaloner had worked independently of him, and the diplomat had rarely given him orders – and suddenly he was faced with the prospect of juggling between two men who would be demanding of his loyalties: the Earl of Clarendon and Thurloe. The count could be raised to *four*, if North and Dalton were to be included. He found himself uncertain as to what to do.

He knew he stood at an important crossroads, and that any decision he made would dictate the rest of his life. He had four choices. He could take the sensible option, which was to return to Buckinghamshire and live quietly. The Chaloner estates at Steeple Claydon were large, if not wealthy, and there would be a corner for him somewhere, although he was loath to inflict himself on his siblings at a time when it was difficult for former Parliamentarians to make ends meet. He supposed he could earn a living by teaching at the local school, or perhaps even enrol in his old College at Cambridge and take a higher degree, although neither prospect filled him with enthusiasm.

The second possibility was to return to the United Provinces. He had friends there, and it would not be difficult to secure a post as a clerk. But administration without the additional thrill provided by spying would be tedious, and there was also the fact that discord was rumbling between the two nations. As part of a diplomatic or ambassadorial mission, he would have an excuse for being there, but it would be dangerous to go alone. He suspected it would not be many months before Englishmen in Holland would be in an untenable position, and it was one thing to be executed as a spy when he was guilty, but another altogether to be shot when he was innocent.

His third choice was to accept the challenge thrown down by the Lord Chancellor. However, he sensed with every fibre of his being that the Earl would not make a good master. His agents would not be safe, and Chaloner would probably spend a good deal of time looking over his shoulder, not sure who to trust – especially if Thurloe wanted him to investigate murders and spy on Royalist fanatics at the same time.

And finally, he could decline the Earl's commission and continue to work for North, his income occasionally boosted by translating for Dalton. But he could not survive long on such meagre earnings, and Metje would never marry him.

He stirred the cold beverage, wondering what Thurloe would say about him being forbidden to explore Clarke's death. The ex-Spymaster was sure to ask what he had been ordered to do instead, and Chaloner had promised not to mention the missing gold. He intended to keep his word, not out of loyalty to the Lord Chancellor, but because the Earl might have ordered his silence to see how far he could be trusted. Or was Thurloe doing the testing, to assess whether Chaloner's allegiance would be with his old master or the new one? He rubbed his eyes. There were no answers, and it was one of few times in his life when he was wracked with indecision.

He had been allotted three independent tasks: unveil Clarke's killer, monitor Kelyng and find some buried treasure. Any investigation involved talking to people and listening to speculation and rumour, and he supposed it was not impossible to research all three cases simultaneously without overstepping the boundaries he had been set. He had juggled a good deal of complex information in the past, and the prospect of carrying out three enquiries at the same time did not daunt him.

He considered what he knew, beginning with Clarke. Perhaps most pertinent were the two messages found in his clothing, written in the kind of code that indicated they had been intended for Thurloe. One had contained the phrase 'praise God's one son' and the other had mentioned the number seven. Both had been written in the same hand as the note on Clarendon's desk that had declared PRAISE GOD'S ONE SON in lemon juice or onion juice – which became visible only when heated, and was a well-known device for sending secret information.

Had Clarke penned them all, or had he taken them from someone else? Chaloner was inclined to believe they were Clarke's, and Clarke had died before he could pass them to their intended recipient. Praising Jesus was also the message breathed by the dying Hewson – or was it Jones? Clarendon claimed he could not decode the cipher, although that was irrelevant, since the presence of the onion- or lemon-juice message indicated the Earl had some knowledge of the odd phrase, and possibly even knew what it meant. Did Thurloe know, too? And was Clarke's death a result of his dabbling with the information they contained, or something to do with the thefts from the White Hall kitchens?

Secondly, he thought about Kelyng. He had learned two things. First, Dalton was passing him Thurloe's secrets, and second, what Kelyng hoped to learn by intercepting

Thurloe's post was the identity of his brothers. What brothers? Thurloe's only male blood kin were the Ewers, whom Kelyng had dismissed as of no consequence. Chaloner wondered whether it was significant that Kelyng had mentioned *six* brothers – which made *seven* when Thurloe was included. And the number seven had been muttered by Hewson as he had died and was included in one of Clarke's ciphered notes. It suggested a connection between Kelyng and the messages Hewson and Clarke had been trying to pass.

And lastly, there was the treasure. If Chaloner was not permitted to speak to anyone connected with the case, it was not going to be an easy nut to crack. But he had faced worse odds in the past, and he enjoyed a challenge. He made his choice: he would remain in London and see what might be done about locating Barkstead's gold, *and* he would try to watch Kelyng and make enquiries after Clarke's killer. It would keep him busy, but he was no stranger to hard work.

A sudden clamour of voices broke into his thoughts. He had been aware of people entering the room, but had taken no notice, concealed as he was inside his booth. Now he lifted a corner of the curtain to look at them, puzzled by the abrupt outburst.

Seven people sat around the largest table, five of whom he recognised. At one end was a man he had last seen drifting on the Thames: the Lord Mayor and Lieutenant of the Tower, Sir John Robinson. Opposite Robinson were four other familiar faces. First, there was Dalton, wafting his orange-scented linen with a trembling hand. Second, there was Chaloner's Puritan employer, North, a stricken expression on his face. Third, there was Robert Leybourn, the bookseller's sardonic brother. And finally,

153

there was Downing, sitting with his arms folded and his eyes flicking around the room as though he were looking for something. Chaloner supposed this was the 'urgent meeting' Dalton had mentioned to his wife. He closed the curtain to the merest slit, and prepared to do what came naturally to him: sit quietly and listen.

'I do not believe it!' one man cried, his voice rising above the others by sheer dint of its volume. He reminded Chaloner of a pig, with jowls that wobbled over his collar and fingers so fat they were elongated triangles. 'You must be mistaken.'

'There is no mistake,' replied Robinson soberly. 'I saw the body myself. So did Dalton.'

'I chanced to meet Robinson when he was going to view the corpse, so I went with him,' explained Dalton. 'It was as well I did, given that it took both of us to make the identification. Recognising a man who has been consumed by flames is not easy.'

So, thought Chaloner, that explained the stench of burning on Dalton. It also accounted for why he had seemed troubled: inspecting a charred corpse was enough to put anyone off his stride.

'Gentlemen!' Downing snapped, when there was another flurry of raised voices. 'This is not Parliament, so do not behave like a rabble, I beg you. All your questions will be heard, and we will answer as best we can. One at a time, please. North?'

'You said the body had been burned beyond recognition, so how can you be sure it was him?' asked North in a hushed voice that had Chaloner straining to hear.

'I tried to do it from the shape of his teeth,' said Robinson, a detail that made North and several others wince. 'But Dalton searched the body for jewellery.'

154

'You saw his ring?' asked North in the same low whisper. His face was ashen, and his neighbour poured him coffee and urged him to drink it. 'The one with the emerald?'

Dalton nodded unhappily. 'On his little finger. There was an ancient mangling of the skull, too, and you will recall that he lost an eye at the storming of Kilkenny.'

Chaloner frowned. The man Bennet had knifed had worn a green ring and was missing an eye – but he had certainly not been near a fire.

'Poor devil,' said Robinson. 'We must stick together now, and allow nothing to break the bonds of our Brotherhood.'

'Our Brotherhood,' said North softly. 'Sometimes, it is the only thing that makes sense in this cruel, wicked city. I am grateful I joined you when I came here from Ely after the Restoration.'

'We are all of the same mind,' said Robinson kindly. 'But we should never give voice to thoughts that may be deemed seditious – it is not safe, not even here, when we are alone.'

There was a general murmur of agreement. 'I shall miss him,' said the pig-faced man soberly. 'He was generous with his donations to our cause.'

'God rest his soul,' whispered North. 'Poor John Hewson.'


Chaloner gazed at the gathering, his thoughts rolling in confusion. He doubted there were two one-eyed, beringed men by the name of John Hewson, but how had the fellow come to be burned? And the gathering at Will's Coffee House comprised wealthy, influential citizens, so why should a servant be mourned in such company? He

155

thought about what had happened in Kelyng's garden. Hewson must have been told to collect the satchel from Snow and Storey, or he would not have known they had it, and the fact that he took it to Kelyng's house suggested he was following Kelyng's orders. Kelyng had referred to him as Jones, indicating he had probably inveigled employment under false pretences. He was really Hewson, member of some mysterious Brotherhood.

Then he had been killed by Bennet, and Bennet had told Kelyng that Chaloner was responsible for the mishap, although Hewson's friends were now saying he had been incinerated. Why had Bennet killed Hewson? Was he just a poor marksman, or had he taken the opportunity to dispatch Hewson for reasons he was unwilling to share with his master? And then what? Had Snow and Storey been instructed to burn the body in an attempt to disguise what had really happened? They had not done it very well, if they had left a ring and other identifying features for his friends to see.

Chaloner recalled what Hewson had muttered as he lay dying. He had recommended trusting no one and he had spoken his own name. Why? Because he had wanted someone to know what had happened to him, perhaps because he guessed what might be done to his corpse? And what about the rest – the mumbling about God's son? The more Chaloner thought about the odd phrase, the more certain he became that it had nothing to do with religion.

He studied Hewson's colleagues. Most seemed genuinely upset by the news of his death, although Downing was already putting the incident behind him, looking to the future. North was the most grief-stricken, but Chaloner knew him to be a kindly man, often moved by the sufferings of others. Dalton, on the other hand, was the most disturbed – a reaction quite different from North's gentle compassion.

'Will this damage us?' asked a hulking man with thick, blunt features. His posture was hunched, as though he was uncomfortable with his size and sought to conceal it. 'Hurt our cause?'

'I do not see how, Thomas,' replied Downing. 'Do you?'

The man cringed under the attention that swivelled towards him. 'I am only a clerk, and not in a position to answer such a question.'

'Has there been any more news about that business in the Tower?' asked the pig suddenly. He looked irritable when Thomas did not understand him. 'Barkstead's gold, man!'

Everyone looked interested in the answer, and there was disappointment all around when Thomas muttered that there had not. Chaloner's first instinct was to assume the Brotherhood's interest in the matter was sinister, but then realised that the affair was probably common knowledge. The Tower's many inhabitants were bound to have gossiped about Evett's activities with spades and hired diggers.

'Damn!' said Downing. 'But it will appear sooner or later, and our cause will benefit eventually. Barkstead was one of us – a brother – and it is only right that his treasure should come our way.'

'It is what he would have wanted,' agreed Robert Leybourn.

'How would *you* know?' demanded the pig immediately. 'You never met him – he fled from England long before you were admitted to our ranks.'

157

Robert glowered. 'You all tell me he was committed to our cause, so it seemed a logical conclusion to draw. Am I wrong about him, then?'

'No,' said Robinson shortly. 'He was a dedicated brother. But we are not here to discuss him and his mythical hoard. I am more interested in Hewson.'

Chaloner watched uneasily. Could he be witnessing the start of yet another rebellion? There had been so many since Cromwell's death that people had lost count of them, and there always seemed to be some group of fanatics who believed the government should be in its own hands. If the Brotherhood was plotting treachery, then its members were taking a serious risk by discussing it in a public coffee house; they had not even searched the room first, to make sure it was empty.

'So, what about Hewson?' asked North. 'Did he fall in the fire by accident?'

'I doubt it,' replied the Lord Mayor. 'But corpses cannot speak, and I suspect we shall never know what really happened to the poor man. Ingoldsby, do you have a question?' He turned to the pig.

Ingoldsby! thought Chaloner. Cromwell's cousin, and the regicide who had managed not only to persuade the King to forgive his role in his father's execution, but knight him into the bargain. He regarded the pig with interest, having heard so much about him, and none of it good.

'Yes,' said Ingoldsby. 'Who wanted Hewson dead?'

'Dozens of people,' replied Downing, startled by the question. 'Do you want me to list them all? He was responsible for putting down a riot, here in London, that left twenty dead. He ousted innocent Anglican priests from their churches and denounced them as agents of the Antichrist. He fought for Cromwell during the wars and

158

killed God knows how many Cavaliers. Shall I continue?'

'We should say a prayer,' said North quietly, raising his hands. 'For his soul.'

Chaloner eased back inside his booth. He suspected it would not go well for him if they discovered the room was not as private as they thought, so he sat still, waiting for the meeting to finish.

'Three,' whispered Thomas, when North had uttered his final amen. No one took any notice of him. 'Three!' he said more loudly.

There was an awkward silence. 'Possibly three,' corrected Robinson. 'We do not know for sure.'

'First Barkstead, and now Hewson,' elaborated Ingoldsby. 'And we have not heard from Livesay in months, so he must be dead, too. Thomas is right: that makes three of us gone.'

'I am not so sure about Livesay,' said Dalton unhappily. 'I think I . . . We do not *know* he is dead.'

'He is,' said North, uncharacteristically firm. 'I have already told you what I heard about him.'

'What?' asked Ingoldsby unpleasantly. 'There have been so many rumours about the fellow that I cannot recall the one that came from you.'

North bristled, but replied politely enough. 'That Livesay boarded a ship for France, but there was an explosion. All aboard were either blown up or drowned. It must have been a dreadful way to die.' He touched the burn on his face, as if recalling his own experiences with fire. Downing placed a comforting hand on his arm, and North shot him a wan, grateful smile.

Dalton was unconvinced. 'It may not have been Livesay who was on the boat. Perhaps he has gone into hiding instead.'

159

'Thurloe never comes here any more,' said Thomas fearfully, after a slight pause during which the seven men considered Dalton's suggestion. 'What should we infer from that?'

'Nothing,' said Ingoldsby firmly, 'other than that he is busy.'

'We are all busy,' said Downing spitefully. 'But *we* found the time to come.'

'The only ones missing today are Livesay, Thurloe and those two silly soldiers who attend meetings only when it suits them,' said Ingoldsby, reaching across the table to claim a pastry. His next words were muffled as he rammed it whole into his mouth. 'We should never have opened our doors to military men. They are shallow beings, interested only in polishing their swords and seducing other men's wives.'

'Livesay *cannot* come,' said North softly, in a world of his own. 'He is dead, poor soul.'

'I think we are in danger,' said Dalton unsteadily. 'We agreed to disband the Brotherhood until times were more settled, but we still meet regularly, and—'

'Nonsense,' declared Robert Leybourn dismissively. 'Livesay – and even Hewson – might have died of natural causes. People do, you know.'

'Someone is *killing* them – us,' insisted Dalton.

'Not so,' said Robinson reasonably. 'Barkstead was executed, Hewson died in a fire, and Livesay was blown up or drowned. You cannot assume a single hand at work here.'

'I know who killed Barkstead,' said Ingoldsby, shooting Downing a look of dark dislike. There was an embarrassed silence around the table.

'Not me,' said Downing indignantly. 'How was I to

160

know what would happen when I invited him to come to England? It was his choice to come back – I did not force him.'

Chaloner felt like standing up and denouncing him as a liar. He had heard some bald untruths in his time, but few as brazen as that one. He clenched his hands into fists, and tried to remember when he had last felt such a strong desire to punch someone. He was certain it had been Downing, back in March. The diplomat was speaking again, and Chaloner forced himself to listen.

'But to return to the matter in hand, I agree with Robinson: we cannot assume Livesay and Hewson were murdered.'

'*I* shall assume what I like,' said Ingoldsby coldly. 'Only a fool would ignore the dangers, and even meeting you is fraught with risk.'

'This meeting is not illegal,' objected Downing. 'We are respectable men with common interests. Why should we not gather in a coffee house? Our Brotherhood is nothing of which to be ashamed.'

'Then why did we not remain downstairs?' demanded Dalton. 'Instead, you dragged us up here, bawling to Master Urwin that we crave privacy. We seem unable to act normally, and we do things that arouse suspicion even when there is no need. And sometimes I feel as though I am being watched.'

'Me, too,' said North quietly. 'I helped a man who slipped on ice the other morning, and I had the distinct sense of eyes in the darkness of his stairs. I am sure someone was spying on me.'

'Kelyng!' breathed Ingoldsby. 'God help us, if *he* is on our trail.'

161

'Pull yourselves together,' said Downing sharply. 'I repeat: we are doing nothing wrong.'

'Are you sure we are alone in here?' asked North, glancing around him. 'Only I have the uncomfortable feeling that I am being watched again – right now.'

'I checked,' lied Downing. 'You can see the place is deserted.'

'The curtains on all the booths are drawn,' said North. 'Did you peer behind them?'

Damn, thought Chaloner.

'No one is going to be in here with the curtains pulled,' objected Downing with exaggerated weariness. 'Get a hold of yourself, man, or you will have us all a pack of nervous wrecks.'

'I will look,' offered Robert Leybourn, making purposefully for the first of the alcoves.

'And what will you do if you find someone?' asked Downing scathingly. 'Batter out his brains with a book? Sit down, man, and stop making a fuss.'

'There is no need for book bashing,' said Ingoldsby, drawing his sword. 'I will take care of any unwanted ears.'

Chaloner heard Robert tear back the first in the row of curtains. His booth would be next.

# Chapter 5

'There,' said Downing, when Robert Leybourn had
completed his search. 'What did I tell you? But we should
part company, before we give each other nightmares. I
wish you good day, gentlemen. Robinson and I apologise for bringing you to hear such sorry news.' He ushered
his colleagues out until he was the only one left, then
waited several moments before speaking. 'Heyden? I know
you are in here. I arrived early for this meeting, and I
saw you go up the stairs. Since you did not come down
again, you must still be here.'

Chaloner made no reply.

Downing sighed. 'You always were slippery – Thurloe
chose well when he appointed you to look after Britain's
interests abroad. We need to talk, so come out, will
you? You heard Dalton: it was I who insisted we meet
in this chamber. I did so because I *wanted* you to hear
what was said. I would not have done that if I intended
to harm you, would I? You have nothing to fear from
me.'

Chaloner did not move.

'Think!' said Downing, exasperated. 'Who persuaded

Robert Leybourn that the mouse droppings next to your pastry were a sign that no one had been in that booth for hours, even though I know it is a ruse you have used before? I suppose they were on the floor and you shoved them on the table, just as you did in Delft, when you were almost caught eavesdropping on the French ambassador.'

When Chaloner still did not appear, Downing grew angry.

'I have just taken a great personal risk, so do not make me use my sword. Come on, Heyden. Out!'

Chaloner heard the scrape of metal on leather as Downing drew his sword, followed by hollow tapping sounds as the diplomat began to jab beneath tables. He crawled away from the bench in his booth, aware that concealing himself under it had been an act of desperation, and one that would have seen him unable to defend himself had his ploy with the droppings not worked. Using elbows and knees, he slithered the entire length of the curtained alcoves, and was brushing himself down when Downing glanced up from his prodding. A dagger was cradled in the palm of Chaloner's hand, and Downing did not know it, but he would be dead the moment he made a hostile move.

'God's blood!' Downing swore, jumping in alarm at his sudden appearance. 'How did you manage that?'

Chaloner shrugged. 'I have some experience of escaping from tight corners, as you know.'

Downing sheathed his sword and sat at the table, indicating Chaloner was to join him. Chaloner stayed where he was, and the diplomat leaned back in the chair and rubbed his eyes.

'I do not blame you for being cautious, after what you

164

have just heard. You probably do not know what to think: Thurloe belongs to a Brotherhood, some members of which are murdered or missing.'

'So do you, Sir George.'

'Yes, but I am in the process of extricating myself.'

'So is Thurloe, if he declines to attend meetings.' His unspoken addendum was that Thurloe had removed himself a good deal further than had Downing, who was still active.

Downing smiled wryly. 'If you were half as loyal to me as you are to him, you and I would have made a formidable team. However, I am not so naïve as to imagine our five years together resulted in any liking for me. I employed you as a favour to Thurloe, but you have never been anything but his man.'

'It was not a favour: you were paid. And, after Cromwell died, you began to pass the information I collected not only to Thurloe, but to his enemies as well.'

Downing shrugged. 'Those were uncertain times, and no one can blame me for hedging my bets. But we are not here to discuss me. I assume Thurloe told you about our Brotherhood?'

'What he and I discuss is none of your affair, Sir George.'

Downing regarded him silently for a while. 'I could reveal your past spying activities to men who would see you executed, Heyden. But I am not a vindictive man, whatever you might think. I suspect Thurloe *has* mentioned our organisation to you, but I would like to give you my version, too, so you have a balanced view.'

'Why?'

'Self-preservation. You intend to work for Dalton, and it is only a matter of time before a spy of your calibre learns the secret of the Brotherhood from him – he is panicky, unreliable and indiscreet. Kelyng is watching us closely, and I do not want you investigating Dalton's frightened behaviour and inadvertently exposing the rest of us. I told Thurloe he should stop you from going to Dalton, but he said that would only arouse your suspicions. However, I will not sit back while you put me in danger.'

'Then tell me what you think I should know.'

Downing poured himself some coffee; it was cold and he winced as he swallowed it. 'The Brotherhood was established after the execution of the old king, thirteen years ago. Its remit was to limit the actions of fanatics on both sides – Parliamentarians *and* Royalists. Its founders were men of vision, who saw that extremes would bring nothing but damage and long-term hatred.'

Chaloner did not believe him. 'Barkstead was a member, and you do not get much more extreme than signing a monarch's death warrant. Ingoldsby also put his name to the deed – and while the King may believe that Cromwell seized his hand and wrote his name, he is the only man who does.'

Downing laughed. 'The notion of a fellow like *him* standing meekly while Cousin Cromwell makes his signature *is* hilarious. However, the King thinks Ingoldsby is telling the truth, so I can only doff my hat in admiration for his gall. If I had half his talent, I would be King of England myself.'

Reluctantly, Chaloner returned the smile. 'It was an impressive feat of perfidy.'

'It saved his life, though. However, he and Barkstead saw first-hand the chaos that arises from fanaticism, and they joined the Brotherhood in the hope of securing more moderate solutions to political problems in the future. They were not the only regicides to enrol: John Hewson, whose charred corpse was found yesterday, was one, and so is Sir Michael Livesay – the member who has not been seen for so long.'

Chaloner was sceptical. 'Hewson and Livesay have been living in London? But any regicide with even a remote sense of his own safety would have escaped abroad years ago. They would be executed if they were caught here.'

'Hewson went to the United Provinces for a while, but was homesick, so came back to live the quiet life of a shoemaker – which was his trade before he rose to power under the Commonwealth. Livesay also returned, although he has not been seen for some time now, and I fear North may be right about his death. With men like Kelyng around, no one is safe.'

'You think Kelyng killed Livesay?' Chaloner realised he knew something Downing probably did not: that Hewson had died in Kelyng's garden.

'It is possible. Kelyng knows the Brotherhood exists, and his hatred of us ranges along two fronts: our desire for moderation, and the fact that our membership includes regicides – men he has vowed to destroy. He is a zealot, and exactly the kind of fellow we oppose.'

Chaloner wondered whether Downing was in his right wits. 'Your association with this group is dangerous. Can you not see what will happen, if Kelyng learns you keep company with regicides?'

'But he will not – not unless *you* tell him. Barkstead and Hewson are dead; Ingoldsby will say nothing, because he is in the same pickle as me; and Livesay is God knows where. The remaining brothers no more want the connection known than I do, so will maintain a discreet silence.'

'Livesay's disappearance must be worrying. He could be sitting in the Tower as we speak, spilling his secrets to anyone who will listen.'

Downing shook his head. 'He would never betray the Brotherhood.'

'Why not? You are.'

'But only to you, and you are too fond of Thurloe to tell anyone else about our little fraternity. I did not keep you under my roof for five years without learning something about you. I am safer confiding in you than in treating you as an enemy.'

Chaloner wondered why so many people assumed his relationship to Thurloe was one of devotion. Also, Thurloe had not mentioned membership of any kind of organisation, secret or otherwise, and Downing was wrong to think Chaloner was his confidant. He recalled the flicker of emotion in the ex-Spymaster's eyes when he had learned about Hewson's death. It had been the perfect opportunity to admit to knowing the man, but he had chosen not to take it.

'Tell me about the Brotherhood's cause,' he said, wondering whether it was wise to ask for more information when common sense told him it would be safer to walk away. But he was an intelligence officer, and asking questions about matters that were none of his concern was a difficult habit to break.

Downing spread his hands. 'We want a government that stands for political and religious tolerance, where men are free to voice opinions without fear of reprisal. Is that such a wicked thing?'

'It depends what you do to make it happen.'

'We reason with influential people. For example, Ingoldsby and I soothe angry voices at Court; North and

Dalton encourage moderation among merchants and aldermen; Robinson, Livesay and Hewson speak to the army; Robert Leybourn prints pamphlets urging patience. I have one here, if you would like to read it.'

Chaloner shoved it inside his jerkin. 'And Thurloe? He is in no position to preach to anyone.'

'He has influence over men still loyal to Cromwell. And I know he is doing his part, because there is not a radical among the people he has recommended for employment in the new government.'

'Does the Brotherhood have a motto – some phrase you use to identify each other?'

'Why would we need that?' asked Downing. 'We know each other – well, mostly. The membership has changed over the years, and the newer brothers may not have met the older ones.'

'How many of you are there?'

'Thirteen now. There were others, but some died or moved on before I was invited to join, and I do not know their names. I can tell you the current members, if you like. We have nothing to hide.'

Chaloner thought of the unease evident at the meeting. 'Your colleagues would not agree.'

'They are afraid of being accused of conspiracy, which is *exactly* why the Brotherhood was founded – so that one day, no one need fear because he meets like-minded men for innocent purposes.'

'There were seven people at the meeting today,' said Chaloner. 'You, Ingoldsby, North, Dalton, Robert Leybourn and Robinson I know. Who was the large man?'

'You mean Thomas Wade? He is the Tower's victualling commissioner.' Chaloner's thoughts immediately became a scrambled mess again: it was Wade who had gone with Evett to recover Barkstead's treasure. 'Robinson recruited him to help soothe the loud-voiced army types that gather in the castle.'

Chaloner was careful to conceal his confusion. 'In addition to those seven, there are Thurloe, Hewson, Livesay and Barkstead. Thurloe stayed away, and the others are dead or missing. That makes eleven. Who are the remaining two?'

'A pair of military nonentities named Clarke and Evett. Philip Evett is the Lord Chancellor's aide, although he invariably forgets to attend our meetings. His task is to influence the Earl, and he is doing quite well, despite his innate stupidity: Clarendon spoke out against vengeance when the King first returned to the throne, and he continues to do so now. But I have answered enough questions, and you must excuse me – I have a funeral to arrange.'

'Just one more,' said Chaloner. 'Who is Clarke, precisely?'

'Colonel John Clarke. He fought bravely in the wars, and was kin to Thurloe.'

'Was?'

'He was recently stabbed by robbers. However, the others do not know – I decided not to tell them when I saw their reaction to the news about Hewson. There is no point in frightening them further.'

'How do you know he was killed by robbers?'

'Because his body was stripped naked and left by the river. I ordered my servants to listen in taverns for thieves bragging about the crime, and when I catch them, I shall have them hanged.'

Chaloner studied him carefully, trying to decide

whether Downing actually believed the story he was telling. The diplomat was apt to draw conclusions before he had all the facts, and it would not be the first time he had made an error of judgement. But Downing was also clever and sly, and who knew what was really in his mind?

'I do not understand why you have told me all this,' he said eventually. 'It puts you at risk.'

Downing pulled a disagreeable face. 'Not as much as keeping quiet would have done. Kelyng has eyes everywhere, although he is less adept at analysing intelligence than at gathering it, thank God. It is safer that you know the truth.'

'Did you tell Thurloe you intended to confide in me?'

'I only made up my mind when I was waiting for the others and saw you walk up the stairs here. You can tell him what I have done. Who knows, perhaps he will ask you to join us. If he does, then come to the Dolphin tavern by Tower Lane at midday the day after tomorrow. The annual conclave of the Royal Foundation of St Katherine is to be held then, and most of the brothers are benefactors – the Queen is the hospital's patron, you see, so it allows us to flaunt our generosity in the right quarters. There is no point in supporting worthy causes if there is no benefit to the giver, I always say.'

'This meeting of selfless donors takes place in an inn?' asked Chaloner dubiously. It did not sound very likely, even though the Dolphin was one of the more respectable establishments in the city.

Downing pursed his lips. 'Of course not. The conclave takes place in St Katherine's chapel, but the Queen always provides a dinner afterwards, as an expression of her gratitude. Obviously, none of us want to eat hospital

171

food, so we suggested the Dolphin as an alternative. But if Thurloe *does* want you to become a brother, come on Wednesday, and I will tell the others he has nominated you as his representative. That will kill two birds with one stone: palliate his annoying refusal to come to our gatherings and eliminate the danger of you interfering from outside. It is an ideal solution.'

'Ideal for you, perhaps,' muttered Chaloner.

It was five in the morning, and Chaloner lay in bed, staring at the shadows on the ceiling. Metje had arrived unusually late – well after two o'clock – and had shocked him from sleep with her bustling arrival and insistence that he light a fire. The flames were devouring the last of the logs, snapping occasionally and making her shift in her dreams. Sleep had eluded Chaloner after her invasion, especially since she could not be deterred from warming her cold feet on his bare skin, so he turned his thoughts to the people he had met since chasing Snow and Storey to Kelyng's house, bemused that so many of them belonged to the Brotherhood – or were dedicated to destroying it. Was someone playing an elaborate game with him, where everything led back to the same men? He sorted them into three categories in his mind, headed by those who seemed to be the main players.

*Thurloe*, whose sister *Sarah* was being pressed on Chaloner as a woman he could trust, and whose brother-in-law *Dalton* was apparently in the process of betraying him. The stolen satchel had led Chaloner to meet the inquisitive *Leybourn* brothers, and to witness the death of the regicide *Hewson*. Thurloe had asked Chaloner to investigate the murder of his kinsman *Clarke*, whose coded

172

messages had contained the same phrases Hewson had muttered about praising God and the number seven. The use of cipher suggested Clarke had intended the messages for Thurloe, which led Chaloner to wonder whether Hewson's desperate last words had also been meant for Thurloe's ears.

*The Earl of Clarendon:* while not a member of the Brotherhood – or at least, not on Downing's list – the Lord Chancellor had links to several members of the group. There was *Evett*, his aide, who was to help Chaloner find *Barkstead's* missing treasure. Another member of the digging party was *Wade*, while *Robinson* was Lieutenant of the Tower, where the treasure was alleged to be buried. *Clarke* had died in Clarendon's service, and Clarendon would also know *Downing* and *Ingoldsby* from Court.

*Downing*, who casually betrayed the Brotherhood to a man he detested. Through Downing, Chaloner had met *Barkstead*, along with the two other regicides who were later executed with him. Why would Downing do such a thing to a member of his own secret fraternity? And why had he arrested Barkstead, but not *Hewson* and *Livesay*, who had also been deemed guilty of king-killing by the courts? Had Livesay gone into hiding, because he was afraid of Downing, or was he dead, as *North* claimed? And what did *Ingoldsby* think of Downing's ambiguous attitude to the men who had signed the King's death warrant?

'You are snoring,' murmured Metje, her voice thick and drowsy. She spoke English, which was rare, particularly when she was not properly awake.

'I am not asleep,' he replied in Dutch, wondering whether his agitation had somehow transferred itself to her.

She opened her eyes. 'Lord! I thought I was in bed with a German!'

173

He smiled and extended his arm. She snuggled into it, sighing her contentment, while he turned his thoughts to William Leybourn, trying to decide whether the encounter in the grocer's shop had been contrived – that Leybourn had deliberately prevented him from eavesdropping on Kelyng. But a good many people had been out that morning, because of the King's paintings, so a chance meeting was not impossible. And what about Kelyng? He had made an enigmatic reference about 'six to go'. Was he referring to the Brotherhood, but did not know there were thirteen members? Or was it something to do with seven, minus one – Thurloe's 'brothers'?

'Only five days to Christmas,' murmured Metje. 'The Court plans another masque. Did you know there was one last night? Everyone went as a wild animal, and when I was shopping yesterday, I heard there were so many lion costumes in the offing that White Hall was predicted to look like a Roman circus. I miss parties and balls, Tom. Mr North's idea of a wild evening is Milton's poetry and a cup of hot milk. I would love to attend a masque, like we did in Holland.'

'I saw a baboon when I was with the Earl, and he seemed rather debauched to me. I do not think you would approve of the Court's revelries.'

'You have been awake most of the night,' she said, propping herself up on her elbows. He could just make out her face in the fading firelight. 'I could tell by the way you were breathing. What is worrying you? The work the Earl offered? You should not take it – accept Dalton instead.'

Chaloner was not so sure, given that the vintner belonged to a secret organisation that included regicides and was busily passing secrets to Kelyng about Thurloe.

'What exactly *did* the Earl offer?' she asked when he made no reply. 'You did not say.'

Chaloner disliked lying to her, but could hardly tell her the truth. 'Supplies clerk.'

'But you seem apprehensive. Why? You have a good head for figures. You found hundreds of mistakes in Downing's accounts, and you are not afraid of hard work.'

'You said yesterday that I was lazy.'

She slapped his arm, to make him see she was entitled to say something unkind and then change her mind. 'I do not want you to work for that Earl, Tom. He is sly – he ordered his own daughter to sleep with the Duke of York and get his child, so the man would be forced to marry her. And, until the King produces a son of his own, the Duke is heir to the throne. Clarendon will be father to a queen!'

Chaloner disagreed with her interpretation of events. 'Clarendon was furious about the pregnancy, because he had a political marriage in mind for the Duke – one that would strengthen England's ties with Spain or France. He was ready to have her beheaded for treason.'

'What kind of man threatens to execute his own daughter? I repeat: I do not like him. There are other things you could do – teach, for example, or go back to your family in Buckingham. I know you have brothers and sisters, but you never talk about them. Have they banished you? Are you in disgrace for some childish misdeed that means you can never return?'

'Of course not!' There were times when he found Metje irritating, and one of them was when she drew bizarre conclusions from half-understood facts. When she did, he was grateful she knew nothing about his work for Thurloe. 'I spent several months at my family's estate

175

after you and I returned from Holland. We are very fond of each other.'

She pulled away from him. 'You did not ask me to go with you.'

Chaloner sensed they were about to launch into one of their periodic arguments, in which she would accuse him of not caring about her feelings, and he would struggle to understand what he had done wrong. 'You said you could not ask for time away so soon after securing your new post.'

She regarded him rather coldly. 'Did you know Preacher Hill comes from Buckingham? He dined with the Norths last night, and when I mentioned in passing that you and he came from the same county – just to make conversation – he said he had never heard of a family called Heyden.'

Chaloner's heart sank when he heard the catch in her voice. He had hurt her and was sorry. However, she had never shown any interest in his family before – she had parted on bad terms with her own, and tended to shy away from discussions about anyone else's.

'It is a big shire, Meg,' he said gently. 'And my family's farm is very small. Hill cannot possibly know everyone in the region.'

'He comes from *Buckingham*,' she said unhappily. 'You said you hail from a village *close* to Buckingham. He knows all the local gentry, and it was vile to be told your family does not exist.'

He wondered what Hill would have to say about a clan of dedicated Parliamentarians called Chaloner, one of whom had been a regicide. If Hill came from Buckingham, he would certainly have heard of them. 'I am sure he and I will unearth some mutual acquaintance if we chat

176

for a while. I do not think this is anything to become upset about.'

She glared at him. 'I have shared your bed these last three years – abandoned my own country to be with you – but you reward me with lies.'

'If you gave up your country for me, then why will you not become my wife?'

She began to cry. 'Marriage is not as important as trust and love, and I have neither from you.'

Chaloner was astonished by the route the discussion had taken. 'That is simply not true.'

'I do not know what to believe about you.' She shoved him away with considerable force. 'I do not want to talk any more. Time is passing, and if I am not kneeling in the chapel before Mr North arrives, I might be without a master, as well as without a lover I can trust.'

Long before the first glimmer of dawn touched the grey city, Chaloner had washed, shaved, dressed and was ready to begin his investigation for Clarendon. Metje readied herself for chapel in silence, repelling his attempts to pacify her, and ignoring him even when he lit the lamp – a vast piece of equipment that would not have looked out of place in St Paul's Cathedral. A nagging guilt made him defensive, and he began to feel annoyed with her for doubting him, although the rational part of his mind told him that she had a perfectly good reason for doing so.

She was so upset that she stormed out of the house and stalked towards the chapel without making sure the coast was clear of Norths, displaying a reckless abandon she had never shown before. Fortunately, the jeweller was still at his private devotions; Chaloner could see his silhouette at an upstairs window, Bible open in front of him. He trotted after her, aware that she was walking very fast for so small a woman, another indication of her anger. They had not gone far when Chaloner felt a pricking at the back of his neck that told him he was being watched. Fearing that it might be North – he did not think Metje would ever forgive him if their argument cost her her job – he spun around, and saw someone standing in a doorway, cloaked and wearing a hat that shadowed his face.

Chaloner's immediate assumption was that it was one of Kelyng's rabble, but the watcher made no hostile move, and when Chaloner took a step towards him, he turned and hurried away. Chaloner watched him go, knowing from his gait that he was not Bennet or Snow. He began to walk after Metje again, then spun around when a stone clipped his shoulder.

The man was standing in the middle of Fetter Lane, and Chaloner was forced to duck when he lobbed another missile. He made a run at the fellow, who promptly fled down the alley by the Rolls House. His first instinct was to set off in pursuit, but he skidded to a halt at the lane's dark entrance and thought better of it. He could detect movement in the shadows, and was not so foolish as to let himself be lured to a place where he could be set upon. He abandoned the chase, and made his way back to Metje, preferring to make sure she was safe than hare after men who threw stones. He walked quickly, suspecting Kelyng's men were responsible for the 'attack': it was the kind of half-baked scheme they might devise. Metje was fumbling with the chapel's lock as he approached and he heard her talking to someone, but when he reached her, she was alone.

'Was someone here?' he asked. The street appeared to be deserted.

'A beggar,' she replied frostily. 'The poor devil ran away when he saw you coming, and I do not blame him. Why have you drawn your sword? You are asking for trouble, wandering around looking as though you are itching for a fight.'

He sheathed it only when he was sure they were alone. 'North is coming. You had better hurry.'

She glanced up the road, then shot inside the chapel when she saw he was right, rushing to light the lamps and set the place ready before her employer arrived. She was lucky, because the Puritan was searching his person for something as he walked. He stopped abruptly and returned to his house, emerging a short while later with a sheaf of paper – the monthly accounts that were to be presented to the community that day. Faith and Temperance were with him. Faith was tugging gloves over her meaty hands, while Temperance appeared to be daydreaming.

Chaloner hid behind a water butt until they had entered the building, and was about to leave when he saw Hill marching from the opposite direction, Bible under his arm. He pretended to be fastening the buckle on his boot, but knew from Hill's sharp, suspicious expression that the ruse had not worked. The preacher was wondering what he was doing lurking behind barrels in the dark.

'Our clerk from Buckingham,' he said unpleasantly. 'God does not like liars, Heyden.'

'I hail from Buckingham*shire*,' replied Chaloner coolly. He went on the offensive. 'But there was no respectable family called Hill that I ever heard of – no teacher in the local school, either.'

Hill was incensed. 'How dare you question my antecedents.'

'I recall an iconoclast called Hill, though – in the stocks for daubing paint on those religious statues the churchwardens deemed exempt from destruction. He raved all through his trial, then recanted pitifully and was never seen again.'

Hill regarded him with dislike. 'It seems we should both turn a blind eye to each other's pasts. However, this is the only agreement I shall ever make with you. If I catch you doing anything to harm my flock, I will denounce you without hesitation.'

'You are the one putting them at risk. It is unwise to draw attention to them with defiant speeches.'

'I speak when the Lord inspires me,' said Hill indignantly. 'North invited me to dinner last night, but the hand of friendship was extended only because he wanted me to curb my tongue – and *you* put him up to it. Well, it will not work. When I preach, I am God's vessel, ignited by the power of—'

'Yes, yes,' said Chaloner, knowing he was wasting his time, but persisting anyway. 'But it would be better if you were to ignite a little more quietly. You can see from here that more chapel windows were broken last night. It is because the patrons of the Golden Lion are tired of hearing your braying voice when they come for a drink.'

'Ale is the Devil's brew,' snapped Hill. 'It is my sacred duty to disturb those seduced by it.'

'Christ!' muttered Chaloner, seeing the situation was hopeless.

'Preacher Hill,' said Temperance, coming outside to see what was happening. Faith was behind her. 'And

180

Thomas, too. Do not stand in the cold, brothers. Come inside.'

'It is no warmer, because there are holes where there should be glass,' added Faith, shooting them both a resentful glare. 'But it is out of the wind.'

'Wind is created by the Lord,' declared Hill loud enough to startle two passing horses. 'And so is inclement weather. It is profane to attempt to ameliorate it.'

'You do spout some rubbish, Preacher,' said Faith. 'But perhaps a decent breakfast will unscramble your wits, so please dine with us after the service. I bought a ham yesterday.'

'Fine food is how the Devil corrupts the weak,' boomed Hill. 'But I shall partake of a little ham, just to demonstrate to you lowly sinners how I accept temptation, then rise above it. However, I shall not come if Heyden is invited, too – or if you tell me I cannot extol the Lord.'

'Are you coming to breakfast, Thomas?' asked Temperance eagerly, her happy tone attracting the immediate attention of her mother. 'What a lovely surprise.'

'I have an appointment at nine o'clock, and I doubt Hill will have finished extolling by then.'

'He might,' whispered Temperance with a mischievous smile, 'if he knows there is food waiting.'

'Has your turkey arrived yet?' asked Hill of Faith. 'I am partial to turkey meat, as well as ham.'

'It has arrived, all right,' said Faith grimly. 'And it has taken up residence in the kitchen, since it decided the yard was not to its liking. That is why we have ham today – it can be eaten cold, and no one will be obliged to encroach what is now the bird's domain.'

'*I* shall deal with it,' announced Hill. 'Once it hears the word of the Lord, it will become compliant, like Isaac

181

did with Abraham. And then I shall crush its skull with my Bible. No turkey defies God.'

Chaloner regarded him uncertainly. 'You plan to brain it with a book?'

'With the Bible,' corrected Hill. 'It is very heavy, and should do the trick nicely.'

'That is horrible,' said Chaloner. 'It probably will not work, and is sure to make a mess. Besides, I doubt you will tame it with scripture. I have met it, and it is not a God-fearing bird.'

Everyone jumped away in alarm when Hill hauled a pistol from under his cloak. 'If it resists, then the Lord has other means of destroying His enemies.'

Chaloner started to laugh after the preacher had strutted inside the chapel. He was surprised to find Temperance smiling, too.

'Is he quite sane, do you think?' she asked, watching Hill reach the pulpit and begin to leaf through the Good Book for a suitably rabid text. Two sections were particularly well thumbed, and Chaloner suspected they were the violently radical books of Daniel and Revelation.

'Not really. If you have any influence over your parents, you should tell them to muzzle the man. He is doing your community no good with his controversial opinions.'

'I know,' said Temperance. 'But unfortunately, they never listen to me. If they did, there would not be a turkey usurping our kitchen.'

After Temperance had gone, Chaloner lingered a while, unsettled by his argument with Metje, by the man who had tried to entice him into the alley, and by Preacher Hill's antics. When other members of the congregation began to arrive and Hill girded himself up for his morning tirade, Chaloner left to walk to Lincoln's Inn. Dawn was late in coming, because of the thick grey clouds that slouched above the city, and it was bitterly cold. A scything wind whipped old leaves and rubbish into corners, and cut through clothes. A pack of stray dogs snarled and worried over something in the middle of the road. They scattered when a coach clattered towards them, and Chaloner saw they had been devouring one of their own. The vehicle's wheel hit the corpse and lurched hard to one side, making the passenger curse at the driver. Chaloner glimpsed the angry face within, and was sure it was the Duke of Buckingham, travelling home after a night of debauchery with his mistresses.

It was early enough that the Lincoln's Inn porter was still asleep, and it was some time before he could be roused. Once inside, Chaloner went directly to Dial Court – it was still too dark for Thurloe to be walking in the gardens – and knocked softly on the door to Chamber XIII. Inside, the piles of completed correspondence on the table indicated the ex-Spymaster had been awake and working for some time. Over his day clothes, he wore a silk dressing gown and a soft white skullcap. A fire roared furiously and the window shutters were firmly closed, so Chaloner thought the room stifling to the point of discomfort. Thurloe beckoned him in and locked the door.

'The Earl of Clarendon sent me a packet of this newfangled stuff called tea yesterday. Would you like some? It is all the rage at Court, and said to be an excellent tonic – much better than coffee, which makes the heart race in those with frail constitutions.'

'I do not have a frail constitution, sir,' said Chaloner,

183

supposing the Portuguese ambassador had declined to accept a package that had already been tasted, so Clarendon had foisted it on Thurloe instead.

Thurloe looked him up and down. 'No, I suppose you do not. But tell me what happened at White Hall. I was astonished Clarendon waited until Monday to summon you – had it been me, I would have had you there the day I received the note. Did he ask you to look into Clarke's death, as I suggested he should?'

'He ordered me not to interfere, because he plans to investigate personally.' Chaloner watched Thurloe carefully as he added, 'With his aide, Captain Evett.'

'Evett,' mused Thurloe thoughtfully, pouring himself some tea. 'I know the name.'

Chaloner's thoughts raced: Thurloe was familiar with more than Evett's name, if they were both members of the Brotherhood. He had planned to describe how he had eavesdropped on the meeting, and to warn Thurloe that Downing was revealing its secrets, but now he reconsidered. Was it wise to bring up a matter Thurloe might want to keep to himself? He had also intended to tell Thurloe about the messages in Clarke's clothes, but hesitated about that, too, although he was not sure why.

Thurloe leaned back in his chair, tea in hand, and stared at Chaloner. 'Did Clarendon tell you *why* he wants to look into Clarke's murder himself? It is most irregular.'

'He said it was an important matter, so should not be delegated to a man he does not know. He feels guilty about what happened, and is determined to provide you with answers.'

'Pride,' said Thurloe with disapproval. 'The undoing of many a good man. But perhaps Evett will accept your help – I shall write to him before you leave, and you can deliver the message yourself. I would send one to Clarendon, too, but I cannot think of a tactful way to suggest he should leave such business to men who know what they are doing.'

'How well did you know Clarke, sir?' asked Chaloner, trying another way to see whether Thurloe was willing to acknowledge the Brotherhood. 'He was kin, but that does not mean you were close.'

'True. I was fond of him, but I did not know him as well as I know you.' He sipped the tea and shuddered. 'Nasty!'

Chaloner was nonplussed. Although they had sent each other hundreds of letters he would not have considered Thurloe an intimate by any stretch of the imagination. Thurloe read his bemusement, and elaborated uncomfortably.

'You wrote kind words to me after the deaths of my two children.'

Chaloner was none the wiser. 'That was years ago, sir.'

Thurloe nodded awkwardly. 'But most of my correspondents did not acknowledge the tragedy, so I was naturally drawn to those who did. Clarke was one of those whose letters were purely professional, with none of the kindly, personal addenda you always included. He was not a friend, not like you.'

This time Chaloner was unable to conceal his astonishment. He had not imagined for a moment that his casually penned postscripts had been taken so seriously. He thought about Thurloe recommending him to Sarah in the event of a crisis – and Sarah's claim that Thurloe was fond of him – and began to wonder whether this dignified, proper man had indeed taken the letters to be genuine expressions of affection.

185

Thurloe became brusque, obviously embarrassed. 'Forgive me, Tom; I am maudlin today. It must be this horrible tea. You were asking about Clarke. He was a soldier who believed in moderation, and was of the opinion that the best future for our country lies in tolerance and forgiveness.'

'Moderation,' mused Chaloner. He decided to test the extent of Thurloe's 'friendship' towards him. 'I know a group of men who try to instil a sense of moderation in those with power.'

Thurloe glanced sharply at him. 'It is a good theory. But, like all ideals, it will become corrupted in the hands of wicked men.'

'Clarke was a member of such a group,' Chaloner pressed on. 'So is Evett.'

Thurloe regarded him appraisingly. 'You have been busy. Do you know who else is in it?'

'Not everyone.'

'A diplomatic answer. However, *I* have not attended a meeting of the Brotherhood since Cromwell died. It started with honourable intentions, but then men like Downing and Ingoldsby enrolled, and it turned sour. Clarke and Evett joined after I ceased to play any real part in it.'

Chaloner nodded, but was not convinced. Downing had given the impression that Thurloe's absence was temporary, although Downing was no great adherent of the truth himself. 'Downing thought you might recommend me for membership.'

'Never,' said Thurloe immediately. 'It would be a mistake for both of us. *I* cannot claim to have ended my affiliation if I nominate new members. And fraternising with men like Ingoldsby and Downing is a risk *you* do not need to take. I forbid you to have anything to do with it, and if you try to enrol on your own, I shall oppose your election. I do not want you involved with such a group.'

Chaloner regarded him appraisingly, surprised by the uncharacteristic passion. Did Thurloe really have his interests at heart, or was there another reason for his vehemence? However, he suspected pressing the man for clarification would lead nowhere, so he turned to another subject.

'You sent Clarke to the Earl to do what, exactly, sir?'

'To use as he saw fit. The last I heard, Clarke was looking into the theft of silver table knives from the White Hall kitchens, which you would not think was terribly dangerous.'

'That depends on the thief – it might be *very* dangerous if Clarendon has a penchant for royal cutlery. But last week, you said you thought Kelyng might have killed Clarke.'

Thurloe sighed. 'It is possible – he knew Clarke was kin, and may have killed him in an attempt to hurt me. However, I am dogged with the sense that *I* sent Clarke to his death. I would like to know the identity of his murderer, if for no other reason that the answer may salve my troubled conscience.'

'Do you know anything about Clarke that might help me catch his killer?'

Thurloe regarded him oddly. 'Are you going to ignore the Earl's wishes and look into Clarke's death anyway?'

'I thought that is what you wanted me to do.'

'But not at the expense of you ruining your future – or risking your life. I do not want to lose another man to White Hall.'

187

'I can look after myself, sir,' said Chaloner, thinking of all the hazardous tasks he had undertaken on Thurloe's behalf in the past. 'Tell me about Clarke.'

'I cannot think of anything that might be of use to you. He was handsome, but aloof, he played the violin, and he worked at being unmemorable – like all good intelligence agents.'

'Could he have been dispatched by a jealous husband?' Chaloner thought about how Clarke had flirted with Metje, who had responded rather too readily to his charms.

'Not in White Hall, Tom. They all bed whoever takes their fancy – even you must have heard *those* rumours. If every jealous husband took a knife to his rival, we would have no Court left.'

'Was his body searched before it was dumped on the riverbank? Did his room contain anything in the way of clues?'

Thurloe shrugged. 'At the time, I suspect the Lord Chancellor was more intent on concealing the murder than in solving it. He has no experience in such matters.'

Chaloner's cautious probing had not told him whether the Earl had shown Thurloe the cipher messages from Clarke's pocket – or perhaps Thurloe was unwilling to admit that he was the recipient of notes containing the phrase about praising God. He tried one last time. 'Do you have an agent whose codename is Seven?'

Thurloe was startled and wary. 'No. Why?'

'Clarke was alleged to have told a friend that he praised God for sending him *seven* pairs of boots, and I wondered if the word held any significance for you.'

Thurloe's suspicion intensified. 'One of the skills developed by a good spy is deciding which information to discard and which to pursue. Your seven pairs of boots are definitely in the former category, and you will be wasting your time if you follow them. Besides, I want to know who stabbed him, not what he was doing for Clarendon. Do you understand me?'

'Not really, sir.'

Thurloe's expression was cool. 'I do not want you asking questions about the case Clarke was working on – these knives – because the Earl may assume I sent you to investigate *him*. I do not want him to think that – it would be extremely dangerous for you and for me. So, no questions about Clarke's business at White Hall, if you please. I want only to know who killed him.'

Chaloner felt this was unreasonable. 'But he may have been killed *because* of what he was doing at White Hall. It may not be possible to look at one without exploring the other.'

'It will have to be,' said Thurloe tartly. 'A night of listening to gossiping servants may well tell you all you need to know. Kelyng and Bennet are not subtle, and someone may have seen them loitering or asking questions. So, will you do as I ask, or shall I recruit someone else to help me?'

Chaloner was tempted to tell him to find some other fool. If he found Barkstead's treasure for the Earl, he would not need Thurloe's good opinion, and he was being given a task with conditions that might make a solution impossible. But he owed Thurloe something for the past ten years, and he had been oddly touched by the ex-Spymaster's shy expression of friendship.

'It will depend on whether I can gain access to the right servants – whether I can talk to them without arousing Clarendon's suspicions.'

'True,' agreed Thurloe. 'So be careful. Concentrate on Kelyng – he should not present much of a challenge to a man who survived Downing for so many years. If he has stepped up his campaign against me, I would like to know, so I can take precautions.' He went to a table and began to write. 'I will tell Evett you have solved murders before. He is a soldier, not an investigator, and will doubtless welcome any help that comes his way. But what *did* the Earl ask you to do, if not look into Clarke's death?'

'Hunt down some missing money,' replied Chaloner vaguely.

Thurloe nodded, not looking up as he dipped his pen into the ink. 'The new government is desperate for funds, and Clarendon is always trying to find ways of raising more. I wish you luck – if you find him a few hundred, he will take you under his wing for certain.'

Chaloner left Thurloe deeply uneasy. The ex-Spymaster had admitted to belonging to the Brotherhood, but only when the alternative was a brazen lie. Was he really in the process of extricating himself, or was he still involved? And did it matter, given that Downing claimed the group's aims were not illegal or seditious anyway? Thurloe had also declined to admit any familiarity with the words 'seven' and 'praise God', although Chaloner still believed the messages from Clarke and Hewson were intended for him. Was he telling the truth, or was Chaloner being unreasonable, since Thurloe could hardly be expected to know the meaning of messages he had never received?

No answers were forthcoming, no matter how many times he pondered the questions, so he walked to Will's Coffee House and read the pamphlet written by

Leybourn, which Downing had given him. He studied it closely, assessing it for the kind of stilted phrase or unusual reference that might be indicative of secret orders to waiting members, but he could see nothing amiss. Perhaps it was just what it seemed: a call for people to exercise tolerance, patience and understanding. He wished there was someone he could discuss it with, but for the first time in years, he did not know whom he could trust. And that night Metje did not come to him.

Chaloner was early for his appointment with Captain Evett the next morning. When Evett had asked where they should meet, Chaloner had suggested the Dolphin, on the grounds that it was near the Tower. It was also where members of the Brotherhood would meet later that day, after the conclave at the Royal Foundation of St Katherine, and although he would not be joining their ranks, Chaloner intended to engineer a meeting with some of its members. There were too many links between them and his three investigations to be innocent, and he would be remiss to ignore them.

The Dolphin was one of London's best taverns, patronised by clerks from the Navy Office, officers from the Tower and merchants from nearby Fishmongers' Hall. The atmosphere was one of genteel civility, and the inn boasted a freshly swept floor, polished oak furniture and two fires burning in separate hearths. It smelled of sweet ale, pipe smoke and freshly cut logs. Chaloner ordered, but then did not feel like eating, a dish of salted herrings and bread, paid for with a shilling he had found in his spare breeches. His thoughts were on Metje, and he was sorry they had argued. He wondered what she would say if he asked her to go to Buckinghamshire with him, so

191

he could abandon Clarendon *and* the awkward situation with Thurloe. He had the feeling she would not agree, and did not blame her. She thrived amid the colourful bustle of London, with its theatres, pageants and fairs, and there was little in the country that would make her love it.

'Are you going to eat that?' asked Evett, sitting down in a flurry of damp cloak and cold air. 'There was only pink pudding for breakfast at White Hall today. Why have you lost your appetite? Worry over this lost treasure?'

'I argued with my woman,' said Chaloner, surprising himself by the confidence. He did not normally open his heart to virtual strangers.

Evett was sympathetic. 'They have a habit of provoking quarrels out of nothing. Does your wife know about her? Or was that what the row was about?'

'Metje is my wife,' said Chaloner. He reflected. 'Or she will be.'

'You intend to marry?' asked Evett. He looked disapproving. 'I would not recommend that. They become different once you wed them. It is better to leave them as mistresses – kept women are more loving and considerably less demanding. Of course, the King would probably disagree, since Lady Castlemaine is *very* demanding.'

'Are you speaking from personal experience?'

Evett nodded, cheeks bulging with fish. 'With both wives. One manages my farm in Kent, while the other looks after my house in Deptford.'

Chaloner did not know whether to be shocked or amused. Bigamy was a capital crime, and he was astonished to hear Evett so blithely confessing to it. 'Does Clarendon know about them?'

Evett shook his head. 'He would not understand. I

was forced into both matches: the first declined to lie with me until she had been to the altar, and the second *did* lie with me, but a child appeared and her father put a gun to my head. They are lovely lasses, but I find myself lonely at Court. Perhaps I should take a third, to tend me in White Hall. What do you think?'

'Managing three wives would require a deviousness beyond my abilities.'

'And you a spy these last ten years,' said Evett with a grin. 'So, I have skills you envy, do I? Will you recommend me to Thurloe, then?'

'I might. However, I understand you know him, so why not ask yourself?'

Evett chuckled. 'I am jesting. I have been Clarendon's aide for years, and it would be folly to leave him now his fortunes are finally on the rise. Of course, they will not continue that way if Buckingham has anything to do with it. He *was* the baboon at the masque, you know. I told you it was he who burst in on us, thinking himself suitably disguised.'

'Thurloe is a good man,' said Chaloner, trying to steer the conversation back in the direction he wanted it to go.

'Is he?' asked Evett, without much interest. 'I see him when he visits Clarendon, but he tends to wait until I withdraw before embarking on whatever it is they discuss.'

'You do not meet on other occasions, perhaps out with friends?'

'Thurloe has no friends – he is not a sociable man. Why do you ask?'

'He sent you a letter.' Chaloner handed Evett the note Thurloe had scribbled the previous day. It contained nothing other than a polite suggestion that Chaloner's skills might be of use in locating Clarke's killer, and ended with the familiarly scrawled *Jo: Thurloe,* a signature that made some recipients imagine the sender's name to be Joseph. Naturally, Chaloner had read it, then repaired the seal, but he had been unable to determine whether its cool professionalism suggested a prior acquaintance.

Evett scanned the few lines. 'He thinks you might be able to help me with Clarke. Good! I am a soldier, not a parish constable and I am not pleased about being ordered to solve murders.'

'The Earl told me to leave the matter alone.'

'He asked *me* to stop looking for treasure in the Tower, too, but I will give you a detailed tour of the places where we dug, if you help me with Clarke. Agreed? Are you leaving that bread?'

Chaloner pushed it towards him.

'So, your domestic dispute deprived you of your appetite, did it? You should recruit a couple of mistresses to take your mind off it. Do you want me to introduce you to some willing ladies?'

Chaloner watched him eat. 'You seem to have very tolerant views of these matters.'

Evett nodded. 'There are far too many fanatics around these days, and they are making life uncomfortable for the rest of us – like those miserable Puritan extremists who banned horse racing.'

'Have you ever met other people who think your way?' asked Chaloner casually.

Evett stopped chewing. 'Why?'

'Because I have. Well, I did not meet them, exactly, but I know what they think, and I know they gather occasionally to discuss their ideas.'

194

'Damn! Who told you? Rob Leybourn? He will land us all in trouble with his loose tongue.'

'What kind of trouble do you anticipate?'

'People are suspicious of secret societies, and always think the worst. But the Brotherhood really does have good principles. I mean, what more can you ask than everyone tolerating the beliefs and opinions of everyone else? I saw Cromwell suppress Royalists in the fifties, and I see Royalists doing the same to Roundheads now. If we are to have peace, then we need an end to persecution.'

'It sounds idealistic.'

'What if it does? Everyone knows about the Court's decadence – animal masques, pink puddings, money spent that is not there. How long will it be before the people object, and we find ourselves with a ruling Parliament again? And then what? Am I to be hanged, because I am Clarendon's man? Are you? How many times can *you* change sides? I just want justice for everyone, no matter who is in power. The brothers are not men I normally associate with – I dislike Ingoldsby, for example – but unpleasant company is a small price to pay for peace and harmony.'

Chaloner rubbed his chin. Evett did not seem the type to harbour such notions – he was a soldier, for a start, and they tended to prefer war and *dis*harmony, when their skills could be put to use. But then he recalled his own distaste for strife after the wars, and supposed the captain might feel the same.

Evett ate more bread. 'And then there is Downing: he detests me *and* Clarendon, and the feeling is wholly reciprocated. I dislike Hewson, too, but Robinson sent me a message last night to say he is dead. Hewson *claimed* to be moderate, but he still said some fairly radical things about religion.'

195

'Do you know Sir John Kelyng?'

'I assure you *he* is not a brother. He is exactly the kind of man we are trying to overturn.'

'Is the Brotherhood open to anyone?'

Evett laughed. 'No, or we would have lunatics like Kelyng clamouring to join. Newcomers must believe in moderation, and they tend to be recommended by other brothers, who know their views.'

'Who recommended Clarke?'

Evett did not seem surprised that Chaloner should know Clarke had been a member. 'I did – to help me with Clarendon. Why? Surely you do not think the brothers had anything to do with his murder? Lord! That would be awkward! But now we are colleagues, and helping each other, I should tell you something important. Clarendon gives the impression he knows what he is doing, but he is not as competent as he appears. Others have misread his abilities, and it has cost them their lives.'

Chaloner regarded him askance. 'That is a singularly disloyal thing for an aide to say.'

Evett grimaced unhappily. 'I know, and it pains me to do it, but it cannot be helped. And anyway, he misuses me. I am a soldier, but he sends me to chase killers and treasure. He says he cannot trust anyone else, but that does not make such base duties any less distasteful.'

'What would you rather be doing?' asked Chaloner, surprised he should think an aide had a choice.

'I want to be Lord High Admiral.' Chaloner struggled to keep the incredulity from his face: it was a lofty ambition for a mere soldier, and the post was currently held by the King's brother. 'I *know* I get seasick when we cross the Channel, but I love ships. However, that is for the future, and we were talking about the present. I am Clarendon's man, but that does not mean I am blind to his faults – or that I am prepared to watch another spy walk blithely to his death.'

'What are you saying?' asked Chaloner, bewildered. 'That your Earl killed Clarke?'

There was a guarded expression in Evett's eyes. 'He did not hold the daggers himself, but it was his orders that led them into the situations that saw them killed. He is liable for—'

Chaloner was acutely uncomfortable with the use of the plural. '*Them?*'

'Thurloe's men. The Earl ordered them to follow certain people – to see where they went and who they met. It sounded easy, the kind of thing you spies do in your sleep. One lasted a month, but the others were dead within days – stabbed in the back in the dead of night with no witnesses.'

'Thurloe sent six men in total,' said Chaloner uneasily. 'Five, then Clarke. How many have died?'

'All of them.'

Chaloner did not believe him. 'The Earl sends Thurloe letters saying they are doing well.'

Evett shrugged. 'Thurloe was furious when he learned about Clarke, and the Earl could not bring himself to admit that the other five are gone, too.'

Chaloner's voice became unsteady when he remembered the man who had shared his love of music. 'Even Simon Lane?'

'All are buried in unmarked graves at St Martin-in-the-Fields.'

'Who killed them?' demanded Chaloner, shocked by the carnage. 'The men they were following?'

197

'Possibly. I cannot imagine they were pleased to have spies dogging their every move.'

'That assumes they knew they were being watched, but Simon was excellent at covert surveillance. No target would have known he was there.'

'Then perhaps someone told them – or they found out another way,' said Evett. 'I am certain someone invades the Earl's offices at night. I try hiding there, to see if I can catch someone in the act, but I never do. I am just not very good at that sort of thing – they must know I am there.'

Chaloner was angry. 'Clarendon has an unfortunate habit of leaving confidential papers strewn across his desk. *I* saw Lane's reports, and so could anyone else who happened to look.'

'Quite. Do you still think me disloyal for expressing my doubts about his competence to you? Or are you just grateful to have been forewarned?' Evett's expression was cool.

'Christ!' muttered Chaloner. A post under the Earl was sounding increasingly unappealing. 'Was Clarke ordered to shadow these men, too? I thought he was investigating a theft.'

'He was looking into the King's missing table knives. Clarendon thinks servants made off with them, but I suspect Buckingham – I think he pays a silversmith to melt them down.'

'Was Buckingham one of the people these agents were told to watch?'

'No – Clarendon is wary of tackling men who are too powerful, although it is obvious that *they* are where the real threat lies. But I do not want to discuss this any more, Heyden. I told you about the risk, because we are supposed to be helping each other, but I dislike being interrogated.'

Chaloner did not care what he disliked. 'Who were they following, if not Buckingham?'

Evett looked annoyed, but answered anyway. 'Kelyng, because fanatical loyalty is just as dangerous as fanatical opposition and he needs to be monitored. And Cerberus . . . I mean Downing, because he is a turncoat.'

Something clicked in Chaloner's mind. Lane's report had said: *C talked all through church with Jo.* It had been about Downing, and Lane had used a codename for him known only to the Earl – or would have been, if the Earl had not been so free with it.

'Who is Jo?' he asked.

Evett shrugged, startled by the abrupt question. 'It is short for Joseph, I suppose. Why?'

'Or it could be an abbreviation of John,' mused Chaloner, running ahead with his analysis without stopping to explain. He thought about the way Thurloe signed his name – *Jo: Thurloe.* Or perhaps it referred to another member of the Brotherhood: John Dalton, John Barkstead, John Hewson or John Robinson. Or perhaps even John Clarke. 'Of course, there is always the possibility that it might mean nothing – that Simon sent the report just to show he was doing some work.'

'Simon's missives were never very helpful actually,' said Evett, trying to conceal his confusion. 'He told us things we already knew – such as that Downing and Thurloe meet. Well, of course they do: one has been asked to provide summaries of foreign policy and the other was a diplomat.'

Was that the answer? Lane was astute, and may have known the Earl was a poor master, so had sent reports that contained nothing contentious – although it had not saved his life.

'You must feel uneasy,' said Chaloner to Evett. 'Downing is a leading member of your Brotherhood, and your Earl was hiring spies to follow him – spies who are now dead.'

'That is coincidence.' Evett hesitated uncomfortably. 'Well, perhaps Downing did object to being followed, but he could not have dispatched *five* men without being caught. Kelyng might, though.'

Chaloner did not think so, given the ineptitude he had witnessed so far. 'Who watches them now?'

'No one – we do not *have* anyone. The Earl has given you other duties, because he knows he needs to be more careful with you than he was with your predecessors – Thurloe's letter of recommendation went on at some length about how fond he is of you.'

'I do not understand why you have told me all this. You do not know me – I could go to the Earl and repeat everything you have said.'

'Well, please do not,' said Evett coolly. 'I am tired of sly murders, and I am tired of attending hasty funerals in St Martin-in-the-Fields. You seem a decent man – an old soldier, like me. Besides, Simon Lane was my cousin, and I miss him sorely.'

# Chapter 6

'Tell me more about Barkstead's hoard,' said Chaloner, as he and Evett left the Dolphin and made their way towards the Tower.

'I have already told you everything. We dug on four separate occasions, but found nothing. When it became clear the gold was not there, Wade tried to locate Mother Pinchon, but failed. Meanwhile, I interviewed Samuel Pepys – the Earl of Sandwich's clerk. I was suspicious of him, because when we were digging by the old Coldharbour Gate, I had to leave for an hour – between you and me, it was when I learned about poor Simon – and it occurred to me that Pepys might have found the cache and spirited it away. But Wade would not have agreed to that, and there would have been too many firkins for Pepys to carry alone. Besides, Robinson's men would have seen him.'

Chaloner slowed as the grim façade of the fortress loomed ahead. It was a formidable mass, with clusters of grey towers and chimneys, all enclosed within curtain walls and an encircling ditch, the latter of which was a vile, grey-brown lake of liquid sewage, entrails, dead animals and kitchen slops. In the summer, when the water evaporated, the remaining sludge stank so badly that people had been known to pass out. Access to the Tower was via a barbican, which led to the causeway that snaked across the moat. As they passed under the first of a series of portcullises, there was a sudden whooping screech. Chaloner looked at Evett in alarm, hand dropping automatically to his sword.

'The royal menagerie,' explained Evett. 'Where the King keeps his wild animals, and I am not referring to Buckingham. I mean real ones – tigers, apes and other nasty creatures. I *hate* them.'

Chaloner regarded him in surprise. 'Why?'

'Foul, stinking things, all fleas and claws.' He jumped when something roared. 'Have you never been? Many Londoners visit it on Saturdays, for something to do.'

Chaloner hoped Metje would not ask to be taken. He disliked places that were difficult to get out of, and the Tower's gates, drawbridges and walls made him distinctly uncomfortable.

'Wade works here,' said Evett, pausing in a way that suggested he was not happy about entering it, either. 'I do not know how I can show you around without *him* guessing what we are up to.'

'Tell him I am a surveyor,' said Chaloner, who had anticipated such an eventuality. 'I borrowed some instruments from my landlord and know enough about the subject to fool most people.'

'No,' said Evett. 'That is boring. We will say you are looking for mushrooms.'

Chaloner gaped at him. 'In December? But if you think surveying is dull, then hopefully other people will, too – and they will leave us alone. The point is to be unobtrusive, and that will not be the case if folk think we are on a fungus foray at this time of year.'

Evett took a deep breath, as if to fortify himself, then shot through the building known as the Lion Tower, running harder still when his pounding footsteps elicited a cacophony of grunts, snorts and growls from its furred occupants. The drawbridge in the Middle Tower led to the causeway that crossed the moat, where three dead cats and a sheep floated in the poisonous waters below. Then came the Byward Tower, a gatehouse set into the massive curtain walls.

'No weapons are allowed from here on,' said Evett. He beamed at the soldier who came to disarm them. 'Good morning, Sergeant Picard. We have come to look for fungus.'

Chaloner shot the captain a withering glance, but the guard just grinned. 'You have come to the right place then, sir. There is a lot that is rotten around here.'

Evett was meticulous, and showed Chaloner all the areas he had dug with Wade and Pepys. At first, people were interested to know what sort of fungus they expected to find, keen to be told whether it represented any danger, but drifted away when Chaloner began a ponderous series of measurements that involved standing still a long time, then writing a figure in a notebook. When the last had left, he listened again to the description of the treasure's hiding place, and agreed that there was only one serious possibility: a cellar in one of the smaller towers near the main gate. It was the only one that contained a 'central grey stone arch with a single red brick in its middle'.

Although Evett had refilled the trenches he had excavated, his workings were still visible. He told Chaloner his pits had been waist deep, and the agent was forced to acknowledge that the treasure was unlikely to have been buried there – Barkstead had been in a hurry in his last night of office, and would not have had time to scrape out more than a foot or two, especially since the earth was hard packed and difficult to move. Chaloner stood in the undercroft and studied his surroundings carefully, while Evett sat on the stairs with Sergeant Picard, discussing the latest Court masque.

The cellar was low and dark, with cobwebs falling like curtains and a floor so ancient that centuries of filth had raised it by several feet. Chaloner's head brushed the ceiling in places, while in others, he was obliged to drop to hands and knees. He crawled for some distance, and when he glanced back, he could see no light from the door, only a vast expanse of blackness. The air smelled foul, and at one point, he discovered a skeletal hand. He scratched a shallow hole with his dagger and reburied it, not liking to think of the poor soul who had died in such a place.

As he explored, he thought about his uncle's treasure. The Banqueting House was a far more sensible hiding place than the vaults of the Tower, because coins under a flagstone were a lot easier to retrieve than butter barrels buried in London's most inaccessible fortress. He recalled a story Temperance had recently told him about a Royalist who had put a hoard in his dead wife's coffin – the fellow had been delighted when he had exhumed her to find it still there.

Water dripped, sending mournful echoes rolling through the arches, and rats lurked in the darker recesses. The cellar was otherwise as silent as the grave. He could hear nothing from outside – no traffic, horses or bells –

and he realised he could no longer hear Evett and Picard, either. Then the lamp went out.

Cursing, he started back to where he thought the stairs were, but after several minutes, there was still nothing but darkness. He tried to stand, but the ceiling was so low that he could not even kneel without cracking his head, and he began to wonder whether he had been going in circles. Then he felt a breeze on his face, which encouraged him because it suggested he was near the exit. He crept along until his fingers touched something soft. At first he thought it was a rat and jerked away in revulsion, but it did not move, so he probed it more closely. It felt like hair, and he supposed someone had lost a periwig after the recent excavations. He shoved it in his pocket, and resumed crawling.

His leg was beginning to ache from the unaccustomed posture, and it protested even more when something sharp dug into his knee. Becoming annoyed, he called out to Evett, but all he could hear was his own muffled voice. He made a right-angled turn, in the hope of locating a wall, and was relieved when he bumped against one, considering a bruised skull a small price to pay for orientation. He yelled again for Evett and was astonished that what had seemed a normally sized vault when he had had a lamp had assumed monstrous proportions in the dark.

The walls were cold and slick under his hands, and the entire cellar had an ancient, disused feel to it. It occurred to him that he could be locked in it for years, and no one would ever know. Perhaps Evett had taken against him for his questions about the Brotherhood, and had decided to prevent him from asking more. Guards could be bribed to overlook the fact that the aide had

205

arrived with a guest but had left without one, and the Tower had a history of stealthy murder. Chaloner began to feel uneasy.

He clambered to his feet and stumbled on, nose assailed by the rank, sickening smell of decaying flesh. The rats were growing bolder, and he could hear their claws on the earthen floor. He comforted himself with the knowledge that if they could get in, then he could get out, but his optimism was abruptly shattered when he trod on something soft, and his questing fingers encountered furry bodies – it was the reek of dead rodents that filled this part of the cellar and made him want to retch. He started moving again, gagging when he encountered something that squelched, then swore when he reached a dead end.

By now, he was genuinely alarmed. He called a third time for Evett, but there was no sound other than his own ragged breathing and the soft, sinister scrabbling of claws. And then he felt something that rose at an angle. The stairs! He began to climb, one hand on the wall for balance. Then he reached the door and saw a rectangle of light around it. It was closed, and he wondered whether anyone would hear when he hammered – and if they would help him if they did. He fumbled for the latch, anticipating that it would be barred from the outside. Consequently, he was startled when it opened. Light flooded into the cellar, leaving him blinking stupidly.

Evett looked up from where he was sitting on the steps that led to the yard. He was playing dice with Sergeant Picard, and was relaxed and cheerful. 'I hope you did not mind us abandoning you, Heyden, but we were cold. I hollered to let you know, but you did not answer.'

'I did not hear you,' said Chaloner, somewhat accusingly.

Evett's expression was hopeful. 'You took longer than I expected. Did you find it?'

'The lamp burned out.'

Evett's jaw dropped. 'Lord! Did it? We closed the door, because it kept banging in the wind, and that would have made it pitch black down there. Why did you not shout for a candle?'

'I did,' said Chaloner tartly.

Picard started to laugh, thinking it a fine joke. 'Barkstead used to shut his prisoners in that cellar when he was Lieutenant of the Tower – he would lock them in at dusk, and by dawn they would be mad or dead.'

'That would not happen after a single night,' said Chaloner. The man was trying to unnerve him.

'It would,' argued Picard. 'You were all right, because you knew you were going to get out. But imagine what it would be like if you thought you were going to *die* down there, alone and forgotten.'

'Believe me, I did,' said Chaloner. 'But I doubt Barkstead would have done such a thing.'

'You are wrong,' insisted Picard, becoming sullen. 'He said it saved money, because he did not have to pay for their food.'

'I think you may be right, sergeant,' said Evett thoughtfully. 'When we were digging last month, we kept unearthing fragments of bone, and I am sure some were human.'

'The cellar is hundreds of years old,' Chaloner pointed out. 'I am sure people *have* died down there, but that does not mean they were Barkstead's victims.'

'What are you, a Roundhead or something?' demanded Picard. 'You take his side very readily.'

'He is just sceptical of ghost stories,' said Evett soothingly. 'Politics have nothing to do with it.'

The sergeant sniffed, then pointed to the hair that tumbled from Chaloner's pocket. 'What is that?'

'Someone dropped a wig,' said Chaloner, removing it to show him. Although matted and muddy, the curls remained a fine chestnut colour, and the piece appeared to be made of real hair. He was surprised someone had not missed such an expensive object, and taken steps to recover it.

'I did! It is mine,' said Picard, snatching it. 'I had a—' He faltered, then let it drop to the ground. 'That is no wig!'

Evett made a choking sound, revolted. 'Jesus God, Heyden! You brought out a piece of someone's scalp. What were you thinking of?'

Chaloner was sheepish. 'It felt like a wig in the dark.'

'Why did it not rot away, like the rest of the corpse?' asked Picard ghoulishly.

'It must have dried,' explained Chaloner. 'There was a breeze where I found it, so it must have desiccated, rather than decomposed. Hair and skin can last a long time under the right conditions.'

Evett was horrified. 'How do you know such terrible things?' he cried.

Intelligence agents collected all manner of bizarre facts during their assignments and, combined with the fact that the work was dangerous and people died, Chaloner knew a good deal about corpses and their various stages of decomposition. He considered regaling Evett with some of his experiences in the arid hills of Spain, but thought better of it when he saw the revulsion in the man's eyes. There was no point in alienating someone who was helping him.

Picard was less squeamish. He picked up the hair,

using the ruff on his sleeve so he would not have to touch it with his fingers. 'It is very *young* hair – brown with reddish glints, like my grandson's. How long has it been down there? A hundred years?'

'Not that long,' replied Chaloner.

'One of Barkstead's victims then,' concluded Picard, rather defiantly. 'We can get ten shillings for this, once we clean it up. That Dutch wigmaker near the Strand pays a fortune for hair, and never asks questions – then one of you could demand *another* ten shillings for keeping quiet about the fact that it came from a corpse.'

'He is French,' said Chaloner, not wanting Jervas's windows smashed for the wrong reasons.

Picard sighed at his irrelevance. 'Do you want in on this, or not?'

'Bury it,' ordered Evett. 'Get the Tower chaplain to say a prayer, for decency's sake. Do not stand gawking, sergeant. Do it!'

Picard slouched away, studying the find as he went, and Chaloner thought that if Evett believed it would ever see a graveyard, then he was a fool.

'Before you started to dig under that arch, did it look as though the ground had been disturbed within the last three years?' Chaloner asked, turning his thoughts back to the treasure.

Evett shook his head. 'We checked for recent upheavals, but it was all uniform beaten earth. We found a few bones that we tossed into a corner, but . . . Oh, Lord!' His hand flew to his mouth as something occurred to him. 'The bones were not all in one place – they were scattered in a way that suggested they had been chopped about.'

'Chopped about?'

'As in disjointed, perhaps because someone was digging through them.' Evett was appalled by the conclusion. 'But we were *so* careful to look for evidence of earlier excavations. Does it mean someone got there before us?'

'It might – although it does not tell us whether this someone also found the treasure. And bear in mind that it might also be evidence that Barkstead really *did* bury something there.'

Evett chewed his lip. 'We could go deeper, I suppose.'

Chaloner shook his head. 'There is no point. You dug for hours, but Barkstead could not have spared that kind of time with the Commonwealth collapsing and so much business to complete. You were right: there is nothing here now.'

It was almost noon by the time Chaloner had finished examining Evett's excavations, and he was eager to return to the Dolphin, to observe the Brotherhood at their benefactors' dinner.

'Good,' said Evett, when Chaloner informed him that he had a sudden desire to watch the Queen leaving St Katherine's hospital. 'I have business of my own at midday, and since you cannot be in the Tower without a military escort, you would have had to leave anyway. Now I need not feel guilty about shoving you out before you are ready. You can wave to the Queen, I can interview these wretched White Hall men, and we can come back here this afternoon to complete your work.'

They left the fortress and walked towards the tavern. 'White Hall men?' asked Chaloner.

'His Majesty's measurers of cloth. They took a liking to Clarke because he played the violin for their musical ensemble. The things you spies do to cultivate contacts!

Anyway, they declined to speak to me in the palace, because walls have ears, but when I told them I planned to be in the Dolphin part of the day, they agreed to meet me there instead.' Evett pushed open the tavern's door and entered the smoky warmth within. 'I would not mind you joining us, actually, since I imagine you are more skilled an interrogator than I will ever be. Would you mind? There they are.'

Chaloner followed the direction of his pointing finger and saw a trio of men sitting with their backs to a wall. They were difficult to tell apart, because they were all middle aged, overweight and wore identical uniforms that comprised grey wigs and blue coats. They exuded an aura of unease, and their agitation increased tenfold when Evett sat at their table. The hands of one were shaking so much that he could barely lift his ale to his lips. Some of it spilled on his clothes.

'I hope this will not take long,' said the tallest, after Evett had introduced Chaloner as an 'associate of Clarendon', which he thought made him sound sinister. The measurers obviously thought so, too, because one turned pale and another looked as though he might be sick. 'The King wants a new cloak, urgently, and our skills are needed to pick the right cloth. We do not know anything that will help you anyway.'

Evett looked annoyed. 'Then why did you agree to meet me?'

'Because you were asking loud questions and it was the only way to stop you,' said the smallest. 'The clock keeper is in *Kelyng*'s pay. We cannot afford to have *him* hear us talk to you about murder – not even when we have nothing of relevance to impart. It would be dangerous to say the least.'

211

'Do you think Kelyng killed Clarke, then?' asked Chaloner. 'You must, or you would not be worried about his spy seeing you with Evett.'

The three hung their heads in perfect synchrony. 'No one believes that tale about Clarke being murdered by robbers,' whispered the middle measurer. 'He was a soldier, and knew how to look after himself. But Kelyng has been lurking around the palace, trying to befriend the law clerks. The clerks say he is just using them as an excuse to be there, though. Him and Bennet.'

'I do not like Bennet,' said the smallest. 'He pretends he is educated – like us – but he cannot even tell you what William Heytesbury said about uniformly accelerated motion.'

'How remiss,' said Chaloner, recalling that Bennet was sensitive about his social standing. 'Did Clarke ever take him to task over his lack of learning?'

'Yes, about a month ago – after Bennet insulted him and us by saying he preferred the sound of yowling cats to our music,' said the tallest. 'And Clarke told *him* that yowling cats always sound attractive to upstart toms. Knives were drawn, but then Sir George Downing came bursting into the kitchen, looking for cream to rub on Lady Castlemaine's ankles, and the quarrel was lost among the panic of finding him some.'

'Sir George is a good man,' said the shortest fondly. 'He was very complimentary about our rendition of Pretorius last month, and the next day, he sent us copies of three new pieces.'

'And he gave me five crowns towards the new transverse flutes we have commissioned,' added the middle measurer, excited. 'He said there is nothing so sweet as the sound of a silver flute.'

212

'What happened after the cream was found and Downing left?' asked Evett. 'Did Clarke and Bennet resume their squabble?'

The tallest shook his head. 'They let it go, but I saw the way Bennet looked at Clarke as he was leaving. It would not surprise me to learn that *he* stuck a knife in Clarke's belly, thus depriving us of the best fiddler in White Hall. I do not suppose you have any talent for music, Mr Heyden?'

'I play the bass viol.'

The tallest beamed, delighted. 'Then visit us any evening, and we shall have a fugue in four parts.'

'Lord!' breathed Evett with strong disapproval. 'The things you spies do—'

'Is there anything else you can tell us about Clarke?' asked Chaloner.

'One thing,' said the tallest hesitantly. 'He was worried something might happen to him, because he asked us to give his wife a message in the event of a mishap. She was to be reached though Mr Thurloe, of Lincoln's Inn.'

'What was it?' asked Evett.

The tall man pursed his lips. 'It was personal, and Mr Thurloe agreed to send it sealed, because its contents were . . . intimate.'

'You can tell me,' said Evett. 'I will not be embarrassed – I am a man of the world.'

'Actually, we were thinking of *her* feelings,' said the smallest. 'I think we can tell Mr Heyden, though. A man who plays the bass viol will know how to be discreet.'

The tallest sighed. 'Very well. Clarke said he would plant seven kisses on her lips when they met in Paradise, and that they would praise God's one son together, well away from the shadows cast by the towers of evil. He

213

was very insistent that she should know those *exact* words.'

The smallest stood. 'And now we must go, or the clock keeper will tell Kelyng we were gone.'

Evett watched them leave. 'That was a waste of time. They were right: they know nothing that will help me, and I suspect they want Bennet blamed for the crime, because he is critical of their music. There is one thing, though. I heard Clarke mention seven of things, too, and I suspect it was his codename – the Earl is fond of allocating such tags to people. He asked me to choose one, but I told him I did not want to be a spy. When he insisted, I opted for Admiral, but he did not take the hint.'

Chaloner's thoughts whirled in confusion. If 'Seven' was Clarke's codename, then were Hewson's dying words intended to be a warning to *him*, because he did not know the colonel was already dead? More to the point, what had Thurloe made of the note the measurers had sent Mrs Clarke? He would certainly have read it – opening other people's letters was second nature to a Spymaster, even a retired one, and he would have wanted to know what Clarke had considered so pressing. And what would he have learned? That Clarke, like Hewson, had turned to religion as death approached? Chaloner rubbed his chin. Praise God's one son *must* be code, but for what? Something connected to the Brotherhood? Downing had denied that members used a phrase to recognise each other, but that did not mean he had been telling the truth.

He turned to the 'brother' who sat opposite him. 'What does "praise God's one son" mean?'

'It is no good looking for sense in messages spoken by men in fear of their lives, Heyden – or ones intended

214

for lovers. If it is not some panicky religious exhortation spoken in the terror of the moment, then it will be some lewd reference to his courtship with his wife.'

'That man is trying to catch your eye,' said Chaloner, nodding across the crowded room to where a clerk was eating veal chops and drinking beer. 'He has been fluttering his handkerchief for the past ten minutes, like a whore recruiting a customer.'

Evett immediately stared down at the table. 'It is Pepys from the Navy Office. We do not want to talk to *him*! He is a sly rogue, and will know in an instant that the Earl has asked us to have another look for Barkstead's cache without his own master's knowledge.'

'He will only know if you tell him,' said Chaloner, suspecting Pepys *would* guess something was afoot if Evett insisted on acting in a way that screamed furtiveness and guilt. 'He is coming over.'

'Damn! What shall we do? The Earl will think we disobeyed him deliberately.'

'Calm down,' ordered Chaloner sharply, knowing perfectly well who would be blamed if Pepys did learn the truth. 'He only wants to pass the time of day.'

'What do you want?' demanded Evett, as Pepys approached. The navy clerk was a short, chubby man who took great care with his appearance and who clearly thought himself something of a devil among the ladies. His progress across the tavern had been punctuated by several attempts to paw the serving women.

Pepys was startled by the hostile greeting. 'I came to enquire after your health. We spent several days chasing phantom gold together, and I assumed that allowed us a certain familiarity. Besides, I am always happy to greet acquaintances from White Hall.'

215

'This is Tom Heyden,' blurted Evett. 'We are here to . . . to discuss viols.'

Pepys smiled. 'I am partial to music myself, and, although modesty prevents me from elaborating, I am something of a composer, too. Did Captain Evett tell you about our treasure hunt?'

'No,' said Evett in the kind of way that made it clear the answer was yes.

Pepys frowned, puzzled by his behaviour, then addressed Chaloner again. 'My Lord Sandwich was very disappointed with the outcome, but the hoard was alleged to have been hidden by Barkstead, and the regicides were slippery fellows. I doubt it was ever buried, and anyone looking for it will be wasting his time. Ha! There is Lord Lauderdale. Excuse me, gentlemen.'

'He knows!' breathed Evett, watching Pepys scurry across the room to bow to an overweight, badly dressed man in blue silk, who did not look at all pleased to see him.

'He does not. He just wanted to renew an acquaintance that might prove useful in the future. You are the Lord Chancellor's aide, and he intended to make sure you remember him – until someone more important caught his attention.'

'He contrived to be here because of the conclave,' said Evett in disgust. 'When they have pledged enough money for the coming year, the hospital's benefactors dine in the Dolphin, thus providing an opportunity for characters like Pepys to come here and toady. You should open the window, by the way, or you will miss the Queen.'

Chaloner unlatched the shutter and peered out, Evett standing close behind him. 'Three of your brothers are about to come in,' he said conversationally. 'Downing, Dalton and my neighbour North.'

'Several of them *are* generous to worthy causes,' acknowledged Evett. 'Especially ones that win them the favour of the Queen. There is her carriage now – the black one. Wave to her, then!'

Chaloner saluted as the vehicle rattled past. A tiny white hand flashed as she waved back. 'She smiled at me!'

'That was a grimace. Can you imagine how tedious it must be, constantly hailing the masses? But we should get back to the Tower. I know most of these benefactors from Court, and some are very difficult to escape from once they start talking. Damn! Lauderdale is in our way. Good day, My Lord!'

Lauderdale was difficult to understand, since his tongue was too large for his mouth, but the gist of his growled diatribe was that there had better be something worth eating, or he would not be so generous with his dona- tion next year, and that if there was any kind of music, he would leave. While Evett tried to stay out of spittle range, Downing took the opportunity to speak to Chaloner. He pulled the spy to one side as the benefac- tors began to stream past, heading for the private chamber above.

'Lauderdale has a poor opinion of music,' he whis- pered, making it clear he considered it a serious defect. His green coat seemed tighter than ever that day, as though he had recently been gorging himself. 'I would recommend you play to him, since you are in need of employment and he is in greater need of education, but I think his ears are past redemption. Well? What did Thurloe say? Will you join us?'

'He does not think it is a good idea.'

Downing sighed his annoyance. 'He is like an old woman these days, afraid to do anything with his friends – not even when it might prove advantageous to him. Well, I suppose I am not surprised, although I think he is wrong. So, we shall have to trust you with our secrets, Heyden, and hope your affection for him will keep you in line. But why are you here, if not to join us? Looking for Dalton, in the hope that he will employ you as a translator?'

'Looking for Barkstead's tr—' began Evett, who had finished with Lauderdale.

'Barkstead's head,' interrupted Chaloner, wondering what was wrong with Evett. Was he trying to land him in trouble with the Lord Chancellor? 'It is still displayed outside the Tower.'

Downing regarded him in alarm. 'Do not bring that subject up here! It still rankles with some people, although I cannot imagine why. He was a regicide, for God's sake, and deserved what he got.'

'He was a brother, too,' said Evett reproachfully. 'He was before my time, but still a brother.'

'You have been discussing our fraternity *together*?' said Downing uneasily. 'I hope you have been discreet – both of you. It will not take much to draw Kelyng's attention in the wrong direction.'

Evett declined to be diverted. 'Why *did* you betray Barkstead, Sir George? It is one thing to catch a fugitive, but you were members of the same secret organisation – one that professes loyalty to its fellows.'

Downing's expression was resigned, and he rubbed his eyes tiredly. 'I have explained a hundred times: I had no choice. *I* was in Holland and *he* was in Holland. How

218

would it have looked – me in the same city, rubbing shoulders with him, as though we were friends? It would have seen me dismissed and disgraced. Besides, there was the Brotherhood to protect.'

'I do not see how arresting him helped us,' said Evett doubtfully.

'That is because *you* joined later, when it was safe,' replied Downing frostily. 'If it had emerged that Barkstead – who was always unrepentant about the old king's death – was one of our members, we would *all* have hanged. It is as simple as that, and I did the right thing. But even so, you cannot imagine how painful it is to see his severed head outside the Tower every day.'

'And what about the Brotherhood's other regicides?' asked Chaloner. 'You dealt with Barkstead, but that still left Hewson, Ingoldsby and Livesay.'

'They signed documents of apology,' replied Downing. 'Besides, Ingoldsby is the King's man now, and the others are dead. Ask North. North, tell Heyden here that Livesay is dead.'

North closed his eyes and breathed a prayer, clasping his Bible as he did so. Although he had dressed well for the conclave, he was still drab in his black suit and plain white collar. 'I fear so,' he said sadly. 'Although Dalton thinks otherwise.'

Dalton was not well. His face was pale and sweaty, and he smelled of wine. 'Livesay is *not* dead. He is in hiding, and who can blame him?'

'He is not hiding,' said North gently. 'I spoke to eye-witnesses. Gunpowder was stored in the forward hold of Livesay's ship and the vessel exploded. There were no survivors.'

Chaloner had learned a lot about explosions during

219

the wars, and knew their outcomes were unpredictable. The ship may well have sunk, and there would no doubt have been a large number of fatalities. But some of the bodies would have been impossible to identify, and there was always the chance that Livesay had used the situation to vanish. Such an opportunity would have been a godsend to a man in his position, and it was not impossible that he had ignited the gunpowder himself. Chaloner was inclined to side with Dalton: an explosion was not clear evidence that Livesay was dead.

'I like Dalton,' said Evett, when he and Chaloner had elbowed their way outside. 'If he offers you work, you should take it. You do not know how this business with Barkstead's gold will end, and even if you do find it, life at White Hall is precarious. Look at what happened to my poor cousin Simon.'

Chaloner spent the next hour examining all the Tower cellars that even vaguely fitted the description given by Mother Pinchon, although none were as promising as the first – there were grey arches galore, but none also had a distinctive red brick. When he had finished, he was faced with three possibilities: first, Pinchon's memory was faulty; second, Barkstead had changed his mind about where he had left his treasure; and third, someone had been there before them.

Evett considered the last option. 'Who?'

'Someone capable of sending a team of diggers inside the castle with the authority to keep them quiet about what they discovered.'

'Robinson?' asked Evett. 'He has been Lieutenant of the Tower most of the time since Barkstead was ousted. You think he spotted evidence that something was buried, and investigated by himself? Perhaps he thinks it is his to keep, since he is in charge of the castle.'

'It is possible, but there is a sizeable garrison billeted here and a lot of people mill around. Folk have been watching us ever since we arrived, and I imagine it would be difficult for Robinson – or anyone else – to retrieve a large number of butter firkins with no one noticing. If someone *was* at the hoard before you, then it is more likely to have been someone from the old regime.'

'But that means we will never have it,' said Evett, disappointed.

'Yes,' agreed Chaloner. 'It does.'

It was nearing two o'clock, and Chaloner was ready to leave the Tower, hopefully never to return, but Evett had other ideas, and led him towards the long, timber-framed house in the south-west corner, where the Lieutenant had his offices.

'The Earl said he did not want—' began Chaloner, seeing what the captain intended to do.

'He said not to talk to Pepys or Wade, who would be clamouring for their share. But Robinson has no vested interest, so I do not see why we should not discuss the matter with him. And you need all the help you can get. Besides, I like Robinson. He is a good man.'

'Can he be trusted?'

'Yes, probably. Incidentally, he is a member of the Brotherhood, but is sensitive about secrecy. If you want his help, you should not mention that you know about it.'

Chaloner frowned. 'This is an odd organisation – some members open, and others furtive.'

'That is why it will not survive long term. It cannot even agree about a basic thing like secrecy.'

Chaloner grabbed his arm before he could tap on the door. 'This is not a good idea.'

Evett shrugged him off. 'Do not be such a lily! You will be all right, as long as you watch what you say. And anyway, if you glance to your right, you will see Kelyng and Bennet standing between us and the gate. Robinson gave them a dungeon here, and they use it to frighten people into giving them information, although Kelyng spends most of his time fussing over the beasts in the menagerie. We cannot leave without passing them, and I do not want that pair quizzing us about mushrooms. We have enough to worry about, without adding them to the list.'

'Why should they care what we are doing?'

'Clarendon's aide and Thurloe's man together? They will be interested, I assure you.'

The term 'Lieutenant's Lodgings' was a misnomer as far as Robinson was concerned. He owned a mansion on Mincing Lane, and declined to reside in the draughty, rambling edifice that had represented home for his predecessors. He agreed to use the building for Tower business, but only after it had been renovated to his exacting standards of comfort.

That day he was working in a large upper-floor room with wood-panelled walls, a fire in the hearth and a Turkish rug on the floor. He was reading, lips moving silently as he deciphered the words. Standing near the window was the plump girl who had been in the boat with him the previous Friday, her eyes fixed on the yard below. Robinson seemed pleased of the distraction when Evett and Chaloner were announced, and rose to greet them.

'Do you know how much salted beef my soldiers eat

222

each week?' he asked, when introductions had been made. Fanny gave a brief smile that showed her to be pretty in a rotund sort of way, and turned her attention to the bailey again.

'No, sir,' said Chaloner, when Robinson waited for a response and Evett did not supply one.

'Lots,' declared Robinson angrily. 'Herd upon herd disappears down their gullets, and Wade and I can barely keep up with the demand. Come away from the window, Fanny. He will come if he can.' He elaborated in a whisper to his guests. 'It is her birthday, and she longs for a visit from her beau.'

'He promised,' said Fanny. 'Perhaps I should write . . .'

'He will come when he can,' repeated Robinson testily. 'Do not send to him, or he will see you as desperate, and might demand a higher dowry.'

'He would not!' she cried, distressed. 'He would take me for nothing.'

'Yes, dear,' said Robinson. 'But come over here or Bennet will think you are pining for him, and we do not want *his* amorous expectations aroused again.'

Fanny shot away from the window as though it were on fire, and came to stand at her father's side. 'I hear you have been looking for fungus,' she said politely to Chaloner.

'There is a lot of it about,' said Robinson. 'Great orange things growing out of the Bell Tower, rot in the timbers of the Wakefield.' He turned to Evett. 'I do not suppose you had another look for Barkstead's treasure while you were there, did you?'

'No,' said Evett, too quickly, and Chaloner thought that if Pepys and Wade did not surmise that another search had been launched, then it would be a miracle.

Robinson seemed to believe him, though. 'Pity. But we considered Pinchon's description very carefully before we dug, and we all agreed that particular arch was the only likely location. When you did not find it in the first hour, I knew you were harking after a lost cause.'

'What would you have done, if you had been in Barkstead's position, sir?' asked Chaloner. 'As his successor, you are in a position to know better than anyone else how he might have acted.'

Robinson went to the window, and was silent for so long that Chaloner began to suspect he had forgotten the question.

'Bennet will think *you* are hankering after him if you stay there much longer,' said Fanny eventually. 'And he will offer *me* forty silver spoons.'

'I am thinking,' said Robinson tartly. 'I have been asked for my expert opinion.'

'Oh,' said Fanny, chastened.

'I would not have buried it here,' Robinson said, after another lengthy pause. 'I would have picked a hiding place where my money could have been retrieved as and when I needed it. It is not easy to gain access to the Tower, and Barkstead could never have returned here with a spade, even if he had been pardoned and granted his freedom.'

Chaloner nodded, thinking it was a sound assessment, mostly because it concurred with his own. 'So why do you think he lied to Mother Pinchon?'

Robinson raised his hands. 'Perhaps Pepys was right: that Barkstead wanted her to keep working for him, even after he had packed up his gold and could no longer pay her. It is a distasteful conclusion, but times were desperate and there was treachery everywhere.'

224

'He was afraid of being betrayed?' asked Evett. 'By his own servant?'

Robinson arched an eyebrow. 'People are always betraying their friends, their kin, their colleagues. You only have to look at what Downing did to Barkstead . . .' He trailed off, and looked as though he wished he had not spoken, shooting Evett a glance to warn him to silence. He continued, slightly flustered. 'Anyway, suffice to say that Barkstead would not have trusted anyone, not even favourite retainers. If you want another example of distrust and treachery, just remember that odd case . . .' He hesitated again. 'I should not resurrect ancient gossip.'

'It might help,' said Evett hopefully. 'And My Lord Chancellor will be very grateful for anything that leads him to the gold – so he can present it to His Majesty, for bestowing on his subjects.'

Robinson did not look convinced – by the notion of the King's largesse or the usefulness of Clarendon's gratitude – but he shared his story anyway. 'It started shortly after Cromwell died, and the Commonwealth was crumbling under Tumbledown Dick, his son. There was a group of seven men so determined to prevent Charles's return, that they were ready to do *anything* to prevent it.'

'There were more than seven men trying to do that,' said Chaloner, thinking about the many plots that had erupted around the time of the Restoration.

'But *these* seven were well-placed, influential and ruthless. It was rumoured that they were the ones who kept the Commonwealth going for so long.'

'The Commonwealth owed its success to dedicated ministers like Thurloe,' said Fanny, displaying surprising insight. 'The same is true of any government: a few strong

225

men lead the rest. I do not see any special role for these seven mysterious people.'

'Perhaps not,' said Robinson irritably. 'But that is beside the point. I am telling a story here – repeating a rumour – not providing facts. These seven men, who called themselves the Seven—'

'Imaginative,' said Evett with a derisive snigger.

Chaloner's thoughts whirled. Could *this* be what Hewson and Clarke meant when they mentioned the number 'seven'? Was he wrong in assuming it was a code-name for Clarke? He thought about Hewson's words and Clarke's cryptic notes: that Seven were in danger. Were they trying to warn these 'well-placed, influential and ruthless' individuals, or was the connection too far-fetched?

Robinson ignored Evett. '—dedicated themselves to blocking the return of Charles.'

'Then they were not as powerful as they thought,' said Evett. 'The King is king now.'

'They failed because of one man, according to the tale that was rumbling around the exiled Court,' said Robinson, lost in memories. 'This fellow found out about the Seven and told the King, who was suitably grateful – he offered a bar of gold for every name revealed.'

'Do you know the identity of this traitor?' asked Chaloner.

'Traitor?' asked Robinson sharply. 'Most men would say he was a hero to confound such a plot. Which side are you on? But I heard this tale more than three years ago now, and my memory of it is hazy. Rumour had it that his name was Swanning or Swanson or some such thing. I saw him once – a young fellow who sang like an

226

angel. Like my Fanny.' He smiled affectionately at his daughter, who had edged towards the window again.

'Did Swanning get his gold?' asked Chaloner.

'Not when I saw him, because he did not know the Seven's names – only that they existed. I heard he had high hopes of learning them, though, because the Seven had scheduled a meeting, and he was going to eavesdrop.'

'How do you know all this?' asked Chaloner. It sounded like the kind of story told in Royalist homes at Christmas – a brave young Cavalier, valiantly taking on sinister Parliamentarian politicians.

'It was not a secret,' said Robinson. 'It probably should have been, given the delicate nature of Swanning's mission, but you cannot keep much quiet in courts.'

'What happened to Swanning?' asked Chaloner.

Robinson shoved his red wig to the back of his head and scratched his shaven pate. 'Swanning: that does not sound right – his name was not Swanning. But as to what happened, I am not sure. He just disappeared and I never saw him again. I wonder if he did reveal the names of the Seven. I suppose he must have done, because Charles is on the throne.'

'Or they discovered they were not as influential as they thought, and their machinations came to nothing,' suggested Chaloner.

'But this tale goes to prove the point I was trying to make earlier,' said Robinson. 'Men are always betraying each other – they cannot help themselves. Do not perch too comfortably on Clarendon's shoulders, Evett. Great men have farther to fall.'

After a short silence, Evett and Robinson began to discuss the disgraceful state of the navy – not paid for two years, and still expected to defend England against her enemies. Chaloner joined Fanny at the window, wishing Evett would put an end to the discussion, so they could leave.

'An ugly man,' said Fanny, looking disparagingly at the loitering Bennet. 'And a stupid one. I told him I was not interested in his advances – that my heart is tied to another – but he refused to believe me.'

'It could have been worse,' said Chaloner. 'Kelyng might have made the offer. At least Bennet is not old enough to be your grandfather.'

She regarded him earnestly. 'Bennet is the nastiest, most vicious man in the city. I only hope he has not done anything to frighten my Robert away from me. I would not put it past him.'

'Is your Robert intelligent?'

Her eyes gleamed with misty adoration. 'The cleverest fellow in London. My father believes so strongly in his prospects at the Treasury, that he is willing to let us wed now, while he is still poor.'

'Then he has nothing to worry about from Bennet.'

She smiled, and was about to add something else, when a soldier arrived, bearing the news that a lion from the menagerie had eluded its keeper and was on the loose. Robinson grabbed his sword, and the interview came to an abrupt end.

'Go that way,' he ordered, pushing Evett towards a narrow passage between two buildings. 'I do not want you savaged. The Earl will be vexed if he loses his aide. Mind the steps – they are slippery.'

Before Chaloner could say he wanted to collect his weapons first, he had been shunted down the passage to

228

emerge in a yard dominated by towering walls. Evett headed for the nearest gate at a run.

'What is the hurry?' asked Chaloner, trying to keep up with him.

Evett regarded him as though he were insane. 'Lions, man! Do you not know how dangerous they can be? And the one in the Tower is particularly fierce, because close confinement has sent it insane.'

'Robinson should give it the run of Barkstead's cellar then. There are enough rats down there to keep it happy for years.'

'It wants human prey,' said Evett, glancing around him in a way that suggested growing panic. 'I am uneasy, Heyden. We have no swords, and it is too quiet here.'

'We should go back to the main gate,' said Chaloner, skidding to a standstill. He did not like the notion of moving deeper inside the Tower, although he was not unduly worried about the lion. The ones he had seen in captivity had been pathetic, mangy beasts, with rotten teeth and broken claws.

Evett grabbed his arm. 'No, come this way.'

Reluctantly, Chaloner followed him through a series of doors, then down some unlit steps. Water slopped on stone, swishing softly in the darkness, and he supposed they were near the Thames.

'Traitors' Gate,' said Evett, indicating a low, river-filled vault dominated by a pair of iron-barred doors. They stood open. 'We can take a boat from here.'

Chaloner shuddered. He had passed Traitors' Gate often enough, although he had never had cause to go through it. He knew only a handful of prisoners had ever made the one-way journey through its dismal portals, and its reputation was wildly exaggerated, but he felt uncomfortable nonetheless. He glanced around, taking in the dripping roof, slick steps and slime-coated walls. A boat was tied to a pier, oars ready. And then he saw something else: a pair of gleaming eyes.

'I think the lion is in here,' he said.

'Stop it,' ordered Evett sharply. 'I am uneasy enough, without you trying to unnerve me.'

'I am serious. It is looking right at us.'

Evett's jaw dropped in horror as the animal began to move. 'Oh, God! What shall we do?'

'We keep calm for a start,' said Chaloner curtly. He watched the beast settle on its haunches and peer at them. It was now close enough to pounce. 'Do you have a dagger?'

'Of course not. I left it at the gate, as we were told.'

Chaloner leaned down and removed the knife from his boot. He handed it to Evett, while he kept the one from his sleeve.

Evett gaped at him. 'You were ordered to disarm.'

'Then we are lucky I declined. Please do not twitch – you are attracting its attention.'

'They will never look for it in here,' said Evett shakily. The weapon slipped from his trembling fingers and he bent to retrieve it, while the lion looked on with interested eyes. 'Cats do not like water. It will kill us long before they search this part of the Tower. Sweet Jesus, Heyden, it is standing up!'

'I thought you were a soldier.' Chaloner was unimpressed. 'Pull yourself together.'

'I *am* a soldier, but I have not been trained to fight slathering beasts.'

'Think of it as Cromwell, then,' suggested Chaloner. The lion was not a particularly fierce specimen, and

230

Evett was armed with a blade. 'Or Buckingham.'

Suddenly, Evett elbowed him out of the way and made a dash for the boat. He did not get far before he lost his footing, and went bouncing down the stairs, wailing as he went. The lion and Chaloner watched his antics in astonishment.

'Robinson told you to mind your footing.'

When Evett seemed incapable of standing, Chaloner walked carefully towards him and took his elbow. As he did so, he noticed a rope had been placed across the third stair. He inspected it curiously. It had been rubbed with slime from the walls, so was virtually invisible to anyone using the steps. It was a potentially lethal hazard, and Evett was fortunate he had not cracked his skull. Chaloner wondered who had put it there, and supposed it was someone's idea of a practical joke, albeit a very dangerous one.

As soon as he was upright, Evett lurched for the boat and tried to push it away from the pier. With silent grace, the lion sprang from its perch and made its way towards them. Evett tore wildly at the knot that moored the little craft, but his fingers were clumsy with terror. The lion swayed towards Chaloner, then pounced, while Evett's shriek of fright echoed shockingly in the damp chamber.

The sudden weight of a fully grown lion was too much for Chaloner's fragile balance on the slick steps, and he went down hard. The dagger flew from his hand. He gripped the creature's throat, fingers disappearing into thick, oily fur as he sought to keep its teeth away from his neck. It batted him with its paw, and he noticed its claws were sheathed. He shoved it, and it backed away obediently.

'It is tame,' he said, beginning to laugh as he stood

up. 'The poor creature probably escaped to stretch its legs. Those cages are very small.'

Evett was unconvinced. He grabbed Chaloner's knife and hurled it at the lion. The weapon clattered harmlessly against the wall.

'No!' snapped Chaloner, interposing himself between them. 'You will hurt it.'

'Then help me with this,' pleaded Evett, scrabbling desperately at the painter. 'I do not trust it.'

Chaloner staggered when the lion placed its paws on his shoulders again. It stank of old meat and urine, and he wondered whether the scent would cling to him, so Metje would notice it that night. If she did, he wondered how he would explain it – and whether she would believe him if he told her the truth. He unravelled the knot that tethered the boat, struggling to keep the lion away from the cowering Evett, then jumped into the craft and propelled it out on to the river. The cat watched, tail swishing behind it. Someone shouted when they emerged, and Chaloner saw soldiers on the wall above, pointing weapons. He supposed, from their hostile stance, that they assumed a pair of prisoners were making a bid for freedom, and was obliged to nudge Evett with his foot, to make him say something to stop them from being shot at.

Evett tried to stand, but his legs would not support him, so he identified himself sitting. Robinson appeared, and ordered his men to stand down. He raised a hand in farewell as they floated away, and Chaloner heard wheedling calls emanating from the gate – the keeper was trying to seduce his charge back into his tender care. Evett made a sudden lurch and was sick over the side. Chaloner looked away as he rowed to the nearest jetty,

232

intending to see the boat returned to its rightful owners as soon as possible. He did not want to be accused of stealing Crown property.

'You must think me a fool,' said Evett in a low voice, wiping his mouth on the back of his hand.

Chaloner nodded. 'A coward, too. I would not like to go into battle with you.'

'Well, that is honest,' said Evett, attempting a smile. It emerged as a grimace. 'I have had a deep fear of wild animals ever since I saw a bear chew the head from its owner as a child. I do not like . . . and a lion . . .' He trailed off with a shudder.

'I cannot imagine you encounter them very often.'

'More than you might think. The King is stocking the royal parks with all manner of dangerous creatures – vicious, bronze-coloured birds with long tails and nasty, slashing beaks.'

'Pheasants?'

'And in White Hall, there are dogs *everywhere*.'

'Dogs are not dangerous creatures,' Chaloner pointed out.

'The King's are: massive things with dripping teeth. I hate them all. Why do you think I want to be Lord High Admiral? Because you do not get rampaging animals on ships.'

'Well, we are away from it now,' said Chaloner, thinking him deranged. 'Who is Lee?'

'What?' Evett blinked stupidly at the abrupt change of subject.

'When I was talking to Fanny, I saw a report you had written for Robinson about your previous searches for the treasures. It was on the window sill, waiting to be filed. It mentioned a Mr Lee, as well as Wade and Pepys.'

233

'Lee is just a clerk. Robinson suggested we involve him, because he is quick at counting money and we were anticipating barrels of the stuff.'

'Why did you not mention him before?'

Evett shrugged. 'Why would I? I did not mention all the soldiers who wielded spades for us, either. None is relevant to the enquiry, and there is no point in me wasting your time.'

Chaloner was not so sure. 'According to your report, Lee lives near the Tower – Thames Street. I suggest we visit him. We cannot talk to Pepys and Wade, but no one has warned us away from Lee.'

'Now?' asked Evett. 'It must be almost three o'clock. It will be dark in an hour or so.'

'Now,' said Chaloner, easing the boat into the dock near Tower Wharf. A man in royal livery was waiting to collect it, although he said he would wait until the lion was in its cage before rowing back.

'But it is tame,' said Chaloner, puzzled.

The man tapped his temple. 'Its wits are stewed. Sometimes it is as gentle as a kitten, but other times it is vicious. Even its keeper cannot predict which it will be.'

Chaloner led Evett along Thames Street until they located the clerk's house. It was a tumbledown affair, leaning precariously between two equally unsteady neighbours, and no one answered their knocks. Evett, regaining his composure, suggested that Lee was probably at work, since it was a Wednesday, and would have no reason to be home. Chaloner stared at the windows.

'No,' said Evett, guessing what was in his mind. 'I will not break in. It is illegal.'

'We should not do it at the front,' agreed Chaloner. 'Too public.'

234

He made his way to the rear of the property, only to find it unlocked. He inspected the door carefully, then stood back to assess the rest of the building. A window was broken, and he could see someone sitting on a chair in the chamber within. He pointed out the shattered pane to Evett.

'So?' asked the aide. 'Glass is expensive to replace, and Lee will not earn a huge salary at the Treasury. We should go *there* and talk to him, since it appears to be important to you.'

Chaloner opened the door, standing well back as he did so. He knew what he was about to find. The familiar odour of death was not overpowering, because the weather was cold, but it was strong enough to tell him that Lee had been past caring about broken windows for several days.

'Is that him?' he asked, pointing to the figure that sat at the table. 'Is that Lee?'

# Chapter 7

For the second time that day, Evett retched while Chaloner looked in the opposite direction. Then the captain hovered in the doorway, offering to 'keep watch' while Chaloner searched the house, although there was no longer any danger – whoever had murdered Lee had been gone for days. Chaloner left the unhappy aide outside and stood next to the body, hands on hips as he looked around.

The little room was the home of a man who lived frugally, either from choice or necessity. There was a table, a chair and a bench, while pots and pans, all scrupulously clean, sat on shelves above the fireplace. A set of stairs, so steep and narrow that most people would have deemed them a ladder, led to an attic. Chaloner climbed them, but the loft was bare except for a bed with neatly folded covers. He poked the floorboards and knocked on the plaster walls, but there was nothing to find.

He returned to the lower chamber and completed a similar search, aware of Evett chatting to a water-seller outside. He knelt in the hearth and peered up the chimney, jumping back when his probing released an avalanche of soot. Then he turned his attention to the table. Three cups stood on it, and when he lifted one and sniffed its contents, he detected the distinctive aroma of wine. Lee had been enjoying a drink with two companions when he had died. However, there was nothing to suggest they had shared his fate. Had one of them killed him? Chaloner tapped a forefinger on his chin, looking from Lee to the broken window and back again.

Then he assessed the body, noting its relaxed posture, with one hand resting on the table and the other folded in its lap, and was sure death had come as a surprise. But what about Lee's companions? Had they expected it? Or had the attack been startling for them, too? Chaloner looked more closely at Lee's hands, and saw something caught between his fingers. He removed it carefully, but the house was no place to study such a find, so he put it in his pocket to examine later.

When he had finished, he rejoined Evett. The water-seller had gone and Evett was full of questions, but Chaloner motioned him to silence as he led the way to Botolph's Wharf, where they hired a boat to carry them to White Hall. The sun had managed to burst through the clouds during the afternoon, and was setting in a blaze of orange. The boatman began to row with clean, strong stokes, hurrying to deliver them before dusk, and they sat in the stern, so they could talk without being overheard.

'Do you know Latin or French?' asked Chaloner in a low voice. 'It would be safer.'

'French would not,' Evett pointed out. 'He would think we were Catholic spies. I speak Dutch, though. I learned when I was in exile with Clarendon, but I do not suppose you—'

237

'Good,' said Chaloner, pleased to use the tongue he knew best. 'Who would want to kill Lee?'

'You cannot assume his death had anything to do with Barkstead's treasure,' said Evett, pronouncing each word carefully. He was not comfortable with the language. 'It was a burglary. There are slums all around here, and that water-seller just told me thefts occur every night.'

'Lee's house was not burgled. When we first arrived, I saw five pounds in coins on the downstairs window sill, and a thief would have had that, if nothing else.'

'Then the villain was disturbed,' argued Evett. 'He killed Lee, but heard someone coming. No man wants to be caught in a house with a corpse, so he fled before he could profit from his crime.'

'That is possible, but when the body went undiscovered, the robber would have returned to finish what he had started. Also, I have never met a thief who would abandon that much silver when it was sitting in full view, no matter how pressed for time – not even a thief who lives in the splendour of White Hall.' He stared hard at Evett, to let him see he knew what the man had done.

Evett had the grace to blush. 'I took the money for Clarendon – to make sure the constables did not steal it. I spotted it when you were upstairs.'

But Chaloner was not interested in Evett's colourful ethics. 'How well did you know Lee?'

'We met on four occasions – the four times I went to dig in the Tower. Robinson told me he was a good man, and he seemed honest enough. He worked in the Treasury, counting money.'

'How did Robinson know him? Surely a Lord Mayor does not mingle with clerks?'

238

'Lee was the kinsman of some friend. You will have to ask Robinson.'

Chaloner was annoyed with Evett. 'Is there anything else about this treasure that may have slipped your mind? You are supposed to be helping me, and neglecting to mention one of the men involved in the initial search is not the way to go about it.'

Evett considered carefully, taking no offence at the accusatory nature of the comment – or perhaps his Dutch was not good enough to allow him to detect it. 'No, there is nothing, and I really do not think Lee's death has anything to do with the treasure. I saw nearly all the soldiers who did the actual spadework today. Why should Lee, who is insignificant, be killed, and the rest of us left alive?'

'We saw Pepys this morning, but what about Wade? Are you sure he is living?'

'He and I exchanged words when you were in the cellar. He came to ask what you were doing.'

'What did you tell him?' asked Chaloner uneasily.

'That I had lost a ring and sent servants to look for it. Do not worry. I can dissemble when necessary. Did you learn anything when you searched Lee's house?'

'No,' lied Chaloner. 'Why? What did you expect me to find?'

'*I* did not expect you to find anything, as I told you to start with. *I* think it was a botched robbery. How did he die?'

'Shot with a crossbow,' replied Chaloner. 'I imagine a gun was not used, because the killer did not want to make a noise. There was no evidence of a fight, and there were empty cups on the table. I think he was drinking wine with guests when it happened.'

239

'And one shot him?' Evett was incredulous. 'Crossbows are large weapons, and I do not see even a gentle clerk like Lee sipping claret while his killer wound and aimed one at him. You do not need to be a spy to deduce that!'

'No one in the house killed him. You remember the broken window? Someone stood outside and shot him, smashing the glass in the process. His drinking companions may have known what was going to happen, or it may have been as big a shock to them as it must have been to Lee. However, if the former is true, then they must be cool customers. I would not sit next to someone about to be assassinated – not unless I had absolute faith in the marksman, and probably not even then.'

Evett was thoughtful. 'So who is this furtive killer? I can tell you think it was someone who believed Lee had information about the treasure.'

'Actually, I do not think that. Dispatching Lee would not help the killer find the hoard, because obviously the information would die with him. So, perhaps the intention was not to *learn* the location of the gold, but to prevent Lee from telling anyone else about it.'

Evett stared at him. 'That is convoluted reasoning.'

'Yes, perhaps it is.' Chaloner leaned back in the boat and tipped his hat over his eyes, not wanting to talk any more. Evett was a pleasant enough fellow, but he was not very bright – or perhaps he was just not at his best after dealing with lions and corpses – and seemed incapable of making insightful suggestions. Chaloner thought about the item he had retrieved from Lee: the scrap of paper. He had no firm evidence, but he believed Lee had been holding a document when he had died. Afterwards, someone – although whether a companion or the killer

240

was impossible to say – had snatched it from him, but in the hurry it had torn, leaving a fragment behind. The writing was tiny, and it was in cipher. He would try to decode it that evening, before Metje came.

'I do not think we should tell the Earl any of this,' said Evett, somewhat out of the blue.

Chaloner was surprised. 'Why not? And speak Dutch, especially when you are talking about Clarendon. He may not be the only one with spies paid to listen to idle chatter.'

'Lord!' muttered Evett. 'And you wonder why I joined the Brotherhood! Are you content to have agents listening to your every word, and never daring to say what you think?'

'I am used to it. And you had better inure yourself, too, if you want to be of use to the Earl.'

'I joined the Brotherhood for him, you know,' said Evett resentfully. 'I believe in its aims, of course, but all they do is talk. They never *act*, because they are too busy arguing with each other.'

'Did he ask you to enrol, or did you do it of your own volition?'

'The former. Downing let slip something about it once, and Clarendon sent me to find out more. I stalked Downing for a few days, and eventually the fraternity met. I told Clarendon it was all perfectly innocent, but he asked Downing whether I could join anyway. Did you know Thurloe founded it?'

Chaloner only just managed to keep the surprise from his face. 'Did he?'

'He seems a decent man. It is a pity he spent the last ten years working for the other side.'

And which side was that? wondered Chaloner. He

241

changed the subject. 'Why should we not tell the Earl about Lee?'

'Because he may order me to look into that death, too, and I have my hands full with Clarke. I do not want to spend weeks probing Lee's personal affairs, only to learn I was right all along, and that he was killed by a burglar. I *hate* that kind of work.' He hesitated, and a crafty expression stole across his face. 'If you agree to say nothing about Lee, I will tell you something about the treasure that Clarendon ordered me to keep to myself.'

'Very well.'

'Can I trust you?'

'You can trust me not to mention Lee to anyone else. What is this secret?'

'Mother Pinchon. Clarendon ordered me to watch Wade's house after that first night of digging, and I saw a crone come to visit him – probably to claim her hundred pounds. When she left, I followed her to the Fleet Rookery, but she ducked down one of those wretched alleys and I lost her. I do wish the Earl would not give me such missions. I hope to God he will pass such tasks to you from now on, and let me learn about the navy instead.'

'So, Pinchon does exist,' mused Chaloner. 'I thought Wade had made her up – that Barkstead had told *him* the location of the hoard, and he invented someone to take the blame if things went wrong.'

'What a suspicious mind you have,' said Evett in distaste. 'She exists, and she probably lives near Turnagain Lane, since that is where I lost her. I would have asked the locals, but they were not of a mind to chat, and I was lucky to escape with my life.'

'Why did Clarendon order you to keep the Pinchon episode quiet?'

242

'He does not want you to think us incompetent. Will you try to find her?'

Chaloner nodded. 'Tonight.'

'Do you mind if I decline to come with you? I did not enjoy it much the last time I went.'

'Not at all.' Chaloner leaned back in the seat again, and closed his eyes, thinking about the cipher from Lee, and wondering whether he would be able to unravel the code. If he could, then he would have two leads to follow: Mother Pinchon and whatever he learned from the document. Or was he being overly optimistic? He had assumed Lee's death was connected to the treasure, but perhaps Evett was right and it was not. He did not dwell too long on the matter. Answers would come soon enough.

Chaloner and Evett did not speak again until the boatman pulled into the pier near White Hall and let them off. It was a long journey, but the tide was with them, so they were able to pass under the London Bridge without disembarking to meet the boat on the other side – the starlings that formed the bridge's feet funnelled the water into treacherous rapids when the river was in full spate. Once the sun had set, the city assumed shades of grey and brown. Red roof tiles showed their dusting of black soot, and the once-pristine washes on the bankside houses became the colour of old pewter. Buildings clawed towards the darkening sky in a confusion of chimneys, gables and garrets, their uneven lines punctuated by the taller, stronger masses of churches. Rising above it all, like a stately galleon on a turbulent sea, was the mighty bulk of St Paul's with its myriad buttresses and pinnacles.

The city rang with sound, even on the Thames.

Hundreds of craft still plied their trade, some carrying passengers, who shouted greetings to each other, and some ferrying the goods that were needed to keep the metropolis grinding on – grain from Lincolnshire, wool from Suffolk, coal from the north. A quay was being repaired, and the rattle of hammers and saws, along with the urgent yells of a foreman keen to squeeze the very last moment of light from the dying day, drifted across the water. Boats were being unloaded by winches that creaked and groaned, and people were everywhere, buying, selling, walking, working, picking pockets, shopping, scavenging.

Chaloner was hungry, and wanted to eat something before he inspected the place where Clarke's body had been found, but Evett was keen to press on, claiming that since Chaloner had managed to deduce so much from the place where Lee had died, then he could now do the same for Clarke. He strode under the Holbein Gate, and opened an inconspicuous door that led to a dank passage and then the servants' quarters. He led the way along several unlit corridors that he said were only ever used by the below-stairs staff, and Chaloner was astonished to see spyholes cut into the wood, affording views of the sumptuous chambers on the other side. He pointed them out to Evett.

'We did not put them there,' said the captain defensively. 'This wing is said to have been built by the eighth King Henry, who was fond of that sort of thing. So was Queen Elizabeth, who also spent money here. Clarendon constantly orders them blocked, but people keep poking them open again.'

'Are they concealed within paintings or murals?' asked Chaloner. As an intelligence-gathering agent, it was the kind of thing that interested him, particularly if he was going to work at the palace.

'Some are, while others are hidden behind statues or furniture. Here is one of the chambers used by Lady Castlemaine. She is in it now.' He swallowed, and his voice became unsteady. 'Naked.'

Chaloner peered through another hole. He had heard a lot about Lady Castlemaine, and was keen to see her for himself. Loyally, he thought she was nothing compared with Metje: her face was small and rather catlike, and it was not difficult to imagine her being spiteful. However, even her harshest critics could not deny that her body was about as near to perfection as it was possible to be, with perfectly proportioned limbs, exquisite curves and alabaster skin.

'Metje is better,' he declared, after a period of detailed study. 'Rubens himself could not have made her more beautiful.'

Evett raised his eyebrows. 'She must be a veritable Madonna. You must introduce us.'

'You have enough women of your own.'

'Two wives and someone special,' acknowledged Evett. 'I am in love again, thinking of extending my harem. But I was not going to seduce Metje: I just wanted to see her. When will you marry?'

'She will not have me until I secure a permanent post with Clarendon.'

'Then unless she wants to be a widow, she should encourage you to look elsewhere. You seem a decent fellow, Heyden, and poor Simon's fate keeps preying on my mind – I do not want you to go the same way. Why not apply to the Treasury? They are always looking for clerks.'

245

'That would be safe,' remarked Chaloner caustically. 'Just ask Lee.'

Evett was suddenly more interested in what was happening on the other side of the hole 'That is Buckingham with her,' he whispered disapprovingly. He squinted and angled his head to one side as she released a moan of delight and Buckingham sniggered. 'What are they doing?'

Chaloner pushed him gently, to make him move on, but Evett was intrigued by the curious positions the lovers had adopted, and refused to budge. Chaloner shoved him harder, then glanced through the gap in alarm when Evett stumbled against the panelling hard enough to make a substantial thud. The two people entwined on the bed either had not noticed or did not care, because they showed no sign of interrupting their antics to investigate.

'This is where Clarke died,' said Evett, when they reached a hallway that was somewhat more public than the ones they had just travelled. 'He was found at dawn, and I was the one who had to take his body to the river – Clarendon thought it was unwise to have rumours about murder in the royal household. All these chambers are used as offices by palace administrators during the day.'

'And at night?'

'They are empty, as you can see. The clerks do not work after dark, because the light in this wing is poor, and it is too expensive to provide them all with lamps.'

'So, these offices are always empty after dusk? This corridor is deserted?'

'Not necessarily. Some of the King's celebrations are very wild, and his barons copulate everywhere – with any woman who possesses the requisite body parts, usually. Because these rooms are relatively secluded, they are occasionally used by those who exercise discretion in their trysts.'

'Using a clerk's office is being discreet, is it?' Chaloner was amused.

Evett nodded with great seriousness. 'Yes, when the rest of them use the public rooms. I like women, as you know, but even I disapprove of the Court's behaviour. The common people are beginning to mutter about it, and the King should be setting a moral example, not engaging in orgies every night of the week – or at least, not orgies that everyone knows about.'

Chaloner shrugged. 'The problem lies not in the Court's decadence, but in the fact that it follows so hard on the heels of Cromwell's strictures. One was too repressive, and the other too free. I think it is the contrast that unsettles people.'

'Moderation,' said Evett with a grin. 'We are there again. At every turn I am proven right.'

Chaloner turned his attention back to the hall. 'So, in essence, anyone can come here? It is used mostly by servants and clerks, but courtiers have access, too? Especially at night?'

'Yes. The killer took quite a risk in choosing it for his crime.'

Chaloner rubbed his chin, thinking about the deserted tunnels he had just travelled, which would have been far better places to commit a stealthy murder. 'Perhaps you should consider the possibility that the culprit is someone who does not know White Hall very well.'

Evett was unimpressed by this. 'But Buckingham knows White Hall like the back of his hand, and so does Downing. Even Kelyng and Bennet have a working knowledge of the place, because they come here to report to the King. Your suggestion will take me away from my main suspects.'

Chaloner pointed to the floor. 'Is that blood?'

Evett nodded. 'The maids scrubbed and scrubbed, but it will not come out.'

Chaloner bent to examine the mark, which was huge and suggested Clarke had bled profusely. 'A proficient assassin would never have made such a mess, so perhaps he was stabbed by someone unused to killing – someone who does not know how to do it with a minimum amount of spillage.'

Evett regarded him askance. 'The things you say! But I suspect few courtiers have experience of actual slaughter, although I imagine Buckingham has done it, and Kelyng and Bennet certainly have. What about Downing? Has he stabbed anyone in the past?'

'I do not know. Was the knife left with Clarke's body?'

Evett pulled a blade from his belt, making Chaloner step back instinctively. 'Easy! I am no silent assassin – especially in a half-public hallway like this one. I have taken to carrying this dagger around with me, in the hope that someone might recognise it, but no one has, as yet.'

Chaloner was not surprised, since recognition might go hand in hand with an accusation of murder. He inspected the weapon. It was a fine one, with a jewelled hilt. He thought it unlikely that a servant would have owned it, because it was far too valuable to have been left behind. He said as much to Evett, who looked pleased.

'Good. That means I can concentrate on my wealthier suspects – such as Buckingham.'

'Do not allow your judgement to be clouded by dislike,' warned Chaloner. 'If you look for clues that point only to him, you may miss evidence directing you towards the real culprit.'

Evett nodded, although Chaloner had the feeling the advice would be ignored, and pointed to the dagger. 'What else can you tell me about it?'

Chaloner turned it over in his hands. 'It is small, which means it was probably concealed. The killer could have hidden it in his hand, then turned and struck upwards. Like this.'

Evett did not enjoy playing the role of victim with a sharp blade slicing through the air towards him. He jumped away in alarm. 'And how does knowing that help us?'

'It suggests a sudden attack, which left Clarke no time to defend himself. It also indicates that he did not suspect the person intended to harm him.' Chaloner was thinking aloud. 'He may have been lured – he followed the killer here, perhaps with the promise of information or a tryst.'

'Not a tryst,' said Evett. 'Clarke liked *women*, and would never have let himself be seduced by Buckingham, Downing or Kelyng's fellows. So, one of them must have promised information – perhaps about the missing knives from the kitchen.'

'Perhaps,' said Chaloner cautiously, thinking about the coded messages discovered in Clarke's secret pocket. He had obviously been investigating something other than the theft of silverware, and might well have gone to the hall in the hope of learning something useful – perhaps about praising God or the Seven.

Evett sighed, then threw up his hands in exasperation. 'Questions and speculation! That is all there is with this case. I *hate* this kind of work! I wish I was someone else's aide.'

Chaloner smiled ruefully. 'And I have no idea how to find Barkstead's treasure, so I suggest we both leave White Hall before the Earl sees us and demands a progress report.'

Evett led the way out of the corridor, and Chaloner was uneasy to note it emerged in the wing where Clarendon had his rooms. Almost immediately, the Lord Chancellor waddled out of his office, driving a crowd of petitioners before him like a flock of geese. Chaloner tried to escape while the rabble took issue about their abrupt dismissal, but Clarendon spotted him and cocked a chubby forefinger, beckoning agent and aide into his office with one hand, while he flapped away his clamouring visitors with the other. Chaloner complied, wishing he had something more to tell his new employer than 'questions and speculations'.

When he entered the Earl's chamber, the first thing he saw was a peculiarly shaped object, crazed with cracks and knobbly with glue: he had been right when he had predicted that repairing the crystal vase was impossible. He also noticed Clarendon's desk had been cleared, and sensitive documents no longer sat in full view. Of course, he thought grimly, with six of his seven agents dead, there were probably very few secret reports coming to him.

'Have you made a will, Heyden?' asked the Earl, closing the door behind them.

Chaloner regarded him warily. 'I do not own any property, sir.'

'None at all? Thurloe told me you had a bass viol.'

'Why do you want to know?' Unease made the question more curt than Chaloner had intended.

'A will would be helpful in the event of . . . well, you do not need me to tell you that your kind of work can be dangerous. Talk to Thurloe. He should be able to draft something out for you.'

'Is life at White Hall so perilous, then, My Lord?' asked Chaloner, aware of Evett's frantic signals, urging him to say nothing that would reveal he had been told about the sad fate of Lane and the others.

The Lord Chancellor gave a patently false smile. 'Not at all, except for poor Clarke, of course. All the others are in fine fettle, and are very happy working for me.'

'Good,' said Chaloner coolly. 'Because Simon Lane is a friend of mine.'

'Was he?' muttered Clarendon unhappily. 'Damn!' He cleared his throat and became businesslike. 'Have you been looking for my treasure today?'

The use of the possessive pronoun did not escape Chaloner's attention, and he wondered whether the man planned to keep the entire seven thousand pounds for himself. His anxiety deepened, knowing perfectly well that while Clarendon was unlikely to be hanged for defrauding the King, the agent who abetted him would be tried by a different set of laws altogether.

'He has not found it yet,' said Evett, when Chaloner did not reply.

'Well, keep looking,' ordered the Earl. He seemed out of sorts, and Chaloner supposed the petitioners' demands had annoyed him, along with the reminder that six spies had died doing his bidding. 'It will turn up. Lost objects always do.'

'We have just come from the Tower,' said Evett conversationally. 'You asked me to show Heyden where we dug for the gold. We met Robinson, and there was a lion on

251

the loose. It had escaped, and was looking for someone to eat. Robinson sent us out through the Traitors' Gate, thinking to keep us from its waiting maw, but it almost had us anyway. Someone had tied a rope across the steps that led to the water, obviously intending to see us fall to its mercy.'

'We do not know it was put there for us,' said Chaloner reasonably. Indeed, he strongly suspected it was not, since no one could have predicted they would leave the Tower that way.

Anger crossed Clarendon's face. 'Let me understand you correctly. A lion – presumably the mad one – was released into the Tower grounds when you were in them? It was inside the Traitors' Gate, and Robinson sent you in there with it?'

'I do not think he did it deliberately, sir,' said Evett, although he sounded uncertain.

'Do you not?' shouted the Earl, his temper breaking. 'Do you not? Well I do! It was a deliberate strike against me! He tried to murder my aide *and* my new spy – to make Thurloe angry with me for losing yet another one.' He grimaced, annoyed with himself for the inadvertent admission.

'Robinson wanted *me* dead?' asked Evett, aghast.

'Of course he did,' hissed the Earl. 'Do you not agree, Heyden?'

'I have no idea, sir,' replied Chaloner, wanting to say that he did not think Robinson would waste his time on Evett. He was a pleasant fellow, but hardly represented a threat. 'We had no appointment to visit the Tower, so it would have been a very last-minute attempt.'

But there had actually been plenty of time to organise it, given the number of hours they had spent there.

Robinson had been very determined that they should leave by the Traitors' Gate, and he would also have known that they had been disarmed before they had entered his castle. Then there was the rope: it had been pure luck they had not been injured by it. And the reason for such an attack? Did Robinson want to find Barkstead's treasure, and either keep it for himself or donate it to the Brotherhood? Chaloner thought about Lee, described as a kinsman of one of Robinson's friends. What was going on?

'Robinson saw an opportunity and he seized it,' declared Clarendon angrily. 'For two reasons. First, to weaken me by depriving me of men. And second, because he wants to prevent further searches for the treasure. Go and fetch me some wine, Philip. I am so angry that my heart is all a-flutter.'

Evett disappeared, and some of Clarendon's rage seemed to go with him.

'I thought Robinson had no interest in Barkstead's money,' said Chaloner. 'He was never in line for a share of it.'

'He will have a share if he finds it on his own. I may not be up to Thurloe's standards, Heyden, but I have a few informants in place, and I know for a fact that he went digging himself one night. And I can assure you *he* was not looking for mushrooms.'

'He will not find it, sir,' said Chaloner, supposing the same people had also reported Evett's excuse for his presence in the Tower that day. 'It is in none of the obvious places.'

The Earl pursed his lips. 'Then you must look in the less obvious ones – before he does. Barkstead had a family. Talk to them and ask where else he might have put it.'

253

'His wife and son – a child of six – are in Holland, and he has no other relatives. Would you like me to travel to the United Provinces and speak to—?"

'No, I would not,' snapped Clarendon. 'Once you are there, you might decide not to come back – I know you are fond of the place and that you keep a Dutch mistress. What about his friends?'

'They were Parliamentarians, either dead, fled or in prison. Those who are incarcerated or in hiding will not betray his trust, and those who are dead cannot.'

'Those in gaol may reconsider their loyalties if we promise them their freedom,' suggested the Earl. 'You can visit them, and see what they say.'

'With respect, sir, they will not parley with me. I do not have the authority to make offers they would trust.'

'I will go, then. I am the Lord Chancellor – they will believe me.'

'I am not sure that is a good idea, either,' said Chaloner, knowing any such approach would be treated with the suspicion it deserved. 'Trouble-makers like Kelyng would accuse you of treason before you had asked Robinson for the keys to their cells.'

Clarendon scowled, giving the impression that promises would have been made with no intention of honouring them. 'He must have had other friends. *Find them.* I want that money!'

Barkstead did have other friends, Chaloner thought, as the Lord Chancellor turned on his heel and stalked away. He had the Brotherhood. Chaloner saw he would be spending the next few days interviewing its senior members, and hoped one would give him a clue that might take him forward. And then there was Mother Pinchon. Perhaps there was a detail she had forgotten, which skilled questioning might shake loose. He was planning his strategy when the Earl turned around.

Chaloner was startled by the transformation. Gone was the fussy little fellow who had almost stamped his feet in impotent rage, and he was replaced by something far more unnerving, leaving Chaloner with the absolute conviction that here was a man who would have what he wanted. For the first time, he understood how Clarendon had risen to become Lord Chancellor of England.

'You had better not fail me, *Chaloner*,' he said in a soft voice. He did not need to add threats. The tone of his voice spoke them all.

Night had fallen by the time Chaloner left White Hall, and lamps were set along some roads in compliance with the city fathers' ordinances. But mostly, the highways were dark, and there was already a different kind of crowd emerging to slouch along them. Chaloner was not worried about street ruffians. One hand rested on the hilt of his sword, and the other on the dagger at his waist, and the weapons would be out without conscious thought at the first sign of danger. One man tried to bump into him as he walked, probably to pick his pocket, but Chaloner side-stepped him and the fellow staggered into nothing. Linksmen with pitch torches wanted him to pay them to light his way, while beggars in doorways snatched at him as he passed. He rummaged for change, but his purse was empty. He was hungry himself and could not even find a farthing for a pie.

He had intended to go home, to resolve his differences with Metje, but first he stopped at St Martin-in-the-Fields, where the vicar showed him five wooden crosses in the churchyard. There was a sixth, too – a mound of earth that the minister said would soon be covered by a stone memorial. It was being prepared at Thurloe's expense, and would be ready the following week. Chaloner was used to losing colleagues, but was unsettled by the graves of so many in such a small space, and was sorry that Simon Lane should be among them.

He took his leave of the priest, relieved to be away from the graveyard. Despite the fact that it adjoined the Strand, with its bright shops and busy traffic, St Martin's cemetery was a bleak place, and the diversion had depressed him. He knew it was the wrong time to repair his rift with Metje, since they would almost certainly argue again if he was morose. So, since Lincoln's Inn was not far, he decided to speak to Thurloe about some of the facts he had learned. He wanted to ask the ex-Spymaster whether he had indeed founded the Brotherhood, whether he knew anything about the Seven, and what Clarke and Hewson – and possibly the five dead agents – might have been investigating on his behalf. Thurloe had not actually lied to him, but he had not been wholly honest, either, and if Chaloner was to solve Clarke's murder, then he needed the truth.

He walked to Lincoln's Inn, keeping to the left side of Chancery Lane, which was better lit and less potholed than the right. It was a cold evening, and he supposed it was clear, but the sky was masked by a pall of smoke from thousands of fires, which blotted out any stars that might have been visible. The air stank of burning wood, overlain with a sharper tang that made him wonder whether more snow was in the offing. For the second time in as many days, a memory surfaced of a childhood Christmas, when the hall of his father's manor was bright gold with candlelight, and the rafters were adorned with holly and mistletoe. Pine cones on the fire, spiced wine and sweet oranges added to the heady aroma of celebration. He remembered laughing at something his oldest brother had said, something that still made him smile, and wondered whether he could share the joke with Metje without revealing too much about his family. He was sure she would find it amusing, and was assailed with the realisation that he missed being able to talk openly about people he loved.

He reached Lincoln's Inn, and trudged towards Dial Court, shivering as the wind gusted hard and cold. Thurloe had seen him coming through the window, and the door to his quarters was ajar. A fire blazed, as usual, and the room was full of the scent of a good dinner – roasted meat, baked parsnips, boiled fowl, and a pear tart to follow – but the dishes on the table were empty, and only a pile of gnawed bones remained.

'I expect you have already eaten,' said Thurloe, going to his customary seat at the hearth. 'But join me in a glass of milk with honey. I always find milk soothes the stomach and reduces night terrors.'

Chaloner accepted – he would have taken anything offered at that moment – and scalded his mouth when he tried to swallow it too soon. Thurloe liked his milk boiling. He also liked it sweet enough to be sickly, so the resulting potion was more syrup than drink. Chaloner set it by the hearth to cool, intending on finishing every last drop, no matter how vile it tasted. There was no food at home, and Thurloe's sugary potion was the only thing he was likely to get that day.

'The Lord Chancellor told me I should make a will,' he said, when Thurloe waited for him to state the purpose of his visit. 'He thought you might be able to help.'

Thurloe stared at him in surprise. 'Why were you discussing such a topic?'

'I imagine because Clarke is not the only agent to have met an early end in his service. The other five you sent are dead, too, and he was advising me to take precautions against intestacy.'

The colour drained from Thurloe's face. 'What?'

'I have just seen their graves in St Martin's churchyard, and their names are in the parish register.'

Thurloe massaged his eyes with unsteady fingers. 'Here is a detail the Earl neglected to mention when he asked for more men. I would not have obliged, had I known. All five are dead?'

Chaloner nodded, and they sat in silence for a while, the only sound being the wind gusting outside and the fire popping in the hearth.

'I sent him about forty names,' said Thurloe eventually. 'Clerks and men skilled at administration. But only six spies, counting Clarke.' He shook his head slowly. 'I should take you away from him before he buries you, too. I knew there was an element of risk – old intelligence officers working for a new regime – but I thought my people could look after themselves. What have I done?'

'It is not your fault, sir. Presumably, they wanted the opportunity you provided, and we all know the dangers of our work.'

'Who killed them?' demanded Thurloe, suddenly angry. 'Kelyng?'

'Possibly. All except Clarke were instructed to watch him or Downing.'

'Downing is a sly villain, but I do not think he solves

258

problems with violence. He was here again today, talking about you. He said you eavesdropped on one of his meetings, and left him no choice but to take you into his confidence.'

Chaloner grimaced at Downing's untruthful version of events. 'He claimed it was to protect himself and his colleagues – by stopping me from asking questions that might alert Kelyng to the Brotherhood's existence. But you never know with him.'

'No, you do not. He has somehow learned that you operate under a false name, and is determined to discover your real identity. He said he would give me fifty pounds if I told him.'

'What did you say?' Fifty pounds was a lot of money, and Chaloner found himself holding his breath for the answer.

'I told him to discuss it with you, although I strongly advise against confiding in him. He will offer protection and friendship, but you should accept neither. Perhaps his intentions are honourable – I think he really does want an end to civil strife – but I cannot forget what he did to Barkstead, Okey and Corbet. He knows he made a serious error of judgement over that, because now even the most ardent of Royalists thinks him a rogue. As regards you, he is probably afraid that the Earl has asked you to catch him out in some way.'

'Then why did he tell me about the Brotherhood? Surely, it would have been better to keep his clandestine dealings to himself?'

'The Brotherhood is not clandestine, Thomas. It is perfectly innocent – which is why he was keen for you to witness a gathering, I imagine. And he is still eager for you to join its ranks, although I stand by my threat

259

to contest your election, should you ignore my advice and decide to accept a nomination. I told him the same thing today: I do not want you involved.'

Chaloner was a little suspicious. 'Why not? People keep telling me its aims are virtuous.'

'For several reasons, the strongest being that Downing is in it, and the less time you spend with him, the better – you made an enemy of him when you argued against his arrest of Barkstead, and I think he means you harm. Another reason is that membership of the Brotherhood costs, and I doubt you have funds to squander in such a way, no matter how worthy the cause.'

That was certainly true, thought Chaloner ruefully, thinking about his empty larder. 'You said you are no longer active, yet it seems Downing still consults you about its affairs.'

Thurloe looked hard at him. 'Because he hopes to entice me back. But I have not attended a meeting in three years – Kelyng watches my every move, and I know exactly what *he* would make of me sitting in a private chamber with Downing, Ingoldsby and the others. He would assume we were plotting, and would order our arrests without bothering to ask what we discuss. It is safer for everyone if I keep my distance. But what have you learned about Clarke's death? Perhaps he and the other five were murdered by the same hand.'

'Evett showed me the place where he was killed. I have scant evidence, but I do not think he was dispatched by a professional assassin. I think he was lured into a hallway, perhaps with the promise of information, and then stabbed. Evett thinks Buckingham did it.'

'Buckingham might hire someone to kill, but I doubt he would bloody his own hands. I appreciate his position:

I have ordered the occasional expedient death myself, but I could never slip my own knife between a man's ribs.'

Chaloner nodded, not sure what to say to such a confidence, and an uncomfortable silence fell until Thurloe spoke again.

'Where did you go today?'

Chaloner recalled his vow to say nothing about Barkstead's gold. He considered inventing a tale that would place him well away from the hunt for the treasure, but several members of the Brotherhood had seen him near the castle, and Robinson had even discussed the matter with him. He decided to stay as close to the truth as possible.

'I went with Evett to the Tower. He was happy to accept my help with Clarke's murder – I do not think he has much stomach for violent death, despite being a soldier.'

'Clarendon told me he has never seen a gun fired in anger. He has great faith in the fellow, so he must have some wits, although he has always seemed rather stupid to me.'

'You know him well?' asked Chaloner, recalling that the last time they had discussed Evett, Thurloe had been wary about admitting an acquaintance with him.

'Well enough to know I would not trust him near my wife. He has two of his own already, and no lady is safe from his amours. I would watch Metje, if I were you, Tom. She is a pretty lady.'

'They will never meet. I do not introduce friends to working colleagues.'

'Very wise,' said Thurloe. 'So, tell me what you did at the Tower today.'

'A lion had escaped, and Evett and I ended up inside the Traitors' Gate with it.'

'Not the mad one?' asked Thurloe, shocked. 'They should shoot the poor thing before it kills someone else. Of course, the problem lies with the King: he does not want a royal menagerie with no lion, but they are expensive and the Court is short of money. What else did you do?'

'Then I went by river to White Hall, where—'

'No prevarication, Thomas, I beg you,' commanded Thurloe sharply. 'Do not forget who I am and what I once did for a living – or the fact that I know you well enough to see when you are lying. I ask you again: what did you do at the Tower?'

Thurloe's blue eyes bored into him, and Chaloner saw it was time to make his choice. He had always known he could not manage two powerful men who demanded his complete loyalty.

'I cannot say, sir.'

Thurloe regarded him expressionlessly. 'Why not?'

'Because I gave Clarendon my word.'

'What about your word to me?'

'I will keep that, too. I would never reveal details of the past – you should know that.'

Thurloe continued to stare. 'Are you sure you are making the right decision today?'

'Not really. However, you told me to do my best for Clarendon – and I made him a promise and I intend to keep it.'

'But you must have broken confidences when you were working abroad. There is no such thing as an honest spy – he would not be able to function!'

'Of course, but that was in an enemy state. And we

262

are not talking about honesty here, but about fidelity.'

Thurloe stared into the fire, and it was some time before he spoke again. 'I own a manor in Essex – one I managed to keep from the Royalists when they confiscated the rest of my property. It is a good place, with fertile soil, streams and woods. You and Metje could live there. You could have children, and let them grow up safely and happily, as you did. What do you say?'

'No,' said Chaloner, acutely uncomfortable. He had been offered bribes in the past, but there was something very sordid in what Thurloe was doing.

'Clarendon will probably cast you aside in a week, and you will be reduced to translating letters for Dalton. But only until Britain breaks with Holland, when you will be lucky not to be hanged as a spy for your knowledge of Dutch. It is not much of a future. Is there *anything* I can offer you, to make you change your mind?'

Chaloner shook his head. 'No, sir.'

'Then we have no more to say to each other. Serve your new master well, Thomas.'

Chaloner stood, a deep sadness washing over him. He had not expected his relationship with Thurloe to end in bribes and corruption, and he was sorry for it. 'Goodnight, sir.'

Chaloner was opening the door when Thurloe called out to him. 'Come back, Tom. You have passed the test – not that I had doubts, but the last three years have made me more suspicious than I once was.'

Chaloner turned to face him. 'Test?'

'Of your integrity. It is difficult to know whom to trust these days, and my friends urged me to make sure of you before I take you further into my confidence. Your uncle would have floundered, but I always knew you were the better man. If you decline to betray someone who has been your patron for three days, then our ten years makes you a true friend. Come and sit, please.'

'I am tired,' said Chaloner coolly. 'And Metje is waiting.'

'She will not arrive until at least ten o'clock,' said Thurloe, standing to close the door. 'Unless she stays away altogether, as she did last night.'

Chaloner gaped in disbelief. 'You sent someone to watch me?'

'Actually, I did it myself. I keep a chamber in the Golden Lion, and I have not entirely forgotten the skills I once taught you.'

Chaloner reached for the door again. 'Goodnight.'

Thurloe's grip on his wrist was surprisingly firm for a man who professed to be delicate. Chaloner could have broken it – and the wrist, too, had he wanted – but although he was angry, his temper had seldom led him to violence.

'I know what you were doing at the Tower,' said Thurloe softly. 'I attended a service in Westminster Abbey this evening, and I met Robinson there. He said you had been looking for mushrooms, but that you, Evett and he discussed matters that had nothing to do with fungus. These included salt beef, a buried seven thousand pounds, and plots against the King.'

'We talked about silver spoons and Bennet's pursuit of Fanny, too.'

Thurloe continued as if he had not spoken. 'And I already know from the loose-tongued Pepys that there were recent excavations for a vast sum of gold, said to have been buried by Barkstead. Since the hunt was unsuccessful, and Clarendon is desperate for funds, I assume

264

he has ordered you to look into the matter. I also suspect he is keeping his new investigation a secret, or Pepys would have been involved – and he is not, because he spent *his* day fawning over Lord Lauderdale in the Dolphin.'

Chaloner said nothing, and Thurloe released his hand.

'I may be able to help you, but not if you scowl at me. Stop it. It is making me nervous.'

'I do not need your help.'

'Every man needs help on occasion, and you need mine more than you imagine. I was telling the truth when I said Downing was very keen to learn who you are. Perhaps he offered to find out for Clarendon, who is naturally suspicious of all my people. I am worried for you.'

'There is no need. Clarendon already knows my real name, and I fended off Downing's enquiries for five years in Holland. He will not best me.'

Thurloe smiled faintly. 'Yes, of that I am sure. Please sit down, Tom. You cannot imagine how unpleasant this has been for me. What would I have said if you had accepted the manor, and I was then forced to admit that it does not exist? Finish your milk. It may soothe your acid temper.'

Reluctantly, Chaloner sat, but he no longer had an appetite for milk or anything else. The first spurt of anger had faded, but Thurloe had fallen in his estimation, and he was not sure the trust the ex-Spymaster seemed to place in his integrity would ever be fully reciprocated. Then he reconsidered. There had been a moment when he had considered confiding in Thurloe, which would have meant defying Clarendon. Perhaps he was not as honourable as he thought, and had no right

265

to sit in judgement of others. Thurloe was in an unenviable position, with men like Kelyng baying for his blood, and others like Downing regaling him with offers of 'friendship'. Chaloner supposed he would be cautious of everyone, too, were he in Thurloe's shoes. He relented, and Thurloe seemed to detect a softening of his mood, because he began to talk.

'I suspect, from some of your earlier questions, that you have stumbled upon various matters that involve me, and you are wondering why I have not mentioned them sooner.'

'The Brotherhood, for a start,' said Chaloner. 'The society *you* founded.'

'Who told you that?' Thurloe sighed. 'Downing, I suppose. Robinson, Ingoldsby and Dalton would not have blathered; Clarke, Barkstead and Hewson cannot; and Wade, Leybourn, Evett and North are late-comers, so I suspect they do not know who started the whole business. Of course, I could be wrong . . .'

'And Livesay? Why not him?'

Thurloe's expression did not change. 'North believes he was killed in an explosion, but you will know for yourself how violent "accidents" often conceal the truth. Personally, I believe he is still alive, and that he used the incident to disappear. Dalton thinks so, too, although none of us knows for certain. What I can say, though, is that Livesay would not have told you I founded the Brotherhood – he was not an original member, and so not in a position to know.'

'Is it true?'

Thurloe stared at the flames for so long that Chaloner thought he was not going to reply. 'Yes,' he said eventually. 'Shortly after the birth of the Commonwealth, although most of the first members are now dead, senile or in exile. I do not really know the newcomers – men like Evett, North and Wade. But the Brotherhood ceased to have any significant function months ago – when England started to slide faster into the pit of bigotry and intolerance – so it is irrelevant who is acquainted with whom.'

'And what about the Seven?' asked Chaloner. 'Are you one of them, too?'

Thurloe gazed at him, bemused. 'The Seven what?'

'The Seven men who were determined to prevent the Restoration. Hewson and Clarke both left messages warning the Seven, and I believe they were intended for you.'

'For me? Why? I did not stand against the Restoration. If I had, I would not be sitting here now.'

That was true, although Chaloner was unwilling to admit it. 'Then what about the cipher I saw in Clarendon's room, about praising God's son? What does that mean?'

Thurloe regarded him uneasily. 'What cipher? If these messages were meant for me, then why does Clarendon have them? And what is it that you think Clarke and Hewson wanted me to know?'

Chaloner saw that interrogating Thurloe was not going to produce many answers. He sighed. 'I saw letters on the Earl's desk, which I assumed were from Clarke. Perhaps I was mistaken.'

'On his desk?' asked Thurloe, appalled. 'You mean lying there, for anyone to read?'

Chaloner nodded. 'They had gone the next time I visited.'

Thurloe rubbed his eyes. 'If I asked you, as a friend, to walk away from Barkstead's treasure, would you do it?'

'That would be impossible. The Earl would demand to know why, and he would guess I have been divulging matters he ordered me to keep to myself.'

'I do not want you associated with this business. It will almost certainly turn out badly.'

'Why do you say that?' Chaloner had predicted Thurloe would decline to admit an association with the Seven, but he had not anticipated a stand over the missing treasure. Surely *he* had not been to the Tower with a spade? As two highly placed ministers in Cromwell's government, Thurloe and Barkstead would have known each other well, and it was entirely possible that the Lord Lieutenant had confided his secret to the Secretary of State and Spymaster General.

'Because treasure comes in a variety of forms, Tom, and not all of it is gold and silver. The Earl may discover he is prodding about with more than he can handle.'

'You are speaking in riddles, sir.'

'I am saying you may well find treasure in the Tower, but it may not be the kind of wealth you hope for. And Clarendon may not be pleased with the result.'

'My remit is to find it, not assess whether it is something he will like. I agreed to undertake this task, sir, and I cannot refuse it now. First, Clarendon is my only real hope for the future. And second, he may assume I *have* located it, but that I intend to keep it for myself. I would spend the rest of my life looking over my shoulder.'

'You do that anyway,' Thurloe pointed out. 'It is second nature to you. I ask you again: please walk away from this dangerous assignment while you still can. I will petition the King on your behalf, and suggest he recommends you directly to Williamson.'

268

'Why would Williamson trust me, when I have failed the Lord Chancellor in a fairly simple quest?'

Thurloe sighed. 'Very well. If I cannot dissuade you, I suppose I must help you. Let us consider Barkstead's damned hoard, then.' He seldom swore, and Chaloner could see he was vexed.

'I would rather not discuss—'

'Do not worry about your vow to Clarendon: it is hardly your fault I guessed what you were doing. But I knew Barkstead, and may be able to answer some questions. Tell me what you need to know.'

'First, it would be helpful to know whether this hoard actually exists.'

'Barkstead was a rich man, and when the Commonwealth fragmented, he knew he would lose everything he could not carry away with him. He would definitely have hidden something somewhere, you can be sure of that.'

Chaloner thought of his uncle's money, tucked inside the Banqueting House. 'Then where is it?'

'I have no idea, although I can be fairly confident in predicting that it will not be in the Tower.'

'Why not?'

'Because he would have known that he was never likely to be in a position to go and get it again. He lived in the Lieutenant's Lodgings, so there is no private London house to excavate, as there would be with Robinson. Perhaps you should look at the place he rented in Holland, before he was arrested.'

'This treasure was packed into butter firkins. Could he have left England with what would have been a sizeable load?'

'He knew a lot of merchants, and merchants excel at transporting goods. Of course he could have spirited his treasure away. If *I* were forced to locate it, *I* would go to Holland.'

Since the Lord Chancellor had forbidden Chaloner to leave the country, it was not an option he could choose. 'I was planning to speak to Barkstead's friends – his fellow regicides.'

'It is a pity we do not know what happened to Livesay, because he would have been your best bet. He was commissioner for the armed forces, and worked closely with Barkstead. They fled to Holland together, although Livesay eventually grew homesick and came back. Did you ever see him there? He spent a few days with your uncle.'

'What does he look like?'

Thurloe shrugged. 'Like a Puritan – sober clothes, grim face, plain features. And he has a thin moustache like the one favoured by the King, which he darkens daily with charcoal.'

The description fitted many men. 'Does he have no unique characteristic or habit?'

Thurloe thought for a long time. 'He clasps his hands when he is nervous or distressed – he interlocks his fingers, and makes a curious rubbing motion with his palms.'

'I do not recall anyone wringing his hands with my uncle. Do you think Livesay is in England?'

'Yes, but not in London. Ingoldsby might have managed to convince the King of his innocence, but the other regicides paid for their crime with their lives or imprisonment. Livesay will be in some remote retreat, using a false name and staying low. As I said, the best way to find this treasure is to go to Holland. I can give you money, if that is what keeps you here.'

'Thank you, sir, but I will talk to Ingoldsby first. Then perhaps Robinson will let me interview—'

'No, Tom! Associating yourself with imprisoned regicides is a dangerous—' Thurloe stopped speaking when there was a soft sound in the corridor outside.

Chaloner was already on his feet, dagger in his hand. 'Are you expecting visitors?'

'No. It is more would-be assassins, I suppose. Will this never end?'

Thurloe, his movements stealthy, retrieved a sword from behind his chair, and took up station on the left side of the door, while Chaloner stood to the right. They waited in silence for several moments, listening hard, and eventually there was a gentle tap – one beat, followed by three in rapid succession, ending with two slow ones. Thurloe sighed in relief, and indicated that Chaloner was to answer it.

'My sister. She always uses that sequence when she visits me.'

Chaloner opened the door cautiously, dagger at the ready, and checked the corridor after Sarah had marched in. There was no one else, but smears of mud on the polished floor indicated that someone had spent some time standing outside in one position. When more dirt dropped from Sarah's shoes as she flounced towards Thurloe, he assumed she had been crouching with her ear pressed against the panels. He wondered whether they had spoken loudly enough for her to have heard them.

Sarah give no indication that she had been eavesdropping, and made for the hearth, tossing her gloves carelessly towards the table. She wore a riding outfit, following the current fashion for masculine coat, doublet, wig and hat, and if it were not for her trailing petticoats, she might have been a man. It was a style favoured by the Queen, although the older members of Court grumbled that such attire made it difficult to discern a person's sex.

'Are you alone?' asked Thurloe, frowning. 'You know I do not like you coming here in the dark.'

'My maid rode most of the way with me – her nephew lives in Shoe Lane. And there are several plays tonight, so the streets are busier than usual. Do you have any wine? I am parched. I have been in the Cockpit watching *Claracilla*. A tragicomedy by Killigrew,' she added, rather condescendingly.

'I trust you enjoyed it,' said Thurloe, while Chaloner went to the wine jug. 'Personally, I dislike the theatre – too many people in too small a space.'

'Quite. That makes them excellent venues for listening to idle chatter. Ask any of your spies.'

'Indeed,' said Thurloe, watching her sip the drink. 'Tom, bring a chair and join us.'

'He and I met near the Strand the day before yesterday,' said Sarah, indicating Chaloner with a flick of her thumb. 'I rescued him from a beggarly pair, who were going to blow out his brains.'

'Snow and Storey,' explained Chaloner. 'Kelyng is now minus a henchman.'

'You killed one?' asked Thurloe worriedly. 'Are you sure that was wise, Tom? Kelyng will only recruit more, and there is a wealth of louts to choose from. And, since they usually work in pairs, the survivor tends to yearn for revenge when his partner dies violently.'

'I should be going,' said Chaloner, unwilling to be preached at when he could be working on the cipher he had recovered from Lee. 'I have a lot to do.'

He caught the spark of interest in Sarah's eye, and wondered yet again what she had overheard. Was she expecting him to visit Ingoldsby that night, and would she try to follow him again? If she did, he sincerely hoped she would not batter the fat knight to death and leave Chaloner himself to take the blame.

'Will you see my sister home first?' asked Thurloe. He raised his hands when both parties began to object. 'I do not care how many people are abroad for the theatre, Sarah. You are precious to me, and I do not want to lose you to a robber who thinks your life is worth his night in an alehouse.'

'I can look after myself,' said Sarah, although there was uncertainty in her voice.

'You can protect Tom again, then,' said Thurloe, unmoved. 'But it is late and I want my bed. I dislike these cold, dark evenings. The only place to be is tucked under the blankets with a book.'

'But I have not said why I came to see you,' said Sarah. She glanced significantly at Chaloner.

'You can trust him,' said Thurloe. 'I have already told you that.'

'You have also taught me to trust no one,' she shot back, not unreasonably.

'True, but we all need friends sometimes,' said Thurloe. 'If anything happens to me, I would like to think you two would turn to each other, and—'

'Stop!' cried Sarah, troubled. 'Nothing is going to happen to you, and I do not like you talking like this. It is unlike you to be maudlin. If I want a friend, *you* are the one I shall visit.'

Thurloe raised his hands to quell the outburst. 'Forgive me, my dear. I am tired, and the news about my poor

273

agents has been most distressing. What did you want to tell me?'

She glanced uneasily at Chaloner, but spoke anyway. 'My husband is becoming increasingly agitated, and has it in his head that Livesay has been passing secrets to his rivals.'

'What secrets?' asked Thurloe, bemused. 'Secrets about his business?'

She shrugged, to indicate she did not know. 'I keep telling him Livesay is either dead or in some remote country retreat, but he will not believe me. Will you speak to him?'

'I will visit tomorrow, if you think it will help. I shall recommend rest – a few days in bed can do wonders for a man. So can a night.' He looked pointedly towards the adjoining chamber, where his manservant had arrived to remove the warming pans.

She ignored the hint. 'It is not easy to live with a man who seems to be losing his mind.'

Thurloe was alarmed. 'Are you in danger? If so, then I shall arrange for you to move to Oxfordshire with my Ann and the children immediately.'

She waved her hand. 'He is not dangerous – at least, I do not think so. We have never been close, as you know, but he barely exchanges a greeting with me these days, and spends hours gazing out of the window. He witnessed two robberies and a brawl last night, and sees them as a sign that London is on the brink of revolution. I tell him it has always been that way, but he will not listen.'

'Perhaps you should both go to Oxfordshire,' suggested Thurloe. 'He clearly needs the peace of the country. And I need the peace of my bed.'

'Poor soul,' said Sarah, going to kiss the top of his

head. 'Sleep well, then, and tomorrow I shall tell you everything I overheard at the Cockpit. None of it is particularly interesting, but I can give you a detailed account of Lady Castlemaine's latest lover.'

'Buckingham,' said Chaloner. 'Late this afternoon in White Hall. And she has a mole on her right thigh.' Leaving them both gaping, he walked to the door and held it open, indicating that Sarah should precede him outside.

# Chapter 8

'You enjoyed that,' said Sarah accusingly, as she and Chaloner walked to the Lincoln's Inn stables to collect her horse. 'I had something interesting to tell him, and you pre-empted me.'

'It was not important anyway – as you said yourself.' He wondered why she was making such a fuss. 'Everyone knows Buckingham harbours a liking for Lady Castlemaine.'

She regarded him curiously. 'The mole . . . did you see . . . I mean, how did you find out?'

'Your brother trained me well. Just as he did you.'

She pouted. 'I wish that were true. You know how to locate birthmarks on royal mistresses, while I can barely decode the simplest cipher. I have begged him to teach me more, but he always has an excuse as to why he cannot.'

'Spying is not a game. It can be dangerous.'

'John has always been good to me, and I would like to return the favour. Bennet and his minions have been loitering near his gate most of today, which is why I have only been able to visit now – I dared not come before.

Is there anything we can do to drive them away?'

'Not without arousing their suspicions. You should not meddle – it may do more harm than good.'

'You said you would help protect him, Thomas *Chaloner*. Are you reneging on your promise?'

He watched her lead her horse into the yard, horrified that she – a woman of whom he was intensely wary – should know his real name. He wished Thurloe had kept the matter to himself: *he* might dote on his sister, but Chaloner had no reason to trust her. He was also puzzled. Thurloe had refused to confide in Downing, with whom Chaloner had worked for five years, but had revealed the secret to Sarah, someone Chaloner had met only twice – and one of those was when she was committing murder. Why would Thurloe be cautious with one person, but so rash with another?

Sarah petted her restless pony, and Chaloner stepped forward to lift her into the saddle. She was surprisingly heavy, far more so than Metje, although he sensed her bulk was more muscle than fat. The blow she had dealt Storey attested to the fact that she was strong. He took the reins and started to lead the horse towards the gate, but she pulled them from him and made a pretence at untangling them.

'Tell me about *Claracilla*,' he said, intending to learn a little more about her character while she kept him waiting. 'I saw *The Parson's Wedding* once, but it was a poor performance.'

She was surprised. 'You are familiar with Killigrew's work?'

Since a spy was obliged to cultivate a knowledge of all manner of subjects, he had acquired a grasp of the performing arts that allowed him to converse about

277

them with at least a modicum of intelligence. 'I met him in Holland once, when Downing invited him to dinner.'

She was impressed. 'What was he like?'

He had been petty, foul-mouthed, sharp-tongued and dissolute. 'A learned gentleman, but passionate in his temper.'

'I heard he was a rake. Look, Thomas, you do not have to walk home with me. My brother is overly protective, and I shall be perfectly safe on my own.' She hesitated, then added in a softer tone, 'But if it is not out of your way, I would not object to your company.'

'It is no trouble.' He tried to take the bridle, but she jerked it from him a second time. He sighed. 'At least, it is no trouble if you allow me to do it tonight.'

She made a noise that sounded something like a sob, and he gazed up at her in surprise. When she spoke, her words emerged a rush. 'Snow is following me, and I am so frightened that I do not know what to do. That is what I came to tell John, but I could not bring myself to do it. He looked so tired.'

'He will not thank you for that – he will want to know. Go back and tell him.'

She shook her head firmly. 'I cannot bother him with my problems. But I dare not go home, because then Snow will see where I live.'

'Did he follow you here?'

'No, I lost him by climbing out of a window at the Cockpit. He had followed me *right inside*, and sat glowering at me all through the second half. I am not easily alarmed, but I do not like this.'

'How did he find you in the first place?'

'He probably loitered at Charing Cross until he spotted

278

me. You will always see the person you want if you wait there long enough.'

Snow had done much the same to catch Chaloner two days before. 'How do you feel about lending me your hat?'

She regarded him uncertainly. 'What for?'

'So I can take your place. Your riding garb is masculine, and the streets are poorly lit. If I wear your hat and keep my head down, I think we can fool him. I shall take your horse – and Snow – on a tour of the city, while you go home.'

'But he means me harm. You will be putting yourself in danger.'

'I doubt he will do anything too outrageous as long as there are people around. I will lead him away from you, then give him the slip. It should not be difficult.'

'What about my pony?'

'I will stable him at the Golden Lion, and you can fetch him at your leisure.'

'And what happens tomorrow? Will you take my place then, too?'

It was a reasonable question, and Chaloner suspected she would not be safe until she had either made some sort of arrangement with the fellow or one of them was dead. 'Stay indoors. If he does not know where you live, then he cannot harm you. He will not linger on the Strand for ever – Kelyng will have other things for him to do.'

'Why should you risk yourself on my account?'

'You came to my rescue in the wigmaker's shop,' he replied, after wracking his brains for an answer. Why *was* he willing to help her? Because he disliked the notion of Snow stalking a woman? Because she was Thurloe's sister and, for all his suspicions and uncertainties, he still felt a lingering affection for the man who had treated him well for a decade? Or because he wanted her to think kindly of him now she knew his real name?

He lifted her off the horse and climbed into the saddle, keeping his elbows tucked in to make himself less bulky. Her wig smelled faintly of a perfume that was sensual, and it carried her warmth.

'Hoist up your petticoats, so they do not show,' he instructed, as he started to ride down Chancery Lane. 'Walk ahead of me – not too far, or I will not be able to help you if he sees through our plan, but not so close that we look as though we are together. And move like a man – do not mince.'

He smothered a laugh when she effected an exaggerated swagger. It made her appear drunk, and one fellow immediately sidled up to her, evidently intent on taking advantage of an inebriated gentleman. Chaloner drew his dagger and the thief melted away into the shadows, holding his hands in front of him to indicate he meant no harm.

It was not long before Chaloner spotted Snow; Sarah saw him at the same time, and tensed perceptibly. The robber was waiting near the Maypole in the Strand, a towering pillar set up two years before to replace the one destroyed during the wars. He was alert and watchful as he leaned against a wall, chewing a stick of dried meat. When he saw Sarah's pony, he pushed himself upright and stretched. A bulge near his waist indicated he carried a pistol. Chaloner scanned the dark street for an accomplice, but Snow made no attempt to pass signals: the stalking of Sarah was personal, not duty, and he was alone.

'Easy,' called Chaloner softly, when he saw her falter, unwilling to walk past the man.

'I cannot let you take the consequences for something I did,' she replied unsteadily. 'It is not fair. I should never have agreed to it.'

'It is too late now. Go home, before your hesitation puts us both in danger.'

Reluctantly, she entered the garden of her house, while Chaloner continued along the Strand. He glanced behind him when he reached the corner, and saw Snow still watching. The ruse had worked. He rode towards the river, then eased the horse into a trot. Snow sped up, and Chaloner took a sharp left, but found himself in an alley barely wide enough for the animal to pass. The pony did not like the sensation of buildings hemming it in, and began to buck. Snow hauled a pistol from his belt and took aim. Chaloner ducked, and the shot blew to pieces a swinging sign above his head. The sound was shockingly loud in the confined space.

The horse bolted. It raced down the alley, and its hooves drew sparks when it reached the end and tried to make a hard right-hand turn. Snow tugged a second weapon from his coat, not taking the time to reload the first. The pony thundered on, then reared suddenly when its path was blocked by a stack of roofing tiles. Snow's footsteps echoed behind, and he gave a brief shout of satisfaction when he saw his quarry trapped. Chaloner tried to turn, intending to ride Snow down, but there was no room for such a manoeuvre and the horse knew it. It started to gallop towards the tiles, and Chaloner braced himself for the impact. Then he was airborne, wind whistling past his ears. A sharp click sounded when a hoof connected with the highest tile, and then they were across. He grabbed the beast's mane to keep his balance as it cavorted back towards the Strand, and Snow's second

281

shot was fired more in frustration than in any real hope of hitting its target.

Chaloner was grateful the landlord of the Golden Lion knew him, because it meant he did not demand advance payment for the horse's lodging. He lingered in the tavern, partly to warm himself by the fire before he went to his icy garret, and partly to ensure Snow had not traced the tortuous route he had taken home. Nothing was amiss after an hour, and he left the inn with some reluctance. He smiled when he saw Temperance returning from a late prayer-meeting at the chapel, although she looked as though she had just spent an hour sitting next to a live cannon.

'What did Hill rave about this time?' he asked, watching her face light up when she saw him.

'Turning the other cheek, although he is actually rather a vengeful man.'

'Why does your father not hire someone more moderate?'

'Hill was once attacked by brutal men who hated his religion, and my father feels a kinship with him because he suffered the same treatment, as did my brother. He knows Hill is a danger to us, and spends a lot of time asking God to make him more temperate.'

Chaloner wondered whether the incident Hill had related to North was actually the time he had spent in the Buckingham stocks for iconoclasm. 'Then let us hope God hears him.'

She brushed aside his concerns. 'Where is your hat? You should not be bareheaded on such a night – you will take a chill.'

Chaloner gave her a brief flash of Sarah's headwear,

which he had shoved in his pocket after the escapade with Snow. 'I was hot.'

'That is not yours,' she said immediately. '*That* belongs to a *woman*.' Her voice fell to a horrified whisper, so the last words might equally well have been 'the devil'.

'I must have picked up the wrong one,' he said, wondering how she came to be so well acquainted with his clothing – it was dark, and he had only offered her a glimpse. 'It happens all the time.'

'Not to me,' said Temperance. She regarded him uneasily. 'Do you have a lady friend?'

'Not one with whom I exchange clothes,' replied Chaloner. He saw she was not amused. 'It belongs to someone you know – Sarah Dalton. She is happily married to someone else.'

'Sarah?' asked Temperance, startled. '*She* is not happily married! Her brother advised her not to take Dalton, but she ignored him and has regretted it ever since. Poor Sarah. How do you know her?'

'I am hoping to do some translating for her husband.'

'Oh.' She sounded relieved. 'Will you come inside? I made knot biscuits today, and I do not think Preacher Hill finished them all when he visited us earlier. He came to deal with the turkey.'

Chaloner accepted willingly, hoping she might provide other food, too, and that Metje might be there. He wanted her to visit him that night, because it would be warmer in bed with two than one, and it was time their differences were forgotten. He followed Temperance into the comfortable sitting room at the front of the house, where the Norths and their servants gathered in the evenings. It was a pleasant chamber, dominated by its hearth and long oaken table. North sat at one end, reading under a lamp, while Faith sat at the other with a pile of darning. The servants ranged themselves in between: as in many Puritan homes, masters and servants mingled, all equal in the eyes of the Lord.

The household was small, but Chaloner had always sensed it was a happy one. The two maids were practising their handwriting under Metje's watchful eye, while the men – named Henry and Giles – sharpened knives. There was a dish of dried fruit to assuage any hunger pangs remaining after supper, and a posset bubbled over the fire, to be drunk before everyone retired to bed. Metje glanced up, then turned her attention back to her students. Her coolness meant nothing, because she always ignored him when they were in the presence of the Norths. Nevertheless, he pushed Sarah's hat and wig further inside his pocket, not wanting accusations of infidelity to add to their troubles.

'Do not go in the kitchen, Miss Temperance,' cried Henry in alarm, as the daughter of the house raised her hand to the latch. 'The turkey is in there.'

'We are lucky it is not in here,' said North, standing to greet Chaloner. 'It had designs on spending the night by the fire, and I was hard-pressed to prevent it from doing so. Wretched beast!'

'It is still alive?' asked Chaloner. 'I thought Hill was going to kill it with his Bible – or his pistol.'

'The gun flashed in the pan, and the Bible only served to annoy it,' replied Faith. She looked furious, and her small eyes glittered. 'It guessed what he intended to do and went for him. I will not shock you with details, Thomas, but suffice to say it is a good thing he stands to preach his sermons.'

Chaloner turned to the menservants, indicating the

arsenal of blades in front of them. 'What about you two? Surely you are not both afraid of a bird?'

'It is not a bird,' replied Henry coolly. 'It is a turkey.'

'And *I* do not kill God's creations, either,' added North, before Chaloner could challenge him. 'I only *eat* them. Besides, I do not mind admitting that the thing has me terrified. It is a demon.'

'I have never had trouble killing things before,' said Faith. 'But I did not like the feel of its neck when I grabbed it. It was like holding a snake, and I could not maintain my grip long enough to cut its throat. It was not like dispatching a person, which I was obliged to do several times during the wars.'

'Where are the knot biscuits?' asked Temperance, while Chaloner regarded Faith uneasily. She had related some of her war experiences before, and he was under the impression that she had endured a bloodier time of it than he had – and he had been in several major battles.

'The bird had them,' replied Faith, looking angrier still. 'What a waste of good butter!'

'The kitchen is now out of bounds for the night,' said North to Chaloner. 'The turkey will forage in the yard in daylight, but it moves indoors when dusk falls, and no Christian soul can stop it.'

Chaloner wondered whether the bird's near starvation had rendered it unusually aggressive, or whether it was common for turkeys to take over a house if they were not executed immediately. He struggled not to laugh at the situation. Faith detected his amusement, and became cool with him.

'Have you eaten tonight? If not, do have some raisins.'

'I am not hungry,' lied Chaloner. She had made the offer from spite, knowing he hated raisins with a passion.

'But I should leave. It is very late and I still have some work to do.'

'Paid work?' asked Metje, rather eagerly.

'He means to practise his music,' said North with a fond smile. 'But choose something more cheerful than the sad piece you played yesterday, Heyden. It was so mournful, it made Metje cry.'

'Did it?' asked Chaloner, startled.

'It reminded me of home,' said Metje uncomfortably. She stood up. 'Do not let us keep you, Thomas. I will see you to the door.'

'You do not have to go,' said Temperance. 'Sit next to me and show me those coin tricks again.'

'Coin tricks?' echoed Faith. She looked uneasily from her daughter to Chaloner, making him wonder what she thought they had entailed. 'What sort of coin tricks?'

'Nothing too debauched. And now he needs to work,' said Metje, elbowing him towards the door. He did not want to go: it was warm and comfortable in the Norths' house, and the prospect of a cold, lonely garret was not an enticing one. But he bowed to the Norths, aware of Faith regarding Temperance in motherly dismay, and followed Metje into the corridor, closing the door behind him. A murmur of conversation began, and he could hear someone stoking up the fire.

'I was in no hurry to leave,' he said, watching her unbar the front door and feeling his stomach growl emptily. 'There was no need to force me out.'

'You should not waste time fooling around with Temperance when you could be earning money for the rent,' she said sharply. 'Go to your translating. I lit the lamp for you.'

286

'Did you really cry last night?'

'It was such a gloomy tune,' she replied, looking away. 'And I keep thinking about what will happen if our countries go to war. Everything is so horribly uncertain.'

'I am sorry, Meg.' He tried to touch her, but she pulled away from him.

'Go to your translating, or Faith will think you are seducing her servants, as well as her daughter.'

Chaloner did not like leaving Metje when she was ridden with anxieties, and was angry with himself, feeling he was letting her down by failing to provide her with the security she craved. A feeling of inadequacy washed over him as he climbed the stairs to his rooms, and he decided he *would* locate Barkstead's treasure, even if it meant a journey to Holland. Clarendon would then pass him to Williamson, who was said to be intelligent, so would see the wisdom of using experienced men to help avert a crisis with the Dutch. *And* he would learn who killed Clarke and watch Kelyng for Thurloe, since two sources of income would surely allay Metje's fears.

'Heyden,' came a soft voice from the stairwell. 'Is that you?'

Stifling a sigh of annoyance, Chaloner retraced his steps. 'Did I disturb you, Mr Ellis?'

The landlord shook his grey head. 'I wanted to make sure you were not a whore. I like your lamp, by the way. I might accept that in lieu of rent, should you find yourself unable to pay this week.'

'Thank you,' said Chaloner, hoping it would not be necessary. Metje would be furious.

He walked back up the stairs, wondering whether he could petition Clarendon for an advance on his pay. It was not something he liked to ask; no man wanted to be a beggar. However, he was not so engrossed in his worries that he did not realise something was amiss in his room when he started to unlock it. The hall outside was always draughty, but when he put his fingers to the bottom of the door, there was a veritable gale whistling under it. There was also no flicker of light from the lamp Metje said she had lit. Had Ellis turned it off? Standing well back, Chaloner opened the door slowly, then waited a moment before entering, alert for any indication that someone was inside.

But the room was empty, and the icy draught was the result of a smashed window. Shards of glass were strewn across the floor, and the lamp had blown out. He walked to the broken pane and looked into the street below, aware that someone might be lurking there to see what would happen when he returned and found the mess – someone with a gun. But nothing moved, and Fetter Lane appeared to be deserted, so he secured the shutters and set about rekindling the lamp. Then he searched for the missile that had caused the damage. What he found astonished him.

He had expected a stone, lobbed by the people who attacked the Nonconformist chapel – either because they had confused his house with North's, or because he was known to be in the Puritans' employ. However, it was no rock that lay amid the chaos of glass and splintered wood, but a black object that emitted the distinctive aroma of gunpowder. Someone had thrown a grenade. He studied it where it lay, turning it with the tip of his sword, and trying to determine why it had not exploded. He saw it was the creation of an amateur, who did not understand that the vessel holding the inflammable chemicals needed to break in order for its contents to ignite, and too sturdy a container had been used.

So, who had thrown it? Clarke's killer, because he intended the murder to remain unsolved? Someone who did not want Barkstead's treasure located? Kelyng, because Chaloner was Thurloe's man, or Bennet, because Chaloner had made a fool of him? Or had someone intended to strike a blow at the Puritans – or worse, at Metje, because she was Dutch?

He dropped Sarah's hat and wig on the table, but then shoved them behind the bed, not wanting Metje to question him about them, as Temperance had done. In an attempt to take his mind off his empty stomach, he drank a lot of water, then sat at the table and stared at the scrap of paper he had retrieved from Lee. It was less than the length of his ring finger and only half as wide; the whole document had clearly never been very large. He assessed the kind of writing materials used, holding it to the lamp to see whether heat might reveal secret marks – some spies still used lemon or onion juice. But there was nothing visible, and the paper was the cheap kind favoured by everyone. Assuming the original document was rectangular, Chaloner had the bottom right-hand corner of it.

The cipher comprised not only letters, but numbers and symbols, too – a system of substitution devised many years before Thurloe's rise and fall. The order of the characters was fixed, but only the sender and recipient knew which letter corresponded to another, and although it was usually possible to break the code, it was a time-consuming process. It was especially troublesome when only fragments of words were available. But Chaloner was keen for answers, and was prepared to work all night if necessary. He found an old broadsheet with a blank back page and began.

He laboured until the church bells chimed one o'clock, when his eyes burned from fatigue and a headache gnawed at his temples. He sat back and rubbed his back, wondering what had happened to Metje. He returned to his task a little longer, then began to worry. She often missed one evening with him, but it was rare for her to forgo two in a row. Had the Norths become suspicious at last, and locked her in? Or had she fallen foul of whoever had lobbed the bomb as she had left North's house to join him?

He tiptoed down the stairs and let himself out through the back door, wincing at the sharp chill of the night. Carefully, he scaled the wall that separated his house from North's, landing lightly on the other side. North's bedchamber was in darkness, but there was a glimmer of light in Metje's. He groped on the ground for a suitable piece of mud – not so small that it would not fly, but not so large that it would make too much noise. He found what he was looking for and took aim.

The clod struck the glass exactly where he had intended, making a soft but distinct tap. He waited, expecting her to answer. She did not, so he crouched a second time and hunted for something larger, supposing she was asleep and had not heard what was a very small sound. His second shot hit the window frame, making a sharp snap. The light wavered, as if someone was on the move, but the window still did not open. Becoming impatient, he selected a third missile, which he hurled with rather more vigour than was wise. The crack was startling in the still night air, and Metje was not the only one who heard it. North's shutters flew open, and he peered into the darkness.

'Cats,' Chaloner heard Faith murmur sleepily. 'That big orange thing from two doors up.'

'It was not a cat.' As North leaned out, the night-cap fell from his head and dropped to the ground below. 'Curses!' Chaloner smiled, certain only a Puritan would use such an expletive.

North's head disappeared, and moments later, came the sound of a key turned in a latch. Chaloner padded to the end of the garden and crouched behind a holly bush, while North retrieved his hat and began to prowl, holding a lamp above his head. He carried a cudgel in his other hand, clearly determined to flush out intruders. Chaloner sighed. It was very late and he was tired: he did not want to be chased by an irate neighbour who thought he was a thief. He was tempted to stand up and announce himself, adding that he was also the man who intended to marry his daughter's companion, but consideration for Metje made him prudent. He edged to one side as North drew closer.

'Come out,' North shouted. His voice was unsteady. 'I am armed and in no mood for felons.'

Chaloner doubted the threat would strike fear into the hearts of many criminals. North moved closer, obviously intending to be thorough, and Chaloner saw he would be caught if he stayed where he was. Keeping low, he crept towards the rear gate. Then he trod on a shell.

'Ha!' shouted North, darting towards the sound. 'You treacherous son of a whore! I shall thrash you to a pulp, and hand you over for hanging. Bastard!'

Chaloner ran, learning that even Puritans could employ salty language when sufficiently roused. He doubted North could best him in a fight, even with his club, but did not want to explain why he was hiding in the man's garden, and flight seemed the best option for everyone concerned. He headed for the gate, North hot on his heels. It was barred, so Chaloner hauled himself up the wall.

'Theft!' screamed North. 'Murder!'

Chaloner reached the top of the wall at the same time that North reached him. The merchant swung with his cosh, hitting the bricks and sending shards flying in all directions. Chaloner pulled his leg out of the way as North aimed again, careful to keep his face in shadow: it would be acutely awkward to be recognised now. Then North abandoned cudgel and lamp, and seized Chaloner's foot.

'Fire!' he howled with increasing fury. 'Arson!'

Lights started to gleam in neighbouring houses, and Chaloner saw shadows in the lane along which he had intended to escape. He was beginning to be annoyed with North. Claims of blazes in a tinderbox like London were taken seriously, and he might be lynched if he ran into the alley now – mobs tended to act first and think later once words like 'arson' and 'fire' were in the air. He struggled, trying to free himself without hurting the man.

'I let our turkey out,' shouted Temperance, stumbling up the dark garden towards them. Faith was behind her, priming a pistol. 'Unhand my father, you vile man, or it will peck you to pieces.'

When she added her brawn to North's, Chaloner felt himself begin to slide towards them. He gripped the wall and resisted hard, hoping Faith would not join the tug of war, because the situation had gone too far to be explained away innocently. Much as he was loath to harm North, he realised he would have to use force if he were to escape, so he reached down and pulled the man's nose. The Puritan shrieked, releasing Chaloner's leg as both hands flew to his face. But Temperance was furious, and with an impressive display of strength, she hauled Chaloner off the wall and into the garden. He landed flat on his back with a crash that drove the breath from his body.

'Wicked man! You hurt my father!' cried Temperance, hurling herself on top of Chaloner to prevent him from standing. Faith hurried forward and took aim with her pistol.

'No!' yelled North, shoving Faith away as her finger tightened on the trigger. 'You might hit Temperance. Leave him to me.' He snatched up his cudgel and advanced with genuine menace.

Chaloner shoved Temperance away from him, and scrambled upright, aware of raised voices from the lane. North lashed out with his club, hard enough to make him lose his own balance and stumble into his daughter. The tip caught Chaloner's knee, and if he had not fallen at that precise moment, Faith's shot would have killed him. He staggered to his feet a second time, and limped to the wall of his own house, scaling it awkwardly while North and Temperance wallowed on the ground and Faith reloaded. But by now, lights were burning in Ellis's chambers, and Chaloner knew he would not be able to reach his rooms unseen. Thinking fast, he flung open the rear door of his landlord's home and began to shout.

'He is over here!' he called to North. 'In Ellis's garden.'

Ellis was soon at his side, clad in a night-gown. 'Where is the fire? Should we fetch buckets?'

'Theft!' screeched North, bobbing up and down on

293

the other side of the wall as he tried to see what was happening. 'Murder. And . . . and treason!'

'Treason?' echoed Ellis, startled. 'Are you sure?'

'Where is he?' demanded Faith, hoisting herself up the wall and peering across it with her reloaded gun. 'Flush him out, and I will shoot him dead.'

'I cannot see anyone,' said Ellis. 'Are you sure he came this way? I do not think so, because—'

'There!' shouted Chaloner, pointing. 'By the gooseberry bush.'

'Well, go and get him, then,' said Ellis, shoving him forward, while Faith took aim at the general area. 'I do not want an arsonist on my property, and *I* cannot go, because I am not wearing any shoes.'

'Yes, by the Devil! Catch the sod!' howled North.

Chaloner moved to the back of the garden and made a lot of noise in the fruit bushes. His leg was numb, it was freezing cold and he was heartily sick of the whole business. It was not long before he returned to where North, Temperance, Faith and Ellis waited expectantly. In the lane at the end of the garden, he could see torches flickering as people ran here and there, looking for the fire.

'I am sorry, sir,' he said to North, who had found a crate to stand on. 'He escaped.'

'Damn!' cried North, wringing his hands in agitation. 'The scoundrel grabbed my nose, threatened me with his pistol and demanded all my money! Did you hear the shot he fired?'

'Horrible!' exclaimed Ellis with a shudder. '*All* your money?'

'We should pray for his soul,' said Chaloner sanctimoniously. 'Poor misguided sinner.'

North took a deep breath. 'Yes, I suppose so, although it is difficult to imagine a creature like that in the Lord's Plan. But, unchristian though it may be, I am glad I gave him a good beating before he got away. That will make him think twice before invading the homes of . . . Ouch! What was that?'

'The turkey!' exclaimed Temperance. When she next spoke, her voice was some distance away. 'I let it out to drive off the burglar.'

North promptly disappeared, doors slammed and there was a lot of agitated hollering. Then it was quiet again, except for North bemoaning the fact that the gun had flashed in the pan when Faith had tried to shoot the rampaging turkey, and Faith complaining that the thief had managed to duck away from the bullet that should have killed him. Shivering in the bitter night, Ellis was not long in returning to his warm bed, leaving Chaloner to tell the people in the alley that there was no fire after all. There were venomous mutters when he explained that the commotion had been caused by a prowler, and someone threw water at him. When he returned, sodden, to his back door, he saw Metje standing on the crate North had abandoned. Even in the dark, he could tell she was angry.

'Where is the turkey?' he asked, not liking to think of her at its mercy.

'In the sitting room,' she snapped, glancing behind her to ensure she was not overheard. 'It is not so stupid as to stay out here when there is frost in the air. It had a go at North, then made for the best room of the house, where the embers of a good fire are glowing.'

'Oh,' he said tiredly.

'What were you doing?' she demanded furiously. 'I

295

*know* all that commotion was your fault.'

'I was worried about you. You did not come.'

'I did not want to come. I am angry with you – and you will not win my favour by hurting the man who pays my wages, either. Are you limping again? What happened this time? Another fall from a cart?' Her voice had a hard, callous ring that was unfamiliar.

'North hit me with his club. I did not know he kept such a weapon in his house.'

'I told you about it when you offered to waylay him by pretending to have the plague. I am going inside now, Thomas. Do not lob any more bricks at my window; I do not want to see you.' Her voice softened. 'But perhaps I will come tomorrow, since you have been to such pains to secure my attention.'

Chaloner fell asleep over his decoding, leg propped on a stool in front of him. He awoke cold and stiff to hear the bells chime six o'clock. He returned to the cipher, and supposed he must have been overly exhausted the previous night, because suddenly there was a pattern that made sense:

> *e*
> *d*
> *y*
> *on*
> *seven*
> *s cache*
> *raise God*
> *r of London*
> *th day of Decbr.*
> *obert Lee, Clerk.*

He gazed at it. Praise God – the phrase Hewson had muttered, the words on Clarendon's desk, and the message Clarke had asked the measurers of cloth to send his wife. He rubbed his leg. Seven what? The Seven? Seven thousand pounds – Barkstead's cache? Without more of the original document, he knew he had taken interpretation as far as he could. However, he could conclude one thing: Lee's paper contained more proof that all three of his investigations were inextricably linked.

Driven by hunger, Chaloner scoured his room for money, but all he found was a token. Tokens were issued by some taverns in lieu of change, since small denomination coins were often in short supply, so he visited the Rose at Covent Garden, and exchanged it for a pie that smelled rancid. He ate it anyway, and walked towards the Thames with the grenade in his pocket. The missile was not something he intended to keep, not just because incendiary devices were inherently unstable, but because men could be hanged for owning items that might be used to ferment rebellion.

A cat watched him hurl it into the river, so hard and far that its splash was inaudible. Then he stood on the Milford Stairs, listening to the water gurgle around the piers, while the cat wound about his legs, purring. It was still early, so the Thames was relatively empty of traffic. One craft rocked towards him, though, its oarsman driven on by a strident voice that made Chaloner jump towards the shadows to avoid being seen. He watched Preacher Hill reach the quay just as a robust recitation of Psalm Eighteen was completed. The boatman was breathless, and slumped on his seat as though he was drained of strength, although this did not stop him from pushing off as soon as Hill had alighted.

'Thank you, my son,' boomed Hill. 'The Lord be with you.'

'Fuck off!' came the reply. 'And never set foot in my boat again, you fanatical bastard!'

Hill grinned, before shifting his Bible to its customary position under his arm. When he passed the cat, it arched its back and spat at him. He stopped walking, then made a sudden lunge that saw the animal grabbed by the scruff of the neck. It yowled and hissed, but was powerless to resist as Hill drew back his arm and prepared to lob it into the river.

'Good morning, Preacher,' said Chaloner, stepping from his hiding place and catching the man's wrist. The cat dropped from Hill's fingers, and scampered away. 'You were not thinking of sending one of God's creatures to a watery grave, were you?'

Hill's eyes narrowed. 'What are you doing here? You should be . . .'

'Be what?' asked Chaloner, immediately suspicious. 'Be dead from the grenade someone tossed into my room last night? You seem to like hurling things around.'

Hill raised his eyebrows. 'Someone tried to blow you up? The Devil must have been watching over his own, then. Who threw it? One of the apprentices from the tannery again?'

'Again?'

'I found a fireball in the chapel last night, although no attempt had been made to ignite the fuse – those stupid lads do not know how such devices work. I took it home with me, and I shall throw it at *them* if they try anything untoward again.'

298

'Temperance said your homily last night was about turning the other cheek.'

'I am the Lord's soldier, and we are sometimes obliged to meet violence in kind. But the reason I am surprised to see you has nothing to do with explosives – North said he was going to ask you to kill the turkey, and I did not think you would survive the experience.'

Chaloner was curious as to why Hill was crossing the Thames at such an odd hour. 'Were you over in Southwark because its whores are less likely to recognise you than London ones?'

Even in the pre-dawn light, he saw Hill's face turn puce. 'Do not make an enemy of me, Heyden. *I* am a friend of Gervaise Bennet, and I will set *him* after you if you make trouble for me.'

'I am not afraid of Bennet.'

Hill was contemptuous as he turned to stalk away. 'Then you are a fool.'

Chaloner watched him go, uneasy with the notion of Hill telling Bennet where he lived. He was not unduly worried for himself, but what would happen if Metje was home when Bennet struck?

He had intended to visit Ingoldsby that morning, but when he reached the Temple Bar he began to feel sick. He returned to his rooms, wondering whether the wretched illness that followed was a result of the Rose's rotten pie or drinking so much water the previous night. He was better by the evening, but did not go out, for fear of missing a visit from Metje. He lit the lamp and played his viol, but she failed to appear, even when he bowed her favourite dance several times in a row.

Unable to sleep after dozing much of the day, he rose at two o'clock and went to the Puritans' chapel, tucking himself behind a water butt and in the mood for confronting louts with grenades. But nothing happened until six, when a lone man approached. He was swathed in a cloak too large for him, and clearly did not want to be recognised. He reached the chapel, then leapt away in alarm when he discovered the hiding place behind the barrel was already taken. His hand dropped to the hilt of his sword, but when he saw Chaloner already armed, he turned and raced towards Fleet Street. Chaloner started to give chase, but his bout of sickness had left him unsteady on his feet, and it was obvious he was not going to catch the fellow. He gave up, and returned to his rooms, annoyed by his weakness, but supposing the fellow might think twice about causing mischief another time.

Seven o'clock saw the beginning of another grey dawn, with the occasional speck of snow drifting down and a bitter, raw feel to the air. The first cart laboured along Fetter Lane, its driver cracking his whip and yelling at his listless horse. A man hollered at a woman for hurling swill from her window, and the altercation developed into a fist-fight when a bellman became involved. A herd of sheep was being driven in a bleating ball to the slaughterhouses, and pigeons flapped and cooed on the rooftops.

Chaloner remained determined to solve his various mysteries, and decided that day would yield some answers. He donned his cloak, found the old horsehair wig, and left the house, aiming for the Fleet Rookery. It was a good time to begin his search for Mother Pinchon, because the gangs that roamed the streets during the hours of darkness would be in their beds, and anyone awake would be the more honest inhabitants, who might be inclined to talk to him.

300

He found Turnagain Lane, which was close to the alehouse where he had listened to Snow and Storey chatting to the dung collector. The tavern was closed, its windows shielded by thick shutters, and was deserted except for a rat that was grooming itself. He began to waylay passers-by. First, he spoke to a flower-seller, but she declined to converse once it became clear he had no money. A butcher in a glistening apron offered to cut his throat, and a ballad-seller spat at him. Then he became aware that three slovenly, dirty men were watching him from a distance. Word had spread that someone was asking questions, and he sensed he would not be left alone for much longer.

'Fresh milk?' came a voice at his side. 'Warm from the ass? Only a penny.'

Chaloner smiled at the old woman. 'Good morning, Mother Greene.'

'You seem to like danger,' she said, regarding him thoughtfully. 'This makes twice you have come to a place where you cannot be sure of your welcome. Snow said you are Whitechapel's parish constable, but you are too well dressed for that. Did you know that Bennet has vowed to kill you?'

'Has he?' Chaloner recalled Kelyng ordering Bennet to forget about him. 'Why?'

'Something to do with St Thomas à Becket. Give us a penny.'

'I wish I had one,' said Chaloner rucfully, 'because I would like some milk.'

She smiled toothlessly and took his arm. 'Come with me. Do not look alarmed. No one will harm you, now you are in the company of Mother Greene.'

The slouching figures in the shadows made no move

to intervene, and he surmised that she had earned herself a degree of respect on account of her age. She also had the look of a witch about her, with her long nose and wrinkled face. She led the way down a street with particularly tall houses, and opened the gate to a tiny garden. It was surprisingly clean, its stones still wet from a recent scouring. She headed for a door and beckoned him to follow. Cautiously, he ducked under the lintel and found himself in a room full of the scent of dried herbs. It contained a table that was scrubbed white, and there were shelves on which stood an array of pots and bottles. The floor comprised red flagstones that were spotlessly clean, and there was a pot simmering over the embers of the hearth. It was a pleasant chamber, and a welcoming one, and not at all what he would have expected.

'Surprised?' she asked, noting his reaction. 'My old man left me something when he died. He was an actor – the best in London, in his day.'

'It is a lovely place,' he said sincerely. 'It smells of home.'

She grinned, pleased. 'That is what my Oliver always said. What is wrong with your leg?'

He had not bothered to hide his limp that morning, hoping it would make him appear less threatening to potential informants. 'I hurt it doing something stupid. I do not suppose you know where I might find Mother Pinchon? I need to ask her some questions.'

'About Barkstead's gold?' She cackled at his astonishment. 'Who do you think told her to go to Wade in the first place? I said to demand a thousand pounds, but she agreed to a hundred, soft cow. And now you have come to ask for better directions, so you can dig it up and give her nothing at all.'

'Yes, I doubt she will see any of it,' he admitted.

'At least you are honest about it. Are you hungry? I got enough stew for two.'

'I cannot take your food. You will need it for tomorrow.'

'You might bring me a penny tomorrow. Besides, it is a pleasure to share food with the man who brained Storey. You did what I asked: you said my boy's name. Snow heard you as he lay dazed.'

'I cannot take the credit for dispatching your son's killer.'

'I do not care – all that matters is that he is dead, and that the last thing he heard was you talking about Oliver. This is hot, so mind your fingers.'

The stew was surprisingly good, and he said nothing until he had finished it, realising it was the first decent meal he had eaten in days. He felt it warming him through, and experienced a reviving of his energies. She returned his smile when he sat back in satisfaction.

'Now we shall go to Mother Pinchon,' she said.


Unlike the fastidious Mother Greene, Pinchon wallowed in her poverty, and cared nothing for the fact that water was free, and that it cost nothing to rinse the filth from the floor. Her hair hung in listless snakes, and her entire person was impregnated with grease. Chaloner found it hard to believe Barkstead had considered her his most trusted servant.

'What about Bennet?' she demanded, when Greene had introduced Chaloner as the man who had given Storey his comeuppance. 'Will you do him too? Storey was a pig, but Bennet is worse.'

'He will see to Bennet in his own good time – and Kelyng, too, I should not wonder,' said Greene comfortably. 'But today, he is here about that treasure in the Tower.'

Pinchon regarded Chaloner with naked hostility. 'Wade promised he would never tell no one about me, so how did you find where I live?'

'Luck,' replied Chaloner truthfully. 'Did you tell Wade everything you know about this hoard?'

Her face was sullen. 'Barkstead said he would bury it under that tower near the gate. There is an arch with a red brick in the middle, but the rest is grey stone. The gold is there, in butter firkins. Barkstead and me packed it in that very cellar – out of sight, so his soldiers would not see us.'

'Why did he choose you to help him?'

'Because his other staff saw how things were going and ran. I stayed, because I wanted the pans he was going to leave – I was his scullion, see. He said I was the best of all his people for staying.'

Chaloner nodded, imagining the situation: Barkstead desperate, reduced to relying on the lowest member of his household, who had remained not out of loyalty but because she had wanted to scavenge. He probably had not trusted her, and therefore may not have told her the truth.

'What was in these firkins? Coins?'

'Coins, plate, jewellery, ivory combs, little pictures, gold crosses, all sorts of stuff. But it was all valuable. He said if we sold it, it would give us seven thousand pound.'

'Did you *see* him bury it?'

'He sent me away at four o'clock that afternoon, because he was afraid they might come for him, and did not want me to suffer, too. He said he would bury it himself. He had a spade hidden, ready.'

'Why did you wait so long before telling anyone? It has been more than three years since this happened.'

'I was scared they would hang me for a traitor, but the treasure was always there, in my mind. A month ago, I decided to tell Ma Greene. She said I should approach Wade – she sells him milk.'

'Why did Barkstead share the secret with you? Why not a friend?'

'Because he did not know who was friend and who was foe by then. He asked me to tell Secretary Thurloe, but I could not, because Kelyng was watching Lincoln's Inn, and only a fool gets in *his* way. I never did speak to Thurloe. But Barkstead said *I* was to have the treasure, if anything bad happened to him. Well, something bad happened, all right, and his head is on a pole to prove it.'

'Can you recall his exact words?'

'What does it matter? The treasure is not where he said. Wade kept pressing for more details, too, but I cannot tell what I do not know. Wade even smuggled me into the Tower one night, after dark, and I pointed out the arch, but he said they had dug there already.'

But Chaloner was not interested in the arch or the treasure; his mind was moving along another avenue. 'What did Barkstead tell you to say to Thurloe – his *precise* words.'

The urgency of the question caught her attention and she regarded him calculatingly. 'What is in it for me? My hundred pound?'

'Your hundred pound is long gone,' said Greene scornfully. 'It is obvious that Barkstead either never buried it, or someone else got it first. But this man has a job to do, so answer him.'

Pinchon scowled. 'Why should I?'

'Because he killed Storey, frightened Snow and annoyed Bennet. What more do you want?'

Pinchon sighed. 'All right. Barkstead said to tell Thurloe that the stuff was buried in the cellar, and bade me mention the arch with the red brick.'

'He referred to his treasure as "stuff"?' asked Chaloner incredulously.

She was thoughtful. 'No, he used a queer expression: his "godly golden goose". He said Thurloe would know what he meant. He made me repeat it, but he was panicky by then, not making sense.'

'When did he say you were to deliver this message?'

'As soon as it was safe. But it was not safe – not after he escaped to Holland, and especially not when he was brought back to die last March.'

'When he said "as soon as it was safe", I do not think he expected three years to lapse.'

'He should have made himself more clear, then,' said Pinchon resentfully. 'If he had given proper orders, I might have found a way to get to Thurloe, and we would have been rich. Now it is too late.'

But Chaloner did not think the treasure had been Barkstead's main concern, and Thurloe would certainly not have wanted the encumbrance of additional wealth at a time when Royalists were confiscating it all. It had been a different message the Lieutenant of the Tower had been passing to the Spymaster General, although Thurloe had never received it, and now Barkstead was long past caring.

Three men shadowed Chaloner until he was out of the Fleet Rookery, although they made no attempt to intercept him. They merely maintained a discreet distance, and seemed interested only in making sure he left. Chaloner thanked Mother Greene for her help, promised

306

to return with a penny as soon as he had one, and took his leave, relieved to be away from the stench of poverty and despair.

He tried to make sense of what he had learned. Barkstead had wanted Thurloe to know he had buried something, but Pinchon had maintained a frightened silence until greed and destitution had overcome her reticence. Why Thurloe? Was it something to do with the Brotherhood, and Barkstead had naturally turned to a man who held similar values? Was it because both had been loyal supporters of Cromwell, or because Barkstead had trusted Thurloe to pass the treasure to his wife and child? Or, perhaps more darkly, did he want Thurloe to use it to oust the King when the time was right? And what had he meant by 'godly golden goose'? Chaloner would never have described money as godly, since it invariably brought out the worst in people. He walked slowly, a sixth sense helping him avoid speeding carts and undersized men with quick fingers, and was startled when he heard his name spoken with some exasperation.

'North,' he said, recognising his neighbour. 'Were you talking to me?'

'I *said* you are limping,' said North irritably. 'And then I asked whether that fellow hurt you the other night – Ellis said you spent all yesterday in bed. He wounded me. Look at my nose!'

'Is it very sore?' asked Chaloner, trying to sound concerned. The appendage was red, but that could have been due to the weather, and he had not pulled it very hard. North was exaggerating.

'Extremely. But I gave him a hiding he will not forget. We live in a wicked world, Heyden.'

'We live in one full of obscene language, too,' remarked

307

Chaloner, not liking the way the incident was being warped so far from the truth. He had not been doing anything so terrible in the garden, and North's vicious club and Faith's gun had been far in excess of what had been warranted.

North looked sheepish. 'I was a soldier during the wars, and learned some ripe expressions that occasionally slip out under duress. However, I regret shocking you.'

'I shall probably recover,' said Chaloner gravely. 'Good day to you, sir.'

They exchanged bows and parted, Chaloner supposing that since he owned so little, he was more sanguine about theft than North. After a while, he found himself near White Hall, so asked one of the palace guards whether Evett was free to see him. He was shown to a tiny chamber near the Holbein Gate and ordered to wait, and while he was fretting about the wasted time, he saw one of the cloth measurers in the street outside. The man greeted him with pleasure, and showed him a transverse flute he had just collected from the artisan on the Strand, who had been commissioned to make it for him. It was a beautiful thing of silver, and Chaloner was charmed by the sweet notes it made.

'Did you recognise the dagger that killed Clarke?' he asked, when the demonstration had ended.

The measurer raised his eyebrows. 'What dagger?'

'Captain Evett has not shown it to you?'

The man shook his head, then backed away when a thickset man strode past. 'Odds fish! There is the clock keeper! I do not want him to see me with you. Next time, bring your bass viol, because at least then we would *look* as though we were doing something innocent.'

308

He hurried away, and it was only a few more moments before Evett arrived, dishevelled and fastening the buttons on his breeches.

'What have you done about Clarke?' asked Chaloner without preamble. 'Have you identified the owner of the murder weapon yet?'

Evett grimaced. 'I have asked half of London, but no one will tell me anything.'

'You failed to ask one of the cloth measurers.'

Evett bristled at what sounded like an accusation. 'Rubbish! I spoke to all three in the kitchens, when the clock keeper was out bull-baiting. Did one tell you I had not? I wonder why?'

'Ask him again,' suggested Chaloner, backing down. Perhaps the cloth measurer had not been telling the truth – and he knew for a fact that the fellow was dishonest, because a silver flute cost a lot more than the four pounds he claimed he had paid. If he was willing to lie about that, then what else might he fabricate?

'I hate murder,' said Evett with considerable feeling. 'Do you know what I was doing before you came? Something a lot more profitable than hawking daggers about – I was listening to a meeting of navy commissioners through one of those holes, learning all sorts of important facts for the future.'

'With your breeches undone?' asked Chaloner, wondering just how much Evett wanted to be Lord High Admiral. 'But never mind that. What else have you done about Clarke?'

'I wrote to his wife, asking if his romantic message meant anything special to her. If it does not, then we shall know it was code – and that it was actually intended for someone else.'

Chaloner suspected Mrs Clarke would tell him to mind his own business, and changed the subject. 'What do you think the Earl will say if he learns Barkstead's hoard does not exist?'

'Mother Pinchon said—'

'She is not the trusted servant we were led to believe. It is true she helped Barkstead parcel up his treasure, but there is no evidence to prove he actually buried it there. In fact, the more I think about it, the more convinced I am that he would never have left it in a place like the Tower. It is probably in Holland, being used to support his family. He was a sensible man, well organised; he would not have left his wife destitute.'

'Then you are in trouble, my friend. That is not a solution that will please Clarendon.'

'But it may be the truth. However, all is not lost, because I think there may be a different kind of treasure concealed in the Tower.'

'If it is not gold, the Earl will not care,' warned Evett.

'I imagine that depends on what it is.' Chaloner shrugged. 'I will continue to investigate and see what emerges. Perhaps it will be enough to see me hired as an intelligence officer again – a proper one this time, not just someone who runs shady errands for the Lord Chancellor.'

'Now you know how *I* feel,' muttered Evett.

'Where does Ingoldsby live? The Earl told me to talk to Barkstead's friends, so I had better do it.'

Evett gave him an address near the Tower. 'And I will interview the cloth measurers *again*, so—'

But Chaloner had spotted Metje walking along King Street with a shopping basket over her arm. He nodded an abrupt farewell to the startled captain and darted after

310

her, weaving through the crowd and calling her name until she looked around. She did not return his smile.

'What?' she demanded crossly.

He took a step back, startled by the hostile greeting. 'I just wanted to speak to you. What are you doing here? I thought you did your shopping at—'

'I came to buy a poultice for Mr North's nose, if you must know – here is the apothecary's receipt. But what about you? You *say* you have secured work, but you have had no money since Saturday, and I came to see you before chapel this morning, but you were already gone and it was far too early for the victualling office. God alone knows where you were and what you were doing at such an hour. How much longer can we live like this, Thomas?'

'Has North been talking about leaving London again?' asked Chaloner gently, suspecting his early departure was not the real reason for her display of temper.

She nodded miserably. 'And it is your fault. You frightened him with your nocturnal invasion, and Temperance has been very outspoken against Preacher Hill over the last week – at your instigation. It is almost as though you *want* them to leave, and me to be destitute again.'

'I am sorry, Meg. I did not want North to know I was trying to see you the other night.'

There were tears in her eyes. 'Perhaps we should part company, Tom. We have been in England for months now, and your situation is as hopeless now as when we arrived.'

He took her hand. 'I am working as hard as I can. Please do not give up on me yet.'

She gave him a wan smile, then glanced covertly behind her. 'You see that man in the red hat? He asked whether

311

I spoke Dutch earlier, and he has been watching me ever since.'

'Go home. I will make sure he does not follow you.'

'How will you stop him – you with your lame leg which does not seem to be getting any better? Perhaps you should give up dashing around dark gardens in the middle of the night.'

He fought down a tart response. 'I will think of something. I am not entirely useless.'

He watched her walk away, then stepped forward to intercept the man who immediately started to follow her. He pushed his dagger against the fellow's ribs, making his captive gasp in alarm.

'I do not have any money! I am just a weaver.'

The accent was familiar, and Chaloner released him. 'Where are you from? Amsterdam?'

The man was appalled, eyes full of naked terror. 'I am Danish – from . . . from Hamburg.'

'It is not safe to accost people and demand to know what languages they speak,' said Chaloner in Dutch. 'You will be shot as a spy.'

The man hung his head, and replied in the same tongue. 'I do not know what to do. My friends shun me and it feels dangerous here. I was just looking for a sympathetic countryman . . .'

'It will get worse,' warned Chaloner. 'Your safest option would be to sell all you have, and leave.'

'Will you give the same advice to that woman you were just talking to? We are all in danger now.'

Chaloner headed towards the Tower, aiming for the street near the Royal Foundation of St Katherine, where Evett had told him Ingoldsby lived, his thoughts a chaos

312

of worry for Metje. As he passed the castle, he paused by the blackened heads on poles, placed to gaze across the Thames. He wondered which was Barkstead's, and joined the gathering of people who gaped at the spectacle, where someone rather more familiar with the heads than was nice told him Barkstead's was the second from the left. The Lieutenant of the Tower had boasted long hair, watchful eyes and a moustache, and the bald skull with its missing teeth and sagging jaw bore no resemblance to the dignified man Chaloner had met.

'What did you want Thurloe to know?' Chaloner asked him softly. 'What was your godly golden goose? And did you praise God, like Hewson, Clarke and Lee? What binds you to the Brotherhood, secrets buried in the Tower and the murder of Thurloe's spies?'

He stared a while longer, then went in search of the regicide who had managed to do rather well for himself, a feat all the more remarkable given that Richard Ingoldsby was Oliver Cromwell's cousin and had made much of that fact when the Lord Protector was in power. Ingoldsby lived in a fine Tudor mansion that overlooked the hospital gardens. Chaloner was about to knock at the door when he heard the clatter of hoofs travelling too fast down the narrow road. He turned to see a stallion galloping towards him, its rider kicking it forward for all he was worth. He saw a chicken disappear in an explosion of feathers, and heard people yell in alarm. The rider's hat was pulled over his eyes and his collar was up – given his cavalier progress, Chaloner was not surprised he did not want to be recognised. He watched him come closer, but it did not occur to him that he was the fellow's intended target until the very last moment – by which time, it was almost too late.

The horseman slashed with his sword as he thundered past. Chaloner threw himself to one side, and the blade missed him by the width of a finger. He scrambled to his feet and watched in disbelief as the rider wheeled around and came at him again. He ducked behind the gatepost, and the blade missed a second time. When the fellow came for a third pass, Chaloner drew his own sword, and was bracing himself for the impact, when there was a shout, and several soldiers began to canter towards them. The horseman glanced at the advancing posse, then spurred his mount in the opposite direction.

'He was after doing you mischief,' said a passing merchant. 'I wondered what he was doing behind that tavern all morning, swathed and silent. I should have known it was nothing good.'

'Have you seen him before?'

The man shook his head and lowered his voice. 'Do not take it personally. None of us like Ingoldsby, and that rider probably decided to deprive him of a caller – to show the world that we do not want the likes of him as our neighbour.'

'Why not?'

The merchant regarded him askance. 'Clearly you have never met the fellow, or you would not ask. We dislike his manners, his greedy wife and his lies. Cousin Cromwell forced his hand indeed!'

He walked on, leaving Chaloner puzzled. Would someone really kill Ingoldsby's visitors to make a point? Somehow, he did not think so. He reviewed the people who knew he had intended to see Ingoldsby. Thurloe did, and Sarah had been listening outside his door when they had talked about it. Had she sent someone to kill him? Had she hoped Snow might save her the bother,

314

when Chaloner had so gallantly stepped in to rescue her? Or was Thurloe angry with him, and wanted rid of a man whose loyalty was no longer assured? Or had Sarah mentioned the matter to Dalton, who did not want anyone interrogating a fellow brother? And finally, there was Evett, who had given him directions to Ingoldsby's house. But Evett was in White Hall, asking about the dagger that had killed Clarke. Chaloner's thoughts returned to the Daltons, although cold logic told him that the main reason for choosing them as suspects was that he did not want to believe the culprit was Thurloe.

He waited to see if the rider would return, but the fellow obviously knew there was no point in mounting another assault when there were soldiers looking for him, so Chaloner knocked on Ingoldsby's door. The politician was at home, but a series of wails suggested it was a bad time for callers. Nonetheless, a servant showed Chaloner into a low-ceilinged, wood-panelled room that was scented with sweet lavender, and asked him to wait. The portraits on the walls were of aloof men on oddly proportioned horses, as if Ingoldsby wanted to impress people with his Cavalier ancestry.

When he came to greet his guest, Ingoldsby looked even more porcine than he had in Will's Coffee House. He was chewing something, clearly having rammed the last of it in his mouth just before he entered the chamber. His cheeks bulged, and when he spoke, he was incomprehensible.

'I said my wife is in mourning,' he repeated irritably when Chaloner looked blank. 'Can you not hear her shrieks of distress?'

Chaloner cocked his head, but the cries had stopped, and before he could answer, the door opened and a woman entered. She carried a handkerchief, but her eyes were clear and blue, and he thought that while a good deal of noise might have been made, very few actual tears had been shed: Ingoldsby's wife was doing what was expected of her, but without genuine sorrow. Her face was familiar, and he knew he had seen her before. After a moment, the memory snapped into place: she had been with the regicides who had escaped to Holland. She had left soon after, when her husband had secured his pardon, but she had been with them for a while.

'I am sorry to come at a bad time,' he said, after she had been introduced as Elizabeth, kin to the wealthy Lees of Hartwell in Northamptonshire. There was no flicker of recognition when he bowed to her, and he knew she had not associated him with the silently unobtrusive nephew of the exiled regicide.

'The deceased is a brother-in-law from my first marriage,' said Elizabeth, her face crumpling into the obligatory mask of grief. 'Some villain shot him with a crossbow.'

'A crossbow?' asked Chaloner, not bothering to hide his shock.

Elizabeth nodded. 'His colleagues from the Treasury came to tell us this morning.'

Chaloner's thoughts whirled. Robert Lee, murdered while in possession of a document bearing the words 'seven' and 'praise God', and who had been digging for treasure in the Tower, was kin to one of the Brotherhood?

'Did he have enemies?' he asked. 'Or was he involved in anything dangerous?'

Ingoldsby glared at him. 'Ours is a respectable family, and although Robert was not wealthy, he was obviously very well-connected, since he is related to us.'

316

'He would have had money eventually,' added Elizabeth. 'A woman with a large dowry.'

'They said a thief killed him for the five pounds he kept on his window sill,' said Ingoldsby, more angry than distressed. 'And a friend in Fetter Lane told me that a prowler fired a great musket at him in his *own garden* the other night! What is becoming of our country?'

Mr North of Fetter Lane is my neighbour,' said Chaloner. 'But how do *you* know him, Sir Richard? He seldom engages in social activities outside his chapel.'

Ingoldsby was not about to admit to being a member of the Brotherhood. 'We are both patrons of the Royal Foundation,' he replied a little defensively. 'I donate money to thank God for destroying the Commonwealth, and he does it to praise God.'

'To praise God?' asked Chaloner, more sharply than he had intended.

Ingoldsby regarded him oddly. 'Most of us do it on Sundays, but he does it with every breath. It is all very laudable, but I could never be a Puritan. I would forget myself and have some fun.'

Was that the meaning of praise God: the way Puritans lived? But Clarke had not been a Puritan, and neither had Hewson, as far as Chaloner knew. Meanwhile, Ingoldsby was waiting for him to say why he had come.

'I am acting on behalf of the Lord Chancellor, regarding Sir John Barkstead's—'

Ingoldsby interrupted in alarm. 'Barkstead was a traitor, so I seldom had occasion to speak to *him*! I know nothing about his evil deeds. I am devoted to the King, and—'

'Your loyalty is not in question, sir. My enquiries do

317

not relate to Barkstead's politics, but to the dispersal of his estate after his death.'

'Oh,' said Ingoldsby, relieved. 'However, I still cannot help you. He was wealthy, but he did not give any of his money to me – not that I would have accepted it, of course, him being a Parliamentarian.'

'Of course,' said Chaloner. 'It seems he spirited some of it out of the country.'

Ingoldsby nodded. 'Most regicides did – they had to. Barkstead smuggled his out on a fishing boat. Old Chaloner routed a cache through Scotland, but spent most of it on high living and died a pauper. Hewson put his hoard inside bales of wool, but the Dutch got wind of it and confiscated it all.'

'Did you see Barkstead with his gold?'

It was Elizabeth who answered. 'My husband was busy persuading the King of his loyalty at the time, but I saw it – in The Hague, when I was waiting to hear whether it was safe to come home. It was packed into butter firkins, and needed *three* carts to transport it. There were bags of money, beautiful jewellery, precious stones, silver plate, crosses . . . It was a fabulous sight.'

'How much do you think it was worth?'

'In excess of thirteen thousand pounds! I know that for a fact, because it was taken to the Jews for investing, and I saw the receipts.'

'How did you come to do that?' asked Chaloner, puzzled.

'Because after Barkstead was arrested, Downing went through his house looking for plunder. He had decided Barkstead should pay for his own transport to London, you see.'

'He said that?' This was low, even for Downing.

318

She nodded. 'But Barkstead's wealth was with the money-lenders and therefore inaccessible to him. Downing toted up the receipts and showed us how they amounted to more than thirteen thousand pounds – a fabulous sum. Barkstead was laughing, because he had outwitted him.'

'What about Sir Michael Livesay?' asked Chaloner. 'Did he send money overseas?'

'Why do you ask about him?' asked Ingoldsby suspiciously.

Chaloner shrugged. 'No reason, other than the fact that he has disappeared and no one knows where. If he is dead, then the Crown would like to liquidate his estate.'

'He is dead,' said Ingoldsby. His tone was wary. 'He was escaping from England on a ship, but there was an explosion. Everyone onboard was blown to pieces.'

'Was the explosion a deliberate act aimed against Livesay, or an accident?'

Ingoldsby effected an attitude of studied carelessness. 'I have no idea – I was not there.'

Every fibre in Chaloner's being knew he was lying. 'Very well,' he said, picking up his hat. 'If you are unwilling to cooperate here, then the Lord Chancellor can talk to you in the Tower instead.'

Ingoldsby was appalled, and reached out to stop him from leaving. 'Wait! All right. I will tell you what I know, but you *must* explain to Clarendon that my role was innocent.'

'Someone seized your hand and signed your name?' asked Chaloner insolently, freeing his wrist.

Ingoldsby glowered at him. 'I was to have travelled on that boat, too, but I changed my mind at the last minute. I am a poor sailor and the forecast was stormy. I saw the ship leave the harbour, and I heard the blast. Livesay did not stand a chance.'

Only if Livesay *was* on the vessel, Chaloner thought. Perhaps he was a poor sailor, too. Or perhaps he had seen a warning in Ingoldsby's abrupt disembarkation, and it had saved his life. Or did it mean Ingoldsby had killed his 'brother' and fellow regicide, by putting gunpowder on his ship?

'I understand you belong to a certain Brotherhood,' he began. 'I have—'

'I know of no Brotherhood,' snapped Ingoldsby. He was beginning to look dangerous. 'And if you accuse me of belonging to secret sects, I shall complain to the King, and not even Clarendon will be able to protect you. So take *that* message to your Lord Chancellor!'

# Chapter 9

After he had been ejected by Ingoldsby, Chaloner went to Lee's house, and watched two constables strip it of anything saleable, then carry Lee's body to the parish church. When they had gone, he knocked at the door of the next building, which was answered by a man with a French accent. The fellow refused to answer questions until Chaloner addressed him in his own tongue, after which the flood of information was difficult to stem.

'Oh, there were odd happenings, all right. Several days ago – perhaps the night Lee died, since the corpse was not fresh when it was found – he entertained a couple. I assumed they were a colleague and his wife from the Treasury. Lee welcomed them like they were the King and Queen of France.'

'Did either carry a crossbow?'

'No,' said the Frenchman. 'I would have noticed that. Poor Lee. He had a young lady, too, and was destined for better things in life, so it is a shame he was murdered.'

'Do you know her name?'

The Frenchman shook his head. 'But she lived on Mincing Lane.'

'Fanny Robinson,' mused Chaloner to himself. 'The Lord Mayor's daughter. Her home is in Mincing Lane, and she said her beau was called Robert and that he was a Treasury clerk. No wonder Robinson did not object to the match: Lee was kin to Ingoldsby, a fellow brother.'

He wanted time to consider what he had learned, so he walked to St Paul's Cathedral, intending to sit at the base of one of its ancient pillars and analyse the confusion of facts that ricocheted around his mind. He had just reached the churchyard, where a lively market had established itself among its lichen-stained tombstones, when he saw Leybourn. The bookseller was with his brother and the hulking Wade, and Chaloner watched them enter Don Pedro's Spanish Eating House together.

Don Pedro's was a place where the respectable classes could buy an affordable meal and eat it in decent company. Unlike the male-dominated coffee houses, women were welcome, which meant the air was not quite so thick with smoke, and the decor was less masculine. Located in Panier Alley, it was owned by Donald Peters, who was no more Spanish than Chaloner, but who liked to maintain the illusion of overseas exoticism by affecting a foreign accent – when he remembered – interspersed with phrases once learned from an Iberian papal legate. 'Don Pedro', as he styled himself, was a source of gossip and information, and Chaloner suspected that a few hours spent listening to him would go a long way towards providing him with the knowledge every other Londoner seemed to take for granted.

The rich scent of baking spilled across the street, enticing customers to sample Señora Nell's pies, infamous for powerful spices and robust pastry. However, it was not a place for men with no money, so Chaloner picked up a pebble and tossed it at a window, not sufficiently hard to break it, but firmly enough to make a sharp crack that had everyone turning towards the sound. When all eyes were looking in the opposite direction, Chaloner slipped through the door and headed for the table next to Leybourn's. The bookseller had just been served a beaker of wine and, as he passed, Chaloner stole it in a sleight of hand that would have impressed the most skilful of pickpockets.

'It was stone from the wheel of a carriage,' announced Pedro in his peculiar London-Spanish. '*Mama Mia!* It happens all the time.'

'Don Pedro,' called Leybourn, when the fuss had died down. 'What does a man have to do to order a drink? Eat one of your pies?'

'Nell's *empanadas* are the best in London,' declared Pedro, offended. 'My wife, she make them fresh, just like she did in España. Besides, I already brought you wine – as soon as you come in.'

Leybourn gestured to the empty table. 'Did it have wings, then?'

'Señor Heyden,' said Pedro, obligingly bringing Leybourn a replacement and recognising another patron at the same time. 'When did you arrive? I never seen you come, but we been busy today, so if I served you without saying *buenos dias*, I apologise. Where is your hair? Are you having it made into a *peluca*? It is a good idea, because us *hombres* never know when it might fall out or turn grey.'

He bustled away, and Leybourn turned around, as Chaloner knew he would. 'Heyden,' he said cautiously, no doubt recalling his curt dismissal when they had met in the grocer's shop. 'May I introduce my friend, Thomas Wade? My brother Robert I am sure you recall.'

Chaloner stood to return the large man's bow. 'Mr Wade.'

Wade read something in Chaloner's bland greeting that was not there. He looked distinctly uncomfortable and began to gabble. 'I see my name is familiar to you. Perhaps you heard it in connection with a small misunderstanding over a consignment of fur. I did not realise she meant me to *kill* the poor beast, and she was angry when I sent only combings.'

'An understandable error,' said Chaloner, wondering what he was talking about.

'For the masque,' elaborated Wade. 'My responsibilities at the Tower include overseeing the royal menagerie. A collection of creatures has resided there since it was built, as I am sure you are aware.'

'I have certainly seen the lion.'

'*She* has seen it, too,' said Wade resentfully. 'And she demanded its fur. I sent her two sacks of hairs, thinking she wanted to stuff cushions for His Majesty or some such thing, but it transpires that she wanted the *skin* for her disguise at the masque. She expected me to destroy Sonya!'

'God forbid,' said Chaloner. 'Not Sonya?'

'He means Lady Castlemaine,' explained Leybourn, reading his bemusement. 'Sonya is a lion, and Lady Castlemaine wanted its fur – a "castle mane", if you see her contorted pun.'

'I thought only males had manes,' said Chaloner. 'Why would Sonya be at risk?'

'There was a mistake when he was born,' replied

324

Wade dolefully. 'You will appreciate it is difficult to get near lion cubs when their mother is present.'

'Will you join us for an apple dumpling, Heyden?' asked Leybourn. His expression was arch. 'I know you have an acute interest in that particular fruit.'

Chaloner accepted, then listened to the banter between the brothers and Wade as he ate, making the occasional comment to encourage them, but preferring to gain their measure than to speak himself. It was some time before Robert realised the discussion was almost entirely one sided.

'You are quiet,' he said coolly. 'Do you have nothing to say?'

'I had an unpleasant experience this morning,' replied Chaloner, taking a sip of wine. 'I was near the Tower, when I saw a body removed from a house. It had been shot with a crossbow.'

'I thought you would be used to that sort of thing,' said Leybourn, surprised.

'What do you mean?' demanded Chaloner immediately.

Leybourn coloured. 'I mean you coped well enough when Kelyng was on your heels. I would not have imagined *you* to be unsettled by the sight of a corpse, no matter what its manner of death.'

'I dislike an excess of blood,' said Chaloner. 'And there was certainly an excess in this case. His name was Lee, and he worked for the Treasury. He was kin to Ingoldsby and lived on Thames Street.'

'God save us!' breathed Wade, white-faced with shock. He started to stand, then sank down again when he realised there was nothing he could do.

'Did you know him?' asked Chaloner innocently. 'I am

325

sorry. I should have guessed that a Treasury man and the Tower's commissioner might have been acquainted.'

'I have not . . .' Wade hesitated, then spoke more firmly. 'I did not know him.'

Chaloner frowned. 'Then you seem oddly moved by a stranger's death. Or are you like me, and have an aversion to spilled blood?'

'I will spill some of yours if you do not leave him alone,' growled Robert.

Chaloner leaned back in his chair. 'I wonder if Lee advocated moderation, like the Brotherhood.'

'Brotherhood?' asked Wade. He turned paler still, while Robert's jaw dropped.

'You and Robert are members,' said Chaloner to Wade. 'I saw you both at Will's Coffee House. I imagine an organisation like that is always in need of funds.'

He knew he was coming dangerously close to letting Wade know the hunt was still on for Barkstead's treasure, but could think of no other way to broach the subject. Wade gnawed on his lower lip and his eyes darted around the room like those of a trapped rat. He was clearly terrified.

'What are you suggesting?' demanded Robert, hand dropping to the hilt of his sword. 'That *we* shot this Lee for his money? If you spied on our meetings, then you will know most of our members are rich, and we do not need paltry pickings from a Treasury clerk to help us.'

'To help you what?' asked Chaloner.

'To help us in our objectives,' snapped Robert. 'To spread the word that the future lies in equanimity and tolerance. Who are you? A spy for the King? One of Kelyng's men?'

'Not Kelyng,' said Leybourn quietly. 'I saw Bennet try to kill him.'

326

'But he did not succeed, did he,' snarled Robert. 'Perhaps it was a ruse, to persuade you that he is a friend. I ought to run him through.'

'Stop,' ordered Leybourn sharply, seeing his brother start to stand. 'Sit down.'

'Practise what you preach,' suggested Chaloner mildly. 'Equanimity and tolerance.'

It was the wrong thing to say, because Robert surged to his feet and hauled his sword from his belt. 'Name the time and place, and I will meet you there.'

'No, Rob!' cried Leybourn. 'You do not know what you are doing.'

'I know I am being insulted.' Robert glowered at Chaloner. 'Meet me Christmas Day at dawn in Lincoln's Inn Fields. We shall see then whether your sword is as sharp as your tongue.'

Because Robert's voice was loud, every one of Don Pedro's customers was listening as he and his brother began to quarrel – Leybourn was urging him to retract the challenge, which served to fuel his temper all the more. Chaloner took the opportunity to escape, disliking the attention Robert was drawing to himself. Craving peace and solitude, which would not be found in the busy St Paul's, he walked instead to his parish church – St Dunstan-in-the-West on Fleet Street. Its rector was Joseph Thompson, who knew unscheduled visits from his congregation usually meant they wanted to escape the noisy flurry of London, and he always left them alone when they pushed open the clanking door and breathed their relief at the echoing stillness within. He nodded a friendly greeting to Chaloner, then turned his attention back to his registers.

327

Chaloner found a bench at the back, leaned against the wall and closed his eyes, wondering why Robert had responded to his questions with such fury. It was scarcely the kind of behaviour one would expect from a man belonging to an organisation devoted to restraint, and the encounter had left him unsettled. To take his mind off it, he considered what he knew about Lee. He was sure the murder was significant, since Lee had been present during the search for Barkstead's treasure *and* he had been killed while holding a document bearing the words seven and praise God. Had the message been intended for Thurloe, as Chaloner believed Clarke's and Hewson's had been? But then who had stolen it from Lee's corpse?

Next, he considered the way his three quite separate assignments were now inextricably linked. Thurloe wanted Clarke's murder solved, but had warned Chaloner against finding Barkstead's treasure; the Lord Chancellor wanted Barkstead's cache, but had denied Chaloner permission to look into Clarke's death; and both men were wary of Kelyng. It seemed Thurloe had been right to advise Chaloner to abandon the search for the hoard, since the Ingoldsbys' evidence put the butter firkins firmly in Holland with Barkstead's wife.

After a while, Chaloner left the quiet confines of the church, and a sharp nip in the air outside told him there would be more snow that night. Although it was only two o'clock, it was a dark day, and here and there the street gleamed yellow from lamps set in windows, while lanthorns – hollow horns containing candles – gleamed inside carriages, giving them a warm, cosy look as they rumbled past. Street traders with packs and trays yelled hoarsely, their breath pluming white before them, and everywhere folk were huddled inside their cloaks. Pigeons roosted in the skeletal oak tree in St Dunstan's church-yard, fluffed up to almost twice their size as the wind blew and the branches swayed.

Chaloner was about to head home, when he became aware of a commotion. It had already attracted spectators, and others were stopping to join them, reminding him of a trick his uncle had often played. Old Chaloner had liked to stand in a public place and point to the sky in an excited manner, asking people whether they could see 'it'. They nearly always could, and he encouraged them to witness all manner of marvels, some of which were then reported as fact in the daily news sheets. His most famous prodigy – as such phenomena were called – had been a complete replay of the Battle of Naseby in cloud formations, and some spectators had even claimed to have recognised the faces of known combatants.

However, it was no wry mischief that controlled the crowd that evening, but something far more invidious. Pulling his hood over his wig, partly for warmth, but mostly for disguise, Chaloner eased his way through the onlookers until he could see. There, at the centre of the group, was a bruised and bloodied man who begged piti-fully for his life. Unfortunately for him, his pleas were in Dutch, which did more to incense the crowd than secure their compassion. Standing over him was Sir John Kelyng, while Bennet and Snow hovered to one side.

'What is happening?' Chaloner asked Joseph Thompson, who had also joined the throng, and was watching with nervous apprehension.

The rector grimaced. 'John Kelyng has found himself another Hollander to torment.'

329

'What do you mean by "another"? Does he dislike them, then?'

Thompson regarded him in disbelief. 'You must have seen him doing this before – and if not, then you definitely heard my sermon reviling this kind of behaviour last week.' He sighed when Chaloner looked blank. 'Sometimes, I wonder why I bother. I might just as well preach to the pigeons.'

'Why has he taken against the Dutch?'

Thompson raised his eyebrows. 'How can you live in London and not know that? He is driven by a deep loyalty to the King, and it leads him to see plots and rebellions in the most unlikely of quarters. These last few months have seen him moving against the Dutch, because Mr Thurloe – whom he detests – once employed Dutch-based agents to spy on His Majesty when he was in exile.'

'Christ!' muttered Chaloner, thinking he and Metje would hang together if Kelyng ever found out about their relationship.

'He will have that poor Hollander transported, I imagine,' said Thompson unhappily. 'And his property confiscated and given to the King. John Kelyng and I have known each other for years – since we were students together at Trinity Hall – and I have tried time and time again to make him see that this kind of activity is unjust. But he just smiles and says we must agree to differ, since neither of us is willing to accept the other's point of view.'

'So, there is nothing you can do to stop this man from being persecuted?' asked Chaloner. 'We are not at war with the Dutch yet.'

'*I* stop it?' asked Thompson uncomfortably. 'One does

330

not simply march up to John and start issuing orders –
at least, not while that loutish Bennet is listening. I would
end up sitting next to the Dutchman on a boat to
Jamaica.'

Chaloner watched as the petrified Netherlander was
invited to accompany Snow to the Tower. Most of the
spectators followed, jeering at the man's naked fright, so
it was not long before Kelyng and Bennet were alone.
No one, it seemed, wanted to linger near them, given
their penchant for random accusations. Seizing the opportunity for some impromptu eavesdropping, Chaloner
nodded a farewell to Thompson and went to lurk behind
a black carriage that was obviously Kelyng's personal
transport. He knelt and pretended to fiddle with the
buckle on his boot. The windows of the vehicle were
open, and it was absurdly easy to hear and even see what
was happening on the other side, making Chaloner think
once again that Kelyng and his retinue were sadly incompetent.

The Reverend Thompson stood thoughtfully for a
moment, then approached Kelyng. Chaloner supposed
he had seen a moral challenge in their discussion: he had
preached against tyranny and then had done nothing to
prevent it outside his own church. He hoped it would
not lead to the man's arrest.

'I must protest, John,' the rector said reproachfully.
'That poor fellow was only buying dried meat.'

'He was victualling himself for a long journey,' argued
Bennet, before Kelyng could speak. 'I have been following
him. He plans to leave England and return to Holland.'

'Is that a crime?' asked Thompson. 'If I were Dutch,
I would want to go home, too.'

'You must have read what the broadsheets say about

331

Netherlanders,' said Bennet. 'They are cheese-worms, who do nothing but eat fat and bathe in butter.'

'No man of breeding and intelligence believes those scurrilous rags,' said Thompson, treating Bennet to a look of utter contempt. 'Let the fellow go, for pity's sake. He is not worth your time.'

'*We* decide who—' began Bennet, angry by the slur on his ancestry and wits.

Kelyng cut across him, waving him to silence in a way that made him seethe with indignation. 'You are probably right, Joseph – the cheese-worm will almost certainly prove to be inconsequential. And I doubt he owns anything worth confiscating, not if he was buying dried meat. It means he cannot afford butter, which all Hollanders prefer.'

'That is true enough,' said Bennet, turning his back on the rector in an attempt to cut him out of the discussion. 'So, we shall have him sent to Jamaica, and then we can concentrate on finding the woman who murdered Storey—'

'You will leave her alone,' snapped Kelyng. 'I could scarce believe my ears when Snow confessed to shooting at her when she was on a horse. I will *not* have my people putting animals at risk. And that goes for you, too. And I absolutely forbid you to kill Thurloe's shorn-haired agent.'

'I do not understand,' said Bennet, scowling. 'He made a fool of me, and—'

'You made a fool of yourself. Thomas from Becket and Guy of Fawkes, indeed! I should never have appointed a chamberlain who is lacking a university education.'

'I went to university,' said Bennet in a strangled voice. He looked as though he was only just in control of himself,

332

and his teeth were clamped so tightly together his jaw muscles bulged. 'Oxford.'

'Three days at Balliol before being expelled for knowing no Latin,' sneered Kelyng. 'That does not count. But you will *not* kill the lame spy: I have questions to ask him, and I cannot trust you to do it, because he will outwit you again.'

'Then I will kill him when you have finished,' declared Bennet tightly.

'No, you will not,' said Kelyng testily. 'And I have explained why at least three times already: I was in Leybourn's bookshop the other day, and I heard him mention a short-haired, limping friend who owns a turkey. It is almost certainly the same man, so you are not to touch him. What would happen to the poor creature if you dispatched its owner? A large game bird would hardly be safe with Mrs Kelyng, given that Christmas is so close. So, you are to bring him to me alive. Is that clear?'

Bennet's face flushed with a deep, dangerous rage, and Chaloner was certain the order would be ignored – if a body was dumped in the Thames, Kelyng would never know he had been disobeyed. Bennet nodded to his master and strode away, holding himself rigidly and barely able to contain his temper.

'You should watch him, John,' advised Thompson, staring after Bennet in rank disapproval. 'He does not like being insulted, and he is vicious, irrational and stupid.'

'That is precisely why I hired him,' said Kelyng. 'He makes people take me seriously. But you are right: he is becoming increasingly difficult to control, although I would be more concerned if his intelligence matched his ruthlessness. But do not worry about the Dutchman: I fully intend to release the fellow. The real point of that exercise was to warn foreign spies that their days here are numbered, and to encourage people to be vigilant against outsiders. I have more important fish to fry.'

'Do you mean Thurloe?' asked Thompson. 'I do not think he—'

'He has powerful friends,' interrupted Kelyng, off in a world of his own. 'Even the Lord Chancellor wants him untouched, "lest we blunder into difficulties with the Dutch and need his advice". But Clarendon is suspicious of him, even so, because I intercepted a report from a spy that described a clandestine meeting between him and Downing. Clarendon's code for Downing is "Cerberus" and his name for Thurloe is "Jo" – which is how Thurloe signs his name – so it was not difficult for me to grasp its meaning. The report said they chat in church.'

'I know,' said Thompson dryly. 'It is hard to concentrate on my sacred duties when they jabber all through the service. But has it occurred to you that the agent might have been reporting on Downing, not Thurloe? Downing did change sides in a rather spectacular manner, and the government would be rash to accept such ready turncoats without some degree of surveillance.'

Kelyng gazed at him in surprise, then shook his head. 'It was Thurloe this spy was watching. I copied down the report, and sent the original to Clarendon, so he would not know it had been intercepted. I have a talent for this sort of activity.'

'I can tell, by the way you keep your secrets,' said Thompson gravely. 'Would you mind if I accompany you to the Tower, to make sure this Dutchman is set free?'

'Not at all,' said Kelyng pleasantly. 'I shall enjoy your

company. Do you remember the time when we rescued those ducks from the Trinity Hall kitchens? Those were the days, Joseph!'

Chaloner watched them leave, then started to walk in the opposite direction, to where his cold rooms awaited him. He took great care not to limp.

Snow clicked against the window all evening, and the wind whined through the pane that had been broken by the grenade. Chaloner had no firewood and no money to buy any, but he refused to let Metje 'borrow' some from North. She was vexed when he elected to spend a night in discomfort when a minor theft would have alleviated the problem, but she was angry with him anyway, and he suspected she would have disapproved of whatever he had decided. He watched her slip out of her skirts – the voluminous undergarments stayed defiantly in place – and dive under the bedcovers, muttering venomously about the fact that they were damp as well as icy.

'What do you want me to do, Meg?' he asked tiredly, not sure how to appease her. 'I understand your worries and will do all I can to protect you.'

'How? You cannot afford to hire a guard. Besides, you have been odd ever since we came to England, and we no longer understand each other. I feel as though I do not know you any more.'

He was puzzled. 'What do you mean?'

'Just that – your family has no farm in Buckinghamshire, and I know nothing about them.'

Chaloner was determined no one would, either – at least, not until the wave of hatred against regicides had eased. He rubbed his eyes, wondering whether he should stay away from her for a while.

335

'You have no answer,' she said sadly. 'Tell me the name of the village where you were born then, or the location of your father's manor. Just tell me *something* about you that is true.'

He was bemused. 'Most of what you know is true.'

'And there is a lie for a start.' She turned her back on him. 'Douse the lamp before you sleep.'

'Can we discuss—?'

'You cannot speak without lying, and I do not want untruths.'

'I may die soon,' he said, thinking about Robert Leybourn, who would probably be sharpening his sword as they spoke. He knew it sounded melodramatic, especially given that he had not told her about the bookseller's challenge, but he did not care. 'I do not want to—'

'All right,' she said, sitting up and eyeing him coldly. 'If you are to die, then we had better talk. Ever since we settled in London, you have been mysterious. You go out at odd times, but you have no regular employment. What are you doing?'

'Trying to earn the trust of men who may employ me in the future.' He wondered why his lifestyle should so suddenly perplex her, since he had kept irregular hours ever since she had known him.

'Once, when I was out with Faith, I saw you go inside Lincoln's Inn. Why?'

'I was visiting a friend.'

She lay back down. 'Vague answers that tell me nothing. I do not want to talk to you, Thomas. I am tired of half truths.'

Chaloner lay awake for a long time, listening to the snow, and when he slept, it was fitfully. Once he dreamed about the Tower, with its great thick walls and dank cellars, and fancied he could hear the screams of prisoners. He came awake with a start, only to hear the mournful cry of the bellman outside, bawling that it was one o'clock and exhorting all to bank their fires and douse their candles.

He slept again, but woke just after four to find himself freezing cold and Metje with all the covers. He tried to retrieve some, but her fingers tightened around them and he did not want to wake her. He dressed, wondering when he had last known such a bitter night, then lit the lamp and sat at the table. It was quiet, and a good time to write to Clarendon about Barkstead's cache, and to Thurloe about Clarke. Such messages would have been a waste of time in daylight, when there were more useful things to do, but it was a good way to pass the hours of darkness. When he had finished, he surveyed the notes critically, thinking them pitifully inadequate.

Using cipher without conscious thought, he reported to Thurloe that he had asked Evett to show more White Hall employees the weapon used to murder Clarke. He also mentioned that Kelyng remained determined to bring Thurloe down and was suspicious of his acquaintance with Downing. He added that Lane's missives to Clarendon had been intercepted, and entirely the wrong conclusion drawn. This was worrying, because if Kelyng could misinterpret one letter, then he could do the same with others, and it was often difficult to correct such misunderstandings once accusations had been levelled.

To Clarendon, he hinted that Barkstead's treasure might have been taken abroad, intending to break the bad news by degrees. He described the interview with 'an unnamed witness' who had seen the butter firkins in Holland, and

337

said he planned to speak to others who would confirm or rebut the story. He did not include Thurloe's theory that Barkstead might have left a legacy of a different kind in London, because his thoughts were full of what his dissolute uncle might have done: left a trail to a hoard that comprised a gloating message or a pot of farthings. Barkstead had not struck Chaloner as a practical joker, but the possibility was in the back of his mind nonetheless.

'What are you doing?' Chaloner turned around to see Metje sitting up and looking at him.

'Writing letters to men I hope will employ me.'

'Such as Dalton? Show me what you said to him.'

He regarded her uneasily. 'Why?'

'So I know you are telling the truth.'

Chaloner was beginning to be annoyed with her, and resented the implication that she could not believe a word he said. He flung them across, and waited for the next round of accusations.

She studied the one to Thurloe for a long time. 'I cannot read this.'

'It is cipher – a kind of shorthand.'

'Why would you write in cipher?' She gazed at him with wide eyes. 'You are a spy, selling your country's secrets. *That* is why you were in Holland. Downing did not know half of what you did – I could see it in his eyes. You are a traitor!'

'Please do not shout,' he said quietly. 'I am not a traitor.'

She sniffed. 'I had no idea you communicated in secret languages. But that should not surprise me, I suppose. What is your name?'

He regarded her expressionlessly. 'You know my name.'

'Preacher Hill asked friends from all over Bucking-hamshire about a family called Heyden, with five brothers,

338

two sisters, and a father and mother who died during the wars. He says one does not exist.'

'You have been investigating me?' Chaloner was aghast, not liking the notion that Hill might now have enough information to connect him with his real kin.

'I *need* to know.' She started to cry. 'I am carrying a child, and its father is suddenly a stranger.'

Chaloner gaped at her, then a smile spread across his face. 'You are pregnant?'

She would not let him touch her. 'I do not know why you are so pleased. It will mean an end to your carefree existence. You will *have* to find proper work now.'

Chaloner ignored her attempts to fend him off, and took her in his arms, cradling her to his chest, fiercely at first, then gently when he thought about the precious life within. 'It will mean a *change* to my carefree existence. This is wonderful news, Meg. How long have you . . . ?'

'A while. And do not ask why I did not tell you before – you who has kept secrets from me for years. I am surprised you did not notice, anyway.'

He inspected her critically. 'You do not look any bigger. Are you sure . . . ?'

'Of course,' she said, a smile tugging at the corners of her mouth. 'I am a woman.'

'You cannot refuse to marry me now. We will name our daughter after you. Meg.'

'Meg what? Meg Heyden? Or shall we just say Meg de Haas, because then we can be sure it is right? Please tell me your name, Tom. Your *real* name? I do not like this secrecy between us.'

'I cannot. It has nothing to do with trust, and I *will* tell you, I promise. Just not now.'

'Why not now?'

'Because it is not safe – not for you or for my family. When the time is right, I shall take you to meet them, and then you will see there is nothing sinister or unpleasant about them. Please trust me.'

'I shall try,' she said, although there was a deep unhappiness in her eyes. 'For Meg's sake.'

While Metje greeted the prospect of a child with mixed emotions, Chaloner did not. He was delighted, and found it difficult to concentrate on anything else. It was Christmas Eve, and although some of the more strict Puritan families still ignored the merry preparations that were taking place around them, it was generally a time for celebration and relaxation. Green boughs appeared in the most unlikely of places, and people bedecked their churches with candles and wreaths. The scent of roasting chestnuts, spiced wine and other seasonal favourites filled the air, and Chaloner wished he had money to buy some for Metje. Feeling he should do something to mark the occasion, he took his much-read copy of Farnaby's *Rhetoric* to Cripplegate, where Leybourn had his shop, as soon as it was light.

There were dozens of booksellers in London, but Chaloner knew why he was drawn to the one run by the Leybourns. When Robert had first challenged him, he had regarded the duel as more nuisance than cause for concern, confident in his superior skills. But Metje's news had changed all that, and he found he did not want to meet Robert's sword at dawn the following day. The chances were that he would win, but supposing he did not? What would happen to Metje without a provider? Would North take pity on an unwed mother and continue to employ her? Chaloner did not think so: it would suggest his household condoned sin, and even if North and Temperance were moved to compassion, Faith would pressure them to reconsider. Metje would be doomed to poverty.

Leybourn's house smelled of paper, ink and the leather used to bind books after they were printed. It was an agreeable aroma, and the shop was the kind of place Chaloner loved, with closely packed shelves and treasures at every turn. It was busy, because several graves in St Giles without Cripplegate – the land had been sold for a new building – had been opened the hour before dawn, and the public had been invited to watch. The exhumation over, folk gravitated towards the nearby shops to escape a sudden downpour, and Chaloner saw a number of familiar faces, including Downing and the Daltons. He glanced out into the street, wondering whether Snow was nearby, but could not see him anywhere.

Since Robert did not seem to be at work that morning, Chaloner decided it was safe to wait inside the shop until his brother was free to talk. He had just taken down a copy of Boyle's *New Experiments* with which to pass the time when Sarah sidled up to him.

'Snow seems to have given up on me. I have not seen him since you so gallantly deceived him on my behalf. I told my brother what you did, and he is very grateful.'

Chaloner was unmoved. 'Did you tell anyone I was going to meet Ingoldsby yesterday?'

She seemed taken aback by the question. 'What are you talking about?'

'You were listening outside Thurloe's door as I confided my plan to see Ingoldsby. When I arrived at his house, someone was waiting with a sword.'

She gazed at him coolly. 'And you think it was my

341

fault? Kelyng and his minions have tried to kill you once already, so have you considered the possibility that *they* are responsible?'

'Snow could never have ridden such a spirited horse, although I suppose Bennet might. But I do not think it was an opportunistic attack: I think it was premeditated.'

'But not by me. Besides, I could not hear what you and John were saying – I tried, but your voices were too low. Why would I harm you, anyway? You rescued me on Wednesday, and John would be upset if you came to grief. He likes you very much.'

Given that Thurloe had deceived him and devised tests to probe his integrity, Chaloner suspected Thurloe's affection was not as deep as she seemed to think.

'Perhaps John mentioned your plans to someone else – innocently,' she went on when he did not reply. 'He came to see my husband, and several other men happened to be there – Downing, Lord Mayor Robinson, Samuel Pepys of the Navy Office, Thomas Wade, Sir Thomas Clifford, Robert Leybourn. It was Leybourn who told us about the grave-opening and suggested we should come. Saturdays are dull, so it was a welcome diversion.'

Chaloner regarded her in distaste. 'Was it?'

'Skeletons are fascinating, although I think most people came because they hoped the coffins might contain a few Parliamentarian hoards. There was a definite surge forward as the lids came off – folk readying themselves to make a grab.'

Dalton reached them before Chaloner could turn the discussion back to Ingoldsby, waving his citrus-scented handkerchief. The rings under his eyes were black as he shot Chaloner a bleak smile. 'Come to see me next week,

342

Heyden. I have several documents ready for translation.'

He spoke in a whisper, and Chaloner understood why when he saw Downing not far away. The diplomat scowled as the Daltons left the shop, and came to take Chaloner's arm in a pinch that was firm enough to make the agent reach for his dagger.

'Do not work for him,' grated Downing, releasing Chaloner abruptly when he saw the weapon start to emerge. 'He does not seem entirely sane these days.'

'I thought he was a member of the Brotherhood, and therefore beyond reproach.'

'Do not be facetious. You think you can hide behind Thurloe's skirts, but his star is fading fast and you may soon find yourself alone.'

'What do you mean?' It sounded like a threat on Thurloe's life.

'Just what I say: without Thurloe, you are nothing. Have you secured employment yet?'

'With Dalton,' replied Chaloner, hoping to annoy him.

Downing's eyes narrowed, and he changed the subject to disguise his irritation. 'Has Thurloe asked you to look into anything of late? I know you have spent time with him.'

Chaloner was surprised he should expect an answer to such a question. 'We discuss pheasants.'

Downing regarded him in confusion. 'Pheasants?'

'He plans to build a volary in Lincoln's Inn.'

Downing regarded him coldly. 'There is a rumour that you spy for the Dutch – you speak their language, and I did not know half of what you got up to in The Hague. I may have to speak in your defence one day, so do not rile me. Once you have earned my dislike, you may never be rid of it.'

Chaloner was puzzled. 'Why should I be the subject of rumours? No one here knows me.'

'But you regularly visit Thurloe *and* the Earl of Clarendon,' replied Downing. 'And that interests all manner of folk. Remember: you do not have to have committed a crime to be taken to the Tower.'

He turned and stalked away, leaving Chaloner wondering why Downing should care what he did. Was it simple jealousy – he did not want a rival to have a Dutch translator? Or was he regretting his exposure of the Brotherhood, and had decided his unwilling confidant represented too great a risk? Eventually, Chaloner was able to corner Leybourn. The bookseller greeted him warily.

'Shall we talk about turkeys?' asked Chaloner pleasantly. 'You told Kelyng I own one.'

Leybourn nodded, but there was no sign of his customary grin. 'It saved your life. He and Bennet were stealing more of my books in the King's name, and Bennet was making a strong case for dispatching a short-haired, limping enemy. It was obvious he referred to you. He had virtually convinced Kelyng of his point of view when I casually informed my brother about your turkey. Kelyng likes birds, and when he overheard my idle chatter, he forbade Bennet to touch you.'

'Why should you help me?'

Leybourn grimaced. 'It was before you goaded Rob into a duel, or I would not have been so solicitous. But I have told you why: you and I both despise Kelyng. Is that why you came? To question my motives in doing you a favour?'

Chaloner handed him the book, feeling a pang as it went. Leybourn took it and ran expert hands across the binding. Then he opened it, and his eyes took on a distant expression as he assessed the fine quality of the work. 'Are you sure you want to part with this? I would not.'

Chaloner nodded, and they haggled for a while until a mutually acceptable price was reached. Chaloner experienced a lurching sadness when he saw it set on Leybourn's shelf, but the deed was done, and there was no point in fretting over it. It was only a book, and Metje was more important.

'Where is Robert today?' he asked.

'Practising his swordplay. He is being coached by Sir Richard Ingoldsby – not that he needs advice. He is already very good.'

Chaloner saw the bookseller was trying to unnerve him. 'Perhaps I shall learn something, then.'

Leybourn sighed. 'You went after Wade like the Spanish Inquisition, and you should apologise. I do not like the thought of Bennet dancing on your grave.'

Chaloner gave a wry grin. 'He would not dare, not while Kelyng frets about my turkey.'

'Rob will kill you,' warned Leybourn, brazening it out. 'He fought in all three wars.'

'So did I.'

'Did you?' asked Leybourn unhappily. 'Christ! Look, Heyden, I will talk to him. I will say there was a misunderstanding. You must put an end to this nonsense before someone is hurt.'

He turned at the sound of footsteps. 'We shall resolve our differences tomorrow at dawn,' said Robert coldly, hand on the hilt of his sword. 'It is too late for apologies.'

\*　　\*　　\*

345

Chaloner spent an hour buying cloth and a selection of treats for Metje, arranging for them to be delivered to his rooms later that day. Then he went in search of Mother Greene, and delivered the promised penny, along with a plum pudding that had her cackling in delight. She spoke softly as he was about to leave.

'Mother Pinchon is dead. They found her by the river.'

'She drowned?'

'That is what we were supposed to think, but there was no mistaking the rope mark on her neck. Young Joe Turner was flush with money last night, and he would sell his grandmother for a jug of ale. Someone came to find Mother Pinchon, and we all know *he* told them where to look.'

'Will you take me to see him?'

'People around here do not like folk who bring about the deaths of old women. Turner is dead.'

Chaloner swore under his breath. 'Did *you* see Turner talking to strangers?'

'He may have been greedy, but he was not stupid. He passed his information secretly to the killers, then spent his dirty money in the alehouse near Turnagain Lane. No one *saw* anything.'

'Then perhaps he was not responsible.'

She regarded him as though he were insane. 'People around here get rich for two reasons: they have stolen something, or they have been paid to break the law. Besides, Turner was ale-soaked enough that he got to bragging. He told the dung collector – Potts – that he had been invited to a very nice house, and given cakes and wine. It was obvious what had happened.'

'Did he say where this house was?'

'Potts asked, but Turner could not remember – he was

346

too drunk. Then news came that Mother Pinchon was dead and he tried to slink away. He did not get far. Potts has a sly knife on occasion.'

'Damn! This means that we have no way to trace the real villain – the man who paid Turner for the information in the first place. Did any of her neighbours see anything, hear a struggle?'

'She went out and told no one where she was going. The next time anyone saw her was when she was on the banks of the Thames, dead.'

Chaloner sighed. 'Will you take me to Potts? Perhaps Turner said something before he died . . .'

'Potts would never tell you anything. He mentioned something to me, but it is probably nothing.'

'What?'

'Turner kept saying the stranger smelled of oranges.'

Chaloner had agreed to meet Evett in the Dolphin mid morning, to discuss their respective cases. He was early, but did not mind waiting, instinctively occupying one of the tables at the rear of the tavern where he could keep his back to the wall. He had done no more than order a jug of ale, when the door opened and Bennet and Snow entered. They were swathed in thick cloaks, and evidently thought themselves well disguised. It was clear from their behaviour that they had been following him, and he realised he had been so engrossed in trying to determine why Dalton had killed Pinchon, that he had let his guard down. It was the sort of carelessness that could prove fatal, and he suspected he had been limping, too, although at least his short hair was covered by his hood. He was furious with himself.

Bennet leaned nonchalantly against a wall, hat pulled

low over his eyes, while Snow pretended to be with someone else. Chaloner read the anti-Dutch broadsheets that someone had thoughtfully left on each table, while he waited to see what they would do. Bennet tried to effect an air of casual disinterest, but could not prevent himself from looking at Chaloner from time to time, while Snow's fingers often twitched around the hilt of his dagger. They made no effort to leave.

Chaloner stood, knowing the only way to be rid of their annoying presence was by losing them in the maze of alleys surrounding Thames Street. It was true they could kill him more easily outside than in a crowded tavern, but he did not want them with him for the rest of the day. He exited through the rear door, Snow following him. Predictably, Bennet ducked out of the front with the clear intention of cutting him off. Chaloner emerged into a narrow lane, with Snow behind and Bennet approaching from his left. He turned right and started to run, then stopped dead when another man stepped in front of him and levelled a pistol. He had not anticipated a third participant, and was trapped.

But although he could not turn right, left or re-enter the tavern, all was not lost. There were doors leading to yards, and walls that could be scaled. He raised his hands in surrender, then raced for the nearest gate when the man lowered his pistol. It was locked, and part of it disintegrated when the gun was fired at close range, sending splinters in all directions. The noise was deafening, and Chaloner heard Bennet ordering the fellow to desist. Chaloner jumped for the wall, and was almost over it when Snow grabbed his foot. For the second time that week, he found himself the subject of a tug of war.

Snow was not North, however, and he and his brawny helpers soon had Chaloner off the wall and wrestled to the ground, despite him using every tactic in his arsenal of tricks to evade them. Snow leapt back with a bloody nose, the third man shrieked over a broken finger and Bennet swore at a kick that caught him on the shin. Chaloner might have escaped had they been alone, but others were pouring into the alley, and he was hopelessly outnumbered. Eventually, seeing further struggles would only serve to tire him, he abandoned the fight. He was hauled to his feet and his hands secured behind him, although not before another tussle that resulted in the rope being far looser than it should have been. Bennet indicated he was to precede them down the lane.

'Where are we going?'

'Just walk. Kelyng has questions for you, although I would sooner slip a dagger between your ribs and leave you for the dogs. Now move, unless you want to be dragged.'

With the odds so heavily stacked against him, Chaloner had no choice but to comply. He began to walk in the direction Bennet indicated, while the men surrounded him closely.

'Left,' ordered Bennet, when they reached a junction. 'Come on, Heyden – yes, we know your name. My friend Preacher Hill was delighted to chat to me, especially when he learned it would see you incarcerated. Hurry up. I do not have all day.'

Chaloner faltered when he saw the road led to the Tower. 'In there?'

'It has nice, quiet cellars, where you and Kelyng can converse undisturbed,' said Bennet with an unpleasant leer.

Chaloner did not like the prospect of 'conversing' with Kelyng in the Tower. He wrenched his hands free, then jerked backwards, bowling over two of the men behind him, and managing to fell Snow with a punch to the jaw. Almost immediately, a gun went off, and people scattered in alarm. Chaloner saw a woman drop to the ground, while a companion stood over her and began to shriek.

He started to run, lashing out with his fists when the men snatched at him, but then there was a sharp pain in the side of his head and he felt himself fall. Dizzy and disorientated, he was hauled to his feet and bundled towards the barbican, vaguely aware of horrified people converging on the prostrate woman. None of Kelyng's men joined them: they did not care who they had killed.

Bennet's mocking voice was a buzz in his ears as they passed through the first of the portals. A gate slammed behind them, and then they were near the menagerie with its growling, snuffling occupants. Chaloner's legs were rubbery, and he was only just regaining control of them when they reached one of the buildings opposite the White Tower. A door revealed a flight of steps, and he was sure it would lead to some dimly lit dungeon full of implements used to extract secrets from hapless prisoners. He resisted Bennet's shoves long enough to look at the sky before he descended, certain it was the last time he would see it. Heart thumping, he steeled himself for what was about to happen.

He was disconcerted when the stairs emptied into a comfortable office with rugs on the floor and paintings on the walls. Cushions had been placed on benches, and the room was dominated by a massive table, on which

350

stood a cage containing a glum pigeon with a bandaged wing. A lamp hung from the ceiling, and braziers in sconces on the walls rendered the room bright and warm. Kelyng was sitting in a chair with a cat on his knee and a dog at his feet. He glanced up in surprise when Chaloner was shoved into the middle of his domain, followed by Bennet and the rest of his entourage.

'Stop!' he cried, when more tried to crowd inside. 'You are frightening the bird. And what have you done to Thurloe's spy? I told you I wanted him unharmed.'

'He resisted arrest,' said Bennet, forcing Chaloner into a chair. 'He grabbed a gun and shot an innocent bystander.'

'And how did he do that, if he was in your custody?' demanded Kelyng. 'Either you were supremely inept, or you are lying. Mind the dog, man!' The last comment was aimed at Snow, who was trying to prevent the mongrel from cocking its leg against his black boots. Kelyng clapped his hands. 'Everyone out! It should not take a dozen fellows to bring me a guest. Be off with you.'

He stood, set the cat gently on his chair and went to the table, where he poured a goblet of wine and offered it to Chaloner. The agent dashed it from his hand in what he imagined would be his last act of physical defiance. Bennet jumped forward with a raised fist, but Kelyng quickly interposed himself between them.

'Why do the people who visit me here always display such poor manners?' he asked irritably.

'Probably because they do not like the way you extend your invitations,' replied Chaloner tartly.

Kelyng sighed. 'And if Bennet had phrased the question nicely, would you have come then?'

Chaloner certainly would not. 'It depends what you wanted to talk about.'

'There are several subjects I would like to air,' said Kelyng, watching his men shuffle back up the stairs until only Snow and Bennet remained. 'I understand you own a turkey?'

Chaloner nodded, unsure of the man and the discussion. 'A great big one.'

Kelyng's expression softened. 'I know little about turkeys. What are they like, as companions?'

Chaloner was aware of Bennet's blazing hatred, while Snow was itching to say something. 'They have a tendency to hog the fire of an evening,' he hedged, not sure how to reply.

Kelyng smiled indulgently. 'Show me a beast that does not, Mr Heyden. I am sorry violence was used to bring you here, but you should not have resisted.'

'He knows where I can find the woman what did for Storey,' blurted Snow, no longer able to contain himself. He cracked his knuckles. 'Let me ask him sir, and then you can—'

'You may leave us, Snow,' said Kelyng sharply, watching the cat jump into Chaloner's lap. 'You, too, Bennet. Wait outside.'

'I do not think that is a very good idea,' said Bennet immediately. 'He is far from pleased about the way he was brought here, and—'

'Go!' ordered Kelyng icily. 'I can look after myself. And anyway, a cat would not sit with a fellow contemplating rough behaviour, which is why she never comes to you. Go away.'

Bennet was seething as he obeyed, while Snow's voice echoed on the stairway, asking him whether Kelyng could be trusted to ask after the woman who had killed his accomplice. Bennet muttered something inaudible, and Snow fell silent.

'I know where Sarah Dalton lives,' said Kelyng, when they had gone. 'But I have no desire to see women killed, not even Thurloe's kin, so I shall make sure Snow never touches her.'

'He came close the other night. You may not be able to stop him.'

'I have informed Bennet that I will dismiss *him* if anything happens to Mrs Dalton. He is inordinately dim-witted, but he usually does as he is told. I will pour you more wine, if you promise not to hurl it at me again. We can talk like civilised men, I hope?'

Chaloner accepted the proffered cup, worrying about what would happen to Metje and their baby when he was not there to care for them. He wondered whether Thurloe could be trusted to help, or whether the information Kelyng extracted would be used to harm him, too. He was not deceived by the lawyer's friendly manner, suspecting he would not remain kindly once he saw his prisoner would never cooperate with him.

'What did you want to talk about?'

'Thurloe. Once I had your name, it was easy to find out about you. I spoke to George Downing, and he said you worked for Thurloe in Holland, and that you continue to visit him in Lincoln's Inn, as a friend. I would like to know whether he asked you to spy on me.'

'Why would he do that?' asked Chaloner, wondering whether Kelyng really expected him to answer such a question honestly.

'He does not like me,' explained Kelyng. 'And the

353

feeling is wholly reciprocated. I vowed to rid England of traitors, and anyone who once expressed loyalty to Cromwell is fair game. I repeat: did Thurloe order you to spy on me?'

'I am sorry if I offend you, sir, but I had never heard of you before last Friday,' replied Chaloner honestly.

Kelyng pursed his lips. 'That is what I thought. He is an odd man, and I do not understand him at all. I am trying to destroy him, but he barely acknowledges I exist.'

'This is a pleasant office,' said Chaloner, changing the subject to hide his confusion. Surely, Kelyng would not believe answers given under such circumstances? He glanced at the man's wolfish features, and was suddenly struck with the knowledge that his single-mindedness was his greatest weakness – he was so determined to carry out his mission that he was incapable of objectivity, and only saw what he wanted to see. No wonder Thurloe had been able to outwit him. Kelyng might have a reputation for violence, because of Bennet's brutal antics, but he was not an artful man.

Kelyng nodded, looking around. 'It is rather nice. Robinson's original plan was to house me in the crypt where Barkstead buried his treasure – a nasty, damp place – but the King intervened on my behalf. There are tales that Barkstead incarcerated prisoners there, but I know for a fact that he did not.'

'Really? How?'

'I studied the Tower's records when I first arrived here. That cellar has never housed prisoners, because it connects to the vaults of adjoining buildings, and felons thus have a tendency to escape. This chamber is much cosier, and I am extremely happy here. Have you ever heard of the Seven?'

354

'The seven what?' asked Chaloner, bracing himself for the real purpose of the interview.

'Just the Seven. They are a group of men who formed an alliance during the Commonwealth, and their intention was to prevent the return of King Charles to the English throne.'

'Then they were not very effective.'

Kelyng rubbed his chin. 'True. Few people know about them, because they are a secret society – not like the Brotherhood, which is about as secret as the existence of White Hall. Most of *its* members gossip about their nasty objectives to anyone who asks, and they meet quite openly.'

'The Brotherhood's "nasty objectives" are promoting moderation and tolerance.'

'Quite,' said Kelyng grimly. 'I abhor moderation and tolerance. I am a man of strong opinions, and I am ready for a society that is extreme and *in*tolerant. I do not want to live in a world where any sinner can do as he pleases. I want one with guidelines, where every man knows his place and what will happen if he transgresses. I want traitors like Thurloe punished for supporting Cromwell, and I want to establish an effective undercover police force, which will infiltrate every aspect of society and keep a watchful eye on its people.'

'It sounds idyllic.'

'It will work,' argued Kelyng. 'We are an unruly species, and we need strong laws to govern us, not foppish, indulgent liberalism. But I did not bring you here to discuss my philosophical ideals.'

'You were telling me about the Seven,' prompted Chaloner, aware that he was eliciting more information from Kelyng, than Kelyng was from him. Was this some

355

subtle interrogation technique, or was the man simply unused to extracting confessions? Chaloner had no idea, but he had seldom felt less comfortable than he did in Kelyng's windowless domain.

Kelyng nodded. 'The Seven did not succeed – obviously – but I have dedicated the last six months of my life to exposing their identities *and* the details of their wicked plot.'

'Who are they?'

Kelyng grimaced. 'You do not know? Damn! I was hoping you might give me a name or two.'

'If they were operative during Cromwell's reign, then the chances are that some will be dead by now, from natural causes.'

'You arc doubtless right, although that would be very annoying. I shall not give up, though, not until I have unveiled every last one of them. Are you sure you cannot give me a clue? I will buy you a new wig – a good one, like mine, which has real hair.'

'I wish I could help, because a new wig would be very welcome.'

'Well, you know where to come, should you learn anything in the future. However, I know the identities of three of the Seven: one was Barkstead.'

Chaloner frowned. 'Why do you think that?'

'Because Downing read his papers when he arrested him. He showed some to me, and they proved Barkstead's membership of the Seven without a shadow of doubt. Unfortunately, he was executed before I could ask him about his six colleagues. The second is Sir Michael Livesay.'

'Who is he?' asked Chaloner, while thinking it was no surprise the man had disappeared if Kelyng's claim was true.

'Another regicide. There is a rumour that he was killed in an exploding ship, but I do not believe it. The last time I fell for a tale in which a man was blown to pieces, the fellow appeared alive and well eighteen months later with a fortune in molasses. I am not *certain* Livesay is a member of the Seven, but it makes good sense.'

'Who else?' Chaloner knew what was coming next.

'I have strong suspicions about Thurloe.'

'Then you would be wrong. Thurloe would never join a group with those sorts of aims. Barkstead and Livesay were different: they were regicides, and had a lot to lose if the King was restored. But Thurloe is not a man to throw in his lot with extremists.'

'He is a member of the Brotherhood.'

'*Was* a member,' corrected Chaloner, hoping Kelyng did not know he had founded it. He wondered why he persisted in defending a man who had been far from honest with him. 'He has not been to a meeting in ages, and has lost all interest in politics. He just wants to be left alone, to live quietly. Surely, that is not too much to ask?'

'It is for him,' said Kelyng. 'He will never have peace, and you can tell him so from me.'

Chaloner stood, not relinquishing the cat. Kelyng would never resort to rough tactics while he held the animal. 'Very well. I will tell him when—'

'In a moment,' said Kelyng, waving him back down. 'So, you have never heard of the Seven and their attempts to keep the King from his throne? Do you know anyone called Swanson?'

Chaloner made a pretence at considering the question, trying to remember what Robinson had said about a man called Swanning or Swanson. Eventually, he shook his head. 'Who is he?'

357

'The man who first became aware of the Seven. He sent word to the King, who told him he should have a gold bar for every name he provided. Incidentally, the King informs me that the offer still stands, although it is a minor incentive in my campaign – I do not persecute for money, but because I enjoy it.'

'Naturally. How much is a bar of gold worth?'

Kelyng shrugged, as if he did not care. 'These would be valued at nine hundred and ninety-seven pounds, seventeen shillings and fourpence-ha'penny each, as a very rough guide.'

'Almost a thousand pounds. So, the total reward would be seven thousand pounds?'

'Minus the odd fourteen pounds, eighteen shillings and fourpence ha'penny. It is definitely a prize worth having. Indeed, men acting for the King and the Earl of Sandwich dug up half the Tower looking for seven thousand pounds recently, although they did not find it, more is the pity.'

Chaloner wondered whether Kelyng really had not made the connection between the two near-identical sums, or whether he was playing some sophisticated mental game. 'Why is it a pity?'

Kelyng gazed at him in astonishment. 'Even to ask such a question is treason! No man loyal to the King could hope he would miss a share of this treasure. It belonged to Barkstead, and it would have been a glorious irony to see *his* money in Charles's pocket. I know what you are thinking.'

'Do you?' Chaloner sincerely hoped he did not. No man liked being considered a blithering idiot.

Kelyng nodded earnestly. 'You think the seven bars of gold and Barkstead's cache are one and the same, but

358

you only need to apply a little logic to see they are not. The King paid Swanson for giving him the identities of the Seven, so there is no way Barkstead could have got his hands on *that* gold, because *he* was one of the men named.'

'Swanson told the King their identities?' Chaloner had been under the impression – from Robinson – that the arrangement had been made, but the information had never been delivered. 'If His Majesty knows, then perhaps you could ask him about it, and save yourself some trouble.'

'The message went astray in transit – I expect Thurloe intercepted it, as he intercepted so much else. So, the King never received the letter, although he was sufficiently confident of Swanson's success to have paid him in advance.'

'Who is Swanson? A courtier?'

'Someone close to Cromwell. But I have not been able to ascertain whether Swanson was his real name or an alias. He is a hero, of course, for exposing the Seven.'

'So it could be Thurloe,' said Chaloner, to confuse him. Thurloe would never have betrayed Cromwell. 'He was close to the Lord Protector.'

It was obviously something that had never occurred to Kelyng. His jaw dropped. 'I hardly think . . . I cannot . . . But of course, it might! Lord, that would put me in an awkward position! I have vowed to destroy Thurloe, but I can hardly do that, if he was the man who foiled the Seven.'

'You had a servant called Jones,' said Chaloner, after several silent moments had passed.

'Actually, his name was John Hewson,' said Kelyng, dragging himself away from his thoughts. 'You chased him into my garden, and he was killed. He had infiltrated my household, which was a stupid thing to do, given my views on regicide: he placed his head in the lion's mouth, so to speak.'

'Did you know he was a regicide when you employed him?'

Kelyng looked annoyed. 'Of course not, or I would have had him executed. I found out when we took his body to the church and someone recognised it. I felt like an ass, I can tell you, especially since the missing eye was something of a giveaway. He told me he lost it fighting for the King, but he actually lost it crushing rebels in Ireland. I had to order Snow to burn the body, lest it was traced to me. But Hewson was a curious fellow. He kept asking whether people knew how to praise God. I think he was addled – the terror of being hunted drew him towards me in a perverse kind of way.'

Chaloner did not think so. Hewson had not seemed addled, and he suspected the man had known exactly what he had been doing. The more he thought about the facts, the more clear it became that Hewson was one of the Seven, and he had taken a post with Kelyng to assess how serious the threat was against its surviving members. It explained his message about the danger 'for Seven' with his dying breath, while 'praise God' was obviously some sort of code known only to him and his six colleagues. But Chaloner had reasoned that Hewson's messages were intended for Thurloe. Did that mean Thurloe was a member of the Seven after all?

He smiled at Kelyng. 'So, Hewson applied to you for employment, and you accepted him. You sent him to collect the satchel stolen by Snow and Storey, and Bennet stabbed him . . .'

'Bennet said you did it, but it was *his* knife embedded in Hewson's chest, and I can usually tell when he is lying. He was aiming for you, but missed, and did not want to admit to his ineptitude. It was a wretched nuisance, because I would have liked to ask Hewson what he thought he was doing, pretending to be a servant – and whether he knew anything about any of his fellow regicides. There are still a number of those unaccounted for, you know. Did he say anything to you before he died? I thought I heard him talking.'

'Just religious exhortations.'

'He *was* deranged,' said Kelyng sadly. He cleared his throat. 'Now, I cannot believe that a man of your obvious intelligence will refuse to hazard a guess at the Seven's remaining members – other than Barkstead, Livesay and Thurloe. Share your thoughts with me, and you will be home with your turkey in an hour.'

Chaloner ruffled the cat's fur, supposing the time for pleasant conversation was drawing to a close, and Kelyng was girding himself up to use rougher methods of persuasion.

'Thurloe is not one of the Seven. But there are two other men who might bear investigation.'

Kelyng's face lit up. 'I *knew* a man close to the ex-Spymaster would be able to help me.'

'This has *nothing* to do with Thurloe,' said Chaloner doggedly, hoping Kelyng could not read his uncertainty. 'And you will be wasting your time if you try to connect him with it. The men you should investigate are Hewson— '

'But he is dead!' cried Kelyng, disappointed.

Chaloner nodded. Kelyng could not hurt a corpse, which was why he had decided to share that particular

361

suspicion. 'And there is another possibility, but he will kill me if he finds out, and I—'

'He will never know,' promised Kelyng. 'I swear on my soul, he will never know.'

Chaloner could tell he meant it. He had dealt with sly politicians and slippery diplomats aplenty, but this was the first time he had ever been obliged to treat with a zealot, and he was finding it a challenge.

'Sir George Downing.' This was pure malice on Chaloner's part, although a man as devious and corrupt as Downing would suffer few ill effects from anything Kelyng might do. Still, it might inconvenience him, and that would be satisfaction in itself.

A slow smile spread across Kelyng's face. 'Downing. Of course! It makes perfect sense – a man once devoted to the Commonwealth, who changed sides when he saw his evil plotting could not keep Charles from his rightful place. A deceitful, cunning fellow, who only goes to church on Sundays – and talks through most of the service anyway. Thank you, Heyden. You have been very helpful.'

'You are welcome.'

'Downing,' grinned Kelyng, delighted with the information. 'I should have worked this out for myself, although one can never go wrong in seeking the help of a fellow liked by cats. Here is a silver crown for your cleverness. And a new wig will be sent to you as soon as I can have one made.'

# Chapter 10

Chaloner was bemused when Kelyng drew the interview to a close and indicated that he was free to leave. He climbed the stairs cautiously, expecting Bennet to be lurking in the darkness with a dagger, but he reached the yard without incident and gazed up at the sky he had not expected to see again. As he did so, he saw Robinson and Dalton hurrying towards him. Dalton looked him up and down, before dabbing a clammy brow with his scented handkerchief. His hand shook, and Chaloner thought he looked as though he might be sick.

'We heard Bennet had arrested you,' said Robinson, rather accusingly. 'How did you escape?'

'Kelyng let me go. Why? What is the matter?'

'One of the guards told Thurloe you had been detained, and he rushed to my house and ordered me to secure your immediate release,' said Dalton. 'Robinson and I have a certain influence over Kelyng, because we all attend St Clement Danes, and he wants to be elected churchwarden.'

'Was Thurloe afraid I might reveal his secrets, then?' asked Chaloner.

'Actually, he was concerned about your well-being,' said Dalton. 'He would have come himself, but that might have made matters worse, so we sent him home. He will be relieved to see you safe.'

'It is extremely distasteful having Kelyng in my Tower,' said Robinson, before Chaloner could reply. 'But the King wants him here, so that is that. I gave him the worst room I could get away with, but he simply redecorated it and seems determined to stay. What did he want with you?'

'He asked about that story you told me a few days ago – the Seven.'

Robinson raised his eyebrows. 'Why should he think you know anything about that?'

The sudden pallor of Dalton's face had not escaped Chaloner's attention. 'He thought I might have heard rumours about its membership, so I made up a few names to confuse him. I told him yours. I hope you do not mind.'

'Mine?' asked Robinson, laughing. 'Good! That will give the nosy little ferret something on which to waste his time, because he will find no treachery in *my* past. But, I see you are in no danger, so I shall return to my poor daughter. She has had some shocking news, and is prostrate with grief.'

'You do not mean my name as well, do you?' asked Dalton in a horrified whisper when Robinson had gone. 'You told Kelyng *I* was one of the Seven?'

'What can it matter, if you are innocent?'

'But I am *not* innocent!' said Dalton in the same strangled voice. 'I *am* one of the Seven, and so is Thurloe. How *could* you chatter to Kelyng about matters you do not understand?'

364

Chaloner was sorry to learn he had been right. 'Thurloe plotted to prevent Charles's return?'

'It was not in our interests to see the monarchy restored – not in our nation's interests. And we were right. Look at the mess we are in: the King and his blood-sucking courtiers squander money we do not have, and the men who run the country should not have control of a barnyard.'

Chaloner was deeply disappointed in his old patron. 'I thought Thurloe had more sense than to embroil himself in that sort of thing. It is treason.'

'It would be treason *now*, but it was patriotic *then*. Cromwell was in charge, and we were fighting to keep the Commonwealth in place. Our actions were designed to support *that* government, and make it stable and secure.' Dalton's voice cracked. 'You have killed me, Heyden.'

'I did give Kelyng some names,' said Chaloner softly. 'But yours was not one of them, and neither was Thurloe's. I told him to look at Hewson and Downing.'

'Truly?' Dalton dared to look relieved. 'Thank God! Downing has nothing to do with the Seven. Hewson did, but he is beyond Kelyng's spiteful vengeance. So, Kelyng does not suspect me at all?'

'He suspects Barkstead, Livesay and Thurloc – and has now added Downing and Hewson to his list. Three of these are dead—'

'Livesay *is not* dead,' interrupted Dalton. 'I do not know why everyone insists he is. I *saw* him. He was in disguise, having created a new existence for himself, but I recognised him noncthclcss.'

'What kind of disguise?' Chaloner did not know whether to believe him.

'He was dressed as a Nonconformist minister – all

shabby black clothes and well-thumbed Bible – but he was wringing his hands in that odd way he has. He looked right at me and smiled. Why would anyone do that, if he were not Livesay?'

Chaloner shrugged. 'Nonconformists probably smile at everyone these days, in the hope that it will make people less inclined to harm them. The community near me is always being attacked.'

'I am afraid Livesay has told . . . There is a secret, which he may have let slip to our enemies . . .'

'What secret?' asked Chaloner, watching him struggle with his emotions.

'*I* will never reveal it,' whispered Dalton. 'But *he* may have done – to men who would see us hanged. Perhaps it was Livesay's ghost I saw, come to haunt me, because of the wicked thing . . .'

'You mean your murder of Mother Pinchon?' asked Chaloner bluntly.

Dalton regarded him in horror. 'How do you know that was me?'

'Why did you kill her? She was no threat. She knew nothing about the Seven – only about some treasure Barkstead told her he was going to hide, but that he never did.'

Dalton was ashen. 'She told Wade where to find seven thousand pounds. How long do you think it will be before Kelyng realises that Barkstead's moveable wealth was worth almost twice that, and the sum Pinchon was urging Wade to locate has another significance?'

'Barkstead's godly golden goose,' mused Chaloner. 'Did he mean the seven bars of gold paid to Swanson, one for each of the Seven?'

Dalton nodded miserably. 'I imagine so. Before she

366

died, Pinchon told me how Barkstead had ordered her to take the message to Thurloe, but she was too frightened. The godly golden goose must have been his discreet way of referring to the blood money.'

'How did Barkstead come to have it?'

'I do not know he *did* have it – only that he was trying to pass a message to Thurloe about it.'

'Then who is Swanson?'

Dalton shook his head. 'I do not know the answer to that, either, although I can tell you he never passed the Seven's names to the King, or I would not be standing here now.'

'You, Thurloe, Barkstead, Livesay and Hewson,' said Chaloner. 'Who are the remaining two?'

'You know too much already,' said Dalton, edging away. 'Downing was right: you are overly inquisitive. Stop prying into affairs that are none of your concern before you land us all in trouble.'

He turned and stalked towards the Lieutenant's Lodgings. Chaloner watched him go, and wondered yet again whether it had been Dalton who had tried to kill him outside Ingoldsby's house. If so, then there were two possible motives. The obvious one was that Dalton wanted to prevent him from drawing attention to the Seven with his questions. But another was that Dalton had not wanted him to talk to Ingoldsby. Was Ingoldsby one of the Seven? He *was* a regicide, after all, regardless of his current affiliations. Or was Ingoldsby actually Swanson, and had kept his own neck from the noose by offering to betray the Seven to the King?

There were far too many loose ends trailing in Chaloner's head, and he desperately needed to sit somewhere quiet and consider them all. He looked around him, and his gaze fell on the chapel of St Peter ad Vincula. The Tower was no place to linger, but he did not feel safe anywhere any more.

He opened the door and approached the chapel's altar, staring at the ornate cross and its golden candlesticks without really seeing them. He placed his hands together and dropped to his knees when the door clanked and Snow walked in. The lout faltered when he saw what his quarry was doing, and withdrew for a muttered conversation with someone else. Then he returned to sit on a bench near the back, obviously under orders to keep watch. Chaloner saw no reason to allow Snow to distract him from his deliberations, especially since the man seemed loath to make a hostile move while his target was in a church. He ignored the shuffling, bored presence behind him, and began to think about what he had learned.

First, the treasure that Barkstead – with Mother Pinchon's help – had packed into butter firkins had been worth thirteen thousand pounds, not seven. Seven thousand pounds was the sum promised to Swanson for unveiling the Seven, of which Barkstead was one. Chaloner thought about the message Barkstead had asked Pinchon to deliver to Thurloe, and the more he considered the 'godly golden goose', the more he became certain that it referred to the bars, and that the butter-firkin wealth had never been part of the story.

Second, there had been a traitor in Cromwell's court. The man had called himself Swanson, but Kelyng believed – and Chaloner concurred – that it was probably a false identity. Spymaster Thurloe's monitoring of letters entering and leaving England had been thorough, and it was unlikely the traitor would have risked using his own name – unless Swanson was Thurloe himself, of course. Robinson claimed to have seen 'Swanson' once – 'a young fellow with the voice of an angel' – but Thurloe had tended to use spies as messengers, and was unlikely to have visited the King himself with an offer to expose his fellow plotters. Simon Lane had sung, so perhaps it was he who Robinson had seen. And then what? Thurloe had accepted the gold, but declined to reveal the names? Kelyng, Dalton and Robinson were all certain the King had never been told the identities of the Seven.

Third, Hewson was a member of the Seven. He had been a regicide, like Barkstead, so it was certainly in his interests to see the King kept from the throne – as soon as Charles had been reinstated, Hewson had been condemned to death at a trial during his absence. He would have been terrified, and desperate to know what Kelyng had discovered about the Seven, so he had devised a plan to find out. He had been killed accidentally by Bennet, but had confided his real name to the man dispatched by Thurloe to retrieve a stolen satchel.

But how could Hewson have known that Chaloner was Thurloe's man? Chaloner reflected, and saw the answer was obvious. Hewson would have guessed that Snow and Storey had been followed, and that it was an agent of Thurloe's who grabbed the bag before it could be passed to Kelyng. But why had Hewson been taking the bag to Kelyng in the first place? The answer to that was obvious, too: Hewson had known there was nothing in it that could harm Thurloe. But that had another implication in its turn: it meant Hewson knew enough about Thurloe's operations to make such an assumption, which led Chaloner to suspect that Thurloe had been aware of what Hewson was doing, too.

Chaloner thought about what had happened in Kelyng's garden. The regicide had been confident and self-assured once the initial shock of being challenged had receded, and had known exactly what he was doing when he had whispered his last words. He had spoken his name, so Thurloe would know what had happened to him – a wise decision, since Kelyng had then burned the corpse to prevent identification – and 'praise God's one son' had been another message. The more Chaloner pondered the phrase, the more certain he became that Thurloe knew what it meant. Should he ask him, or would that be dangerous?

Lastly, he considered the Seven. Barkstead and Hewson were dead, Livesay missing, and Thurloe and Dalton trying to stay one step ahead of Kelyng, although Dalton was crumbling under the strain. He thought about Lee's parchment, and the ends of the words that had included reference to 'seven' and 'praise God'. He smiled as something else became clear. The first few lines were the ends of names. He pulled the paper from his pocket and supplied the blanks:

$$e = \text{Thurlo}\underline{e}$$
$$d = \text{Barkstea}\underline{d}$$
$$y = \text{Livesa}\underline{y}$$
$$on = \text{Hews}\underline{on} \text{ or Dalt}\underline{on}$$

So, who were the last two? There had been a dozen executions since Charles's coronation, so perhaps they were already dead, and Kelyng's hunt was in vain. And perhaps 'Swanson' was sitting with his gold, enjoying the benefits of his betrayal. Did Thurloe have that sort of money? Chaloner supposed that if he did, he would be careful how he spent it. He was far too clever to make such an elementary mistake. And why had he sent Dalton to rescue Chaloner from Kelyng? Was it affection, as Dalton claimed? Chaloner did not think so. Thurloe had denied knowing about the Seven, and had virtually ordered Chaloner not to investigate Barkstead's hoard. It had been self-preservation that had prompted Thurloe to arrange his old agent's release, afraid he might have learned enough to be a liability. It was disappointing, but Chaloner supposed he should not be surprised that an ex-Spymaster still involved himself in plots and intrigues, despite his claims to the contrary.

There were no more answers, and the only thing of which Chaloner was certain was that he felt more vulnerable in London than he had ever done in Holland, an English spy in an enemy country. He stood and walked outside, watching Snow snap awake as he undid the door.

For some time, he had been aware of yells coming from the bailey, but since the open space was used for military drills, he had thought little of it. The hollering had faded, and there was now nothing but silence. It was deserted, too, without a person in sight. Chaloner started to walk across it, aiming for the gate. He was passing the White Tower when he heard an urgent shout. Wade was racing along the top of a nearby wall, gesticulating frantically, and when Chaloner followed the direction of his jabbing finger, he saw a pale brown shadow. Sonya was on the loose again.

Since the lion was between him and the barbican, Chaloner set off towards the Traitors' Gate again, feeling uncomfortably exposed in the middle of such a large

371

expanse of ground. He glanced behind him and saw he was not alone: Bennet was also out, sword drawn. Snow joined his colleague, and bellowed to catch the lion's attention. Bennet then ran a few steps in Chaloner's direction, urging Sonya to follow. Chaloner was puzzled, wondering what they intended to do.

'Stop!' yelled Wade in a hoarse scream. 'Do not attract his attention. He has not been fed.'

Snow ignored him and broke into a sprint, while the lion trotted after him with its ears pricked, indicating it was interested. Meanwhile, Bennet circled behind it, shouting and slapping his sword on his boot. Gradually, both men and the lion came closer to Chaloner, who was walking steadily towards the gate, fighting the impulse to run. He glanced behind him and saw the lion veer to one side, but Bennet immediately drove it back on its original course. Chaloner tried to move faster.

Meanwhile, Wade was still atop the wall. He bent across it, exhorting them to leave Sonya's capture to the keeper, who knew what he was doing. It had not occurred to him that Bennet and Snow were deliberately driving the beast towards a victim. When they failed to acknowledge him, he leaned out farther. Suddenly his legs flew up behind him and he cartwheeled to the ground. He landed so close to Chaloner that one of his flailing hands clipped the agent's shoulder. When Chaloner glanced up at the wall-walk, he caught a glimpse of someone running away. Keeping a wary eye on the lion, he crouched next to Wade, although he could see there was nothing he could do: it had been a long drop and Wade had fallen awkwardly. Wade muttered something, then lay still.

'God's blood!' exclaimed Snow, gazing upwards. 'Did you see that? It was— Hey! Watch it!'

372

Sonya had swiped at him, and its claws were caught in his coat. The lion struggled to free itself, and Snow staggered away. Bennet raced forward and poked the animal with his sword, forcing Sonya away from Snow and towards Chaloner again. His face wore a triumphant grin.

'This is not wise,' called Chaloner. They were now in an elongated enclosure, with the Bloody Tower at one end, and Bennet, Snow and the lion at the other. Chaloner was in the middle. The gate through which he had escaped with Evett was blocked with a portcullis, presumably to confine Sonya to the bailey. 'It is just as likely to attack you as me.'

'But *we* have swords,' Bennet pointed out. 'And *we* know how to handle Sonya.'

'Kelyng will not be pleased,' warned Chaloner. 'First, he has asked me to investigate something for him; and second, I do not think he would approve of you maltreating an animal.'

'Kelyng is no longer important,' said Bennet tautly. 'He hunts the King's enemies, but wants them tried in a court of law, when it is better to kill them. He has lost his way, but I have not. Besides, this beast escapes all the time, and it is unfortunate you will be savaged before it can be recaptured.'

'We are abandoning Kelyng to follow our own path,' added Snow, lest Chaloner had not understood. 'Me and the men want a strong leader – and besides, Mr Bennet said he would pay us double.'

'Do you think Fanny will accept you if you make a name for yourself in rebel-hunting?' asked Chaloner in distaste. 'I doubt she will change her mind, no matter how many "traitors" you murder.'

373

Bennet shrugged. 'She will have to marry someone, and there are not many who will take her now she carries a dead man's child.'

'Lee's?' asked Chaloner. Several facts snapped together in his mind. 'Did *you* shoot Lee – to eliminate a rival? That will not make her love you. Robinson said she is grief-stricken.'

'She is not in a position to be choosy. It will not be long before I prove myself Kelyng's superior in every way, and Robinson will be only too grateful to have me as his son-in-law.'

'When you killed Lee, who was with him?'

Bennet shrugged. 'A couple. My argument was not with them, so I let them live.'

Chaloner saw he had been wrong: Lee's *death* had nothing to do with Barkstead's treasure, but his meeting with the 'couple' had, as attested by the fact that he had been holding a document containing a list of the Seven. Were they Ingoldsby and his wife? But why would they run away and leave their kinsman's body to be discovered by someone else? Robinson and Fanny? But Chaloner recalled Fanny's eager happiness as she waited for her lover to pay her a birthday visit: she would not have done that had she known he was dead. Dalton and Sarah? That certainly held all manner of possibilities, since Dalton's own name was on the list snatched from Lee's dead hand.

'Who killed Storey?' asked Snow, waving his sword when Sonya moved towards Wade's body. 'If you tell me her name, I will . . .' He trailed off. There was really very little he could offer, since Bennet clearly had no intention of sparing his victim.

'I do not think Kelyng will be easy to depose,' said

374

Chaloner, taking several steps away while Sonya was preoccupied. 'It has nothing to do with personality or suitability, but with resources: he is wealthier than you.'

Bennet made a lunge that frightened Sonya away from Wade and back towards the agent. 'He will have an accident when he goes to feed your bird. And your pet will fall foul of a blade, too. Fanny likes turkey meat, and it will be a good way to begin courting her again.'

Sonya gave a low growl. Its tale swished this way and that, and its eyes held a wild, opaque look. When its head gave a curious twitch, Chaloner saw it was definitely one of its bad days. He backed away until he reached the portcullis, then began to ascend the metal-studded framework. Snow poked the lion with his sword. It trotted forward and made a half-hearted swipe at Chaloner that missed, then padded off in the opposite direction. Bennet yelled and banged his dagger against the wall. Alarmed by the noise, Sonya veered back towards the gate. Chaloner continued to climb, but the portcullis was not high enough to keep him out of claw range. Bennet struck Sonya with the flat of his sword. The lion roared its outrage, and turned in a tight circle.

'In a moment, it will lose what vestiges of reason it has left,' said Bennet, his face split in a savage smile. 'And you will be ripped from the gate and torn limb from limb. It happened to one of His Majesty's measurers of cloth only yesterday.'

'If you tell us the name of the wench, I will call the beast to heel,' offered Snow unconvincingly.

Chaloner began to tire of the game. 'This has gone far enough. Stop, before you are hurt.'

'Sonya would not dare touch us,' said Snow, although he shot the animal an uneasy glance.

'It is exactly the kind of inept scheme I would expect from men who have never heard of St Thomas à Becket,' Chaloner went on, disgusted with them both. 'Back off, while you can.'

'It is all right,' said Snow sympathetically, when Bennet's jaw dropped in astonishment at the insult. 'I do not know this so-called saint, either.'

Bennet's expression was dangerous. He jabbed Sonya. 'Don't you *dare* accuse me of stupidity.'

The lion's tail was twitching faster. It stood on its hind legs and swiped, catching a claw in Chaloner's boot and almost dragging him down. He saw yellow teeth, chipped and broken, and recalled its heavy body when it had jumped on him before. He jerked his foot away, and Bennet darted forward to jab the hapless beast again. Sonya dropped to all fours and snapped round to face him.

'Do not run,' advised Chaloner, knowing what would happen if he did. He saw men converge at the far end of the enclosure. 'The keeper is coming. Back away, before it is too late.'

'Hey!' shouted Bennet, as the sword was knocked from his hand by a powerful paw.

'Stand still,' suggested Chaloner. 'And do not make—'

Bennet took three rapid steps backwards before turning to flee. Sonya tensed, and then its huge body hurtled through the air to land in the middle of Bennet's back, sending him crashing to the ground.

'—any sudden moves,' finished Chaloner, looking away.

That evening, Metje escaped early from her duties by claiming she did not feel safe with the turkey roaming the house, and asked permission to spend the night with a friend. North had refused at first, on the grounds that it was already dark, but then Chaloner had arrived – invited by Temperance to taste her new batch of knot biscuits – and Metje had asked him to escort her.

'This is decent of you, Heyden,' said North gratefully. 'I cannot countenance a woman going out alone at this time of night, but I have been uneasy every since that villain attacked me with his gun, and I do not want to be out there myself. He may recognise me and try it again.'

'Can I come?' asked Temperance eagerly. 'I do not like the turkey, either.'

'Next time,' replied Metje gently. 'It would be unfair for us both to arrive at my friend's home unannounced.'

Temperance's face fell, but she managed a smile. 'Please arrange it, then. I am bored with spending *every* evening at home or at chapel.'

'Child!' admonished North. 'Think about what you say. Your poor brother would be saddened to hear you speak so. What else would you be doing on a winter evening?'

'The theatre would be nice,' replied Temperance wistfully. 'Or, if those are too full of sin, then a night of music, or perhaps a visit to Mr Heyden's rooms to play cards.'

'Play *cards*?' echoed Faith, shocked. She gazed at Chaloner as though he had put the idea into her daughter's head. 'But that would entail *gambling*!'

'I do not own any cards,' said Chaloner, not wanting to be considered a source of vice. He tried to think of something innocuous to offer as an alternative. 'But I will read Hobbes's *Leviathan* to you.'

A wary silence greeted his offer. 'Do you have nothing

else?' asked North eventually. 'I have seen that book, and it is awfully thick. We will be listening to you for months, and it is dull stuff.'

'Seditious, too,' said Faith accusingly. 'You are trying to corrupt us.'

'We should be on our way or Mrs Partridge will be abed before I arrive,' said Metje, after Chaloner had suggested several safe alternatives that included Gratian's *Decretum* (in Latin) and a collection of erudite essays entitled *Sophistic Recollections*. 'We should let Temperance select one of these fascinating epistles, since she was the one who suggested the diversion. Chose well, though, dear. An evening is a long time in winter, and we shall rely on you to see us all pleasantly entertained.

Temperance was perturbed. 'Lord! Perhaps I will ask Preacher Hill to lend us something instead. He has some books in his room.'

'Religious ones,' said Chaloner dismissively, before it occurred to him that the Puritans would probably prefer them to philosophy or legal texts.

'His room?' pounced Faith, eyes narrowed. 'How do you know?'

'He told *me* about them,' said Metje quickly, earning a grateful smile from Temperance. 'Where is the turkey? Is it safe to leave through the front door?'

'It is in the kitchen eating nuts,' replied North resentfully. 'We shall have nothing left soon.'

Once away from the North house, when he was sure Temperance was not watching from her window, Chaloner grabbed Metje's hand and pulled her up the stairs to his room, wanting to give her the gifts he had purchased. She was delighted, and they ate some of them sitting on the floor in front of the fire. Then, since he

378

still had Kelyng's silver crown, she declared Temperance's musings had put her in the mood for a play, so he took her to see *The Villain* by Thomas Porter at the Duke's House in Lincoln's Inn Fields. He fell asleep during the second act, although she was captivated until the closing curtain. After, they returned to his rooms, and he played Dutch folksongs on his viol.

Metje seemed happier than she had been in days, and confided that her ill temper had arisen from the fact that she had not known whether he would be pleased or angry with the news of the baby. He stroked her hair while she told him how the turkey had stood defiantly in the sitting room that morning, daring anyone to lay a hand on it while it gobbled its way though a bowl of chestnuts. North had responded by going to buy a chicken – a dead one – so they would at least have something to eat in the event of a postponed execution.

'He thinks you might be persuaded to dispatch it,' she said with a giggle. 'When I asked him why, he said he thought you might like to redeem yourself after losing his burglar the other night.'

'I am not killing it,' said Chaloner sleepily. 'He can do it himself, if he wants to eat it that badly.'

'If you will not oblige, he says he will hire the Tower's executioner. Sir John Robinson said that man will kill anything for a shilling. Mr North will devour a roasted bird tomorrow, regardless of whether or not you accede to his request.'

'Poor turkey,' said Chaloner.

'You are sorry for a turkey? Is it because you spent time with Kelyng, and his fondness for dumb creatures rubbed off on you? Tell me the tale again – from the beginning.'

379

'Not tonight,' said Chaloner, aware of what happened when an untrue story was told more than once: inconsistencies crept in, and he did not want her to catch him in even the smallest of lies.

'It is a bad idea to keep a menagerie in a castle. The King should send the animals back to where they came from – especially the lions. Those tiny cages are cruel.'

He regarded her in surprise. 'You have seen them?'

She nodded. 'One Saturday, when you were off on some mysterious jaunt, and the Norths were at chapel. Will Bennet die, do you think – like that poor man Wade, who fell from the wall?'

'No, although his days as chamberlain are over. Kelyng was furious when he learned what had happened. He is fond of Sonya – probably recognises a kindred spirit in its damaged mind.'

She twisted around to look at him. 'It was not Kelyng who invited you to the Tower, was it? I would not like to think you were so desperate for work you that would take Bennet's place.'

He shuddered, genuinely appalled. 'God forbid! When I meet people like Kelyng, I understand why gentler souls have taken a stand against his brand of militancy.'

'What are you talking about?'

He shrugged, and wished he had not mentioned it. 'There is a certain society that preaches against fanaticism. But let's not talk about religion tonight. It is Christmas.'

'But Christmas is . . .' She saw he was laughing at her, and slapped him on the knee before settling again. 'So, you bought me a brush for my hair. Do you think it a tangled mane, then? I always imagined you considered it rather beautiful, like a painting by Rubens.'

He smiled, thinking about what Sarah Dalton had thought of the old Dutch Master. 'You are not fat enough to be one of his subjects.'

'It is nice in here with you tonight, Tom – quiet, safe and warm. I wish it could last.'

'It will,' he said. 'We have the rest of our lives together.'

'Yes,' she said, but her voice was wistful and held no conviction. 'I suppose we do.'

On Christmas morning, Chaloner rose hours before dawn and scrambled over the wall to the back door of North's house, hoping there would be no repetition of the furore that had ensued the last time he had done it. He fiddled with the lock, working quickly and silently in the darkness. When the door was open, the turkey marched past him, its head held high, as though it had business of its own planned for that day. Then he returned to his rooms before Metje realised he had been gone.

He insisted on walking with her to the chapel, claiming he did not care if North saw them. He pointed out that it was only a question of time before she could no longer conceal what was happening to her, while she maintained she would rather inform North herself than be seen stalking brazenly out of his neighbour's bedchamber. Chaloner felt his spirits soar, making plans and thinking about the pleasant changes the future would bring.

'Marry me today,' he said, taking her hands and stepping inside the chapel's dark porch. 'We can ride to Buckingham tomorrow, and Meg can be born on my family's manor.'

She smiled, although there was a sadness that should not have been there. He understood her unease: she was past thirty, and the two boys from her previous marriage had died in infancy. 'I thought you wanted to be a London clerk.'

Chaloner thought about his unsettling interview with Kelyng, Bennet driving lions at him, Snow blasting away with pistols, horsemen with swords and Robert Leybourn challenging him to duels, and realised he no longer wanted the life of a spy. Suddenly, nothing seemed as important as Metje and the spark of life inside her. Thurloe and Clarendon would not miss him, and he certainly would not miss them. In fact, ever since he had chased after Thurloe's empty satchel, events had spiralled out of his control, and he no longer wanted any part of them.

'My brother will give us a few fields,' he said. 'And I can teach.'

'But I do not want to be a farmer's wife, thinking about chickens and pickled apples. I want to shop in busy markets, see plays and watch the King go riding. I would suffocate in the country.'

'Then I will ask Dalton if he can find me something more permanent.'

'You said you had already spoken to him,' she pounced accusingly.

'I mean I will ask again,' he prevaricated.

She looked hard at him, then relented. 'Meanwhile, I can earn a little more before Mr North realises he has harboured a harlot all these months. And then I will marry you.'

'Chaloner,' he said suddenly. 'My name is Thomas Chaloner. My uncle was a regicide, and I worked as an intelligence officer under Spymaster Thurloe. That is what I was doing in Holland – gathering potentially damaging information about your country.'

She gazed at him. 'So I was right when I accused you of underhand activities? You really *are* a spy?'

Chaloner pressed on with his confession, wanting to finish now he had started. 'I sent weekly reports to Thurloe, telling him all I had learned about the movements of Dutch ships, militia and arms. Although I worked for Downing, Thurloe was my real master. He secured me a post with the Lord Chancellor on Monday, although I am not sure how long I can keep it. These are the reasons I go out at odd hours, and why I have never been able to tell you what I do.'

She continued to stare. 'Is it dangerous?'

He shrugged, then nodded. 'My family sided with Cromwell during the wars, and my regicide uncle was passionate about the cause, so most Royalists would be extremely suspicious of a Chaloner once employed by Thurloe. One day, there will have been enough bloodletting, but now there are still too many people who would like to punish me for what my uncle did.'

She sighed. 'Is that all? I thought it was something terrible – you had another wife or were an escaped felon. But you are just a spy and the nephew of a king-killer?'

He wondered whether she was being facetious. 'You do not mind?'

'I mind you not trusting me sooner. But I must go, and we shall talk about this later. Kiss me, then go to see Dalton – or demand more work from Thurloe.'

'I cannot work for Thurloe. It is unreasonable for him to assign me an investigation and then only give me half the facts. It might see me killed, and I want to see Meg born.'

She regarded him soberly. 'If Thurloe offers you the best opportunity, you should take it. If it proves to be risky, then you will just have to be careful.'

383

He was startled. 'That is rather callous advice.'

'I shall be making sacrifices, too – such as giving up a life I love. Faith believes a wife's place is in her own home, and will never condone me leaving mine to sit with Temperance.'

To Chaloner, such considerations paled into insignificance when he considered what they would gain. He kissed her with a wild, happy passion that left her breathless, then laughed as he released her, grateful to have shed his burden at last and pleasantly surprised she was not angry about it. He would not have been so sanguine, had she announced that she had been spying on *his* country.

The door clanked, and Metje flew away from him. North stood there, Faith and Temperance behind him. Temperance beamed at Chaloner, and did not seem to think there was anything odd in him being in a dark porch at such an hour. Faith did, though, and Chaloner watched her face crease with concern when it occurred to her that he might have been lying in wait for her daughter.

'God's blessings, Thomas,' she said in a voice that was far from benedictory. 'You are up early.'

Chaloner was tempted to announce that he was on his way to fight a duel in Lincoln's Inn Fields and that, assuming he survived, he and Metje would marry. He also experienced a strong desire to describe how he intended to tell Thurloe to find another fool to investigate Clarke's death, but that he still planned to locate some treasure for the Lord Chancellor, in the hope that it would eventually see him sent to The Hague. Holland would be a safer place for his new family, and Metje would not spend her life in fear of an attack by people who detested Dutch Puritans. But he was not in the habit of acting on reckless whims, and settled for nodding agreement.

'Why are you here?' demanded Faith suspiciously. 'To see Temperance?'

'Are you?' asked Temperance, eyes shining with pleasure.

Before he could think of a reply that would mollify one and not hurt the other, the door clanked a second time, and Preacher Hill entered, resplendent in a large white collar and a new hat.

'God's greetings,' he boomed. 'Killed the turkey yet? They need a lot of roasting, so if you plan to eat it today, it should be in the oven already. I am something of an expert on turkey meat, and—'

'Well?' demanded Faith, cutting across him and glaring at Chaloner.

'Mr Heyden has been very kind,' said Metje, stepping forward to smile at Faith. 'He was worried about me walking from Mrs Partridge's house in the dark this morning, and came to accompany me. Then he refused to leave until you arrived, and he knew I was safe from bomb-throwers and window-breakers.'

North nodded his thanks, then pointed upwards. 'Another pane was smashed last night, and it is only a matter of time before a person is hurt. It is good of you to be solicitous, Heyden.'

'It is a pity you were not as determined with that burglar,' remarked Faith unpleasantly. 'You should have dragged him back to face the justice of my gun.'

'He is *so* brave with the ladies, but a rank coward with felons,' sneered Hill. 'He has designs on their virtue, no doubt. Gentle Puritan women are considered fair game these days, among his kind.'

385

'His kind?' asked Faith in alarm. She clenched her fists, and Chaloner took a step away from her.

'Catholics,' said Hill in a low, vicious whisper that hissed around the chapel.

'I thought you were Anglican,' said North, regarding Chaloner uneasily. 'Perhaps you should join us for our morning service, and we shall pray for your release from the tyranny of Rome.'

'He has an appointment with his *Anglican* priest,' said Metje. 'He is going to ring the bells.'

North wrung his hands unhappily. 'Bells are *Roman* fripperies. But we must be about our business, or the congregation will arrive and we shall be all confusion. Good day, Heyden.'

Chaloner left, disconcerted by Faith's simmering hostility, and took a series of shortcuts to Lincoln's Inn Fields. Despite the fact that he was slowly losing the favour of the family that paid him a regular income, there was a spring in his step and he sang to himself. His daughter would be born in the summer, when the sun shone and the days were hot and sultry, and each year they would celebrate her birth with a feast under a shady tree.

Lincoln's Inn Fields comprised a substantial expanse of land, some laid down to agriculture, but most left wild or as grazing for cattle. It was the haunt of robbers during the hours of darkness, and was used by turbulent men to gain satisfaction at daybreak. Thurloe once wrote in a letter to Chaloner that he often heard firearms discharged or the clang of steel as the first tendrils of dawn appeared.

Chaloner reached the place where Robert Leybourn had suggested they meet, and set himself to wait – dawn was still some way off. The trees were winter-bare and dusted with frost, and although the snow had not settled on the streets, it had done better on the grass, and lay in gauzy sheets. It made the ground slippery, and Chaloner knew he would have to watch his footing when he fought. Eventually, he saw a shadow moving towards him, so he stepped into deeper shadows. It was William Leybourn, looking terrified. When Chaloner emerged from his hiding place, the bookseller jumped in alarm.

'Where is your brother?' asked Chaloner, resting his hand on the hilt of his sword, and ready to react immediately if Leybourn informed him he was taking his sibling's place.

Leybourn gave a sheepish grin. 'I slipped a dose of something in his wine last night, and he is now sleeping so soundly that his wife is alarmed. But better the sleep of Lethe than the sleep of death, which is what he would be doing if he crossed blades with you.'

'You said he was a good swordsman. He may have won.'

'He would not, and you know it. He has a hot temper and regrets challenging you, but he is not a coward. He was determined to see the matter through. But his boy is not yet a year old, and I refuse to scc him grow up without a father, not over such a petty quarrel.'

'No,' agreed Chaloner, thinking of his own circumstances. 'That would be a pity.'

Leybourn swallowed uneasily, and took a deep breath. 'Are you going to insist honour is satisfied with me, or can we agree to forget the matter like civilised men?'

'That depends. Will you answer some questions?'

'What sort of questions?'

'About the Brotherhood, mostly.'

Leybourn seemed relieved, and Chaloner wondered what sort of interrogation he had anticipated. 'All right. We will talk about the Brotherhood, and then I want this spat forgotten – no resurrecting it if Rob annoys you in the future. The Brotherhood then. Ask away.'

'How long has Robert been a participant?'

Leybourn thought carefully. 'For about a year.'

'How many members are there?'

'Thirteen or fourteen. There were others, but it was founded many years ago, and some of the originals have died – natural deaths, before you jump to the wrong conclusions.'

'What is its purpose?' Chaloner did not point out that Barkstead's death was hardly natural, and neither were Hewson's, Clarke's or Wade's.

'To promote moderation and tolerance – nothing sinister. But you know that already.'

'Then why the secrecy?'

'Because some of its most powerful members – men like Downing and Robinson – maintain it will have a greater impact if it keeps out of the public view. People are more likely to resist an openly vocal group, than a string of individuals all saying the same thing. Or so they say.'

'Name the other members.'

'Lord, Heyden! You certainly expect your pound of flesh! You must never tell Rob what I did today – he may forgive me for drugging him, but revealing the confidences of his friends is another matter entirely.' He saw Chaloner's cool expression. 'All right, names. I have mentioned Downing and Robinson, and you know about my brother. Dear Thomas Wade is also a member, while two men named Livesay and Hewson are dead.'

388

'They were regicides,' said Chaloner, not mentioning that Wade should also be counted among the late members. 'Dangerous characters with whom to form an alliance. Who else?'

'A Puritan called North, who thinks the world would be a better place if everyone prayed more. A stupid soldier called Evett, who wants to rule the navy. Ingoldsby, on the other hand, owns a deadly deviousness – like Downing – and is Cromwell's cousin, so not to be trusted. Then there is a vintner called Dalton, who has a pretty wife – Sarah.'

'Is she a member?'

'Do not be ridiculous – she is a woman. And those are all I know. I am not a member myself, do not forget. Just the brother of one.'

'You do not believe in moderation and tolerance?'

'Of course. But I do not think it will be achieved by throwing in my lot with regicides, greedy merchants, devious diplomats and brainless soldiers.'

'What about Thurloe? You did not mention him.'

'Oh, yes,' said Leybourn, as if he did not matter. 'And John Thurloe.'

'I think I will demand to see your brother. You reneged on your side of the bargain by lying.'

'I have not,' said Leybourn indignantly. 'I just forgot to mention someone. You cannot kill Rob over a slip of my mind.'

'Thurloe is a man of considerable presence, worth all these others put together. He is not easily overlooked, as I am sure you know only too well.'

'I do not know what you mean.'

'Come on, Leybourn. I know you are his spy, just as you know I am.'

The bookseller looked as though he would argue, but

saw the harsh expression on Chaloner's face and thought better of it. 'How did you guess?' he asked in a voice full of resignation.

'You made several mistakes. First, I claimed to be distressed when I saw Lee's murdered body, and you said I should be used to it. You should not have known anything about what I had experienced in the past, so it was obvious someone had told you: Thurloe.'

'That is not true!' declared Leybourn. 'You have no evidence to—'

'Second, London is a large city, and before last Friday, we were strangers. But, over the past few days, we have met in the street, in shops, and I even spotted you watching my room from the chamber Thurloe rents in the Golden Lion. And did you enjoy the play last night?'

'It was dire,' said Leybourn, capitulating with poor grace. 'I credited you with more taste.'

Chaloner raised his eyebrows. 'Metje said it was the best thing she had ever seen, so one of you is wrong. Perhaps we should ask Thurloe to decide. He might even give us an honest answer for once.'

'Please do not tell him you smoked me out,' said Leybourn sulkily. 'You obviously care nothing for his good opinion, but I do. For some unaccountable reason, he likes you, Chaloner. Why do you think I was told to follow you? Because *he* was concerned for you after your encounter with Kelyng.'

'I suppose he told you my real name, too? He has been rather free with it of late. But never mind him, tell me about the day we met. Your appearance outside Kelyng's house was no accident.'

'I was posted there, because Thurloe had anticipated the satchel would be stolen – he had agents in place all

390

across the city, since he did not know which of his enemies would be responsible. I saw Snow and Storey arrive, and then I watched you follow Hewson inside Kelyng's garden. At the time, I had no way of knowing whether you had been sent by Thurloe or were one of his foes. I manoeuvred my way towards you, and . . . well, we became friends.'

'Friends?' Chaloner did not think so.

'Colleagues, then. Why do you think I told Kelyng you owned a turkey? I was protecting a fellow spy. And I still have the book you sold me. I will not sell it – I will keep it until you can pay me back, no matter how long it takes. A man should never part with books, and I could see you did not like doing it.'

Chaloner relented slightly. It was a generous offer. 'You asked a lot of questions that first day.'

Leybourn's grin was rueful. 'And you answered none of them properly. But what happens now? Shall we work together, to find out what Kelyng plans for Thurloe?'

'No,' said Chaloner firmly. 'I intend to break with him today, and concentrate on persuading the government to send me to Holland with my family. I want no more to do with Thurloe and his lies.'

'You will upset him if you phrase your resignation like that,' said Leybourn unhappily. 'He has always been more fond of you than the rest of us – perhaps because of your uncle.'

'My uncle,' said Chaloner bitterly. 'Will I never be free of the man?'

It was still early – there was not the slightest gleam of silver in the sky – and Chaloner did not feel inclined to hammer on Lincoln's Inn's gate until one of the porters

391

woke to let him inside. The foundation was surrounded by a high wall, but this was no obstacle to a man who had made a career out of finding ways inside places that wanted to exclude him. He selected a spot where the bricks were old and crumbling, and was over it in no time at all. He was surprised to find armed men prowling the grounds, but put their presence down to an increased concern about burglars – crime rates always rose when villains knew there was a good chance their victims would be out at church, and Christmas Day was an important religious festival. But it was not difficult to evade the guards in the darkness, and he reached Dial Court unchallenged.

He was about to walk up the stairs and knock at Chamber XIII, when he saw a shadow cross Thurloe's sitting room window – a shape too bulky to be the ex-Spymaster. Chaloner hesitated, then went to stand under it, listening intently. A rumble of voices told him Thurloe had more than one visitor. Curious, he began to climb the wall outside, using cracks in the masonry to pull himself upwards. It was not long before he had ascended high enough to look in.

The usual fire was burning in the hearth, but Thurloe was not in his favourite chair. Sarah sat in it, eyes on a book that lay open on her knees. Thurloe was at the table, a man on either side of him, and all three heads were bent in earnest conversation. Chaloner took a firm grip on the sill and eased into a position where he could see them better. On Thurloe's right was Ingoldsby, his jowls quivering as he devoured nuts from a bowl. Opposite was Dalton, pale and nervous.

Chaloner took his dagger and inserted it in the window frame, jiggling it until he had eased it open. He jerked out of sight when Sarah glanced up, then pushed it open a little wider when she turned her attention back to her reading.

'So, we are agreed,' Thurloe was saying. 'You do nothing, and I will resolve the matter.'

'No, we are *not* agreed!' said Dalton in a furious whisper. '*I* do not agree.'

Thurloe made a placatory gesture to indicate the vintner was to calm himself. 'If you become any more agitated, you will not need Tom Chaloner to give you away – you will do it yourself.'

Ingoldsby tossed almonds into his mouth. 'You are worrying over nothing, Dalton. Kelyng is too stupid to reason sense into the mass of disparate facts he has unearthed, and you have already murdered that poor old woman – to cover tracks that did not exist.'

'You should not have done that,' said Thurloe, and Chaloner knew from the way his eyes bored into Dalton that he was angry about it. 'It was totally unnecessary.'

'It was totally stupid, too,' said Ingoldsby, scoffing more nuts. 'It was the needless murder of Pinchon that led Chaloner to draw the conclusions he did. Thurloe is right: we should leave this to him – he knows what he is doing, and you most certainly do not.'

'I will not rest easy until Chaloner is dead,' protested Dalton. 'I should have put a knife in him at the Tower, but Robinson was watching. I *knew* I could not trust Bennet to see him quietly dispatched.'

Thurloe was livid. 'Are you saying it was *your* idea to let the lion out? God's grace, man! It might have savaged anyone. What were you thinking of?'

Dalton was unrepentant. 'Bennet told me at a Royal Foundation conclave at St Paul's on Thursday how he had almost killed Chaloner when he let the lion loose before – he had tied ropes across stairs and all sorts – so I asked him to try it again. I was in a panic, and did not think Wade would end up falling to his death. I am sorry. What more can I say?'

'You are *sorry*?' echoed Thurloe, appalled. 'I—'

'The Royal Foundation?' interrupted Ingoldsby, cutting across him in horror. 'Are you telling me *Bennet* is a member of the Royal Foundation? Ye gods! I thought it was an organisation that enrolled respectable men. We sit in company with the Queen, for Christ's sake. I shall resign if *he* has been elected.'

Dalton grimaced. 'His coins are silver, just like yours, and he was desperate to join us. But never mind him – I am more concerned with Chaloner. We are in danger as long as he lives. He tricked me into exposing my membership of the Seven, but he already knew about Thurloe's.'

Thurloe rubbed his eyes. 'Time is passing, and you should be on your way. Do as I say, Dalton, or I will go to Kelyng and tell him everything myself. You know me well enough to appreciate that this is not an idle threat.'

Ingoldsby reached across the table and grabbed Dalton by the lace at his throat. 'And since that would harm me as well as you, I strongly recommend you do as he says. Do I make myself clear?'

Dalton nodded resentfully.

Ingoldsby released him and lowered his voice, indicating Sarah with a jerk of his thumb. 'And next time, do not bring *her* with you. There should be *three* of us who know about this business, but thanks to you there are four. It was wholly unnecessary to confide in her.'

'I beg to differ,' said Dalton coldly. 'Thurloe cares

nothing for us, but he loves his sister. He will think twice about betraying us if he thinks she might come to harm, too.'

Thurloe's face wore an expressionless mask that Chaloner thought made him look more dangerous than he had ever seen him. Had he been in Dalton's position, he would have been seriously worried. Ingoldsby stood, took the last of the nuts and stalked towards the door. Before he opened it, he turned and spoke in a voice that carried enough menace to make Chaloner shiver.

'None of this can be proven, and if you two keep your heads, we will come through it unscathed. But be warned: if *you* break and try to implicate me, I will fight with all I have. I will destroy you, your families and everything you hold dear, so think twice before your resolve weakens.'

A few moments later, Chaloner saw him stride across the courtyard and shout to the porters to let him out. Meanwhile, Dalton snatched his hat from a hook on the wall, and jammed it on his head in a way that suggested he was livid. Sarah set down her book and swung her cloak around her shoulders, while Chaloner recalled guiltily that her hat and wig were still stuffed behind the bed in his room.

Dalton turned to Thurloe. 'I did the right thing by killing Mother Pinchon. I made everything safer.'

'You did immeasurable damage,' countered Thurloe coldly. 'It was a bad decision and you precipitated a chain of events that brought two people I love into grave danger. I shall never forgive you for it, and I meant what I said just now: if you make any more mistakes, I *will* go to Kelyng. Leave Chaloner to me. I will do what is necessary to silence him.'

Dalton left without another word. Sarah kissed her

brother's cheek before she followed, and then Thurloe was alone. When he went to wash his face in the bowl of water that stood near the fire, Chaloner used the noise of splashing to cover the sound of the window opening further still. Then, when Thurloe's face was buried in the linen he used for drying, he climbed inside.

'You do not need to send armed horsemen after me this time,' he said. 'I have come to you.'

Thurloe jumped in alarm, then relaxed when he recognised the intruder. 'Close the window, Tom. There is no need for us to freeze to death.'

Chaloner obliged, and Thurloe went to his usual place by the hearth. Chaloner remained standing, although he edged closer to the fire. It had been cold outside, and he was chilled through.

'I tried,' said Thurloe wearily. 'I tried so very hard. Damn Dalton and his stupidity! I thought I could trust him, but fear has unhinged the fellow, and he threatens to destroy us all – including two people who should be nowhere near this mess – you and Sarah. I could kill him for it.'

'The Seven,' said Chaloner. 'You, Dalton, the four regicides – Hewson, Barkstead, Livesay and Ingoldsby – and one other. Barkstead's seven thousand pounds – his godly golden goose – was the money Swanson earned for revealing your identities. Swanson sent his letter, but the information never reached the King. Kelyng thinks you intercepted it at the General Letter Office.'

Thurloe nodded, and closed his eyes. 'The duties of Postmaster General fell to me during the Protectorate – obviously, they sat well with my role as Spymaster – and it was my job to prevent such intelligence reaching our enemies. The gold had already been paid, but I was able to prevent the letter from reaching the wrong hands – just.'

'I do not understand,' said Chaloner. 'Why would you become involved in such a thing?'

'Because I was trying to preserve the Commonwealth. It was what I believed in. I did everything in my power to see it continue after the Protector's death, but once Richard Cromwell had abdicated and Charles was invited home, I saw it was a lost cause and gave it up. The Seven operated *only* during the Commonwealth: we have done nothing since the King returned, and nor will we.'

'That is not surprising,' said Chaloner harshly. 'At least three of you are dead.'

Thurloe did not acknowledge the comment. 'All I want is to live quietly – there will be no more plotting from me. I believe Ingoldsby and Dalton feel the same.'

'You used the Brotherhood as a shield,' said Chaloner, thinking about what he had reasoned. 'The Seven was a sub-group within it, so you could meet without arousing suspicion. Other men joined later – Downing, Robert Leybourn, North, Evett and Wade – and their open ways concealed the fact that there was something other than moderation and tolerance in the offing. But you have not been to recent meetings because there is no longer any need to maintain the pretence: the Seven are defunct.'

Thurloe inclined his head. 'It worked well: one secret organisation within another.'

'All your loose ends are tied,' said Chaloner. 'Mother Pinchon is dead, so she will not be telling anyone else about Barkstead's message. Her contact, Wade, is also dead. Do you know who killed him – who pushed him to his death as he was trying to warn Bennet about the

397

lion? I glimpsed him on the wall-walk, but Wade told me anyway, just before he died.'

'Dalton,' said Thurloe heavily. 'You were not the only one who saw what happened. Robinson did, too, although he will not bring an accusation against another member of the Brotherhood.'

'Even though it was a brother who was murdered?'

'Dalton spun some tale about Wade selling the fraternity's secrets, which Robinson seems to have accepted. Dalton will say anything to protect himself, even defame the name of a dead man.'

'He is not the only one to resort to desperate measures,' said Chaloner accusingly. 'You sent Hewson to spy on Kelyng, to see how much *he* had learned about the Seven. But I cannot imagine you were overly distressed when you heard another potential risk had been eliminated.'

Thurloe gazed at him in disbelief, then anger blazed in his eyes. 'Hewson was my friend. I was *devastated* when I learned he was dead. We were coming close to knowing the extent of Kelyng's knowledge about us, and another day would have seen Hewson back to safety.'

Chaloner did not know whether to believe him. He returned the discussion to Dalton, thinking about what else he had learned. 'Kelyng believes he has recruited Dalton to spy on you. I heard him talking about it to Bennet a couple of days ago, in the grocer's shop on the Strand. He said he has received information about you from Dalton—'

'Information invented by me, using Dalton as a conduit. It was a carefully controlled leak, so Kelyng's reaction would tell us more about him, than he would learn about us. I was a spymaster, Thomas: I know how

398

to manage these things. Dalton passed Kelyng this information on my orders.'

Chaloner was becoming confused. 'But Dalton tried to kill me, and not just with the lion at the Tower, either. The horseman who attacked me at Ingoldsby's house was his doing.'

'I doubt it. And it was not Sarah, either, although she tells me you believe it was. It is a pity you two cannot be friends, because you may need each other one day.'

'I do not need her, and I do not need you, either.' Chaloner started to leave. 'You have lied to me from the moment I chased your empty satchel. I cannot do this any more, Thurloe. I do not want to be in a position where I do not know who to trust.'

'Trust no one,' said Thurloe with a sad smile. 'Then you will never be disappointed.'

'That is what Hewson said before he started to mutter about praising God and the Seven.'

'Did he?' Thurloe sighed. 'You refused to tell me his dying words, and I was afraid I would arouse your suspicions if I pressed you too hard. I suspected then that you might be curious enough to probe further, although I did my best to dissuade you. Please sit down, Tom. At least do me the courtesy of listening to my explanation.'

'I do not want an explanation. You may use the opportunity to slip a knife between my ribs, since you just promised Dalton you would "do what is necessary to silence" me.'

'That is not what I meant,' said Thurloe, sharp and indignant. 'On the contrary, I have done all I can to protect you. I warned you away from Barkstead's cache, and asked you to investigate Clarke's death instead. I blocked Downing's attempt to enrol you in the

Brotherhood. I even offered to pay your fare to Holland, to remove you from danger. You defied me at every turn – almost as if you wanted to become more deeply involved.'

'That was because I did not understand *why* you issued those orders,' objected Chaloner. 'And Clarke's death *was* connected to Barkstead's treasure, anyway.'

'It most certainly was not,' stated Thurloe firmly. 'Whatever gave you that idea?'

'I saw the documents Clarendon found on his body, and I know about the message he asked White Hall's measurers of cloth to give his wife. They were intended for you: they all mentioned the Seven, and reiterated the phrase 'praise God', which is obviously code for something I have yet to uncover. If you tell me you did not know, I will not believe you,' he added, when Thurloe looked bemused.

'I do not care what you believe. And how do *you* know what words Clarke passed to his wife via the measurers? The letter they wrote to her was closed with so much sealing wax that it would have been impossible to open – not that I tried. There are some things that remain inviolate, and loving words between spouses is one of them. I ordered Clarke to stay away from the Seven, and he promised me he would.'

'Then it seems your agents seldom obey you.'

Thurloe rubbed his eyes. 'Clarke was grateful when I recommended him to the Earl for employment, so I suppose I should not be surprised to learn he tried to help me in return – disregarding my warnings in the process. He told *me* he was investigating cutlery stolen from the White Hall kitchens.'

Chaloner was rueful. 'I wish the Earl had asked me

to investigate *that*, because it was easy to solve: the table knives are being pilfered by the cloth measurers, and melted down to make silver transverse flutes for their musical ensemble. They showed me one of the instruments, and it was far too valuable an item to cost what they claimed – or to have been purchased on a measurer's salary.'

Thurloe's expression was bleak. 'But instead of looking into a simple theft, Clarke wasted his life in a misguided attempt to learn about the Seven. I am heartily sorry he tried to intervene. His wife will miss him, as will I.'

'Simon Lane's wife will miss *her* husband, too,' said Chaloner coldly.

'She died a year ago,' replied Thurloe. 'Simon had no living kin, although that does not mean he is unmourned; I grieve for him *and* the others who died in Clarendon's service. Will you tell me what was in Clarke's messages?'

Chaloner was inclined to refuse, because he was angry and it was a way he could annoy Thurloe, but suspected the man would have the information one way or another, and it would be easier to tell him now and have done with the whole business.

'They were in cipher, and they said to "praise God's one son". Those were the exact words Hewson whispered as he died, and they were also on part of a document I found with Lee's corpse. Will you tell me what they mean, or is this exchange of information only to be one way?'

Thurloe frowned, puzzled. 'Praise God's one son? Do you mean Praisegod Swanson?'

'Swanson?' Chaloner was confused. 'The man who told the King about the Seven?'

'I suppose so. You know how we Puritans occasionally baptise our children with intensely religious names, and Praisegod was an appellation that enjoyed a brief popularity – indeed, one of London's best-known fanatics is Praisegod Barbon, in and out of prison for his extreme political views. So, that was the message Clarke and Hewson were trying to pass me – Praisegod Swanson?'

'I do not understand. Why would they do that?'

Thurloe shrugged. 'Because no one knows what happened to him after he collected his gold, and Hewson was afraid he might emerge to betray us again. Perhaps he was warning me to be alert for him. I imagine Clarke, like you, had discovered the phrase, but had not unravelled its meaning.'

'What do *you* think happened to Swanson?' asked Chaloner, not sure whether he really wanted to know. As Spymaster, Thurloe would have been adept at making people disappear.

'I assume he was afraid the King would be angry with him because he took the seven bars of gold but did not keep his side of the bargain. He ran away and has not been seen since.'

'But he *did* keep his side of the bargain. He wrote his letter, but you made sure it did not arrive. Which is not the same thing at all.'

'True, but he could have sent a second missive, and he never did. He probably felt he had risked himself enough the first time and, since he already had his gold, there was no need to do it again. But Swanson is no longer the problem. There is another man trying to expose us.'

'Who?' asked Chaloner.

'I am not sure, but I think he was responsible for blowing up Livesay's ship, and I think he knows about

Dalton, Ingoldsby and me. Perhaps he stabbed Clarke, too. I sense he is moving in for the final kill, which is why Dalton is so desperate to take defensive action. He does not understand that the best way to weather a storm is to rise with the waves.'

'Is it Kelyng?'

Thurloe raised his hands, palms upwards. 'Possibly. Or Downing, who has spent rather more time with me of late than is warranted. But I do not want you involved any further. You will leave the city today, and if I am still alive when you return, I shall try to find you a post worthy of your talents. Here is gold. Take Metje with you.'

Chaloner stood. 'I do not want your money.'

There was a sudden smashing sound as something hurtled through the window. Flames immediately started to lick across the floor. Thurloe snatched up a rug to smother them, but Chaloner had seen other shadows moving in the garden below.

'No!' he shouted, wrestling Thurloe to the floor. At exactly the same time, there was a deafening roar and something struck the panelling where Thurloe had been standing just an instant before.

# Chapter 11

Even after he was sure the flames had been doused in Thurloe's room, Chaloner was reluctant to leave the shaken ex-Spymaster to the care of the porters who came racing to his aid. There were more of them than usual; some lingered to put his chamber to rights, while others began a search of the grounds, although Chaloner knew they were too late to catch anyone. Bennet had fled long ago.

'There are more outside,' said Thurloe, shivering next to the fire. The broken window meant cold air was flooding into the room, although Chaloner imagined shock was more responsible for Thurloe's pallor and unsteady hands than the chill. He poured wine, and watched him sip it.

'More what? Armed porters?'

Thurloe nodded. 'Clarendon recommended I employ extra when I confronted him over the deaths of my five spies. I misjudged Kelyng: I thought he would prefer to see me arraigned in a court of law, but it seems he has finally realised I have too many powerful friends – or too many nervous enemies – so has decided assassination is

404

the only way forward. This is the second attempt since yesterday.'

'What happened the first time?'

'A gift of dried fruits that reek of poison. They are on the table, if you do not believe me.'

'It was Bennet who fired the musket at you,' said Chaloner, going to inspect the offering. There was a dish filled with dried plums, and the stench of the toxin added to them was enough to make his eyes water. 'I recognised the bandages from his encounter with Sonya. Kelyng has pushed him too far, and he has decided to usurp his master's power in order to ingratiate himself with Robinson – and claim Fanny.'

'He will not do it by taking shots at me. Robinson is one of those who would rather I was alive.'

'Bennet's ambitions have taken him beyond reason. He is running amok.'

There was a commotion in the corridor outside, and Sarah burst in, Leybourn at her heels. She ran to her brother's side and put her hands on his shoulders, peering anxiously into his face, while Leybourn inspected the damage to the room.

'Bennet threw a fireball through the window, knowing my natural instinct would be to quench the flames,' explained Thurloe. 'Then, when I was nicely framed against the light, a musket was fired. Had Tom's wits been as slow as mine, I would be dead.'

Sarah hugged Thurloe, while Leybourn went to the window and scanned the grounds below. 'The porters said Bennet brought ten men with him, and they made no attempt to disguise themselves as they ran away.'

'When I left you earlier today, Snow was hiding opposite your front gate, John,' said Sarah in a small voice. 'I did not see him until it was too late, but he recognised me instantly. I galloped my horse away, but I think he knows who I am now.'

Chaloner recalled Kelyng's promise to protect her. It was worth nothing now Bennet had broken with him.

'You must stay here, then,' said Thurloe. 'My chambers are surrounded by armed guards – who will doubtless be a good deal more vigilant now they appreciate the threat is real.'

'I will fetch some clothes and be back in an hour. Will you come with me, William?' Sarah did not wait for Leybourn to reply before turning to Chaloner. 'Will you return my wig when you have a moment? I lost my spare when I escaped from Snow, and now I have none. I left yours at the Golden Lion, and was rather surprised when you did not do the same with mine. Where is it?'

'Behind my bed,' Chaloner admitted sheepishly.

She regarded him askance. 'If you put it there to hide it from your woman, I advise you to move it at once. She will never believe the truth if she finds another lady's apparel stuffed in such a suspicious place.'

Chaloner changed the subject, wondering how she had arrived so quickly after the attack on Thurloe. 'Did the porters send you word about what happened this morning?'

She shook her head. 'They sent a message to William, and I happened to be in his shop.'

'Does he usually open his doors to customers so soon after dawn on Christmas Sunday, then?'

'My business hours are none of your affair,' said Leybourn coolly. 'But she came to me because her husband is beginning to frighten her. She was lucky to catch me in: I had only just returned from an unpleasant dawn assignation.' His expression gave nothing away.

Thurloe regarded Sarah anxiously. 'Why did you not mention this when you were here earlier?'

She winced. 'Claim my husband is losing his wits when he is standing right beside me? You saw how he is – strangling old women and ordering you to murder Thomas. He says he saw Livesay again this morning. I thought Livesay was dead.'

'Dead or deep in hiding,' said Thurloe. 'Your husband is imagining things.'

'Actually, I think I saw him, too,' said Leybourn. He held up his hands when Thurloe eyed him a little accusingly. 'I did not tell you, because I was not sure. I thought I saw him standing outside Dalton's house once, but decided I must have been mistaken. Perhaps I was not.'

'I think you were,' replied Thurloe firmly. 'Dalton would be the last man Livesay would approach. They often quarrelled and each detested the other. He would come to me first.'

'Perhaps that is why Dalton has become agitated,' suggested Leybourn. 'He *believes* Livesay has returned to make life difficult for him, regardless of whether or not it is true.'

'Dalton always was the most nervous and least committed of the Seven,' admitted Thurloe. 'But it is irrelevant, because Livesay – if he is alive – would not go to the trouble of concealing his identity, then risk exposure by playing games with an old rival. He is not stupid.'

Chaloner started to move towards the door. There was nothing more he could do, and Thurloe was now among friends. The ex-Spymaster rose unsteadily, and came to take his arm.

'I appreciate what you did for me today, Tom. You had just refused funds to leave London, but I urge you to reconsider. I do not think Dalton will harm you after my threat to expose him, but the man is not in his right mind, and you will be safer away from the city.'

'No, thank you, sir,' replied Chaloner. 'It is best we part company. We do not trust each other, and I will fare better with Clarendon.'

'You will not,' warned Thurloe. 'Not if you have committed yourself to finding Barkstead's treasure. I asked Ingoldsby about it, and he says it is in Holland with Barkstead's wife. And do not even think about looking for Swanson's gold. *That* will see you in a church-yard next to Clarke for certain. But what makes you think I do not trust you?'

'Because no one lies to friends, and you have been dishonest with me from the start of this affair.'

'That was for your own safety. I did the same to Clarke – although it did not stop him from dashing into an investigation of his own, either. But please take my advice, because it *will* save your life: leave the city, and take Metje, Sarah and Will with you. I would be a lot happier if you all went away for a few weeks.'

'I cannot leave London,' said Leybourn, startled by the suggestion. 'What about my bookshop?'

'And I will not go as long as you are in danger, John,' said Sarah firmly. 'You may need me.'

Thurloe closed his eyes. 'I was once Secretary of State, with legions of men under my command. Now I cannot even persuade my sister, a bookseller and a former spy to do as they are told. Very well, since none of you will see sense, stay a few more days, but if there is even the slightest hostile move towards any of you, I want you gone. Is that clear?'

Leybourn and Sarah nodded. Chaloner started to move towards the door again.

Thurloe gripped his hand. 'Thank you again.'

'It was instinct, sir. You trained me well.'

Thurloe looked hurt. 'Christmas greetings, Tom,' he said softly.

Chaloner was almost in Chancery Lane before Sarah and Leybourn managed to catch up with him. He had heard them calling his name, but had not shortened his stride. He had had enough of Thurloe and his devious associates, and wanted no more to do with any of them. Sarah grabbed his arm and swung him around roughly.

'You did not have to be unkind,' she snapped, ignoring his irritation as he freed himself. 'You know he is fond of you.'

'I know nothing of the kind.'

'You would, if you used your wits. You overheard what happened in his chamber this morning when my husband wanted to kill you – John was ready to sacrifice himself to Kelyng to stop him. Does that count for nothing?'

Leybourn joined in. 'He told us your real name, because Sarah and I have each other to turn to in times of crisis, but you were alone and he wanted to rectify that. He thought that by telling us your true identity, you would see the depth of his confidence in us. Think about it: he has kept your secret for a decade, and the fact that he has chosen to reveal it now – and to us – is significant.'

Chaloner was not convinced. Sarah sighed heavily at his reluctance to see their point of view. 'He is trying to protect you, Thomas. Surely, you have worked out why by now? I thought you were supposed to be astute.'

'I have worked out nothing at all,' said Chaloner wearily.

'The Seven,' explained Leybourn patiently. 'Think about them. Thurloe, the leader, trying to preserve the Commonwealth. Barkstead, Hewson and Livesay, three men who believed so strongly in an English republic that they were willing to behead a king. Ingoldsby, also a regicide, but who, like Thurloe, sees the futility of further plotting and just wants peace and stability . . .'

'Dalton,' said Chaloner, looking hard at Sarah. 'Who is so eager to ensure the Seven's secrets are kept that he murdered Wade and Mother Pinchon.'

She gazed at her feet, chagrined. 'Yes, he killed them. And do you know what else he did to save his skin? He told *me* and then William about the Seven and Praisegod Swanson, so John would think twice about going to Kelyng – lest John's sister and dear friend be implicated, too. And that is how *we* come to be involved – not because of John, but because of my loving husband.'

'Praisegod Swanson,' mused Chaloner. 'No one seems to have heard from him since he wrote the letter Thurloe intercepted. Is he dead, do you think? Did one of the Seven kill him?'

'William has been trying to find out, although John does not know it,' said Sarah. 'He would not approve of William putting himself in danger – like Clarke did.'

Chaloner was thoughtful. 'I think Praisegod is dead.'

'What makes you say that?' asked Leybourn. 'I was

410

under the impression you had never heard of him before today.'

Chaloner began to sort through the chaos of facts he had gathered, beginning with Barkstead's curious behaviour during his last night in power. 'Barkstead tried to send Thurloe a message via Mother Pinchon, not knowing she would be too frightened to deliver it. He asked her to say his "godly golden goose" was buried in the Tower. She assumed, as he intended, that this referred to the butter-firkin treasure, but of course it did not. Barkstead meant Praisegod.'

'*Praisegod* is buried in the Tower?' asked Leybourn, startled.

'Evett unearthed bones and I found hair that Sergeant Picard said was young, like that of his grandson.' Chaloner wondered whether the guard had sold the grisly find to the wigmaker. 'I suspect Praisegod was dismembered before he was buried, because small pieces are easier to hide than a whole corpse, especially in a place where the earth is hard-packed and difficult to excavate. Evett assumed, as I did, that the fragments were from prisoners who had died in captivity, but Kelyng has studied the Tower's records, and he said that particular cellar has never been used as a dungeon.'

'Except by Barkstead,' said Sarah. 'You must have heard the stories about what he did down there.'

'Not even by him. He sited the grave well, because the passages that make the cellar an unsuitable prison also allow rats to come and go, and they have been destroying any evidence inadvertently exposed by Evett and his treasure hunters. Clarke must have guessed this, because the message he sent to his wife via the White Hall cloth measurers said he would "praise God's one son . . . well

411

away from the shadows cast by the towers of evil". Now I know exactly what he meant by his reference to towers of evil: London's Tower.'

'How can you be sure the bones belonged to Praisegod?' asked Sarah.

'I cannot, but it is the obvious conclusion. Did you ever meet him?'

'Once,' replied Sarah. 'My husband brought him home, about four years ago. He was a young fellow with chestnut-brown curls, which may match the hair you found, and a pleasant, eager face. He sang religious songs for Cromwell. I suppose Barkstead was making covert reference to Praisegod's name when he used the word "godly".'

'Or perhaps he buried the ingots with Praisegod's body,' suggested Leybourn. 'Perhaps *that* is what he meant by the word "golden".'

'There is no treasure in the cellar,' said Chaloner. 'Evett was very thorough.'

'So, Barkstead killed Praisegod,' mused Leybourn. 'I suppose it makes sense. He would not bury a murdered corpse for anyone else, and his message to Thurloe indicates he wanted someone to know a problem was settled.'

'Will you dig again, Thomas?' asked Sarah. 'The Earl of Clarendon will be delighted if you find these ingots, although I imagine he will be less thrilled if you also present him with Praisegod's bones.'

'I hope you do not plan to tell Clarendon any of this,' said Leybourn unhappily. 'Because you still do not have all the information you need to make a rational decision. You know six members of the Seven, but you seem blissfully unaware of the last.'

412

'That is not true,' said Chaloner, as strands of information merged and the name of the seventh member
finally became clear to him. 'You are right about Thurloe
never revealing the identities of his spies lightly, but
Ingoldsby and Dalton know about me – I heard them
when I listened outside his window today. I doubt
Thurloe told them, but my uncle was very free with the
information, and—'

'My husband said you looked familiar when you first
met last Friday,' interrupted Sarah, recalling the exchange.
'He knew your uncle, and recognised some of him in
you.'

'He knew him, because my uncle was the last member
of the Seven,' said Chaloner.

'Exactly,' said Leybourn. 'So *now* do you see why
Thurloe has tried to keep you from becoming involved?'

A good many things became clear once Chaloner understood his uncle's role in the affair, all of which Sarah
reiterated with a good deal of recrimination. Leybourn
was more gentle, although even he seemed to think
Chaloner a fool for not guessing sooner.

'Your uncle and Thurloe were close, and Thurloe
promised to protect you when the Commonwealth
collapsed,' explained Leybourn. 'Old Chaloner knew that
if the identities of the Seven ever became public, then
his whole family would fall under suspicion – especially
a nephew who worked for Thurloe's intelligence service.'

'You were with Downing in Holland, and when
Downing changed sides, John assumed you would
change with him and so be safe,' Sarah went on. 'But
you did not: you shared enough information to keep
Downing happy, but your real reports still came to John.

Then Downing arrested Barkstead, and you found yourself back in London, needing employment. Recalling his promise to help, John recommended you to Clarendon, assuming you would prove yourself and make your own way in the new order.'

'It was also a good opportunity to ask a reliable man to look into Clarke's murder.' Leybourn took up the tale. 'If Thurloe had thought for an instant that Clarke had died investigating the Seven, he would *never* have asked you to look into the matter. Worse, Clarendon then ordered you to hunt for Barkstead's treasure, and Thurloe knew you were tenacious enough to uncover the truth.'

'Obviously, he did not want that,' said Sarah. 'So he asked you to leave England or decline Clarendon's commission. You refused both, and now you know everything he tried to keep from you – for your own good. And before you claim he did all this because he loved your uncle, not you, let me remind you of your letters to him. You wrote sympathetically, and he interpreted this as a sign of friendship – he did not append personal paragraphs to the missives he sent to his other spies. He is not a naturally affectionate man, but the sentiments he expressed to you were real. He assumed yours were, too.'

'All right,' said Chaloner, finally accepting Thurloe's motives had been benevolent. 'But what happens now? Where do we go from here?'

'You seem to have an understanding with Kelyng,' said Sarah. 'You can tell him to call off his brutes and leave John alone.'

'That will not help. Bennet is no longer under Kelyng's control.'

414

'Well, we must do something,' said Leybourn. 'I refuse to sit back and wait for the next attack.'

'I will be here,' said Sarah. 'I shall collect a few clothes and return with one of my husband's pistols – then I can shoot Snow, if he comes after me, and protect John at the same time.'

'What will Dalton say when he learns you are leaving him?' asked Chaloner curiously.

She shrugged. 'We quarrelled violently when I learned he has taken to strangling old women and pushing clerks over castle walls. I do not want him near me, and I do not care what he thinks.'

'Will you go with her?' asked Leybourn. 'Or will you guard Thurloe while I do?'

'I will stay here,' said Chaloner, seeing Sarah about to object to his company. She was still annoyed with him, and he did not want to listen to any more recriminations. His feelings were ambiguous about what he had been told: on the one hand, he was angry that Thurloe had not taken him into his confidence, but on the other, he was ashamed that he had not handled the matter with more grace. Thurloe had offered a friendly hand, and he had slapped it away.

Leybourn and Sarah left Lincoln's Inn, and Chaloner locked the gate behind them. He glanced up at the sky. Clouds hung thickly overheard, casting a dull, grey light over the city, and there was drizzle in the air. The gloomy weather did nothing to dampen the spirits of the people, though, and bells rang all over London. In Chancery Lane, carriages and horses clattered as their owners went to church, and folk greeted each other with cheerful calls; there was an atmosphere of celebration as citizens prepared to enjoy a festival that had been deemed illegal not many years before.

415

Aware that another attack would be rendered easier by the fact that the streets were unusually busy, Chaloner ordered the porters to vary their patrols and sent two men to hire dogs from the Golden Lion. Then he prowled the Inn's gardens, looking for weaknesses in their defences. Mixed among the scent of drenched grass and dripping trees was the acrid reek of smoke, as fires were kindled across the city. Someone was roasting meat in the kitchens, so the smell of burning fat mixed with the yeasty scent of proving bread. A scullion started to warble. It was a carol, although the words had been changed to make it a coarse alehouse ballad, and the lad's friends began to cheer. Chaloner smiled, recalling one of his brothers once chanting the same song to a deaf elderly aunt, who had applauded politely and asked him to sing it again.

The clocks struck ten, and Chaloner began to be restless, keen to be away from Lincoln's Inn, either to resume his search for Praisegod's gold or to spend time with Metje. It should not have taken long for Sarah to select a few clothes and return to Thurloe. He wondered whether she and Leybourn had stopped to visit a church or to enjoy breakfast with friends. But then he recalled their concern for Thurloe, and knew they would not have dallied as long as they believed he was in danger. Something was wrong. He abandoned his post and went to Chamber XIII.

'Thomas,' said Thurloe guardedly. He was wearing his cloak. 'You should be with Metje today.'

'Where are you going?'

'Sarah and Will should have been back an hour ago. I am worried.'

'I will find them, sir. You stay here.'

416

Thurloe reached for the sword he kept behind his chair. 'I can manage, thank you.'

'It is not safe. Bennet may be waiting.'

'I will leave by the back gate. Stand aside, Thomas. You are in my way.'

Chaloner staggered as Thurloe thrust past him. He was not the only one who objected to Thurloe's departure: the porters clamoured at him to return to the place where he would be safe. The ex-Spymaster regarded them coolly and they fell silent, awed by the sudden force of his personality. Then he strode into the garden, leaving them staring at each other helplessly.

'Make sure no one enters his rooms,' ordered Chaloner, thinking of bombs with long fuses, the rims of goblets dipped in poison and myriad other modes of assassination. 'I will go with him.'

Thurloe was walking briskly, so he was obliged to run to catch up. He followed him through a gate so cunningly masked by brambles that it was invisible to anyone who did not know it was there. It was similarly concealed outside, emerging in a thicket of hawthorns that clawed at hands and faces. Thurloe fought his way through them, then set off towards Fleet Street. Shouts and cheers emanated from a nearby gaming house, suggesting some players thought it was still night.

'That would not have been permitted under Cromwell,' said Thurloe without breaking his stride. 'This licentiousness and wild liberty will bring the new government trouble for certain.'

'Yes, sir,' said Chaloner. 'Slow down. You are drawing attention to yourself.'

Thurloe complied, although not by much. 'Go home, Thomas. This is not your concern.'

'You should have told me,' said Chaloner. 'About my uncle and the Seven. Then I would not have assumed you were trying to mislead me for sinister reasons.'

'I did not want you to know,' replied Thurloe tartly. 'You had enough to worry about, what with Downing undermining your career and Metje's . . . wavering affections. Obviously, I was overly protective, although there was certainly no malice involved, as you seem to assume.'

'I know,' said Chaloner. He corrected himself. 'I know now. I am sorry I doubted you.'

Thurloe raised his eyebrows. 'Then will you tell Clarendon that you have reliable witnesses who saw Barkstead's butter firkins arrive in Holland, and ask him to allot you another task?'

Chaloner frowned. 'That witness was Ingoldsby, one of the Seven. Did you ask him to——?'

'Stop it, Thomas,' said Thurloe sharply. 'No, I did not ask Ingoldsby to spin you a yarn. I know what he said to you, because he told me you had been to see him. I am sure that what his wife told you was the truth. What is wrong with you? Do you not trust me, even now?'

'I am sorry.' Chaloner frowned. 'What do you mean by Metje's "wavering affections"?'

Thurloe shrugged. 'I met her at the Nonconformist chapel in Fetter Lane, and she seemed . . . seemed less fond of you than you appear to be of her.'

Chaloner knew this was true, although he was surprised Thurloe should recognise it. 'Her first husband died, and it has been difficult for another man to take his place. But we will be married soon.'

Thurloe smiled wanly. 'Then I hope you will be happy, although I think you should leave England. You have been saying for weeks that there will be a war with the

418

Dutch, and you are right. She will not be safe here.'

'When did you first guess Barkstead's buried treasure was different from the treasure he sealed in his butter barrels?'

'On Wednesday, when Robinson mentioned that you and Evett had been hunting for seven thousand pounds in the Tower. You will appreciate that sum holds a particular significance for a member of the Seven, and I suspected immediately that it might not be coin-filled kegs you found. I did not want *you* to be obliged to tell Clarendon that Barkstead's cache might be a body.'

'But you never received the message Barkstead sent to you via Mother Pinchon?'

'No. But I did not need it to piece the facts together. I knew Barkstead had been on the trail of the man he believed had betrayed us – who transpired to be Swanson – and I simply assessed the situation logically. I heard from Sergeant Picard at the Tower that bones and hair were unearthed, and it did not take a genius to work out whose.'

'Smoke,' said Chaloner suddenly. 'I smell smoke.'

'It is Christmas, and every house in London is preparing meals. Of course you can smell smoke.'

'This is from a different kind of fire,' said Chaloner uneasily. 'A big one.'

Thurloe glanced at him, then broke into a run. Chaloner sped after him, wincing when a cloaked pedestrian coming from the opposite direction did not move quickly enough, and Thurloe crashed into him, making them both stagger. The man started to curse, but then thought better of it and backed away. He carried something heavy, concealing it under his cloak in a way that suggested he had just stolen it. That day was perfect for

419

crime, when people were at church or celebrating the festival with friends. The fellow kept his face hidden as Chaloner passed, obviously unwilling to be seen.

'Oh, no!' whispered Thurloe, stopping abruptly. 'Dear God, no!'

Smoke poured through the windows of Dalton's grand home. A crowd had gathered, and there was an attempt to organise buckets and water, although the house was well past rescue, and the main objective was to prevent the conflagration from spreading. People were running, some converging on the site, and others racing in the opposite direction, lest the blaze run out of control and put their own properties at risk. Chaloner took Thurloe's arm and pulled him forward, still alert for Bennet. He saw that although flames raged through the windows on the left side of the house, the right was as yet untouched. There was still a chance that lives might be saved, if prompt action was taken.

'Stay here,' he instructed, shaking Thurloe's shoulder to gain his attention. The ex-Spymaster's expression was glazed. 'Watch yourself among the crowd. Bennet may be here.'

'What are you going to do?'

'See if anyone is inside.'

Thurloe pulled himself together, and the appalled help-lessness was replaced by resolve. Together, they dodged through the hands that would have stopped them, and Thurloe hammered on the front door. Chaloner heard people yelling that he was wasting his time – the fire had taken hold and nothing could be saved. He took aim and kicked the door. It did not budge, and he could tell by the way it shuddered that it was barred from the inside.

420

'The back,' he shouted, shouldering his way through the onlookers a second time, aiming for the narrow passage that led to the rear of the house. People were there, too, watching window frames become charred and blackened, and glass melt in the heat.

There was a small garden behind the house, dug over to receive vegetables the following spring. It was surrounded by a wall of shoulder height. Chaloner scaled it quickly, pausing to help Thurloe, who was out of practise. The back door was less robust than the handsome affair at the front, and shattered under Chaloner's first kick. Immediately, smoke poured out, driving him back.

'You watch for Bennet,' gasped Thurloe, plucking at his sleeve. 'I will go in.'

There was a butt in the garden, placed to collect rainwater. Ignoring Thurloe, Chaloner hauled off his new cassock, dunked it, and wound the sodden garment around his head. He watched Thurloe do the same, then dropped to his hands and knees and crawled inside the house, Thurloe behind him.

He moved quickly, aware that they did not have much time. He took a breath to shout Sarah's name, but his lungs filled with smoke, and the sound he made emerged as a croak. There was an almighty crash from somewhere ahead, indicating a ceiling or a wall had fallen. His eyes smarted too much to open, and would have done him no good if he had, because there was nothing to see but a dense whiteness. His outstretched fingers encountered a door, but wood and latch were searing hot, and he knew better than to open it: anyone inside was long past help, and the sudden inrush of air from the corridor would produce a fireball that would incinerate him on the spot. He moved on until he encountered a body. He forced his

421

eyes open a crack. It was Dalton. There was blood on his chest, and Chaloner could feel a knife still embedded in him.

'Where is Sarah?' he asked, when he saw the man's eyelids flutter.

'Upstairs,' whispered Dalton. There was another creaking groan as something else readied itself for collapse. The flames roared louder still, and Dalton spoke again. 'Live . . . I saved . . . her and . . .'

But Chaloner knew Dalton would not live. The wound had pierced a lung, and blood was frothing through his mouth. He also knew that if he took the time to drag the vintner outside, he would never be able to fight his way back to help Sarah and Leybourn. He ignored the desperate scrabbling of Dalton's fingers and prepared to crawl on.

'No!' gasped Dalton, distraught. 'Do not . . . leave . . .'

'Take him out,' Chaloner ordered Thurloe.

He did not wait to see whether Thurloe obeyed. He located the stairs, took a slow, careful breath through the waterlogged cloth, then stood and ascended as fast as he could. The smoke was so thick he could not see his hand in front of his face, and he was soon light-headed from lack of air. He dropped to his knees, and began to cough. He groped his way along the upper hallway, trying to recall from the arrangement of windows outside how many rooms there might be. He decided there were two – one on each side of the house – with a further two on the floor above.

An orange haze through the grey-white indicated the chamber to the left was already blazing, while the door to the right was closed. He reached up to the latch. It was cool. He tried to open it, but his fingers were thick

422

and clumsy. Someone collided with him, knocking him to the ground. It was Thurloe, staggering and disoriented. He shoved Chaloner out of the way, stepped back, and crashed into the door with his shoulder. The latch splintered, and the door flew against the wall with a resounding crash that was, even so, barely audible above the deep thunder of flames.

The smoke was thinner inside the room. Thurloe gripped Chaloner's shirt and hauled him in, while Chaloner slammed the door behind them, hoping to exclude the fumes for a little longer. The room contained a bed and several large blanket chests, but not Sarah or Leybourn. Chaloner sagged in defeat, knowing that if they were anywhere else, they were doomed. The desperate journey had been for nothing, and he could tell by the growing warmth of the door against his back that he and Thurloe would not be leaving the way they had entered. Even in those few moments, the fire had claimed the hall to the point where it was impassable.

'You should have helped Dalton,' he said hoarsely to Thurloe, who was gasping at his side.

'I tried, but a great gout of blood flew from his mouth – something ruptured when I moved him. What now? We cannot go back the way we came.'

Chaloner assessed their situation through smarting eyes. Clothes and bedcovers had been dumped on the floor, as if someone had been rummaging through the chests in a hurry – Sarah, making a rapid selection of clothes, so she could leave her husband and go to her brother. But there was something odd. Surely, she would not have wasted time closing and latching them again, especially when half their contents were strewn across the room? Chaloner staggered towards the first one, and unfastened the lid. Leybourn's white face gazed out at him. While Thurloe searched for Sarah, Chaloner tugged the gag from the bookseller's mouth and cut through the rope that bound his hands and feet.

Leybourn hauled himself upright. 'Christ in heaven! Dalton was going to leave us here to burn!'

'We might burn yet. The stairs have gone, and the only escape is through the window.'

'Knotted covers,' croaked Leybourn, lurching towards the bed. 'In a rope.'

Thurloe had freed Sarah, who flung herself into his arms, sobbing her relief, although not for long. She was made of sterner stuff and soon pulled herself together, wiping away the tears to leave smudges across her cheeks. She coughed. 'The smoke is getting thicker.'

'It is unbreathable in the hallway,' said Thurloe. He flung open the window, then staggered back as there was a sharp crack. 'Bennet!'

'Surely not!' cried Sarah. She edged towards the window. 'I can see a bandage around his head.'

'It is me he wants,' said Thurloe. 'If I go first, he may leave the rest of you alone. And anyway, he cannot pop away at survivors indefinitely. Someone will stop him.'

'They will not,' said Chaloner, who had seen the way the onlookers had scattered when Bennet had appeared with his gun. 'They are too frightened of him. Besides, it is not just you they want. Snow is waiting for Sarah, and Bennet hates me as well as you.'

There was another roar, and the door began to smoulder. Then flames licked up it, and Chaloner saw the smoke in the bedchamber drift towards the crack under the lintel. The fire was greedy for air, and it would

424

not be many moments before the fragile barrier disintegrated, and the room would be full of flames.

'Hurry with your rope,' he instructed Leybourn. He took a chair and used it to smash the window, glass and frame together. Immediately, there was another crack, and a chunk of plaster was gouged from the ceiling.

Thurloe shoved him to one side. 'Do you want them to hit you? What are you doing?'

'Preparing for a clear shot. Give me your gun.'

'Wait,' shouted Sarah. She snatched up one of her discarded dresses. 'You only have one chance, and you will certainly miss if he is shooting at you at the same time. I will distract him.'

She waited until he nodded that he was ready, then hurled the dress out of the window. Bennet fired almost immediately. Simultaneously, Chaloner aimed and pulled his own trigger. A second later, a bullet slapped into the wall, missing him by no more than the width of a hand.

'They must have several guns each,' said Thurloe, 'which is why they do not need to reload.'

'Did you hit either of them?' asked Leybourn, as he ripped and knotted blankets with hands that shook with fear.

Chaloner peered out of the window, then jumped back when two more shots sounded. One tore into the jagged remnants of the window frame, while the other cracked into the wall outside. Meanwhile, the door was burning more brightly. 'Unfortunately not.'

'We could just throw ourselves out,' suggested Leybourn, tying one end of his rope to the bed. 'We may survive the fall, assuming Bennet does not shoot us as we drop.'

Chaloner took the dagger from his sleeve. He held it

425

by the blade, then stepped forward and hurled it to where he could see Snow leaning across the garden wall. It glinted as it sped towards its target, and then was lost. He heard the sound of jeering. The flames were almost through the door. He retrieved the knife from his boot and hurled it towards the laughter with all his might, more from frustration than any genuine attempt to hit anyone. The taunting cries stopped abruptly.

'You got one,' said Thurloe. He coughed. 'Snow, I think. Bennet is running away.'

'Quickly,' said Chaloner, grabbing Leybourn's rope. 'Sarah.'

She did not waste precious time arguing about priority, but scrambled on to the window sill, and clambered down the rope, hand-over-hand, like a sailor. She released it and dropped the last few feet, to give the others more time. Leybourn was next, slower and more clumsy.

'Go!' shouted Chaloner to Thurloe, before Leybourn was more than halfway down.

'You first,' said Thurloe. 'Hurry.'

Chaloner began to climb. Then there was a low, ominous roar, and he knew the door had finally given way. He looked up, waiting for Thurloe to appear. He did not.

'No!' cried Sarah. She reached for the rope, her face twisted into an agony of grief. 'John!'

Chaloner hauled himself upwards, reaching the sill to see the room full of flames. Thurloe was lying on the floor. Raising one hand to protect his face, Chaloner forced himself back inside the chamber and grabbed the inert body. He cursed his clumsy hands as he knotted the blanket around Thurloe's chest, then straddled the

426

sill, heaving the older man out of the window like a sack of grain.

It was an awkward way to move a person, and Thurloe was heavy. The knotted strips shot through his hands and he lost his grip. Thurloe plummeted downwards, where his fall was broken by Leybourn. Chaloner glanced behind him, seeing nothing but a wall of orange.

'Jump!' screamed Sarah.

Feeling his shirt begin to smoulder, Chaloner let himself drop.

As soon as Chaloner landed, Leybourn was on him, smothering the flames with his cloak. Sarah had already run for water, and upended a pail over both of them, making them gasp in shock at the sudden chill. While Sarah made sure Chaloner was fully doused, Leybourn went to Thurloe, assessing him for damage, then dragged him to the comparative safety of a nearby alley, away from the inferno that had once been a fine house, and from men with guns. Chaloner, with Sarah clutching his shoulder for support, limped after them.

Once he was sure they were well hidden, Chaloner donned his sodden cassock, relishing its coolness against his hot skin, and left them to recover while he went in search of Bennet and Snow. The back of the house was deserted – none of the crowd had lingered once the bully boys had arrived. He found Snow propped against a wall, a crude bandage around his leg. His face was white, and too much blood seeped from the wound. Chaloner's dagger lay on the ground next to him.

'Where is Bennet?' demanded the agent, leaning down to retrieve it.

'Gone for help,' said Snow, wincing as he tried to grab

the knife first and failed. 'You clipped his shoulder when you shot at him, so I hope he does not faint along the way.'

'Why did you set the fire?'

Snow shook his head. 'That was not us. We were waiting for the woman to come out, and the place started to burn as we watched. I saw a man leave through the front door, though, before it started.'

'Who?'

Snow grinned mirthlessly. 'Got any money?'

Chaloner rummaged for a shilling. 'Who?' he repeated.

Snow stretched out his hand for the coin, but fell back when Chaloner declined to relinquish it before he had his information. 'I did not recognise him – his hat hid his face.'

'Describe him, then. Was he tall? Fat? Thin?'

Snow screwed up his face and gripped his leg with both hands. His face turned from white to a sickly grey. 'Christ, Heyden! You did not have to hurl your dagger quite so hard! I think you have done for me. I told you, I did not see him properly.'

'There was nothing unusual about him? No uneven gait or oddly coloured clothing?'

Snow was about to say no, when he reconsidered. 'His coat was green – and tight, as if he had grown out of it.'

Chaloner knelt next to him and slipped the hilt of the man's dagger through the bandage, twisting it tight enough to make him shriek. 'Hold this. It should stem the bleeding until Bennet comes back.'

Snow was beginning to be frightened. 'What if he does not?'

'I will fetch someone else – but only if you agree to

428

stop stalking Sarah Dalton. She did not kill Storey – I did. I hit him when you were stunned.'

Snow stifled a groan. 'No one will help me, Heyden. We drove everyone off – or Bennet did.'

Chaloner dropped the shilling into his callused hand. 'Then I will tell them you can pay.'

Snow coughed weakly. 'That might do it. People will do anything for money.'

Chaloner was sure he was right. He walked to the front of the house, where a fascinated crowd was watching the houses on either side of Dalton's begin to smoulder, although soldiers under a competent-looking captain had arrived and were organising a bucket chain. Chaloner told a bulky matron about Snow's predicament – and his shilling – then limped back to where Leybourn crouched over Thurloe. Sarah stood next to them, her face a mask of shock.

'Is he all right?' asked Chaloner, indicating the prone ex-Spymaster with a nod of his head.

'Yes, he is,' said Thurloe, opening his eyes. 'Wet, sore and dishevelled, but nothing a few days by the fi . . . in bed will not cure. And you? Did you hurt your leg when you jumped?'

Chaloner shrugged. 'It has been worse.'

Sarah raised a shaking hand to her head. 'It was like a nightmare, being trapped inside that chest and smelling smoke. I do not suppose you saw my husband, did you? Did he escape?'

Thurloe looked away. 'He is dead.'

A loud explosion boomed from the house, raising a collective shriek from the onlookers. Sarah watched the black smoke that billowed into the grey sky. 'There goes the first of his gunpowder.'

Chaloner gaped at her. 'His what?'

'He always keeps two barrels in the house. He says you never know when it might come in useful. That was the first one blowing. The second will not be far behind. How did he die? Was it the fire?'

'He was stabbed,' said Thurloe. 'Who did it? Bennet?'

'Bennet was never in the house,' replied Leybourn. 'I saw him and Snow lurking in the street outside when Sarah was packing her clothes. They must have followed us – I am not very good at detecting that sort of thing. She should have taken Thomas instead.'

Sarah drew a shuddering breath. 'Thomas may have been able to prevent my husband from forcing me into a box and leaving me to burn, too.' She swallowed hard, and tried to steady her voice. 'He said he could not afford to let me live. He also said it was only a matter of time before Bennet finished *you* off, John, and he planned to strangle Thomas when he came to translate letters tomorrow.'

Thurloe frowned. 'But if Bennet was outside, and Dalton ambushed you, then who killed Dalton?'

'Someone he knew,' said Leybourn. 'Before the fire started – while Sarah was collecting her clothes and I was waiting on the landing – there was a knock at the door. The servants were at church, so Dalton answered himself. I heard him wish someone a good morning, and then everything went quiet. I do not think he would have addressed a stranger in that friendly way.'

'Who was it?' asked Thurloe. 'Did you recognise the voice?'

'I did not hear it,' replied Leybourn. 'Perhaps it was Ingoldsby.'

'Ingoldsby is trapped at Westminster Abbey with the

430

King all this morning,' said Thurloe. 'I know for a fact he was invited, and he dares not refuse. Ingoldsby is not the culprit.'

'I heard voices in the room below my bedchamber,' said Sarah. 'But my husband was not *arguing* with this visitor: he was discussing business. I heard him mention his new trade agreement with the Dutch, and how wealthy it will make him.'

'It was Downing,' said Chaloner quietly. 'Snow told me he saw someone wearing a tight green coat emerging through the front door before the fire started. Downing owns such a garment.'

'Downing stabbed Dalton?' asked Leybourn. 'But why?'

'He has always been jealous of my husband's good relationship with the Dutch merchants,' said Sarah. 'But I did not think he was envious enough to kill him over it.'

Clutching Leybourn's arm for support, Thurloe staggered to his feet. It was the first time Chaloner had seen him less than perfectly attired, with his crumpled clothes, matted hair and smoke-blackened face. 'Then we shall have to ask him about it.'

Leybourn gaped at him. '*Ask* Downing whether he stabbed Dalton?'

'I will not put it quite like that,' said Thurloe dryly. 'You can credit me with a little subtlety, Will – I was not appointed spymaster for my habit of barging into delicate situations with bald questions. But it is cold here, and I do not want to take a chill. Come to my chambers.'

Chaloner shook his head. 'I want to see Metje.'

'Yes,' said Thurloe, regarding him oddly. 'That is probably a good idea.'

431

Chaloner frowned, knowing there was more to the comment than he understood. Was Thurloe relieved to have him gone, so he could be with real friends? Or was there something else? 'I do not—'

'We should not stay here,' said Leybourn. 'Bennet might come back, and while Thomas seems awash with demonic energy, I have had enough. An afternoon with roasted chestnuts and a glass of spiced wine sounds more appealing than you can possibly imagine.'

Sarah agreed. 'We will take a carriage, and hang the expense. It is Christmas, after all.'

Chaloner returned to his rooms, intending to rinse the stench of smoke from his hair and change his clothes, hoping Metje would agree to spend a quiet hour with him. He was sore from his jump, his leg ached, and he wanted to lie down and talk about their future – although, he admitted ruefully, just lying down would suffice. He climbed the stairs slowly, and was pleasantly surprised to find her already there. She was standing in the window, which Ellis had 'repaired' with the cover from an old book. She held the lamp in her hand and, when he opened the door, he was taken aback when she turned suddenly and hurled it at him. He ducked instinctively, and it smashed against the wall.

'What are these?' she demanded, brandishing Sarah's hat and wig.

He glanced at the bed, and saw she had been in the process of changing the linen. 'They belong to Thurloe's sister,' he said, one ear cocked for Ellis coming to investigate the noise. 'Mrs Dalton.'

'And what are they doing behind our bed?'

Several stories presented themselves to him as possible

explanations before he recalled that there was no need for prevarication, because she knew what he did for a living. 'There is a man in Kelyng's retinue who wants to kill her, because she brained his partner. I helped her escape by donning her headwear.' Even as he related the tale, he knew he would have been better off with a lie.

'Then what about this?' demanded Metje, tears starting in her eyes. She waved another wig, this one a luxurious brown affair, which had arrived in a box bearing Monsieur Jervas's mark. It was the same colour as the hair he had found in the Tower, and he sincerely hoped it was not Praisegod's.

'Kelyng promised to send me one,' said Chaloner. 'I thought he was just talking.'

'Kelyng,' she said flatly. She did not believe him. 'Kelyng bought you an expensive wig, and Mrs Dalton's personal effects are hidden behind our bed because you saved her life.'

'The problem with the truth is that it is sometimes more difficult to believe than a lie.'

'Your truths certainly are,' she said tartly. 'I thought we had reached an understanding, and that fibs were a thing of the past. I would be better off with . . .'

'With what?'

'With Mr North and his family. They have decided to return to Ely at the end of the month. Temperance has asked me to go with her, and I think I will.'

'But you are expecting our child.' He was appalled she should consider leaving him. 'And North will know it in a few weeks.'

She rubbed her eyes. 'I am so confused, I do not know what to do. People throw things at me in the street because I am Dutch. Then I learn you are a spy – and a penniless

433

one, at that. And if there is a war, I shall be lynched, because you cannot buy the protection I need. My other . . . my other . . .'

Chaloner stared at her, thinking about Thurloe's veiled references over the last week – mention of 'wavering affections', and advice to go to Holland or spend time with her. His stomach churned as he began to understand what the ex-Spymaster had been trying to tell him. 'Your other what? Lover?'

She stared at her feet. 'I was frightened, Tom. And you were always out, going about strange business that you declined to share with me. I needed to be with someone I could trust.'

Chaloner regarded her in dismay. 'Who is it? North?'

'Do not be ridiculous. But it does not matter anyway, because I went to see him today and he was with a woman – his wife. He could not be trusted either, so now I have no one. Do not look accusingly at me, when you have not been faithful, either. At least you can go to Mrs Dalton now.'

Chaloner went to stand by the hearth, his thoughts in turmoil. Had his secretive behaviour really driven Metje into the arms of another man, or would she have gone anyway?

'Someone is coming,' he said, hearing footsteps. 'Probably Ellis, wanting to know what broke just now. What do you want to do? Hide under the bed? Or shall we let him see us together?'

There was a soft tap on the door.

'I do not know,' said Metje tearfully. She still held Sarah's wig. 'He—'

'Mr Heyden?' came Temperance's voice. 'Are you there?'

Chaloner went to let her in, while Metje stood next

434

to the window, hairpiece dangling from her fingers. Temperance was surprised to see her in a man's bedchamber, alone and with the door closed, but was too polite to comment on it.

'Metje tells me you are going to live in Ely,' said Chaloner, offering Temperance a chair.

Temperance winced as she sat. 'I do not want to go. It is full of pirates, who sail through the Fens at full moon and abduct young ladies for wicked purposes. And I will miss you.'

Chaloner was still too stunned by Metje's revelation to offer any words of comfort. 'What can I do for you, Temperance? I will not kill the turkey, if that is why you came.'

'The turkey is no longer with us. But I came to invite you to dine with us anyway.'

'Thank you, but not today,' he said, sorry when her eyes brimmed with tears.

'Please,' she said in a low, choked voice. 'There will not be many more occasions, because father says we shall leave in a matter of days. He thinks it is too dangerous here.'

'You should accept, Tom,' said Metje, not looking at him. 'Mr North has always been good to you, and who knows, perhaps you will be his neighbour in Ely.'

'Will you?' asked Temperance, hope bright in her eyes.

'I doubt it,' said Chaloner. He saw Temperance's smile fade, and chided himself for being such a misery. How would he see his daughter unless he travelled? 'But anything is possible, I suppose.'

Chaloner flung off his smoke-soiled clothes, rinsed the stink of burning from his hair, and donned his Sunday

435

best, knowing it would be expected of him, although he was careful to temper his costume with his plainest collar. Also in deference to the Norths, he left his sword behind, along with the dagger he wore in his belt. The one from his sleeve was lost somewhere outside Dalton's mansion, but the one he wore in his boot remained in place. He did not like the notion of being totally defenceless.

Each time he considered Metje's betrayal, a pang shot through his stomach, and he wondered how far his occupation was responsible for the collapse of their relationship. Because they had spent two carefree years in Holland, he had not expected anything to change when they moved, but of course it had. She had told him she was lonely and frightened, and he should have anticipated she might seek solace from other quarters if he did nothing about it. She had not trusted him to look after her, and he had given her no reason to think otherwise.

So what happened now? Could he forgive her? And what about the child? Was it his or the other man's? He supposed he might know the answer when it was born, if it possessed some feature identifiable as his own, but he would have to make a decision sooner than that, and so would she. However, they were not compelled to make it that afternoon, and he supposed it would be wise to let a few days pass first, so that neither would commit to hasty agreements they would later regret.

When one of the maids opened the door to his reluctant tap, he found the North household waiting for him. His dark blue doublet and breeches were hardly gaudy, but even so he felt like a peacock in a flock of pigeons as he approached the black-clad gathering. A single sprig of holly comprised their Christmas decorations – although some effort had been made to celebrate the festival like Anglicans, an excess of merry-making was still anathema to Puritans – but there was a spotlessly clean tablecloth and all the spoons and knives gleamed.

As usual, the room was bright and welcoming, which was more than could be said for the room's occupants: North and Faith were grim-faced and quiet, Temperance was distressed, and the servants – Metje among them – made no bones about the fact that they wished they were somewhere else. Chaloner was relieved the gathering did not also include Preacher Hill.

'You are still limping, Heyden,' said North, standing to greet him with a forced smile. 'Are you not recovered from your encounter with our burglar?'

'There was a fire this morning,' said Chaloner, seeing no reason why he should not tell them what he had been doing. He was tired of lies. 'At the house of John Dalton, the vintner.'

'What a thrilling life you lead,' said Metje, regarding him coolly. 'Each time we meet, you have been involved in some dramatic incident or other.'

Chaloner shrugged. 'London can be a dangerous place.'

'It is indeed!' declared North, rubbing his hands together. 'Very dangerous. In fact, I feel we can no longer live here, and plan to leave in a matter of days.'

Temperance regarded her parents with tearful defiance, and Chaloner sensed they might be about to face a rebellion from their normally dutiful daughter. 'Why so soon?' he asked.

'Robbers stalk our streets as bold as brass, and sin is

everywhere,' replied North. 'Did you hear Lord Mayor Robinson's unwed daughter is with child? I cannot imagine how.'

'It is very simple, sir,' said Chaloner. 'It happens when a man and a woman lie together.'

There was a startled silence. Then one of the maids stifled an embarrassed giggle, Temperance clasped a hand to her mouth in shock, and Faith came to her feet with a carving knife in her hand.

'Keep a decent tongue in your head,' she said icily. 'Or I shall chop it off. I should have known to expect that sort of quip from a man who plays cards and reads Hobbes's *Leviathan*.'

'Would you care for some chicken, Heyden?' asked North hastily, gesturing for his wife to sit again. She complied, although reluctantly, and he noticed she did not relinquish the knife.

Chaloner was ashamed of himself. The Norths were good people, and he had no right to behave boorishly. It was hardly their fault that he had endured such a wretched morning. He rubbed his eyes and coughed, feeling a residue of smoke scratching his throat. 'I am sorry. I am out of sorts today.'

'The fire?' asked Temperance sympathetically, while Faith and Metje exchanged the kind of glance that indicated they thought he was making excuses.

Chaloner nodded, and coughed again. He could not expel the taste of burning from his mouth, and wished North would offer him some wine, knowing it would ease the ache in his leg, too.

'I trust no one was hurt,' said Temperance, passing Chaloner an empty plate, ready for the roasted chicken her mother was viciously hacking apart. It did not escape

438

his notice that Faith looked as though she wished she were dismembering their guest instead of a bird.

'Dalton was – he died.'

North stared at him in horror, and Chaloner recalled that both were in the Brotherhood, so were comrades. He should not have broken the news so bluntly.

'Died?' asked Faith, while her husband clasped his hands and chafed them, as if the news had chilled him. 'How awful! Shall we abandon this dreary feast and say a prayer for his soul?'

Everyone joined hands. Chaloner's left was seized by Temperance, who gripped it warmly, while Metje slipped cold, hesitant fingers into his right. Faith took a deep breath and launched into a lengthy intercession that seemed to go on for ever. Chaloner shifted uncomfortably, trying to find a position where his leg did not hurt. She stopped when he moved, and only resumed when he was still again.

The ordeal might have gone on a good deal longer, but there was a knock on the door, and within a few moments, a visitor was ushered in. It was Downing, resplendent in green coat and new hat. He grimaced when he saw Chaloner.

'We were praying,' said North. 'Would you like to join us?'

'No, I have just eaten,' replied Downing obscurely. 'I was passing, so I came to tell you that another brother has died in flames. Poor John Dalton.'

'Yes,' said North sadly. 'Heyden was telling us about it. It was shocking news, and we have been asking God to look with mercy on his soul.'

'Then I shall leave you in peace,' said Downing. He frowned at the savaged chicken. 'I thought you said you had purchased a turkey for today.'

439

'We sent it to the poor,' said North, with the air of a martyr.

'Actually, it went of its own accord,' contradicted Temperance, in a rare display of spirit.

'You mean it escaped?' asked Downing, raising his eyebrows and trying not to look amused.

'It unlocked the kitchen door and walked out,' replied Faith stiffly. 'Preacher Hill saw it marching along Piccadilly, scattering all in its path, at six o'clock this morning.'

'It was heading towards Knightsbridge,' elaborated Temperance wistfully. 'And its taverns.'

'On its own?' Downing glanced at Chaloner. 'Are you sure it did not have human help?'

'I do not see how,' said North. 'Our locks are the best money can buy – unpickable, even by the most determined of thieves, although I was alarmed to learn they were no match for that bird. I suspect it knew I had booked the London executioner for eight this morning.'

'I should go,' said Chaloner, uncomfortable with the discussion. It was only a matter of time before accusations were levelled, and the turkey had probably been expensive. He stood up.

'Go where?' asked Metje icily. 'To offer Mrs Dalton your condolences?'

'I will come with you,' offered Temperance, making for the line of cloaks that hung on the wall. 'Sarah is my friend, and she might be in need of Christian comfort.'

'Sit down, Temperance,' snapped Faith. Temperance looked as though she might refuse, but returned to her seat when Faith stood up with a fierce expression.

North saw his guests to the door. 'We have enjoyed

your company, Heyden, although I imagine you would have preferred turkey to chicken.'

'It does not matter, sir,' said Chaloner, wondering whether the man was aware that he had only been provided with a plate, and that prayers had started before there was any kind of dead bird on it.

'I provided you with an escape route,' said Downing, when North had closed the door behind them. 'Although you should not have accepted an invitation from Puritans in the first place. After ten years, I am glad to see the back of gloom and austerity. Give me a merry monarch any day.'

'Is he?' asked Chaloner absently, his thoughts on the unreadable glance Metje had shot him as he had left. 'Merry?'

'Outwardly, although his father's fate is never far from his mind. But you know this, *Chaloner*. You know all about regicide.'

Chaloner regarded him uneasily. 'Did Thurloe tell you—?'

'You do not know who you can trust, do you?' said Downing, taunting. 'But I have been watching you – long before Preacher Hill told me you were an impostor. I always did have an inkling that you were not who you claimed, although I am impressed that you managed to deceive me for quite so many years. Who is your real master? Some Dutchman? I dislike traitors, Chaloner.'

'I am not a traitor,' said Chaloner tiredly, supposing that guilt or innocence would not matter now someone like Downing had discovered his identity. He would be used like Barkstead had been – to 'prove' to the King that Downing was a loyal subject who exposed dissenters.

441

Downing regarded him thoughtfully. 'Then you should choose your friends with more care. I tried to help you – to warn you against meddling where you are not welcome – but you insisted on ignoring my advice, and now you must pay the price. You have only yourself to blame for your misfortunes.'

Chaloner raised his hands in a shrug. 'I have no idea what you are talking about. However, while you dislike traitors, I dislike murderers, and you killed Dalton. You went to his house and discussed his business with him. What did he do? Jibe you about his superior contacts?'

Downing regarded him in disbelief. 'What?'

'You stabbed him and left him to burn.' Downing had a sword and a dagger, and Chaloner wondered whether he would be able to reach the knife in his boot if the diplomat turned violent.

'You have a fertile imagination, Chaloner! I did visit Dalton today, but I assure you he was alive when I left. He was fiddling with the gunpowder he keeps in his house, and I imagine *that* is what caused the fire. If he was stabbed, then it had nothing to do with me.'

He spoke with such conviction that Chaloner began to waver. Then a thought occurred to him. 'You left through the front door. You were seen by Kelyng's men.'

'Ha!' said Downing. 'There are your culprits. Bennet is dizzy with outrage, because Robinson's daughter has refused him a second time. If *he* was lurking near Dalton's house, then *he* will be your culprit. And, yes, I left through the front door. I am not a servant, to slink through the back.'

But the front door had been barred, because Chaloner had failed to break it down, and that meant someone had secured it *after* Downing had left. Dalton could have

442

done it, but Chaloner did not think a man playing with gunpowder would have blocked a means of escape.

'Live,' he said, his thoughts tumbling ahead of him. 'Dalton said "live" when we found him. I assumed he meant he did not want to die – that we should save him because he told us where Sarah was, and he thought we owed him something – but that was not it. I think he was saying Livesay – the man he claims to have seen recently, and who seems to have driven him into such a panic.'

Downing shrugged. 'It is possible that Livesay visited him after I left. I know the fellow is alive, because I had a letter from him yesterday. It came as something of a surprise, since I have always believed North's tale that he died in an explosion.'

'Have you seen him?'

Downing pulled a letter from his pocket. 'No, he communicated in writing. How do you think I know your real name at last? Thurloe would have died before letting that slip.'

Chaloner was bewildered. '*Livesay* told you? But I have never met him. Why should he be party to such information?' He wondered how well Livesay had known his uncle.

Downing gave an enigmatic smile, which suggested he did not have an answer, either. 'I know all manner of damaging facts now – I know the identities of the men who formed an organisation called the Seven; I know Praisegod Swanson was murdered by Barkstead in the Tower; and I know the brotherhood was established by Thurloe to conceal what the Seven were doing.'

Chaloner's heart sank for his old patron, although he

443

fought to hide his unease from Downing. He tried to sound sceptical. 'Livesay has been sentenced to a traitor's death. Fear of capture has led him to imagine all manner of conspiracies that do not exist.'

'I have no reason to disbelieve him. I joined the Brotherhood because I support peace, and I am appalled to learn that my honourable intentions might have seen me associated with treason. The same is true for the others who have nothing to do with the Seven – North, Robinson and Leybourn, to name but a few. But thankfully, Livesay has seen the folly of his ways, and has told me everything.'

If he had suspected that Downing was after him, then it was small wonder Dalton had been terrified, thought Chaloner. 'What else did Livesay tell you?' he asked, still trying to sound dubious.

'That the two surviving members of the Seven – Ingoldsby and Thurloe – will kill the King.'

Chaloner gaped at him, then laughed in genuine disbelief. 'They will not!'

Downing raised his eyebrows. 'You *would* say that. Perhaps you plan to help them, and take up your uncle's mantle. Your family always were fervent Parliamentarians, and I cannot believe I harboured one under my roof all those years.'

'At the time, you were a fervent Parliamentarian yourself.'

Downing regarded him with dislike. 'But I saw reason and changed sides. However, *you* hark back to a regime that no longer exists, and so do Thurloe and Ingoldsby. Why do you think Dalton died? He was playing with gunpowder – no doubt making explosive devices with which to assassinate the King – and one must have ignited

444

and set the house ablaze. It was divine justice at work.'

'Why would Livesay tell you all this?' demanded Chaloner, still far from convinced.

'Because he is attempting to buy his life. He offered the information in exchange for a pardon, and I accepted on the King's behalf. Of course, when he comes to collect his reward he will be in for a shock – I do not negotiate with traitors. When he accuses me of false dealing, I shall point out that it is his duty to expose plots that harm the King, and that he should not have sought recompense for what should have been freely given. Everyone will agree with me.'

'As they did when you arrested Barkstead? That made you the most despised man in Britain.'

Downing's expression was dangerous. 'I did what was right with those damned regicides. But I have wasted enough time here. I am going to give Livesay's letter to Clarendon, and put an end to this treachery once and for all.'

'You would betray your friends? Members of your Brotherhood? Again?'

'I have no friends – it is safer that way. Besides, only a fool turns a blind eye to plots these days.'

In a smooth, sinuous movement, he unsheathed his dagger, just as Chaloner, seeing the blade, twisted to one side. Chaloner staggered, then slumped to his knees, gripping Downing's arm.

'I am sorry,' said Downing, trying to free his hand. People were beginning to stare. 'But when I go to the Lord Chancellor, there will be a frenzy of arrests and hangings. It is better you die now.'

'Better for you,' gasped Chaloner, slipping further towards the ground.

'Better for you, too,' said Downing, tugging away from him. Chaloner could tell from the earnestness in his voice that he believed it. 'You would not have thanked me for leaving you alive.'

When Chaloner finally crumpled, Downing sheathed his dagger and walked briskly away.

# Chapter 12

When Downing's footsteps had receded, Chaloner climbed to his feet, ignoring the astonished stares of people who thought they had just witnessed a murder. He brushed himself down and set off in pursuit, grateful but not surprised that Downing had not bothered to check his victim was dead before leaving the scene of his crime. He had predicted the way the discussion would end as soon as Downing had spoken his real name, and had been ready for an attack. He had let the blade pass harmlessly under his arm, and grappling with Downing as he had slumped to the ground had been designed to ensure the man did not notice a lack of resistance when he tugged his weapon from the 'body'. It was another trick learned from Thurloe, and not the first time he had used it to his advantage.

Downing strode along Fetter Lane, then turned into Fleet Street, his green coat billowing around him. The roads were full of people in their best clothes, and entertainers were out in force, filling the streets with music of varying quality. A dancing bear performed near the Maypole in the Strand, although it was obvious from its

447

odd gait that there was a man inside its skin. Chaloner followed Downing at a distance, taking care to remain hidden among the jostling, bustling crowds.

But when Downing headed towards White Hall, Chaloner hung back uncertainly. Was the diplomat right? Would Thurloe and Ingoldsby really try to kill the King? Thurloe had been devoted to Cromwell, and Ingoldsby had been the Lord Protector's cousin, so it was not an impossibility, but would they be so foolish? Chaloner realised that, even after all that had happened, he was still not sure of Thurloe's true mind, and cursed him for being such a complex man. He leaned down to rub his leg, trying to reach a decision. Should he prevent Downing from going to the Earl? He could have a knife in Downing's portly frame without too much trouble, but then what? It might take several minutes to locate Livesay's letter, during which time the murder would be noticed – and there was no point in killing Downing if he could not retrieve the missive. Should he try to reason with him, or delay him? Chaloner straightened slowly. Neither would work, because he had nothing with which to bargain.

But, if the accusations were true, should he be contemplating ways to prevent Downing from doing his duty anyway? Chaloner had not approved of the execution of the first monarch, and he would certainly not condone the murder of a second. He hung back, irresolute and unhappy, and aware that he had never experienced so many conflicting loyalties.

Downing marched towards the Banqueting House, which was busy that day, because the King had ordered another Touching Ceremony. Crowds had gathered, not only to be blessed by royal hands, but to watch the monarch at work among his people. Soldiers in buff cloaks and the Lord Mayor's men in scarlet were plentiful, but their presence was more ceremonial than protective, and Chaloner imagined any attack on Charles would throw them into a chaos of confusion. It would be easy for determined men to kill him as he moved among his subjects.

The King had not yet arrived, although judging by the atmosphere of tense anticipation, the milling crowds would not have long to wait. A number of barons were already there, clad in their finery, and presenting a stark contrast to the scrofula-stricken hopefuls, most of whom wore the dull browns and greys of poverty. The grandest noble of all was Clarendon. His blue robe was liberally adorned with gold ribbon, while a collar frothed with lace beneath his ample jowls. He wore a wig of pale yellow, which sat oddly with his dark moustache and tiny beard. There was an ornamental 'town sword' at his side, which glittered as he moved, and looked as though it would be next to useless in a fight. He carried a leather bag, which was old and scruffy enough to look strangely out of place with the rest of his glorious attire.

He and the other courtiers huddled at the Banqueting House door, waiting to greet their monarch, and guards had been ordered to keep everyone else out until the ceremony was due to begin. Chaloner tensed as Downing stalked towards the gathering, and watched with a feeling of helplessness as the diplomat tapped the Lord Chancellor's shoulder and whispered something in his ear. Clarendon nodded assent to whatever he had been asked, and followed Downing inside.

Chaloner took the last of the money Kelyng had given

449

him, and tossed it towards the door. There was an immediate commotion, during which the crowd surged forward with a yell of delight and the soldiers fought to keep the rabble away from the noblemen. While everyone was otherwise occupied, Chaloner slipped into the Banqueting House porch, just in time to see the tip of the Earl's cloak disappear through a door to his right. He set off in pursuit, and found himself in the undercroft, a vaulted chamber that had been designed as a drinking den for King James. Charles II used it for lotteries, although that day it had been designated a storeroom, and housed furniture stacked to keep the main hall clear for the masques, balls and dances planned for the Christmas period.

Neither Downing nor the Earl bothered to check whether they were alone, and it was easy for Chaloner to step into the room undetected, remaining out of sight behind a pile of benches. He did not know what he hoped to achieve by eavesdropping on the Lord Chancellor and the diplomat, and was acutely aware that it would probably mean his death if he were caught.

'. . . letter from Sir Michael Livesay,' Downing was announcing in his loud, confident voice, 'about seven men who plotted against the King's return. In exchange for his liberty, Livesay names then all: himself, Thurloe, Ingoldsby, Barkstead, Hewson, Dalton and Chaloner. He also outlines details of a plan to hurl grenades at the King – perhaps when he comes for the Touching Ceremony today.'

'I see,' said Clarendon. He sounded bored. 'Another tale of a threat on His Majesty's life. That will make five this week, and every one has been a hoax.'

450

'This is not, My Lord,' said Downing stiffly. 'It is perfectly genuine.'

Clarendon snatched the paper from his hand. 'These assassins will be somewhat thin on the ground – Hewson, Barkstead, Chaloner and Dalton are dead, and Livesay obviously will not take part, since he has given you advance information about it.'

'Just Thurloe and Ingoldsby,' agreed Downing. 'Livesay says they intend to hurl their fireballs, then escape in the confusion. If you want to catch them red-handed, he will tell me the place where they have stored their deadly weapons – a room they rented together for that express purpose. Dalton *was* helping them – I saw him with gunpowder myself – but he met the end he deserved.'

Chaloner closed his eyes in mounting despair. Fireballs. Gunpowder *was* needed to make fireballs, and Sarah had said Dalton had kept two barrels in his house. Therefore, Downing must have been telling the truth about the vintner making grenades. He reflected on what he knew of Dalton's arsenal. Sarah had expected a second explosion after the first, but it had not come. Was it because the other keg had been moved, perhaps to the 'rented room'? Chaloner recalled the man with whom Thurloe had collided on his way to the fire, who had something hidden under his cloak. The ex-Spymaster had been so intent on his sister's rescue that he had taken no notice, but the man had seen something in Thurloe to check the torrent of abuse he had been about to hurl. At the time, Chaloner had assumed it was Thurloe's grim expression that had stopped the fellow, but now he reconsidered. Perhaps it was because he had recognised a colleague. The man had been Ingoldsby's height, and he had taken care to conceal his face.

451

'Livesay does not say where these weapons are hidden,' said the Earl, as he read the letter. 'He obviously does not trust you, because he is holding back.'

Downing glared at him. 'With respect, My Lord, that is *not* the reason. He is just trying to secure himself the best possible bargain before he plays all his cards. It is blackmail, in essence.'

Clarendon scanned the letter again. 'This is a very malicious piece of writing. It does not smack of a man seeking to redeem himself, but of vindictiveness and spite. I do not think Livesay composed it.'

Downing was startled, and so was Chaloner. 'What are you saying?' demanded Downing, affronted. 'That I wrote it myself?'

The Earl grimaced. 'You *are* spiteful and vindictive, but that was not what I meant. A man cannot believe everything he reads, and I do not see why Livesay should trust *you* to accommodate him. You arrested three of his fellow regicides, and consigned them to a dreadful death. I am simply not convinced that Livesay would choose you as a means to help him.'

Downing was horrified. 'But it is true, My Lord, and if you ignore my warning, the King will be in grave danger. Then it will be *you* enduring a dreadful death – for treason.'

Clarendon's eyes glittered. 'Watch what you say – it is not wise to clamour treason against the King's chief advisor. But I shall keep this letter and consider its claims. You may leave.'

'Leave?' spluttered Downing. 'Is that all you have to say? I risked a great deal to bring you this informa-tion. For all his shorn powers, Thurloe still has claws, and I have just been obliged to stab his favourite spy.

*My* life will be in danger if you allow him to remain free.'

Clarendon regarded him in distaste. 'You killed a man?'

'On my way to see *you*. It is only a matter of time before Thurloe learns that Chaloner's nephew and I left North's house together, and within moments one of us was dead. He will guess what happened, and I do not want him coming after *me* with one of his damned fireballs.'

'You killed Thomas Chaloner?' asked Clarendon, aghast. 'Then you are in trouble indeed. He was working for me.'

'He never left Thurloe,' said Downing, unable to keep the contempt from his voice. 'What did you ask him to do? I will wager anything he did not succeed – not because he could not, but because it is in Thurloe's interests to thwart everything the King's ministers do.'

The Earl waved the satchel, and there was no mistaking his fury. 'You are wrong. I asked him to locate a missing seven thousand pounds and, just moments ago, I received this.' He groped inside the bag and produced a block of gleaming yellow metal. 'It is part of a hoard I ordered him to find, and Buckingham tells me it is worth a *thousand pounds*. Chaloner wrote to say he is hot on the trail of the other six, and now *you* have killed him?'

Downing gazed at the gold bar in horror. 'My Lord! I did not know—'

'You know *nothing*,' snarled Clarendon, white-faced with rage. 'You come with tales of treachery, but offer no evidence to back them up, and now you kill a man who was about to provide the King with a fortune. And you call *me* a traitor? I should have your head for this!'

'But Chaloner's uncle was—'

'His uncle's crimes are not his own, and he has demonstrated his allegiance to the King with this gift. It represents a good deal of money to a penniless spy, and he could have made off with it. But he chose to be honest. I *need* men like him and I do *not* need men like you. You are dismissed.'

Downing was livid. 'I know a lot about this Court. Do not make an enemy of me.'

The Earl looked bored, and waved a hand to indicate Downing should go. There was no more to be said, so the diplomat turned and stalked out, almost knocking Evett from his feet as he did so. The captain had obviously been waiting outside, listening.

Chaloner tried to assemble his tumbling thoughts, recognising the satchel as the one Kelyng had tried to steal from Thurloe. But how had Thurloe come by a bar of gold? There could not be many such items in existence, and he could only assume – as the Earl had done – that it was one of the seven that had been paid to Praisegod. Did this mean Thurloe had taken it after Barkstead had killed Praisegod and buried his body in the Tower? But why would he send it to the Lord Chancellor? Chaloner was so engrossed in trying to see sense that he almost did not notice what was happening in the undercroft, not registering the fact that Evett had locked the door and drawn his sword.

'That ingot, sir,' he said, moving towards the Earl. 'Where did Chaloner find it?'

'He did not say,' said Clarendon. 'Damn that meddling Downing!'

'He must have said something,' said Evett, continuing his advance.

454

'Just that he hoped to find the others. What are you—?'

'That gold does not belong to you,' said Evett, gripping his sword in readiness for a lunge. 'It belongs to another man, and I intend to take it to him. Stand still, or your end will be a painful one.'

Chaloner eliminated the chaos of questions from his mind, and concentrated on the situation that was unravelling in front of him: the Lord Chancellor backed against the wall, his face a combination of alarm and disbelief, and Evett with a sword in one hand, and a long knife in the other. Chaloner had a single dagger. He leaned down and removed it from his boot, then stepped from behind the benches and took aim. Unfortunately, it flew from his hand at the same time that the Earl lashed out with the satchel, and when Evett ducked away from the bag, the dagger embedded itself in the wall behind him. The captain gaped in astonishment.

'I thought you were dead!' cried the Earl, equally startled. 'Downing just said—'

'Downing is a poor judge of corpses.' Chaloner backed away, as Evett, seeing he carried no sword, prepared to make an end of the threat he represented.

Clarendon bustled forward. 'I do not know what game you two are playing, with drawn weapons and tales of false deaths, but I do not like it. Have you lost your senses?'

Evett swung around so fast that the Earl jerked backwards and almost fell. 'I have gained them, My Lord Chancellor!' he spat. 'I have been in your service for ten years, and what am I? An aide! A servant, dispatched to hunt murderers like a parish constable. I thought my

455

future lay with you, but I was wrong. It is time I took matters into my own hands.'

'Who has been filling your mind with this nonsense, Philip?' demanded Clarendon impatiently. 'Sheath your sword, and let us talk. What do you want? A larger salary? A different title?'

Evett's eyes glittered. 'Even now you do not understand. I want to be Lord High Admiral.'

'Do you?' asked the Earl, amazed. 'I thought you were jesting! I often claim that I would like to be Archbishop of Canterbury – to sort out the Church – but I do not actually *mean* it.'

'Well, *I* do,' said Evett, while Chaloner assessed his chances of reaching the door before the captain speared him. They were slim. 'But it does not matter what you think. I have met a man who appreciates my talents, and who will help me to greater things. Ironically, I met him through the Brotherhood – the organisation *you* made me join when you tried to turn me from soldier to spy.'

'The Brotherhood?' asked Clarendon, bewildered. 'It corrupted you?'

'It opened my eyes,' corrected Evett.

'Enough!' snapped the Earl, his confusion giving way to anger at last. 'Put down that weapon immediately, before someone is hurt.'

'Someone will be hurt, all right,' muttered Evett. 'But it will not be me.'

'It might,' said Chaloner, taking several steps away as Evett advanced on him. The captain was wisely concentrating on the opponent he considered the more dangerous. 'There are two of us.'

'An old man and an unarmed spy,' sneered Evett. 'Against a soldier.'

456

'A soldier who has never seen a battle,' countered Chaloner, trying to undermine his confidence. 'And one who is frightened of the pheasants in Hyde Park with their "nasty, slashing beaks".'

'*You* are the coward,' snarled Evett. 'I sensed, the day we met, that you would be a nuisance, so I tried to entice you down an alley where my soldiers were waiting. But you were afraid of the dark and refused to follow.'

'Paying others to do your dirty work?' asked Chaloner, disgusted. Several facts came together in his mind. 'I suppose you tried that tactic on me, because it had worked on poor Clarke?'

He darted behind the benches, wincing as the sword gouged chunks from them as Evett made a series of determined slashes. He grabbed a pole that was used for opening windows, and jabbed back. Evett's attack faltered at the sight of a weapon.

'*You* killed Clarke, Philip?' asked Clarendon, shocked. 'But I asked you to investigate his death!'

'And he was no doubt relieved, despite his claims to the contrary,' said Chaloner, 'I should have known why a straightforward enquiry was progressing so slowly. For example, he "forgot" to show the murder weapon to the measurers of cloth – probably because he thought they might recognise it as his own. I assumed it was simple incompetence, but it was something far worse.'

'I did not kill Clarke,' said Evett, licking dry lips. 'I liked him. I even introduced him to the Brotherhood, and backed his election as a member.'

'To gain his trust,' countered Chaloner, gripping the pole like a stave. 'You probably befriended Simon Lane and the others, too, to lull them into a false sense of

457

security. You tried it with me – you claimed Simon was your cousin, but it was a lie; Thurloe told me Simon had no kin following the death of his wife last year. And you kindly "warned" me about the deaths of my predecessors, urging me to take care. It almost worked – I was beginning to like you.'

'None of this is true,' said Evett uneasily. 'Why would I kill six men?'

'You tried to ride me down outside Ingoldsby's house, too,' said Chaloner. 'As a palace captain, you have access to good horses, and I had asked you for directions, so you knew where I was going. And you certainly tried to thwart my investigation into the treasure – you deliberately aroused the suspicions of Pepys, Robinson and Downing with stupid comments and odd behaviour, and you made up that ridiculous story about mushrooms when you showed me around the Tower. You did it to hamper me – to have me dismissed.'

Evett sneered. 'You cannot prove any of this.'

Chaloner ducked away from the sword. Evett was right, but he continued with his analysis anyway. 'Only the murderer would know Lane and the others were "stabbed in the back in the depths of the night with no witnesses", to quote your own words. If there were no witnesses, then how did you know they died at night? But I do not think you killed Clarke – at least, not alone – because you would not have chosen that public passageway. Your accomplice knew no better, though, because *she* was a stranger to the back corridors of White Hall.'

'She?' asked the Earl, appalled. 'Please do not tell me it was Lady Castlemaine!'

'I mean Evett's new woman,' said Chaloner. 'The one

458

he professes to love. You have to be impressed, My Lord, because she comes in addition to his two wives.'

'Two wives?' echoed the Earl, while Evett lunged at Chaloner and swore furiously when he was rewarded with a crack across the shoulders with the pole. 'Philip!'

Chaloner found he could marshal sense into some of the mysteries, now he knew Evett's role in them. 'Clarke was killed because he was unofficially investigating Barkstead's affairs and you decided he was coming too close to the truth. You were right: he had already prepared messages for Thurloe, mentioning connections between the death of Praisegod Swanson and the Seven and he probably knew about the seven gold bars.'

'So? What does Barkstead's nasty business have to do with me?'

'You want the treasure yourself – presumably for this new master of yours.' Chaloner blocked a wild and undisciplined swipe. 'You pretended to help me, but only so you would know how the investigation was proceeding. It was also you and your lady who were with Lee when he was shot.'

'The three of us were drinking wine together,' admitted Evett cautiously. 'We did not kill Lee, though. I was shocked when that crossbow bolt came through the window.'

'That was Bennet, dispatching a rival for Fanny Robinson's affections,' explained Chaloner to Clarendon. He turned back to Evett. 'But it was you who snatched the document from Lee's corpse.'

Evett shrugged. 'It does not matter what you think, since you will not live to tell anyone. But, yes, it was I who took the paper. Lee had learned the names of the Seven from his kinsman, Ingoldsby, and wrote them in

459

a code only I would be able to read. I said he would hang for treason if he did not do it. He told me what happened to Praisegod, too.'

'What did happen to him?' asked the Earl, shocked by the magnitude of the betrayal. He looked at the gold bar in his hand, and finally understood. 'Seven thousand pounds – seven bars of gold . . .'

'Poor Praisegod,' said Evett. 'It was his hair you found in the cellar, Heyden – you got his scalp and I unearthed his bones. Barkstead murdered and buried him. There is often truth to rumour, and you heard Sergeant Picard saying Barkstead's victims were down there. Praisegod was one of them. I wonder whether there will be similar rumours when I bury you two under White Hall?'

Evett took his sword in both hands and made a concerted effort to drive Chaloner away from the shelter of the benches. He lunged hard and in a direction Chaloner did not anticipate, making the agent lose his balance. When Chaloner tried to parry the next blow, he did so clumsily, and the pole broke in two. The captain moved forward with a grin, taking advantage of the fact that Chaloner had lost his longer reach. When Chaloner met the next slashing swipe, the remnants of the stick fragmented in his hand. He stumbled awkwardly, and pain jolted through his weak leg. The Earl drew his little town sword and swished it ineffectually, to draw his attention away from the fallen spy, but Chaloner could tell by the way he held it that he would be cut down in moments, even by a poor fighter like Evett.

'You disgust me,' said the Earl, backing away when the captain turned on him. 'Lord High Admiral, indeed! I would not appoint you master of a barge.'

Evett turned on him, blazing fury, while Chaloner crawled towards the broken pole. 'Leave him alone,' he shouted, struggling to his feet. He jabbed Evett with the pole. 'Fight me instead.'

'Here!' shouted the Earl, flinging him the sword, and clearly relieved to pass the challenge to a more experienced brawler.

Chaloner lobbed the stick at the furious captain, and snatched up the weapon. When Evett saw they were more evenly matched, he became cautious again. Chaloner blocked a tentative prod, then went on an offensive of his own, although the slender town sword was no match for Evett's heavy blade. Evett soon knew it, and his confidence returned.

'When I have killed you, the King will die,' he said gloatingly. 'You heard what Downing said. My friends are making fireballs even now, and England will have new masters – ones who will not squander public money on masques in which barons pretend to be animals.'

'You mean fanatics?' asked Chaloner. 'I thought you disapproved of extremism.'

'Not all Puritans are fanatics. Some are reasonable men, who just want a return to decency.'

Chaloner was inclined to tell him that such people would almost certainly be opposed to bigamy, and that his new world order might not be all he hoped for. 'Who?'

'Not Buckingham?' asked the Earl. 'You hate him – or was that just a ruse to mislead me?'

'He will be the first to go,' said Evett coldly.

'Downing will stop you,' warned the Lord Chancellor, although he did not sound convinced.

Evett laughed, then swung so hard that Chaloner's blade snapped in two. 'Downing will change sides again,

461

and the next time I see him, he will be a Puritan, claiming he has always been an honest man of simple tastes.' His voice was mincingly mocking, and a fair imitation of the slippery diplomat.

'Your friends?' asked Chaloner. The game was up: his leg and broken sword meant he could not win. 'You mean Ingoldsby?' Even now, he could not bring himself to name Thurloe among traitors.

'You will never know,' said Evett jeeringly. 'You will die wondering, and—'

'The Brotherhood,' said the Earl suddenly. 'You said you met him in the Brotherhood. You *must* mean Ingoldsby. It cannot be Downing, because he brought me that letter. Wade and Hewson are dead . . .'

Chaloner was backed against the stacks of benches, and there was nowhere else to go. 'Livesay,' he said quietly. 'He is playing a double game.'

'Shut up,' snarled Evett, gripping his sword in both hands and preparing to strike.

Chaloner braced himself, resting his hand against the seats for support. Then his fingers brushed something soft: a dead rat. He grabbed it and held as he might a live one, so Evett could see its nose and whiskers. 'Does your terror of wild creatures extend to these, Evett?'

Evett's gaze slid towards the rodent, and he released a yelp of disgust when Chaloner hurled it at him. It caught on his tunic, and while he scrabbled to brush it off, Chaloner pushed forward, seizing his wrist and forcing him to drop the sword. The captain fell, dragging Chaloner with him, and then they were on the floor, rolling and grappling like tavern brawlers. Chaloner was aware of the Lord Chancellor, dancing this way and that with the broken hilt clasped in his chubby fingers.

'No!' he gasped, seeing what the Earl intended to do. 'We need him alive.'

But Evett went limp anyway, and when Chaloner struggled away from the inert form he saw a spreading pool of gore. He heaved the captain on to his back and tried to staunch the flow of blood, but it was no use. The wound was too deep, and it was not many moments before the feeble heartbeat fluttered to nothing. Chaloner staggered to a bench and sat, rubbing his knee. He looked hard at the Earl.

'It was him or you,' said Clarendon defensively. 'And *you* might find the rest of the gold.'

'But *he* knew the identity of the man who intends to kill the King,' Chaloner pointed out, wondering exactly where the Earl's priorities lay. But there was no point in recriminations, and what was done was done.

Clarendon sat next to him. 'I knew Philip lacked the skills required for the kind of work you do, but I decided to give him a chance anyway, and asked him to infiltrate the Brotherhood. I thought he was strong, but he was weak and corruptible. I suppose I bear the responsibility for his death.'

'Well, you did put a sword through his back, My Lord,' said Chaloner, tartly insolent. He rubbed his temples, feeling exhaustion wash over him. 'You may have trusted *him*, but I was beginning to trust *her*. I even risked my life on her account.'

'Who?' asked the Earl, raising a shaking hand to adjust his wig. 'Evett's lady?'

'Sarah Dalton. Perhaps *that* is why her husband tried to kill her – not to eliminate loose ends, as she claimed, but for infidelity. She told me on two separate occasions that she owned a liking for handsome young soldiers. I suppose she meant Evett.'

The Earl pursed his lips. 'It is possible. She does visit White Hall on occasion, and Evett did flirt with her when the King exhibited his paintings last week. He has always been fond of women, and, with the benefit of hindsight, I suspect he had wives in France and Holland, too.'

Chaloner stood, feeling his leg protest against his weight. He needed to confront Sarah and demand the names of her accomplices before a plot swung into motion that might see the death of a second King Charles. What would Thurloe say when he learned his sister had been having an affair with Clarendon's aide and helped murder his agents? Or would he already know, because Sarah's actions were part of a greater, more sinister plan?

'Thurloe is not a traitor,' he said aloud, although he was aware his voice carried scant conviction.

'I know,' said Clarendon. 'I would not have asked his advice all these months if I thought he were. But tell me about this gold. The bar you sent me is definitely one of the ones paid to Praisegod Swanson in return for the identities of the Seven. I assume that is the nature of Barkstead's cache?'

Chaloner rubbed his eyes reluctant to admit to Clarendon that he had no idea where the ingot had come from – and was equally clueless regarding the location of the remaining six. But he had the feeling that he would be safer – for the moment, at least – letting the Earl believe he was more knowledgeable than he was. 'Yes, along with Praisegod himself. Praisegod dead was treasure indeed to the Seven, whose lives he threatened.'

'Will you be able to find the remaining gold? Your note said you might.'

'I will try,' replied Chaloner warily.

'That is all I ask,' said Clarendon. 'However, if you fail, I promise not to hold it against you – you saved my life, and you deserve some reward for your courage. What will you do now?'

'Go to see Thurloe,' said Chaloner, retrieving his dagger. 'Try to think some sense into this mess, and work out who really wants to kill the King.'

'I know two men who will be innocent.' Clarendon indicated the letter Downing had given him. 'Thurloe and Ingoldsby would never embark on such a stupid venture.'

'You seem very sure.'

'I am. Thurloe foiled God knows how many plots like this when he was Spymaster, and has more wits than to join one himself. Meanwhile Ingoldsby has too strong a sense of self-preservation.'

'The culprit is Livesay. He did not die in that explosion, and he is here, in London. He is Evett's new master, and is behind all this mayhem. The only question is: how do we recognise him?'

The Earl straightened his wig. 'I will advise the King to remain indoors today, but I doubt he will listen. So, go to Thurloe and tell him everything you know. He may see answers where you and I cannot. We shall foil these traitors' plans yet.'

Chaloner limped out of White Hall, feeling every muscle burn from fatigue, but when he groped in his pouch for coins to pay for a carriage, he found it empty – he had hurled the last of them away in order to gain access to

465

the Banqueting House. He started to walk towards Lincoln's Inn, mentally sorting the mass of information he had acquired, trying to understand what had happened.

First, his three separate investigations had converged: all were connected to the Seven and the gold Praisegod had been paid for betraying them. Barkstead's godly golden goose was Praisegod's death; Clarke had been killed when he had seen the connection; and Kelyng had been perfectly justified in intercepting Thurloe's post, because his kin were indeed dangerous to the King – although it was not brothers who represented the threat, but a sister.

Second, Praisegod had been murdered by Barkstead and buried in the Tower. Thurloe had had nothing to do with the killing, or Barkstead would not have tried to send him the message via Mother Pinchon – he would have known already. Had the gold bars been interred with Praisegod? They had not been with his fragmented remains when Evett had excavated the cellar. So when had they been retrieved, and by whom? The obvious answer was that Thurloe had done it, which explained why he had been in a position to send one to Clarendon. Chaloner did not dwell on the uncomfortable questions that conclusion raised.

Third, Sarah was Evett's lover, and Livesay was the latest threat to the lives of the Seven. Chaloner supposed he should not be surprised that Sarah should prefer a 'handsome young soldier' to her ageing, selfish husband. Evett must have introduced her to his fellow brother, Livesay, and they had then killed Clarke on his behalf. But surely Livesay would not have attended Brotherhood meetings at which Downing was present, given what the diplomat had done to other regicides? Chaloner could only suppose he had been in disguise – but that in turn meant he would have had to be a recently enrolled member. Most brothers had known each other for years, while some of the newer participants – such as Clarke, Evett and Wade – were now dead. Those remaining were Robert Leybourn and North. Robert was too young to be a regicide, so Chaloner turned his thoughts to the jeweller.

North had arrived in London shortly after the Restoration, and was sufficiently unnerved by the city's violence to want to leave it again. Were his chapel's broken windows the sole reason for his pending departure? What if he was not moving to a safer home, but fleeing the scene of a crime he was about to commit? Chaloner thought about what he knew of North. He had been a soldier in the wars, and bad language bubbled to the surface when he was agitated; he kept a leaden club in his house, which he did not hesitate to use on intruders; and he was, for the most part, a kindly, gentle man who was devoted to his God. Could North and Livesay be one and the same?

Chaloner recalled how Thurloe had described the missing regicide – a Puritan in sober clothes with a plain face, dour features and a moustache darkened with charcoal. A man aiming to change his appearance would dispense with the moustache, and North was certainly both plain and dour. He was also a Nonconformist, prepared to risk physical abuse in order to adhere to his religious convictions. His most notable feature was the burn on his face. Had he been telling the truth when he claimed he had been the victim of an anti-sectarian mob, or had he earned his injury when his ship had exploded?

467

Chaloner remembered something else Thurloe had said – Livesay had rubbed his hands in a certain way: 'he interlocks his fingers, and makes a curious rubbing motion with his palms'. He had a sudden vivid recollection of North chafing his hands over the news of Dalton's death earlier that day.

He broke into a trot when he became more certain he was right: North was indeed Livesay. And Metje was with him. His breath came in ragged gasps, and pain burned in his leg as he tried to run harder. He powered through the people in his way, thrusting them aside and oblivious to the furious indignation that followed. One man stood his ground and looked as though he intended to bring him down, but the sight of a dagger in Chaloner's hand made him think again.

He turned into Fetter Lane, racing along it without thinking about what he would do when he arrived. His only thought was to reach Metje. Then a foot shot out from the alley next to the Golden Lion, and he went flying head over heels to crash into a water barrel. His senses reeled, and he was powerless to resist being hauled to his feet and pushed against the wall. When his vision cleared, he found himself facing Kelyng.

'I have a bone to pick with you,' said Kelyng coldly. 'It involves a certain turkey, which you claimed to own, but which transpires to be no man's bird – it has taken up residence in Knightsbridge, and defies all attempts to catch it. You lied to me, Heyden, and I dislike liars.'

Chaloner struggled, but Kelyng was stronger than he looked. 'I can explain,' he said, trying in vain to break lose. 'But not now.'

'Yes, you will explain,' agreed Kelyng acidly. 'In the Tower.'

'No! There is a plot to kill the King. Fireballs.'

'Yes, yes,' said Kelyng, bored. 'Downing came with a similar yarn about an hour ago, but I no more believed him than I do you. You are all trying to take advantage of me today, sending me on fools' errands that will make me look stupid in front of the King, because you know I have lost all my men to Bennet. But *you* will not succeed, because *you* are under arrest.'

'Please!' gasped Chaloner, trying to prevent himself from being dragged away. 'I am telling the truth! Sir Michael Livesay is plotting as we speak, and I think his plan will go into action at the Touching Ceremony.'

The grip slackened slightly. 'Livesay?'

Chaloner nodded fervently. 'He is one of the Seven. I have been looking into the affair, just as you asked. He is not dead, as everyone believes, but alive and in the guise of a Puritan called North. If you are really loyal to the King, you must help me.'

'Must I now?' said Kelyng icily. 'And how do you propose I do that? I have no men, remember? Or are you suggesting you and I should confront these villains single-handed?'

'Thurloe,' said Chaloner desperately, still trying to wriggle free. Was it wise to send Kelyng to Thurloe? Would Thurloe believe him, and what if Sarah was there? 'He has armed porters. Tell him about Livesay and North – say he has a barrel of gunpowder, because I am almost certain it was he we saw near Dalton's house after the fire started.'

'You want me to secure help from Thurloe?' asked Kelyng incredulously. 'But we detest each other.'

'North has a chicken,' said Chaloner, grasping at straws. He did not add that it was a dead one, and had

469

already been roasted. 'You do not want a hen in a house with explosives.'

Kelyng released his vice-like grip a little further. 'A chicken?'

'Martha,' elaborated Chaloner wildly. 'She is called Martha.'

Kelyng released him so abruptly he stumbled. 'My first wife was called Martha. She died just after the Restoration. Go and rescue this chicken, Heyden. I will gather reinforcements.'

'You will go to Thurloe?'

Kelyng shrugged. 'I might. Or I might see what Bennet is doing. He dislikes king-killers, too, and it could be a way to entice him back into my fold. Or perhaps I will ask—'

Chaloner did not wait to hear. He tore away and staggered across the road to North's house, uncaring that a cart was obliged to swerve violently to avoid him. He thumped on the door, thinking nothing other than that he wanted Metje out. There was no reply so he hammered again, battering with his fists in increasing agitation. Eventually, it was answered by Faith, who raised her eyebrows in surprise when she recognised him. She held a pistol under her apron.

'Thomas!' she exclaimed. 'When we heard such dreadful pounding, we thought the apprentices had come to hang us for being Nonconformists. What is the matter?'

Chaloner shoved past her and darted into the sitting room, knowing that if he was wrong, he was going to have some explaining to do. What he saw stopped him dead in his tracks.

The remnants of the Norths' meagre Christmas meal had been cleared away, although the cloth was still in place. In the centre of the table was a barrel, and the entire chamber reeked of gunpowder. There were wicks soaked in saltpetre, fist-sized ceramic pots, a pan of thick oil and a heap of a white substance he took to be quicklime. North was busily assembling grenades, while his manservant Giles mixed the compounds in a bowl. Metje sat between them, cutting lengths of twine, and the second servant, Henry, packed the completed items into boxes that had been lined with straw. Two people were not involved in the activities. One was Preacher Hill, who sat on a bench near the window with his Bible on his knees, and the other was Temperance, red-eyed and regarding her parents with sullen defiance.

'Our neighbour is here,' announced Faith, pushing Chaloner so roughly that he fell into the table, drawing gasps of alarm from the others. When he turned around, he saw she had drawn her gun and was pointing it at him. 'However, there is no Christmas dinner for you this time, Thomas Chaloner.'

There was nothing Chaloner could do to prevent Henry from confiscating his last dagger when he was searched, and there was little he could have done with it anyway. Faith's pistol was fixed unwaveringly on him, while North had grabbed his club and wielded it menacingly. He saw he had been a fool to dash into such a situation unprepared, and should have known better. And he doubted help was on its way: even if Kelyng did go to Thurloe, the ex-Spymaster would regard the tale with perfectly justifiable suspicion. He had thrown away his life and Metje's by behaving like a greenhorn.

'Sit down,' said North. He sounded firm, but his eyes were uneasy. 'Next to Preacher Hill.'

471

'I will kill you if you make trouble,' said Faith, determined where her husband was uneasy. 'I used this weapon to protect my family during the wars, and I will not hesitate to do it again.'

'You would shoot me?' asked Chaloner, hoping his unfeigned shock would bring them to their senses. 'I thought we were friends.'

'He is right: he *is* our friend,' said North quietly to his wife. 'He has always been—'

'He corrupted our daughter,' said Faith, her voice dangerously low. 'And he is dishonest, a liar.'

'I do not believe he defiled Temperance,' said North. '*She* says it was someone else.'

Faith raised an authoritative hand as Temperance started to speak. 'I do not want to discuss it again. It is too horrible.'

Chaloner wondered what they were talking about. He glanced at Metje, who refused to look at him, so he addressed his remarks to North. 'Whatever you are doing, it is madness. The Earl of Clarendon knows there is a plot afoot, and—'

'Of course he knows,' snapped Faith. '*I* sent Downing the letter telling him a group of renegades intends to kill the King, and urged him to inform the appropriate authorities. I *want* them to know. It is part of our plan.'

Chaloner gaped at her. '*You* are Livesay?'

She glowered, offended. 'Do I look like a man? Now, sit next to Hill before I shoot you.'

'No!' cried Temperance, stepping between them. 'You said if I went willingly to Ely, you would leave him alone. I will go, but you have to keep your side of the bargain.'

Hill's face was sweaty with fear. 'You can let me go, too – I only came to see if there was any turkey to eat.

You can trust me not so say anything – far more than Thomas Chaloner here. I know *that* family. Regicides and Parliamentarians. No wonder he has been lying to you.'

'Shut up!' shouted Temperance, snatching Hill's Bible and bringing it down sharply on his head. The blow did no damage, but it startled him into silence.

Chaloner was bewildered. He sat next to the subdued preacher in a daze, most of his attention on Metje. 'You could have run away when they started this . . .' He gestured vaguely, not sure how to describe what was happening.

Faith raised her eyebrows. 'Why should she do that? It is *you* who has been deceiving her with your false identity and underhand activities. *We* have always been honest with her.'

'It was you who told them my name?' asked Chaloner, regarding Metje in horror, scarcely believing she could do such a thing, regardless of what else had passed between them.

North cleared his throat uncomfortably when Metje declined to answer. 'A few days ago, Downing told me he had entrusted the Brotherhood's secrets to you. Naturally, I asked why *you* should be the recipient of such confidences, and he said you had been Thurloe's man for the past ten years. Thurloe! A traitor to the King!'

'But it does not mean Thomas is also a traitor,' objected Temperance. 'Lots of men worked for the old government – it does not make them rebels.'

'Hush, child,' said North gently. 'You do not know what you are talking about.'

'I have known for some time that you seduce Metje on a nightly basis,' said Faith coldly to Chaloner. 'But I

473

overlooked the matter, because we are fond of her. In return, though, I suggested she look more closely at the man on whom she bestows her favours. I advised her to question the odd hours you keep, the mysterious people you meet and the tales you tell her about your kin.'

'When I did as she said, I learned our life together was a tissue of lies,' said Metje, finally looking at Chaloner. 'It was a shocking blow to learn the man I slept with was a *spy*.'

It had been a shocking blow for Chaloner to learn he was not her only lover, but he did not think this would be a good time to mention it. He spoke Dutch, in the hope of appealing to some ember of affection for him. 'You cannot stay with these people, Meg. Leave now, while you still can.'

'Speak English,' said North sharply. 'It is rude to gibber in a foreign language.'

Metje was pale, and Chaloner suspected she continued to speak her native tongue without realising she was doing so. 'You deceived me for years, Tom, so do not look at me as though this is my fault.'

'But the child—' Chaloner saw the way Faith's finger tightened on the trigger, and kept to English.

'There is no child. I wanted to know the truth about you, and Faith said a pregnancy would make you relent – which it did. But you must understand why I lied to you. I was frightened and confused, and needed to know which of you to marry – who would be safer. I seldom make good choices where men are concerned. My father always said one would bring me to a bad end, and he was almost right. You were a spy, and Philip was married already.'

'Philip?' asked Chaloner, wondering whether he would

474

wake up and find the whole thing was a dreadful night-mare. 'Surely, you cannot mean Captain Evett? I thought his new love was Sarah Dalton.'

'Sarah?' asked Temperance, struggling to follow the bilingual discussion. 'She would never entertain a man like Philip Evett. She likes soldiers, but not silly, weak ones like him.'

'Mr North belongs to a brotherhood,' Metje went on, still in Dutch. 'He introduced me to Philip, and we became . . . I thought he was the answer to my prayers – wealthy, strong, able to protect me.'

Chaloner's thoughts were in chaos. Hill had edged towards him and was sitting too close; he tried to elbow the man away as he attempted to distil sense into what Metje was telling him. 'Then you were the woman with Evett when he visited Lee. I suppose you are the reason he speaks Dutch – after a fashion – too. He said he learned in exile, but he was lying. Christ, Metje! What have you done?'

'Do not listen to him,' ordered Faith. 'He is a seducer, and you should believe nothing he says. Look what he did to Temperance.'

Chaloner glanced at Temperance, but could see nothing amiss. 'Is it the coin tricks I showed her?' he asked, confused. 'I assure you they were nothing—'

Faith's face was a mask of barely controlled fury. 'We learned today that she is with child, and I have seen the way you look at her. You are lucky she pleaded for your life, or I would have blown your head from your shoulders the moment you knocked at our door.'

Hill immediately began to pray in an unsteady voice, while Temperance stared at her feet, cheeks burning with shame. Chaloner, looked from one to the other in disbelief. 'You are . . . with *Hill*?'

475

'It was *him!*' shouted Hill, jabbing both forefingers in Chaloner's direction, abruptly abandoning his devotions. 'Not me. I would never lie with lonely members of my flock in chapel after prayers.'

Temperance began to sob, and Chaloner wondered whether the man had been obliged to drug her or make her insensible with strong wine first.

'Since she could not have you . . .' said Metje softly, leaving the rest of the sentence unspoken.

Chaloner tugged his thoughts back to Metje and her other lover. 'I almost caught you with Evett – twice. The first time was when he and his men tried to entice me down an alley. And the second time was when he came half-dressed to the door when I called on him unexpectedly. I should have known you would not walk all the way to White Hall to buy a poultice for North's nose. You waved the apothecary's receipt . . .'

She winced. 'It was a shopping list. Please do not talk about this any more.'

'Evett gave you a lamp,' said Chaloner, as more facts became clear in his mind. 'Do you know why? So it would illuminate my room and make it easier for him to kill me with his grenade.'

There were other clues, too. He recalled singing her praises to Evett, comparing her to a painting by Rubens, and she had cited the compliment back to him when he had given her presents – Evett had reported the conversation. Then there was her vivid account of the masque: Evett had taken her to watch it through the holes in the corridors – and it was the night she had arrived cold and unusually late in Chaloner's rooms. She had also taken to speaking English instead of Dutch when she was half asleep, and she had visited the Tower menagerie,

476

suggesting Evett swallowed his distaste for its furred inhabitants and escorted her there.

'Philip is a gentle man,' she said quietly. 'The apprentices threw the bomb – they lobbed one at the chapel too, although it did not ignite.'

'That is what you were supposed to think.' Chaloner felt sick as he watched her work with deft fingers. She had made such devices before. Hill pressed something into his side, making him wince. He tried to move away, but there was nowhere to go. He reverted to Dutch. 'I do not know what these people think they are doing, but it will end in disaster. Leave them, while you can.'

North stepped forward, club raised. 'I told you to speak English. Do you want to die?'

'Father!' cried Temperance, jumping towards him. 'You promised!'

Hill jabbed again, urgently and hard enough to hurt. When Chaloner put his hand to the spot, he felt metal. The preacher was trying to pass him his gun. He took the weapon and held it behind his back, although he barely registered what he was doing. There was a lurching sensation in his stomach when he considered the implications of Metje's relationship with Evett.

'But this means you killed Clarke! I said the killer was unfamiliar with White Hall and its customs, and I was right. *You* lured him to that corridor and killed him.'

'You do not need to answer, Metje,' said North, wielding the cudgel menacingly.

'It does not matter,' said Metje. She looked Chaloner in the eyes. 'Yes, I killed Clarke. Mr North needed to know what he had learned about the Seven, but he refused to tell me. We were lucky: the Earl assigned Philip to investigate his death, and you were told to look for

Barkstead's treasure. We were able to provide Mr North with details of both cases.'

'I am weary of talk,' said Faith. She came to loom over Chaloner. Hill cringed away, but she ignored him. 'We shall have silence now, if you please.'

'Do not speak, Tom,' said Metje softly in Dutch. 'She wants you dead because of Temperance's condition, and you should not give her an excuse.'

'What do you intend to do?' asked Chaloner, unwilling to sit still while they manufactured the devices that would hurl his country into another maelstrom of civil war.

'I warned you,' said Faith, taking aim.

'Stop,' ordered a stern voice from the doorway. It was Thurloe, with Leybourn behind him, and both carried firearms. 'Your nasty games are over, madam.'

Faith moved faster than anyone would have expected of such a thickset woman, and screwed the barrel of her gun against Chaloner's temple before he could stop her. She forced him so firmly against the wall that the hand with Hill's pistol was trapped uselessly behind him.

'Put it down, Thurloe,' she said calmly. 'Or I will blow away your agent's head.'

'Do not do it, sir,' warned Chaloner. 'They intend to kill the King.'

'We do not,' said Faith, leaning even more heavily against him, to squash him to silence.

'You do,' said Chaloner in a gasp. 'Evett said—'

'Evett is not party to all our secrets – not because he is disloyal, but because he is apt to make stupidly careless remarks, as he seems to have done to you, since you are here challenging us. However, our real plan is to leave these grenades in a place associated with

478

Thurloe and Ingoldsby, and Downing will see to it that they hang. Downing believed my letter purporting to be from Livesay, just as he did my missive in March, which told him where Barkstead might be found on a certain night in Holland. Now, put down the weapon, Thurloe.'

'No!' shouted Chaloner in despair, when Thurloe placed his gun on the floor and Leybourn followed suit. North hurried forward to collect them, and Temperance's sobs became louder and more distraught. 'Now they will kill you, too.'

Thurloe did not reply, and Faith's eyes glittered. 'It is not pleasant, is it, Thurloe? To see those you love in danger? Remember that when you face the King's mercy at Tyburn.'

A shadow appeared at the window. 'Kelyng is outside with Thurloe's porters,' said Chaloner, glancing at it. 'Put down the gun, Faith.'

North looked alarmed, but Faith was made of sterner stuff. 'Kelyng? Helping the man he hates above all others? Do not be ridiculous!'

Chaloner glanced at Thurloe and was shocked to see defeat. 'Kelyng came to you—'

'We thought he was trying to trick us,' explained Leybourn in a voice filled with self-disgust. 'So we locked him in a cupboard and came to investigate on our own.'

'Sit down,' said Faith, abruptly releasing Chaloner and waving her pistol at Thurloe. Chaloner flexed his fingers and leaned forward, hoping he would be fast enough to put his own weapon to good use – and that it was loaded. Faith was the most dangerous person in the room, so she would be the first to die. 'All of you in a row. No, not you, Temperance.'

479

Defiantly, Temperance sat next to Chaloner. 'I do not know what you are doing, but I want no part of it.'

Faith hauled her daughter to her feet, then held her across her own chest in an awkward hug. Chaloner cursed silently. He could not be sure of hitting Faith when Temperance was pinned in front of her.

'You will understand in time, child,' said North kindly, keeping Thurloe's gun for himself and passing Leybourn's to Henry. 'Our revenge is a holy, just thing.'

Chaloner frowned in confusion. 'Revenge for what, Livesay?'

Thurloe glanced at Chaloner as he sat. 'He is not Livesay, Tom. There is a fleeting likeness in their shape and manner of dress, but that is all.'

Faith laughed harshly. 'Livesay is dead, burned in the ship he thought would carry him to safety, although I have borrowed his name to write notes to men like Downing and Dalton. We might never have learned about any of this, were it not for Livesay. He turned to religion in his guilt and confessed everything to his preacher.'

'Not me,' said Hill in a squeak. 'I know nothing about any of this.'

'Another minister,' said North. 'He was an old friend, and he wrote to me about it – in exchange for a donation to his favourite charitable concern, of course. Even men of God have their price.'

Chaloner looked at the burn on North's face. 'Did *you* ignite Livesay's ship?' He thought about what he had heard, and answered his own question. 'Yes, of course you did. You said someone had put gunpowder in the ship's *forward hold*. How would you have known such a detail, unless you had placed it there yourself? You have an affinity for explosions – there are grenades here, and you set Dalton's house alight. I saw you running away with his gunpowder under your cloak. Snow did not see you, but that is because you used the back door – barring the front one first, to make sure no one would be able to go in and extinguish the fire. You wanted Dalton's body burned, to conceal the fact that he had been stabbed. I suppose Hewson's corpse gave you that idea?'

Faith pulled an unpleasant face. 'I could have saved myself the bother. Dalton would have killed himself anyway, had we waited. He was preparing a firebomb to kill his wife, and was so agitated that he was all fingers and thumbs – not a good way to be with explosives. But, like Livesay before him, he told us a lot about the Seven before I dispatched him to Hell.'

'I suppose that is why Metje – and Evett – kept encouraging me to work for Dalton in preference to the Earl,' said Chaloner bitterly. 'They claimed he offered better prospects, but in reality they wanted me to provide them – to provide *you* – with details of his activities. Likewise, Metje urged me to work for Thurloe when she learned I had been his spy, even though I told her it was dangerous and I wanted to see our daughter . . . But why did you always insist that Livesay was dead?'

But he did not need North to answer. The truth was that impersonating a man almost everyone else thought was dead had been a good way to send Dalton mad.

'No more questions,' snapped Faith. 'Thurloe's unexpected appearance means we need to review our plans. I cannot think with all this chatter, so sit quietly, or I will shoot you.'

'When Praisegod Swanson sent the—' began Chaloner. Faith jammed the barrel into his temple and pulled the trigger. There was a sharp click. The gun had misfired.

481

Temperance screamed and tried to struggle free. Chaloner started to draw his pistol, but could not be sure of shooting Faith while Temperance flailed. Then he saw the shadow in the window again – a silhouette with a bandaged head. It was Bennet, and he was busily winding a crossbow, clearly intending to shoot someone inside the room. When the man glanced up and glared directly at him, Chaloner had the feeling he would be Bennet's first victim.

'You do not mention Praisegod,' snarled Faith, white-lipped with fury. 'His name is too good to be on the tongue of a Chaloner.'

'My God,' breathed Thurloe, gazing at North. 'I thought you seemed familiar, and now I see it. You are Praisegod's father! And his mother and sister – Temperance, with Praisegod's chestnut hair. That is why Livesay's minister told you what the man had confessed. He was telling you what had happened to your son!'

'All this is for Praisegod,' said North softly, gesturing around him. 'We changed our names and came to London for him. He was a child – an innocent child. He went to the Protector's court to sing, because he had such a sweet voice. Someone betrayed the Seven, and Barkstead killed Praisegod for it. But Praisegod was not the traitor.'

'How do you know?' asked Chaloner. He glanced at the window. Bennet was still arming his weapon, pausing occasionally to glower. Chaloner considered pointing him out to the others, but hesitated, wondering whether he could turn the malignant presence to his advantage.

'Because he was not interested in politics,' shouted Faith, tears starting in her eyes. 'He *sang*. He liked music. That was his life. Music.'

'Then why did Barkstead believe him guilty?'

'Ask Thurloe.'

Thurloe shook his head. 'I was preoccupied with a Dutch crisis at the time, and only heard later that Barkstead had uncovered the man who told the King about the Seven. Barkstead said he had found seven gold bars in Praisegod's room, and a few days later I intercepted a letter signed by Praisegod, listing our names. I had no reason to disbelieve Barkstead's conclusion – but I only learned this week that Barkstead had actually killed him.'

Faith closed her eyes. 'Barkstead was wrong!' She hugged her daughter tighter still, and Chaloner saw Temperance struggling to breathe under the force of the embrace.

Leybourn appealed to the servants. 'And you are content with this? You are willing to risk hanging to avenge an ancient murder?'

'It is not ancient,' said Faith bitterly, taking a gun from Henry and indicating he could resume his work on the grenades. 'And if God does not strike his killers, then I shall be His instrument.'

'Let Tom and Will go,' said Thurloe quietly. 'Any crime committed here is mine, not theirs.'

'You are beginning to understand,' said Faith with a smile that was chillingly malicious.

Bennet took aim and Chaloner ducked behind Hill. He saw Bennet's lips move in a curse. But something was wrong anyway, and the chamberlain shook the weapon before beginning the process of rewinding, his face a mask of fury.

'Two of your friends will die today for what *you* did,' Faith continued, addressing Thurloe. 'You should not have embroiled them in your business, just as we should not have sent Praisegod to the wolves of Court.'

'We should finish this, Faith,' said North quietly. 'Time is running out.'

Faith directed her gun at Leybourn. 'We will lock Thurloe in the cellar until Downing has done his work with "Livesay's" letter. Chaloner and the bookseller can die now – we do not want them in our way, and we will tell everyone that Livesay killed them, before he disappeared never to be seen or heard of again.'

'But Thurloe will tell his accusers what really happened,' blurted Leybourn, ducking away from her. 'And he still has powerful friends. Someone will believe him.'

'No one will speak for a man accused of high treason,' said Faith, squinting at him down the barrel. 'It would be suicide. And it will be too late for you, anyway. Stop fidgeting or I may miss.'

Leybourn jumped into the centre of the room and dropped to his knees. 'Allow me to say a prayer first. You are Puritans – you will not deny a doomed man a word with God.'

Faith's gun tracked his movements, but North stepped forward and pushed her hand to one side.

'We are not Barkstead,' he said softly. 'Let him have his say with the Almighty.'

Irritably, Faith pulled her arm away from her husband, and fixed the cowering bookseller in her sights a second time. Meanwhile, Bennet had finished arming his crossbow, and took aim at the man who had made a fool of him over his list of Thurloe's 'brothers'. Temperance began to struggle furiously, but the arm that held her was like a vice, and she was powerless to do anything to prevent her mother's finger from tightening on the trigger as she prepared to dispatch Leybourn.

'Bennet!' shouted Hill suddenly, as he caught sight of the figure in the window. 'My old friend!'

Instinctively, North turned, and Thurloe launched himself at his back. Faith yelled a warning and tried to fling Temperance away from her. Chaloner brought up his own gun and fired at Bennet, but not before the chamberlain had released one of his deadly bolts. It sliced through the window and punched into Hill's Bible. The preacher dropped it with a shriek of terror. Bennet disappeared, although whether he had been shot or had gone to reload, Chaloner could not tell. Meanwhile, Thurloe and North were entwined in a deadly embrace, and Faith had rid herself of the squirming Temperance. She aimed her pistol at Chaloner, but the shot went wide when Thurloe inadvertently stumbled into her.

When Faith turned on the ex-Spymaster with blazing eyes, Chaloner grabbed the tablecloth and hauled with all his might. Fireballs, oil and powder spilled everywhere. Henry released a cry of alarm and leapt away, while Faith hurled herself at Chaloner, clawing his face and flailing with her fists as she vented her rage. Leybourn was on his feet, laying about him with a chair, and everywhere was chaos. Metje had a dagger, although Chaloner was not sure whom she intended to stab. Temperance was trying to haul her mother away from him, while Hill lay on the floor with his hands over his head. Then Henry collided with a lamp, knocking it from its moorings and sending it crashing on to its side. Fuel spilled, and flames followed.

'Douse it! Douse it!' cried North in alarm, abandoning his skirmish with Thurloe. 'Quickly, or we are all lost. The gunpowder!'

'Metje!' shouted Chaloner. He pushed Faith away from him. 'Come with me.'

485

'I do not want—' She backed away.

'Just come,' he yelled, watching the flames creep towards the first of the fireballs, despite North's attempts to smother them with aprons, cushions and bare hands. 'Do not die in here.'

The door crashed open, and Sarah stood there, a number of the Lincoln's Inn porters ranged behind her. She was breathless and her hair was awry. Kelyng stood next to her, sword in his hand.

'Where is the chicken?' he demanded, eyes darting around the room. 'Martha?'

Sarah shoved him back into the hallway. 'Fetch water,' she ordered, taking in the situation at once. 'Organise the men, or the entire street might be lost. Hurry!'

Her voice carried such authority that Kelyng obeyed without another word. Chaloner glimpsed a flicker of movement at the window. It was Bennet, and he had reloaded. When he spotted Sarah, his eyes gleamed with evil delight. Chaloner grabbed one of the spent guns and lobbed it as hard as he could. It cartwheeled through the glass and struck the chamberlain's head. Chaloner saw him drop away with a howl before Faith fastened her hands around his own neck and began to squeeze. She was as strong as any of the men he had ever fought, and he felt himself losing ground.

The first of the grenades popped with a deafening crack. One of the maids screamed, blood pouring from her throat. Sarah dealt Faith a hefty thump with a serving bowl, and the older woman fell away, dazed, allowing Chaloner to struggle away and breathe again. Henry picked up another fireball and hurled it at Thurloe, putting all his frustration and fury into the throw. It missed the ex-Spymaster and cracked into the wall behind him,

486

setting the panelling alight. Time was running out. Chaloner seized Temperance's wrist and shoved her towards the door.

'Take her out!' he yelled to Hill, who was making his own bid for freedom on hands and knees. The preacher obeyed with what seemed like agonising slowness. 'Hurry!'

He looked around for Metje, and saw her on the far side of the room.

'The barrel will go up soon,' shouted North, flailing desperately with his cloak. 'It—'

Another fireball ignited, and Metje's hair erupted in an orange blaze.

'No!' yelled Chaloner. He started to move towards her, but someone gripped his ankle. It was Faith again, and he wasted valuable moments trying to extricate himself from her clawing hands.

'Everyone run!' shouted North. He collided with Chaloner, breaking Faith's hold, but knocking the spy to the floor. 'Everyone outside!'

Chaloner struggled towards Metje, but another grenade exploded killing North and throwing his body into him. Henry, burning like a torch was rushing around in a shrieking frenzy, setting furniture alight. Flames began to lick across the keg of gunpowder. Chaloner tried to stand, but his movements were uncoordinated, and North's shattered corpse lay heavily across him. By now, the barrel was well and truly ablaze, and Metje was motionless as flames engulfed her.

Someone seized Chaloner's arm and tugged him towards the door. Other hands helped, and then he was outside in the cool, clean air. Yet another grenade ignited, and this time he could feel its blast vibrate through the ground. Then he was staggering across the street and

487

tumbling behind the shelter of a dung cart. He tried to stand, but someone held him fast.

'Easy, Tom.' It was Thurloe. 'Stay down.'

'The gunpowder,' said Chaloner hoarsely. 'Metje.'

'It is too late,' said Sarah gently. 'Too late for her.'

Thurloe put an arm around his shoulders and shielded him as the first of several large explosions ripped towards them.

# Epilogue

It was several days before Chaloner felt like going home. He stayed with Leybourn at Cripplegate, trying to take his mind off Metje by reading. The Lord Chancellor sent two messages, both asking whether he had recovered the remaining six bars of gold, and Chaloner furnished him with curt replies saying he had not. Temperance visited once, and her white face and red-rimmed eyes moved him to pity. A sheepish Hill had arranged for her to lodge with a sympathetic Puritan widow until lawyers had decided what should happen to North's estate – Downing claimed it should be forfeit to the Crown, while Thurloe was firmly asserting that it should be devolved on his surviving daughter.

Eventually, Chaloner decided he had imposed on Leybourn's hospitality long enough, and left early one afternoon to return to his rooms. Leybourn offered to accompany him, and they walked through streets that were full of people, all talking about the grand audience of the Russian ambassador in the Banqueting House, which had taken place that day.

North's once-fine home was a mass of blackened

timbers. The fire had been fierce but brief, and although the building would have to be demolished, it had not damaged the neighbouring houses – or at least, not damaged them to the point where the authorities deemed them uninhabitable. There were new and alarming cracks in Ellis's walls, and Chaloner was sure the roof was sagging in a way it had not done before. Ellis waved a dismissive hand, and declared it was natural subsidence – his tenants had nothing to worry about. And there was certainly no reason to reduce the rent.

Chaloner climbed to the top floor and unlocked his door. He was glad Leybourn was with him, because even the stairs evoked sharp memories of Metje, and the bookseller's aimless chatter was a welcome diversion. He stopped abruptly when he saw what stood on the floor by the bed. Leybourn pushed past him, and went to inspect the two boxes.

'Grenades,' he said, startled. 'I assume they do not belong to you? We were lucky the fire did not spread to this house, because there are enough of them here to eliminate half of London.'

Chaloner pointed to the side of the box, and started to laugh. 'That is one of the least subtle things I have ever seen! Did they really expect that to work?'

Leybourn read the offending label aloud. '*To be delivered to Thomas Chaloner of Fetter Lane, on behalf of Mr John Thurloe and Sir Richard Ingoldsby*. So, this is what they were doing. They claimed they were going to leave weapons in a place where the last two members of the Seven would be hopelessly implicated, and where better than with Thurloe's spy? You laugh, but we are fortunate Kelyng did not find them. He would have seen nothing staged about this.'

'What shall we do? If we dispose of them legally, Kelyng may leap to the wrong conclusion. He may have saved us by extinguishing the fire, but he wasted no time after in telling us that he intends to resume his persecution. You should not have locked him in that cupboard and incurred more of his wrath. He is still angry about it, even though Sarah believed his story and let him out as soon as you had left Lincoln's Inn and included him in her rescue plan. Damned fanatic!'

Leybourn was thoughtful. 'We shall do what North – I cannot call him Swanson – intended.'

'Use them to have Thurloe and Ingoldsby accused of high treason? That is not a good idea, Will. Think of something else.'

Leybourn was impatient. 'You just said that Kelyng still intends to hunt Thurloe, and I want him to stop. We shall send these infernal devices to *him*, with a message from Thurloe saying he has uncovered another devilish plot to kill the King, and these are the proof.'

'But there was never a plot to kill the King. All North and Faith wanted was to have Thurloe and Ingoldsby executed for it.'

'I know,' said Leybourn with a weary sigh. 'You are very dim-witted this morning, Tom. You should not have abstained from dinner last night – turkey meat is good for the brain. But, as I was saying, we shall send these to Kelyng, with details of a regicidal plot that Thurloe has uncovered. Its ringleader was the last surviving member of the Seven: William North.'

Chaloner nodded, finally understanding. 'I will forge some documents to "prove" it. We shall invent a new Seven for Kelyng, leaving off Thurloe, Ingoldsby and my uncle.'

'We shall include Downing, though,' said Leybourn, eyes gleaming with the prospect of revenge. 'That will teach him to try to stab you.'

'We cannot. Kelyng might learn he is innocent, which may lead him to question the rest of the list. We need him to accept it without reservation, and consider the case closed.'

'Who, then?'

'They all must be dead, so he cannot ask them questions. I suggest Barkstead, Hewson, Dalton, North and Faith. And Praisegod, who then betrayed them and was killed for his treachery.'

'That is only six.'

'And Philip Evett,' added Chaloner with bitter satisfaction.

'North said Praisegod was innocent.'

Chaloner shrugged. 'He was a much-loved son. But Kelyng does not have the wits to probe too deeply, and all we are doing is drawing him away from Thurloe. He will read the documents, accept he is too late to bring the Seven to justice, and move on to persecute some other hapless soul.'

'But hopefully less vigorously, now his army of felons is disbanded and Bennet is dead of a broken skull. Can you make your false letters look as though they were written three years ago?'

Chaloner nodded. 'The result will be a lot more convincing than this ridiculous label.'

'Good,' said Leybourn. He went to sit at the table, shivering as he looked around him. 'It is damned cold in here. No wonder you did not want to come back. Have you no logs for the fire?'

Chaloner offered him a cup of the wine he had bought

492

to share with Metje. He needed a drink. 'We could throw a couple of fireballs in the hearth. That would warm it up.'

Leybourn smiled, then became serious. 'Are you ready to talk about what happened? There are details I still do not understand.'

Chaloner sipped his wine. 'It started with the Seven – men who believed England's future lay in a republic, and who were prepared to go to any lengths to prevent a Restoration. But when it became clear that the Commonwealth was irretrievably lost, they disbanded. However, Praisegod Swanson found out about them, and tried to tell the King. Barkstead killed him and buried him in the Tower.'

Leybourn took up the tale. 'Praisegod's father learned *some* of what had happened from Livesay, but not all of it. He and Faith then killed Livesay, sending him out on a ship loaded with explosives, and decided to have their revenge on the rest of the Seven, too. They returned to London with new identities, and he joined the Brotherhood.'

'But there was little else they could do for a long time. Then Mother Pinchon appeared, and rumours began to circulate about seven thousand pounds in the Tower. Faith and North knew exactly what that meant. One of the secrets they learned from Livesay must have been that Dalton was a member of the Seven, so North started pretending to be Livesay, hoping to frighten him into exposing the others, while at the same time claiming Livesay was dead. Dalton panicked, and killed Pinchon and Wade. Then he tried to kill you and Sarah, and it would only have been a matter of time before he turned on Ingoldsby and Thurloe. But North and Faith wanted that honour for themselves.'

493

'They were ready to use anyone to fulfil their objectives – Evett, Metje, you. You told Metje things you should have kept to yourself, so she and Evett were able to monitor your various investigations – partly thanks to Thurloe, who innocently encouraged you and Evett to join forces.'

Chaloner poured more wine. His hands were shaking. 'I thought Sarah was Evett's lover. It never occurred to me that Metje would fall for him – an empty-headed coward who was frightened of pheasants. Christ, Will! What does that say about me?'

'That you need to develop an endearing terror of birds.' Leybourn clapped a comforting hand on his shoulder. 'It says she was a foreigner in a country about to go to war, and that your duties prevented you from giving her what she needed. Do you think the Earl will send you to Holland now? We need good men to be ready as relations disintegrate.'

Chaloner shook his head. 'I do not want to go – there is too much of Metje there. But, to return to the Seven, North only killed Dalton and Livesay. My uncle died of natural causes, Barkstead was executed, Bennet killed Hewson by mistake in Kelyng's garden, and Ingoldsby and Thurloe are still alive.'

'North should have gone to Kelyng with his information. *He* would have seen "justice" done. Thank God he decided to take matters into his own hands, or Thurloe might have joined Barkstead.'

Chaloner nodded. 'I suppose we could say Thurloe owes his life to the single-mindedness of fanatics.'

Chaloner did not stay long in Fetter Lane, although his reluctance to remain had little to do with Metje and a lot to do with the fact that the room was so cold. He parted from Leybourn and went to visit Thurloe, where there was sure to be a good fire and perhaps mulled wine. The ex-Spymaster greeted him affectionately, and poured him something hot and brown. It tasted better than it looked, although he did not notice a perceptible 'strengthening of the inner fibres' when he had finished it.

He told Thurloe what he and Leybourn intended to do with the grenades, a plan that was met with wry approval. Thurloe offered to help with the documentation, pointing out that he had some experience of forgery himself, and that he could pen some very convincing lies. Then he talked about the deaths of his two children – the event that had turned Chaloner from spy to friend in his mind. Eventually, he stood and stretched.

'Walk with me, Tom. I need some fresh air.'

They strolled west, then turned towards White Hall. The Russian ambassador and his fabulous retinue had long since gone to the King's private apartments, and the Banqueting House was deserted. Thurloe gave Chaloner a detailed description of the splendour he had witnessed that day, with every courtier in his finest clothes and the King so swathed in gold that he might have been an angel. He pointed to where the ambassador had prostrated himself on the ground after he had delivered his ruler's letters, much to the consternation of onlookers, who were not quite sure how to respond to such an odd expression of homage. Eventually, Thurloe's perambulations led to the flagstone under which Chaloner's uncle had left his silver. He stopped, looked directly at it, then turned to Chaloner with raised eyebrows.

'You know?' asked Chaloner, startled. 'He said he would never tell anyone else.'

495

Thurloe smiled. 'He said the same to me, but that would have been stupid. Such a secret needs two people, in case one dies. I suppose he confided in you after he fled to Holland?'

Chaloner nodded. 'On his deathbed. He asked me to make sure it went to his children – my cousins.'

Thurloe poked about with his dagger, and Chaloner was surprised at how easily the stone yielded. Below it was a recess, where, lying neatly side by side, were six bars of gold. He gazed at them in shock.

'I sent one to Clarendon,' said Thurloe. 'I felt your cousins could spare you that, given the trouble their father has caused you.'

'Gold bars?' asked Chaloner numbly. 'He told me his cache comprised five hundred silver pieces in a leather bag.'

'He lied – obviously, or you would have seen the connection much sooner. He told *me* he had buried a psalter of great antiquity, given to him by his grand-father. He deceived us both.'

'But this means . . .' Chaloner faltered.

'It means it was your uncle who killed Praisegod, not Barkstead. And it was your uncle who betrayed the Seven and was paid for his treachery. Barkstead – who almost certainly did not know what had really happened – helped him hide Praisegod's body, then tried to send me that message through Mother Pinchon.'

'North said his son was innocent.'

'He was right. Praisegod was a scapegoat, chosen at random, because he was young, dispensable and unable to defend himself – and your uncle sacrificed him to make Barkstead think the traitor was dead, so he would stop hunting for him. *I* knew nothing about Barkstead

496

and the "godly golden goose" – this callous murder – until you told me about it on Christmas morning, but Dalton did, which accounts for his growing unease.'

'So, when did you work out that my uncle was the villain in all this?' asked Chaloner uncomfortably.

'After the fire at Dalton's house. I suddenly understood that guilty knowledge of an ancient murder was the cause of the man's instability. But I needed proof, and suspected this was where I might find it. Then, since the flagstone was up, I decided to send Clarendon a gift, in the hope that it would secure you a permanent place with the new government's intelligence service. I have been an ass: I should have made sense of all this ages ago.'

'Did I tell you my uncle came to me for help when he arrived in Holland?' Chaloner felt like a fool, too. 'I gave him everything I had, which is why I have been so impecunious since arriving in London. I squandered it all to aid and abet a murderer.'

'We cannot choose our kin, Tom. I understand he died a few weeks later. Perhaps shame hastened his end, or perhaps guilt drove him to a surfeit of wine. He always was a drunkard.'

'Despite this, you still . . .' Chaloner was not quite sure how to say what he meant.

'Extend the hand of friendship towards you? It was hardly your fault he turned rotten, and you wrote me those kind letters – something he would never have done. You are a different man.'

'What shall we do?' asked Chaloner, looking at the gold in its earthen sarcophagus. 'I shall never give *that* to my cousins. It is tainted, and they will not want it.'

Thurloe replaced the stone when he heard a party of

497

courtiers approaching. 'We shall think of something. But for now, I suggest we do nothing.'

'You mean just leave it there?'

Thurloe smiled. 'Why not? It has been quite safe for the last three years.'

# Historical Note

When Charles II made his triumphal return to England after a twelve-year exile, he was relatively forgiving of the men who had supported the Commonwealth. The only crime he could not overlook was the execution of his father. Hence the fifty-nine men who had signed the order for his beheading, along with a handful who had played significant roles in the old king's trial, were in deep trouble. Some were already dead from natural causes, while others gave themselves up and appealed to his mercy. Others still escaped abroad, where a few were murdered by vengeful Royalists, and the rest lived in nervous obscurity.

In a distasteful piece of skulduggery, three men were hauled from their Dutch sanctuaries in March 1662 by a one-time Parliamentarian called Sir George Downing. The Dutch authorities were shocked by Downing's actions, and were reluctant to give the order for Sir John Barkstead, John Okey and Miles Corbet to be extradited to England. Downing applied considerable pressure, and they relented unwillingly. Within a month of their return, Barkstead, Okey and Corbet were hanged, drawn and quartered at Tyburn, and Barkstead's head was displayed outside the Tower of London. If Downing thought this would gain him popularity among Royalists, he was sadly mistaken. Samuel Pepys notes in his diary that 'all the world takes notice of him for a most ungratefull villaine for his pains' (17 April 1662).

In autumn of that same year, another series of events is written in Pepys's diary. On 30 October, he records with great excitement that treasure worth seven thousand pounds had been buried in the Tower, and that his patron, the Earl of Sandwich, was to have two thousand of it. A man named Mr [Thomas] Wade of Axe Yard, who came up with the story, was to have a finder's fee of two thousand, while the King was to have the remaining three thousand. Pepys met Wade, a man called Mr [Robert] Lee (or Leigh) and one Captain [Philip] Evett in a tavern named the Dolphin, where they planned their strategy. Sir John Robinson, Lieutenant of the Tower and Lord Mayor of London, encouraged the men to dig wherever they wanted.

The first attempt revealed nothing, but, undaunted, they returned two days later and tried again. By now, Pepys was becoming sceptical. He had learned from Wade that the hoard had been hidden by the executed regicide Barkstead, when he had held the office of Lieutenant of the Tower, and that a female servant had helped him pack it into butter firkins. She had not seen it buried, but Barkstead had told her where he intended to leave it, on the understanding that she should have it if he was not in a position to claim it himself later. Two more searches were made before Pepys and his companions gave up in disgust. Other people have looked for the treasure since, but to no avail. Perhaps Pepys was correct in assuming it was never there.

Most of the people in this story actually existed. John Thurloe was Cromwell's Secretary of State, Spymaster General and loyal friend. He was consulted about British foreign policy after the fall of the Commonwealth, and lived in quiet obscurity at Lincoln's Inn until his death in 1668. He was always regarded with suspicion, though, and there were reports to the new government that he was engaged in secret meetings with seven men, including his kinsman Colonel John Clarke. These were said to have taken place in the home of a man called Gervaise Bennet. Thurloe's sister is thought to have been called Sarah, and parish records indicate she may have married a man called John Dalton. Thurloe lost two children, who died in infancy in the 1650s.

Sir Richard Ingoldsby was one regicide who managed to escape retribution, and who even contrived to have himself knighted. He made the unlikely claim that his cousin Cromwell had grabbed his hand and made his signature on the old king's death warrant against his will – although there is nothing in the writing on the original document to suggest this – and the King believed him. John Hewson, a one-eyed religious fanatic, escaped overseas, and there are conflicting accounts about where and when he died. The same is true of Sir Michael Livesay, who was at one point a commissioner for the armed forces; some witnesses say he died soon after the Restoration, while others claim to have seen him some years later. The real fates of Hewson and Livesay remain a mystery.

William and Robert Leybourn were booksellers, whose shop was in Monkwell Street in Cripplegate. In the late 1660s, William was the surveyor employed to work on Ogilvy and Morgan's famous post-Fire map of London, now republished as *The A–Z of Restoration London*. Sir John Kelyng spent time in prison during the Commonwealth, and, when he emerged, it was as a rabidly devoted servant of the King. He presided at the trial of the writer John Bunyon, and was later lampooned by Bunyon as 'Lord Hategood'. Kelyng also headed the official inquiry into the Great Fire of 1666. Sir Edward Hyde, the Earl of Clarendon, was the King's Lord Chancellor until his fall from grace in the late 1660s, after which he went abroad and wrote a rather bitter history of his times.

The regicide Thomas Chaloner (1595–1661) was the third son of the famous Elizabethan naturalist, also named Thomas Chaloner (1561–1615). The older Chaloner married twice and sired eighteen children, and opened alum mines on his Yorkshire estates, but these were later confiscated by Charles I. It was probably the dispute over the mines' revenues that led the family to support Cromwell during the civil wars, and encouraged the younger Chaloner to sign Charles's death warrant and act as one of his judges. He was exempted from the pardon issued by Charles II at the Restoration, and fled to Holland, where he died the following year. He was a colourful figure in the drab days of the Commonwealth, who played practical jokes and was publicly denounced as a drunkard by Cromwell. Little is known about his last days in the pretty Dutch town of Middelburg, although one biographer claimed he died in abject poverty.